MY TOUCH BRINGS DEATH

And Other Stories

The Weird Tales of
Russell Gray
Volume #2

The **DANCING TUATARA PRESS**
Books from **RAMBLE HOUSE**

CLASSICS OF HORROR

CLASSICS OF SCIENCE FICTION AND FANTASY

DAY KEENE IN THE DETECTIVE PULPS

MY TOUCH BRINGS DEATH

And Other Stories

THE WEIRD TALES OF

RUSSELL GRAY

Edited and Introduced by
John Pelan

RAMBLE HOUSE

2014

Introduction © 2014 by John Pelan

Cover Art © 2014 Gavin O'Keefe

ISBN 13: 978-1-60543-755-2

Edited by: John Pelan

Stories from *Dime Mystery Magazine, Terror Tales, & Horror Stories*
reprinted by arrangement with Argosy Communications, Inc.
Copyright (C) 2014 Argosy Communications, Inc. All Rights Reserved.

Dancing Tuatara Press #51

TABLE OF CONTENTS

BRUTAL BRUNO — FOUNDING FATHER OF SPLATTERPUNK

Fawcett's Gold Medal line was one of the main sources for hardboiled crime fiction in the 1950s and 1960s. Authors such as David Goodis, Jim Thompson, Gil Brewer, Peter Rabe, Dan Marlowe, and John D. MacDonald all plied their trade there, turning out dozens of novels that have become the foundation stones for modern crime fiction. One of the most able practitioners was Bruno Fischer, who left the legion of authors cranking out paperback originals for more lofty positions in the publishing business. However, Fischer is still fondly remembered for novels such as *More Deaths than One*, *The Spider Lily*, *Fools Walk In*, and *Murder in the Raw,* to say nothing of his large volume of short stories, many of which appeared in *Dime Mystery* and *Dime Detective*. Fischer's novels generally featured ordinary people dropped into extraordinary situations and having to make choices that often compromised or tainted their pre-existing moral code. Nothing too unusual for the genre, and always superbly executed.

However, in 1950 readers must have received quite a shock when confronted with *House of Flesh* and (under Fischer's pseudonym from the pulp era, Russell Gray) *The Lustful Ape*! Both were published as paperback originals from Gold Medal, but in tone, content, and style were a throwback to a genre that had vanished just over a decade previously, the weird-menace or "shudder pulp". Readers with a long memory might well have remembered "Russell Gray" from the pages of *Dime Mystery*, *Horror Stories*, and *Terror Tales*; after all, once Fischer started having work appear under his real name, there was little effort made to conceal the fact that he had cut his teeth as "Russell Gray" and "Harrison Storm". To say that these two novels were lurid is an understatement, however, while pretty brutal and over-the-top for Gold Medal, they would have been considered pretty low-key compared to the monthly mayhem that was served up under the Russell Gray byline from 1936-1941.

While the weird menace genre started in 1933, 1936 marked a sort of changing of the guard; several of the main-stays of the field began to curtail their output or walk away entirely as new endeavors beckoned. Authors who had ap-peared monthly in one of Popular Publications three titles devoted to the genre were now appearing only sporadically, and some, like Paul Ernst, moved on to other fields entirely. While an exodus of talent like this could have been disas-trous, waiting in the wings were several authors who stepped up to the plate and produced excellent work from the very start. These authors included J.O. Quinliven, Mary Dale Buckner (Donald Dale), and of course, "Russell Gray".

Fischer's first story as "Russell Gray", "The Cat Woman" caused little excitement; it was a competently written short story, but nothing exceptional. However, by the end of the next year with stories such as "Girls for the Pain Dance", "Death Sends His Mannikins", "Venus of Laughing Death", and "Darlings of the Black Master" under his belt it was nec-essary to create another pseudonym, that of "Harrison Storm" in order to accommodate the volume of quality mate-rial that Fischer was churning out. In less than a year he'd gone from writing filler short stories to being one of the heavy hitters of the genre.

The period of 1936-1937 also saw a slight change of edito-rial direction on the part of Rogers Terrill. While the basic form of rationalized supernatural tales and lurid murders still held sway, there was an emphasis on ratcheting up the titilla-tion and torture elements and downplaying the gothic atmos-phere which had been prevalent in the first three years. The pace of the stories was picked up, the dialogue became crisper and more realistic and the heroine nearly always faced a "fate worse than death". What's more, with the violence cranked up to the end of the dial these changes in tone made for powerful fast-paced tales of mayhem, exactly the sort of thing that Bruno Fischer excelled at.

Of all the authors who contributed to the weird menace genre, Fischer stands alone as being without question the most brutal of them all. The previous collection featured "Fresh Fiancées for the Devil's Daughter", a tale which may well be the single most repellent piece of horror fiction published until the advent of Edward Lee's "Stick Woman" or *The Bighead* . . . I would say that this piece displaces the previous title holder, Aleister Crowley's "The Testament of Magdalen Blair", written some twenty years earlier. Gray's exercise in perverse revenge held the title with no contenders for over fifty years! Considering the wave of "splatterpunk" and the earlier work of Sir Charles Birkin, that this piece could maintain its place as the singularly most over-the-top piece of horror fiction for that length of time is truly remarkable.

While nothing quite equals that particular tale for sheer perversity, the only other author who came close to Fischer was Wayne Rogers, whose lurid visions not only enlivened the weird menace magazines, but also provided some of the most memorable moments in the long-running sagas of Operator #5 and The Spider. The stories in this volume range from several selections from 1937 (including two from the very same issue of *Terror Tales*!) to two late pieces from 1940, published in two of the lower-tier competing magazines, *Sinister Stories* and *Real Mystery*, to be precise. While neither of these magazines enjoyed the success or longevity of the three Popular Publications titles, they do demonstrate that Fischer was still at the top of his game even as the genre was dying out.

The weird menace genre was, by definition, too self-limiting to have survived a long time. Added to that the pressure from various self-appointed arbiters of the public good and the paper shortages caused by the looming war, the small timers like *Real Mystery* and *Sinister Stories* lasted only a few issues. *Terror Tales* and *Horror Stories* were both gone by the end of 1941 and the flagship, *Dime Mystery Magazine* changed its focus in 1939 to presenting detectives that were every bit as unusual as the crimes that they were confronted with. True to form, Bruno Fischer (still under the Gray by-line), created one of the most memorable of these "defective detectives", Ben Bryn, three of whose adventures can be sampled in the collection *More Tales of the Defective Detective in the Pulps* (Popular Press 1985). While Bryn's cases are certainly macabre, they are toned down considerably from his earlier material. However, we do have the evidence of those two Gold Medal thrillers from a decade later as proof positive that Bruno Fischer was still a master of the form.

John Pelan
Midnight House
Gallup, New Mexico
Winter Solstice — 2010

SHE-DEVIL OF THE SEA

Chapter 1: The Dead Stand Guard

WHEN MY FEET touched the bottom of the ocean, a strange chill coursed through my veins. It was the sudden touch of fear.

But, hell, a diver can't afford to be afraid. There are too many ways a diver can die; some sudden, some a little more slowly—but all horrible. There is only one way to conquer fear, and that is not to think of it.

But this was different. This wasn't fear of dying.

A small shark floated up to me, peered into my face through the glass plate of my helmet, and drifted lazily away. On my left tall grass swayed before the current. On my right was the rotted wooden hulk of the wreck.

Some eighty years ago, a newly built barkentine, the *Happiness* had left California carrying bullion and jewels valued approximately at one million dollars. Off the western coast of Mexico it had sunk in a hurricane. For eighty years the sea, which holds so large a part of the world's wealth in thousands of similar wrecks, had held that gold to its bosom, and now we were attempting to take it back.

They say that the sea is a miser reluctant to give up the gold it has seized. Jinxed treasure, they call the fortunes which are locked in the hulls of sunken ships, and there are some who say that the souls of the dead who died with the treasure guard it from the greed of the living. The usual superstitious talk attending any dangerous enterprise. Yet . . .

Well, the fact is that we weren't the first to try to salvage this gold. Two other expeditions had located the ship, had had the treasure almost within reach, and each time something had happened.

Five years ago the two divers of the first salvage crew had been killed by a killer whale, one of the most vicious creatures in the sea, just as they had been about to board the wreck. Two years later three divers of a second expedition had actually made their way into the ship. And then, inexplicably, the compressor engine had exploded, the tender had burst into flame, consuming all but one man who managed to reach a small fishing boat and tell his tale of horror before he, too, died. The divers, imprisoned on the bottom of the sea, must have slowly perished in their helmets from lack of air.

Few men could be hired to go near the wreck after that, and divers are as fearless a group as can be found. The sea and the dead were holding onto their gold.

But a million dollars is a lot of money, and there we were, the three of us, approaching the bare ribs and rotted beams of what had once been the stout ship *Happiness.* This morning we had succeeded in locating the wreck, and now in the late afternoon we would try to enter it.

On either side of me Bob Shiller and Juan Pietro walked slowly, ponderously, in their 212 pound suits, as in a nightmare or a slow motion picture. Except for the chugging of the air compressor on the tender above, there was no sound. The insulation of our heavy helmets made the bottom of the sea seem as quiet as death.

And it was then I felt the slimy hand of fear close about my heart. Was I afraid of the jinx? My derisive laughter filled my helmet. I, Ethan Thorne, having stared a score of times into the hideous grimace of death in every part of the globe, had ceased to acknowledge fear. I was not afraid to die.

And yet I had a feeling that there was something worse than death down here. Something . . .

At length we three were on the wreck itself. It was tilted at a slight angle on its side. Carefully we moved over its rotted planks. If we fell through or ripped our inflated rubber suits or fouled our lines, we were done for.

A voice squeaked into my ear, asking me if we were all right. That was Steve Hacker, who was tending our lines, speaking from the tender through the telephone which was built into each of our helmets.

"Everything's fine," I replied. "We're standing on the deck in front of the door of a cabin. Maybe the gold is in here. Juan is unhooking his hatchet from his belt and is about to knock in the door."

The wood was rotted and the hatchet tore through it as if it were paper. Juan Pietro knocked the whole side of the wall in. We needed plenty of room to keep our lines from tangling. We stepped in.

"Well," Hacker's voice came impatiently. "What'd you find?"

"Hold your horses," I snapped. "Can't see a thing yet." Then after a minute I said: "Now I'm beginning to make things out. Just an ordinary cabin. Something like a chair seems to be floating by. And there's . . . Good Lord!"

Steve Hacker's voice became tense. "What is it?"

"Bodies," I said. "Two bodies floating in here."

"Is that all?" Hacker said, relieved. "I thought something was wrong. Just bodies."

Then I just stared. The other two divers were motionless too, their heavy helmets facing the bodies. And again I felt that sensation of fear creeping up on me.

Finding bodies imprisoned in wrecks was nothing new. The water pressure doesn't smash a drowning person if his lungs are filled with water as he goes down. And if the fish don't get at it, a body can stay in a state of preservation for an incredibly long time.

That's what had happened to these two bodies we saw floating before our staring eyes in the shimmering, uncertain light. A man and a woman, their arms appearing to be about each other. They must have been in this cabin when the ship had sunk. Locked in each other's arms, perhaps with their lips in a final kiss, they had gone down to their death. And here they had been together, united even in death, for eighty years—until this moment.

I felt, somehow, as if we had violated a grave. We couldn't take them up to the surface and give them decent burial. Accustomed as the bodies were to the pressure which existed under fifty feet of water, they would burst as soon as we got them up, as happens to deep-sea fish which are brought too near the surface.

So we had to leave the bodies there. Sooner or later they would drift out through the opening we had made and the fish would get them. Or else the fish would come in here for them. We had disturbed their eighty years together in each other's arms.

We left that part of the ship and continued our search for the gold. Suddenly, as I made my way along the deck, I went down on my back with a jerk. My head began to throb and no air came to me.

Somehow my lines had fouled on a jutting beam; later I found that my airline had been slashed by the ragged edge of the beam. Automatically my outlet valve had closed, keeping air imprisoned in my suit, but no more air was coming in, and in a few minutes I would be a goner. My head was already hurting like the devil.

Fortunately Bob Shiller and Pietro saw my predicament and freed my life line. Then I signaled to be pulled up. By the time I broke through the surface, I had fainted.

A little later I lay in the tender nursing a terrific headache-but I had escaped the 'bends', that curse of all divers, resulting from too quick decompression. Steve Hacker was watching the lines and muttering over and over to himself: "The jinx, the jinx."

"Jinx, hell!" I burst out. "This isn't the first time my lines got fouled."

Judy Howell slid over to me and asked: "Are you all right, Ethan?"

Just looking up at her sea-blue eyes, her bronze-gold hair, her perfect figure, helped my headache. I lay there watching the way her superb breasts rounded the material of her thin sweater, and I thought the greatest thing that could happen to a man would be to rest his head in her arms.

There was one other person in the tender, Anson Goddard, a handsome, athletic young chap who had obviously come along on the expedition only because Judy was there. He was trying to make himself useful, though, and was at present watching the compressor. That was probably the first useful thing he'd ever done in his life. He was a member of Judy's social set in New York, and I gathered that they were more or less engaged to each other.

Hacker suddenly tensed at the telephone, listening intently, and we all turned to him, waiting. Then he yelled: "They found it! They found the gold!"

We almost capsized the tender in our excitement. We shot questions at Hacker and didn't bother to wait for answers. He waved us to be silent.

Then all at once I saw one of the airlines jerk violently, frantically. "The lines!" I cried, and moved across the boat.

I glimpsed Hacker's face and saw it go deadly white. He hunched over the telephone. "God!" he shrieked.

"What's up?" I shouted.

I snatched one of the phones from Hacker. A single choked scream came from the floor of the ocean—then silence, utter silence.

Judy and Goddard were pressing around us, demanding to know what was happening. I felt the softness of her body against my shoulder as she strained to listen in.

Then words came up from the ocean. It was Bob Shiller speaking in a voice I could hardly recognize. It was an insane muttering, the ravings of a madman.

"Get back!" the hysterical, cracked voice came up. *"You're dead! You can't walk! You're dead! Get back! Dead! . . . Mother in heaven!"*

"Pull up!" Steve Hacker cried.

I grabbed a life line, tugged. It came easily, too easily. Suddenly one end snaked up, writhing, loose. The line was broken!

Hacker and Goddard were pulling at the other line. It seemed to be all right.

"Bob's coming up," Hacker panted. "But Pietro!"

I was still in my diving dress. "Help me on with my helmet," I said to Hacker. "I'm going down."

Through the thick rubber of my suit I felt the pressure of Judy's grip.

"No!" she said. 'There's something terrible down there."

I didn't say anything. My heart was pounding violently against my ribs. God knows I didn't want to go down. It wasn't that at that moment I was afraid of sharks or killer whales or octopi, or any other natural enemy of divers. I knew it wasn't anything like that which had caused Pietro to scream and Shiller to utter those incredible words. I thought of those two bodies whose grave we had violated, and I shuddered.

But I had to go down. No diver would leave a comrade helpless on the bottom of the sea without trying to go to his aid. And something had happened to Bob Shiller so that he was no good down there.

My helmet shut out Judy's plea. I threw off her arm and went over the side of the tender. As I went down through the ghostly green water, I passed the shadowy figure of Bob Shiller being hauled to the surface. His lines were intact, but he seemed to be unconscious.

I found Juan Pietro on the sloping deck of the wreck. Or rather, what was left of him. There wasn't much, just disintegrating pulp inside his crumpled diving suit. A part of the rubber was torn in front, as if ripped by a hand of incredible strength. From the dress oozed a grey substance, the color of blood under water.

I've seen divers die like that before. The slightest rip in the suit, and the water pressure that far down crushes the diver into a jelly.

I had taken an extra line with me. I tied it around the gruesome remains and gave the signal to pull up. Over the telephone I told Steve Hacker what was coming up and to see to it that Judy wasn't looking when it broke through the sur-face.

"I'm going to look around," I told him.

Half a minute later Judy's pleading voice came down to me. "Don't, Ethan! Please come up!"

I didn't bother arguing. My knees were weak as I made my way along the deck. I was afraid. I, who had thought I had conquered fear, found that fear had seized me, was filling me, turning my blood to water.

Fool, I said to myself. Why scare yourself? The bodies are still in that cabin. They couldn't have floated out from the cabin and all the way through the passage in so short a time. They've got to be in there.

I reached the opening to the cabin, hesitated, then stepped through. The bodies weren't there.

Chapter 2: Horror in the Sea

WE DIDN'T SAY ANYTHING on the way back to the yacht. What was left of Juan Pietro lay under a tarpaulin in the stern of the tender. I suppose I must have looked pretty bad, but Bob Shiller—well, I've seen men scared before, but never as badly as he was. His face was green and he couldn't utter an articulate word. Just lay on the bottom of the boat mumbling to himself.

It wasn't merely because Pietro had died. Divers are a fa-talistic bunch. It was something that had happened in the wreck fifty feet under the sea which had been so terrifying and utterly incredible that his mind couldn't grasp it.

As we neared the *Judith*, the 85-foot Diesel yacht owned by Judy's father, Noah Howell, we saw everybody lining the rail, peering excitedly at us.

Howell, yelled, "Did you locate the gold?" and when none of us answered him, he shouted out the question again. Well, we'd found the gold all right in the wreck—and something else. Would we ever get the gold? That was something I couldn't answer.

Hell, I don't believe in jinxes. Yet soon after we boarded the wreck my lines had fouled, and soon after the gold was discovered Pietro had died. And those bodies had disappeared from the cabin . . .

Noah Howell needed that gold badly. He had been wealthy, but he had taken a bad licking on Wall Street, and about all he had left was the yacht. He had raised every cent he could for this expedition, and if it failed he'd be wiped out. Well, that wouldn't be so bad from my point of view. A guy like me who had never been able to save more than a couple of hundred dollars would have more chance with Judy poor than with Judy rich.

Bob Shiller talked when we got on the yacht. He lay propped up on the deck and we all stood about him—Judy and Anson Goddard clinging to each other's hands; Steve Hacker; Noah Howell, his florid face going suddenly flabby when he'd heard what had happened; slim, youngish Captain Brundy; Joseph Legg, the mate; the steward, the two engineers, and the rest of the crew.

"They killed him," Bob Shiller said. "Those two we found floating in the cabin, the man and the woman, they came into the strong-room where we found the gold and they said: 'The gold is not for you; you must not touch it!' "

"You're crazy!" Goddard exploded.

Bob Shiller nodded. "Yes, I'm crazy. But there they were. You don't believe me. I don't believe myself. They weren't floating any more. They were standing up, walking; and they stood there looking at us, and they had their arms about each other, and they said—"

"Wait a minute," I interrupted. "Even if somehow they were there and could talk, you couldn't hear them through your helmet."

"I know it," Shiller asserted. "But, nevertheless, I did hear them. Don't ask me how. People who have been dead eighty years aren't human. They can do things humans can't. They could get up and walk after all that time, and they could make me understand them. Their words reached directly into

my brain, somehow. And the woman said: 'Why did you disturb us? We wanted nothing but to be left in peace.'

"And the man said: 'You have come here to rob us.'"

"Juan and I just stared at them. Then we started to move
away. We couldn't get away from them. We made our way
up to the deck, but always they were there, following us.
God, how I wanted to run! But I didn't even have the power
to open my mouth or to signal to be pulled up. It was like a
nightmare the way we had to move so slowly—and they
were always there.

"Then at last we were on the deck, and I thought: Now we
will be pulled up and get away. They can read thoughts,
those two, because then the man said: 'No, we cannot let you
go. You would come back and bring others. Because we
know how men are when there is gold. We want peace and
we want our golden treasure.'

"Then the woman spoke. 'No, they mustn't go,' she said.

"Juan was nearest the man. The man reached out and dug
his nails into Juan's suit. Juan fell back and smashed against
the man with his fist. You wouldn't believe me, but the man
tore a big piece out of Juan's suit. Don't ask me how he had
the strength because I don't even want to guess. Juan's suit
suddenly collapsed and he collapsed inside of it. Pressure
smashed his face plate, squeezed his body terrifically in
every direction.

"Then the man came for me. His hand went out, and at that
moment the lines yanked me off my feet. I was being pulled
up. I thought surely they would go after me, but they just
stood there, looking up at me."

He lay back with a sob. We looked at each other, and I saw
in most of the faces the belief that he had become stark raving mad down there in the sea. Maybe. But those two bodies
which had disappeared from the cabin and the way Juan
Pietro had died! That meant something which had to be explained. Bob Shiller had the only possible explanation—and
that was utterly illogical.

"The jinx," Hacker muttered.

"Sheer nonsense!" Noah Howell exclaimed. "Pressure under water turns nitrogen in the air into liquid which enters the blood stream with the result that the brain gets sluggish. Isn't that right, Thorne?"

I nodded.

"Then somehow," Howell went on, "those two bodies floated in there while you and Pietro were looking at the gold—"

"Floated down to the hold?" Hacker interrupted. "They'd float up, not down."

"All right, then you and Pietro didn't see those bodies till they returned to the deck. On the deck Pietro tripped and ripped his suit. You were worrying about the jinx anyway and the accident to Thorne and the sight of those two bodies in the cabin had made you jittery, and on top of all that your mind was sluggish anyway; so when you saw Pietro die and those two bodies floating nearby, this fantastic story popped into your head."

"No," Bob Shiller said in a voice that seemed to come from far away. "I saw them. They were walking. They said . . ."

"How'd they look?" I cut in. "Bloated, like when we saw them in the cabin?"

"No," Shiller said. "They'd changed. She was young and beautiful, and he was a handsome young fellow. But their eyes weren't young. Not old either. They weren't human— something so terrible, so fixed in them, like a corpse staring."

Captain Brundy said: "My God, I've heard crazy stories about the sea, but this is the craziest. The poor fellow will be all right by tomorrow. Shock at seeing his pal die, that's all. Tomorrow he'll be anxious to go down again."

Shiller let out a shriek and sat up. "Don't send me down there again! I won't go! They'll get me next time. They tried once and failed. Maybe they'll even come on board here after me. Oh, God, don't let them get me!"

The poor chap was out of his head. The mate and I helped him into a cabin and left the steward with him. When I came out on the deck again, they were all standing where I'd left them. They'd been talking, but suddenly stopped when they saw me. I had a feeling that they were looking at me as though they felt I was going to die shortly.

"Now that the gold's located, Thorne," Noah Howell said, "do you think you can bring it up alone? Shiller is useless now."

I wet my lips. "It's a big order," I said.

"But you can manage it, can't you?" Howell asked. "There will be a fat bonus."

I looked about the circle of faces. I was afraid and they knew it, and I knew too that every man on deck considered himself lucky that he didn't know how to dive. Then my eyes met Judy's and our gazes held. She stood a little distance from Goddard, leaning against the rail. I'd been watching her with Goddard on the ship. I was sure she didn't love him. She seemed to care more for my company. With that extra bonus I might . . .

Judy's words came so quietly that only those nearest heard. "Don't go down. Please. I don't care about the money. Dad is unfair to make you want to go."

I knew then that no matter what she said, I'd dive tomorrow. I didn't want to appear a coward in her eyes. Or in my own. I knew that once I admitted to myself that I was afraid, I'd be no good any more. I'd have to give up diving.

"Haven't enough men died trying to get that accursed gold?" Judy pleaded.

"Six," Steve Hacker said softly. "And there'll be more."

I turned to Noah Howell. "All right," I said. "I'll bring up the gold for you. I'll go down first thing in the morning."

The meal that night in the very modernly decorated dining room of the yacht was eaten in brooding silence. It might be my last supper, I thought. At dawn tomorrow they would all gather on deck to watch me die.

My head was still throbbing and I felt pretty groggy from my accident under the sea, so I went to bed early. A couple of minutes after I went into my cabin there was a gentle knock. When I opened the door, Judy stood in the passage-way.

"I just came to say good-night and to tell you that you are very foolish."

There was not a woman in the world as lovely as she was. She stood there in that thin sweater which revealed every delicate curve of her sweet breasts, and her red, half-open lips were very close to mine.

"But very courageous and very sweet," she whispered.

I kissed her then, held her fiercely to me, and her throbbing warmth against me was the grandest thing in the world. Then a man coughed and we broke apart, flustered and confused. It was Anson Goddard.

"Pardon me," he said in a voice that was cold with anger. "I was on the way to my cabin and I can't get through with you two standing there." His eyes, as he squeezed past us, were venomous with hate.

Judy flushed deep scarlet, turned, and strode out to the deck. I went back into my cabin, cursing Goddard under my breath, in the same way, I thought with a grim smile, as he must be cursing me.

I went to bed, but I couldn't sleep. I kept seeing two dead bodies walking on the floor of the ocean. After a while there was another knock on my door. This time it was Anson God.

"You know, Thorne, I've been thinking," he said. "Maybe Bob Shiller killed Juan Pietro."

Strange man. He seemed to have forgotten the incident in the passage.

"That's a possibility," I agreed. "But why?"

"Shiller wants the gold for himself."

"How'll he get it?" I said. "He can't take it out himself. He'll need a boat, a crew. And anyway, he won't be able to kill every diver that goes down. He must have known that tomorrow I'll go down alone, and there won't be another *living* human being down there."

I realized when I'd finished that I had stressed the *living*. Goddard noticed it too and grinned sickly.

"Well, it's something to think about," Goddard said. "Good night."

After he left there were more wakeful hours. Nerves, I told myself. The cabin became stifling, seemed to be closing in on me. Finally I couldn't stand it anymore. I stepped into shoes and pulled on a pair of white ducks over my pajamas and went out on the deck for a midnight stroll.

A mist layover the sea. There was no moon, but I could see by the light of dim electric bulbs which lit the deck. I pulled a cigarette from my pocket and struck a match. The match never reached the cigarette. Out of the mist a woman came toward me.

Judy, I thought, and stood there waiting for her. There wasn't any other woman on board the yacht but Judy. But why the strange dress? Why would Judy be wearing a skirt that flared so?

Then I saw her face. The burning match was still in my fingers and it scorched my skin, but I wasn't aware of pain. I was suddenly cold all over. The woman wasn't Judy.

Instinctively I knew who she was.

Chapter 3: The Dead that Walk

SHE SEEMED as insubstantial as the mist itself. I told myself that my hand would go right through her. Yet my flesh shrank at the thought of touching her.

Then she spoke. "Tom," she said. "I'm looking for Tom."

It was a voice that seemed to come from very far away and was hardly audible. Tom must be the other one, the man. They had left their grave in the sea and had come up here. Looking for what?

"Tom," she said again, and now she was very close to me. I wanted to run, but my muscles would not obey me. I stood paralyzed, looking at her.

She was beautiful. Not that bloated thing I had vaguely seen floating through the deep green water in the cabin through the thick glass of my helmet. She was the way she must have been when she had died eighty years ago. She was of medium height and rather dark and full-bodied. She wore a wide hooped skirt, with a tight, low-cut bodice which thrust the upper slopes of her plump breasts into view. Her hair was a black pile on her head and in it was stuck a diamond-studded Spanish comb.

But her eyes! I hardly looked at the rest of her because of her eyes. Bob Shiller was right; they weren't human. If the eyes are truly the mirror of the soul, then this woman had no soul. She was a husk of what appeared to be living flesh, but inside that husk was something which had been dead for eighty years. Her eyes were staring, vacant, without life.

"Tom," she said a third time, and she placed a hand on my arm.

My flesh crawled. She was not insubstantial; she was as solid, as real as—death. Her hand was as cold as the bottom of the ocean and as clammy as the things that crawl in it. With a little cry I jerked my arm away.

"Suppose Tom does not come back to me?" she said in a voice quivering with fright. "Then I'll be all alone down there. Tom was never an easy one to hold. But he had to stay with me—down there. Nobody could take him away from me. And then you came and broke open our home and wanted to take our gold. 'We must kill them,' Tom said. 'Then we'll have no more peace.' So Tom killed one. But there are many more."

The words were tight in my throat and I had to force them out. "So you came up here to kill the rest of us?"

"Yes. Don't you see that we have to? Then we can go back to our rest."

She looked around, listening, but her eyes showed no change of expression. They remained always staring, dead.

"But what if Tom finds another woman here?" she said. "Then he'll leave me alone."

Another woman! Judy! God, I must go to her, protect her—if it were possible to protect anybody from these creatures who had no right to walk among the living.

Suddenly she flung herself on me, crying, "You'll help me find Tom! Please! I can't stand the thought of being alone down there."

It was horrible, feeling her wet dress and her skin as clammy as death against me. Revulsion numbed me. Then her lips were groping up for mine and—God help me!—I kissed her! Kissed a woman who was eighty years dead!

And yet when my lips were against hers I felt flames of passion burning within me. Passion for the dead! And through the cold clamminess of her I felt responding flames. Fires of desire which had been kindled in hell!

"If Tom does not come, you will take his place?" she whispered. "You will stay with me?"

Why I did not break away from her then, I do not know. My brain shrieked to me that madness was closing in on it, that in a short while it would be too late to free myself. Yet I crushed her to my arms, feeling her full breasts flatten against the thin material of my pajama jacket, and I drank the nectar of the damned from her dead lips. It was as if some eerie power in her staring, expressionless eyes had completely hypnotized me.

The scream knifed out from the heart of the yacht, keened out through the silence of the night. A girl screaming, and the only live girl on the boat was Judy! "What if Tom finds another woman here?" this dead creature in my arms had said. I had been warned and had *stayed* to make love to the dead!

The spell which had held me shattered, and I flung her from my arms, whirling. "Come back," she pleaded. Again that scream of utmost terror came. I pounded in the direction of Judy's stateroom. In the passage another form was right behind me—the steward. I tore the stateroom door open and plunged in.

Judy was in there, alone. She lay at the foot of the bed, her lacy nightgown torn to her waist, baring her firm round breasts. I dropped down beside her, took her in my arms.

"Judy, are you all right?" I asked. "What happened?"

"I was awakened by water dripping on me," she gasped. "Then I saw that face. The light was on and the face was only a few inches from me, and his terrible eyes were staring at me. Then a hand touched me. It was cold and horrible. I screamed and he disappeared."

She shuddered in my arms. Then she became aware of the other voices in the room, demanding to know what had happened. Almost everybody on board the yacht had crowded into the large stateroom. All but a couple of sailors were in pajamas or bathrobes or in hastily pulled on trousers. Judy covered her breasts with her palms and, jumping on the bed, pulled the covers up to her chin.

"Who was the man?" her father demanded, coming forward with clenched fists.

Judy shook her head. "I don't know. I never saw him before. All I saw were his eyes, those terrible eyes which couldn't see but which were staring at me. Before I could scream he pulled me off the bed and started tearing my nightgown off. It was awful."

Cold sweat plastered my pajamas to my skin.

A man shrieked. "They're here! They've come up after us. Oh, God, they'll get me!"

It was Bob Shiller, and his face was a contorted mask of sheer terror.

"Get a grip on yourself, man," Captain Brundy snapped. He had an automatic in his hand. "What are you talking about?"

"Those two we found in the wreck," Shiller said wildly. "They killed Pietro. Now they're coming after me and the rest of us. The girl is on the ship too. I saw her on the deck." He turned, leveled an accusing finger at me. "I saw her standing with him."

Every eye was on me. I ran my tongue over my lips and said: "Yes, I saw her. I even spoke to her. She said that they had come on the boat to kill us so that we could not disturb them anymore."

"Are you all mad?" Captain Brundy asked. "First the fantastic story Shiller told, then Miss Howell thinking she saw a dead man, and then you saying you spoke to a ghost."

"Mad?" I said. "Maybe we are."

I didn't know. But I did know that if we weren't mad, it wouldn't be long before we were—if we weren't dead first.

Anson Goddard said in a sneering tone: "What were you doing on deck, Thorne?"

The man hated me, of course. He had seen me kissing the girl he thought was his, and a few minutes ago he had seen her almost naked form clinging to me.

"I couldn't sleep, so I went out on deck," I explained.

"And saw a dead woman walking about," Goddard sneered. "And then you were the first one in here. How do we know you weren't in here before Judy screamed?'

His meaning was clear enough. I took a half step toward him and stopped. No sense fighting among ourselves when all faced a common danger.

"No," Judy cried. "It wasn't Ethan. It was a face I'd never seen before."

"Then where is he?" Goddard said. "Did he simply disintegrate?"

"He went out through the porthole," Judy told him.

Shiller started to shriek again. It's even more terrible to hear a man scream with terror than a woman. Shiller's nerves were completely shot, and a diver isn't supposed to have nerves.

"He went back into the sea, back to his home!" Schiller wailed. "But he'll come up again whenever he wants to. And his woman's still here!"

That was when Captain Brundy gave the order to search the boat. We should have done that at once, but in the excitement none of us had thought of it. I waited outside the stateroom until Judy dressed and came out. I didn't want to leave her alone. The *thing,* having seen her charms, might come back for her.

We made a thorough search of the ship, and to the relief of all of us, I confess, found nothing. Every electric light throughout the entire vessel had been put on, banishing the night and, to a lesser degree, the mist.

When at last we had given up the search as futile, Judy and I stood on the deck, her arm tucked through mine. Feeling her so close to me, I found my mind returning to normalcy.

My experience on the deck with that dead creature had been, after all, an hallucination, a bad dream. Judy might have been attacked by one of the crew. And as for the story Bob Schiller had told about how Juan Pietro had died—well, it was possible Shiller had killed him himself. His insane terror didn't strike me as being entirely genuine. A danger-hardened diver doesn't go to pieces as completely and as quickly as any hysterical girl.

An urgent, horror-laden shout came from the direction of the dining-room. "They've found something!" I cried. Grabbing Judy's hand, I raced with her to the dining-room. Other feet besides ours hurried over the deck.

We went through the door in a rush and pulled up sharply. Judy screamed and buried her face in my chest. Every face in the room was chalk-white. Noah Howell stared at the thing at his feet and muttered over and over: "Oh, my God! Oh, my God!"

Bob Shiller lay in a corner of the room in a pool of his own blood. Under his chin was a raw, gaping, bleeding hole. His throat had been torn as if by fingers of incredible strength— the kind of strength which could mock the toughness of a diving suit.

Chapter 4: Creatures from Hell

I WENT TO MY CABIN and got the revolver which I always carry in my bag. There was something reassuring about the hard feel of the steel against my palm.

Everyone, even the members of the crew, was gathered in the cozy, intimate cocktail lounge. They stood about the bar, seemingly huddled together, as if there were protection only in their nearness to each other. The steward was freely dispensing drinks to everybody. There wasn't a person there who didn't need a stiff one.

For the second time within twelve hours a silence fell at my appearance. I knew what they were thinking and had been talking about. Two of the three divers who had broken into the cabin of that wreck had died violently. I was the third.

Judy, white-faced and tense, was facing her father. Evidently my entrance had interrupted an argument between the two.

"Can't you see, Dad, that if you stay here you'll only be endangering more lives?" she pleaded.

There was a worried frown on Noah Howell's face. He was drinking straight whiskey out of a highball glass. His hand holding the glass was unsteady. He needed that money badly, and there it was, a million dollars, within reach.

Captain Brundy said: "I hope you won't let yourself be frightened away, Mr. Howell. I don't like to be master of a ship that flees at the slightest sign of trouble."

Noah Howell turned to me. "What's your opinion, Thorne? You're the man who has to bring up the gold." He coughed. "Besides, you're the one everybody thinks is in most danger."

The silence was suddenly profound. Judy slipped around to my side and placed a small moist hand in mine. I wished to heaven I knew how Juan Pietro had died. I'd just about made up my mind that Bob Shiller had killed him when Shiller himself was killed. Danger wasn't so bad if you knew what you were facing and if you thought that you had a chance in the world of coming out on top. But if there was something you couldn't fight . . .

Steve Hacker leaned over the bar and started to mumble: "The jinx! You can't beat a jinx!"

I took a deep breath and said: "I'll bring up the gold for you tomorrow, Mr. Howell."

Anson Goddard laughed harshly. "Heroics! You're scared crazy. You just want Judy to applaud you, but tomorrow you'll be singing a different tune!"

I turned my back on him and went to the bar for a drink. But I didn't reach it. A man shrieked horribly on the deck. I flung myself out ahead of the others, cocking my revolver as I ran. The scream had stopped abruptly. If I could get there before whatever was attacking him had a chance to flee . . .

As soon as I burst out on the deck I saw that it was too late to save the third victim. Joseph Legg, the mate, lay against the rail, a gruesome hole in his throat. Blood spilled in a stream over his chest. He had died the same way as Bob Shiller.

And then I saw the creatures who had killed him, the dead things which walked among the living. They stood about twenty feet away, that woman whose living-dead body I had held in my arms, and the man whom she had called Tom. The mist swirled gently about them as they stood with arms about each other. Their dead, expressionless eyes were fixed on me.

By this time the others had come on deck. And for what seemed eternities, but could not have been more than a few seconds, there was no sound or movement. Then somebody gasped and Judy whimpered softly. But nobody moved toward those two. We were held in an icy clutch of terror.

The thing called Tom shifted his head slightly. My own head moved also. Judy stood a little behind me and to my side, her fingers digging into her father's arm, and it was at her that he was staring with those terrible dead eyes. He had seen her loveliness once—and he remembered!

Deliberately I raised the revolver and aimed at where a mortal's heart would be. I am pretty good with a gun, and even by the dim electric lights I wouldn't have missed a dime at twenty feet.

Yet after the roar of the gun died away he was still standing there. He was still staring at Judy as if nothing had happened. Horrified, I fired again—and he simply ignored the hot lead which would have brought instant death to any mortal.

Mad with terror, I leaped forward. I shot another bullet into him and then poured two into the girl.

Then I stopped frozen, not daring to go any further. The bullets had had no effect on them. It was useless. The dead cannot be killed, and we were at the mercy of things which did not know what mercy was.

Slowly they turned and began to walk aft, their arms still about each other. It was infinitely horrible the way they turned their backs insolently on us, as if to demonstrate that they had no reason to fear us, and to sear into our tormented minds the grim knowledge that they would be back whenever they chose.

Captain Brundy was at my side, cursing and desperately emptying his automatic into the backs of the retreating figures. The mist thickened about them and it seemed they walked on air. Maybe they did. They could do anything they wanted.

Then they disappeared around the foredeck.

None of us made any attempt to pursue them. Suppose we caught up with them—what then? They couldn't be killed, but they could kill.

Voices started behind me, hysterical, gibbering crazily—fear-maddened voices. Judy still whimpered. At my side Captain Brundy stammered: "My God, it's impossible! It's absolutely impossible!"

I stared down at my revolver. No, it wasn't possible, yet it had happened. Five shots I had fired into them, and the slugs hadn't bothered them as much as a blade of grass thrown at a mortal. Impulsively I broke the revolver. Yes, five bullets had been fired.

Suddenly I spun on my heels and ran to my cabin. I heard Judy call my name as I rushed past her, but I didn't stop. My place at that moment, of course, was with her, and she must have wondered if I had become panic-stricken. But I had something more important to do.

After a few minutes in my cabin, I went into Noah Howell's stateroom. He was something of a hunter and there was a rifle rack on one side of the wall. Carefully I examined the rifles. Nothing wrong with them, but there weren't any cartridges. After a frantic hunt, during which I almost turned the stateroom upside down, I found a box of 30-30 cartridges in a corner of a dresser drawer. I selected a Winchester 30-30 rifle, loaded it, and went out on deck. My revolver I stuck in a pocket of my ducks.

Panic ruled the yacht. It was something one sensed rather than saw, for the members of the crew were at their stations. On the deck, Judy and her father and Anson Goddard were huddled together. I pray that I shall never again see such stark terror on human faces.

"You're running away?" I snapped at Howell. "You gave the order to leave?"

"Of course." He looked at me as if he thought I was crazy to suggest anything else. "I know when we're licked."

Judy wailed: "But will they let us alone now? Will they stay on the boat with us? Ethan, what are you going to do with that rifle?"

Goddard laughed. He tried to make it a derisive laugh, but he couldn't bring it off. I knew he was laughing to bolster up what courage, if any, was left in him. He said: "Thorne thinks a bigger bullet will kill ghosts. Why not try a cannon?"

I was already moving away before he had finished. Again 1 heard Judy call after and again I ignored her ... There wasn't any time to lose. In a few minutes the yacht would be under way.

I took the stairs up to the bridge two at a time. Captain Brundy, as I had expected, was up there.

I leaped to the searchlight and said: "How do you work this damn thing?"

"Why? What are you after?"

"You'll see."

In a couple of seconds a piercing beam cut through the night and the mist. I placed the rifle at my feet and swung the beam in a circle. Both the captain and I cried out when the light picked out the vague form of a motor launch—he with astonishment, I with triumph.

I fixed the beam on the 16-foot launch which rode the sea about a hundred feet from the yacht. They were in there, those two who had played at being the walking dead, the man paddling noiselessly, the woman sitting at the wheel.

They turned, staring bewilderedly at the light. The man dropped the paddle and leaped to the wheel. Roughly he pushed the girl aside. The starter turned over, the motor coughed, and died. Again the starter turned. I snatched up the rifle, dropped to one knee, and took careful aim. Strange how steady my hands were. His back was toward me. I pulled the trigger.

The screams of the man and the girl reached my ears at almost the same time as the roar of the gun. Then there was only the rising, shrieking wail of the girl. The man's body was slumped half over the gunwale of the boat.

I stood up, my knees wobbling. "There are your ghosts," I said to the captain.

Chapter 5: Greed is A Fiend

TWO OF THE CREW rowed one of the lifeboats out to the launch, while I sat in the prow with the rifle on my knees.

The girl wasn't trying to start the motor and get away. The searchlight was stilt focused on the launch, and I could see the girl bending over the man. Her frantic sobs came clearly over the water.

When we reached the launch, she gasped: "He's dying!" Then she turned her eyes toward me. They hadn't changed. They still weren't human; they were as dead as the eyes of a corpse.

A brief examination of the man showed that my bullet had torn through his right lung. It had entered his back at an angle and cut through his side, doing a lot of damage on the way. He was coughing up blood with every agonized breath he took. I saw he couldn't last long. His eyes were like the girl's. It gave me the shivers.

"You'll save him!" she begged. "You'll take him to the ship?"

I stood up. Her agitated breathing pushed most of her full breasts out from her low bodice. I didn't have the stomach to look at her eyes. There was something damn queer about the eyes of those two, something which didn't yet make sense.

"Please!" she entreated. "You can't just let him die."

He hadn't a chance in the world of surviving as much as an hour, but there was something I had to know. So I said: "Will you tell us who was behind these murders? Whom you were working for?"

"Yes, yes!" she moaned. "I'll tell you everything you want to know. Only save him."

"All right," I said.

We tied the lifeboat to the prow of the launch. I started the motor, turned the boat, and eased it alongside the ladder dangling down from the yacht. Above everybody was lined up along the rail. Their faces were frightened, strained, and I saw Captain Brundy's lips move wordlessly. I didn't catch on. I thought they were just getting over the shock of the horror they'd been through.

The two members of the crew carried the dying man up the ladder. Then the girl went up and I brought up the rear, holding on to the rifle with one hand.

As soon as my waist was above the deck, a voice said: "And now, Thorne, be good enough to drop that rifle into the sea."

Fool! I should have known. The conversation between the girl and myself on the motorboat had carried, as sounds will over the water, to every part of the yacht. The one behind the horrors had known then that the jig was up and had taken a desperate step.

I shrugged and dropped the rifle. It made a remarkably small splash in the water. Then I climbed up on the deck and stood there, looking at a Thompson sub-machine gun held in the unwavering hands of Steve Hacker.

"So it's you," I said. "I wasn't sure." He had lined everybody on the yacht against the rail. All were unarmed, of course, and the slightest movement toward him by any of us would bring a burst from the gun. There were fifty .45 caliber bullets in that clip, and while some of us might get to him before we were mowed down, it wasn't likely. He had us all right.

"You were a sap!" Steve Hacker spat out. "If you'd let well-enough alone, you'd have gone away and none of you would have been hurt. Now . . ."

Out of the corner of my eye I saw Judy edging toward me. She wanted to be by my side when we died. Stay away! My mind shrieked. But there wasn't any way I could let her know that her one chance of safety lay in not being too close to me.

"What are you going to do?" I asked. "Mow us all down and then burn the ship, or simply try to make a get-away?"

Hacker smiled crookedly. "What would you do in my place? A million bucks is a lot of dough to run away from."

Judy was at my side now, grasping my left arm. Lucky that she was at my left side. But how could I make her go away? I sparred for time.

"It was beautiful the way you figured this," I complimented him. "You hadn't the money to fit out an expedition to raise the gold. And even if you could raise the money, chances were you couldn't get to the gold, or maybe there wasn't any gold after all. You preferred to let somebody else take the risks. Once the gold was located and easy to get to, you set about trying to scare us away. Was it Bob Shiller who murdered Juan Pietro?"

The others were listening open-mouthed.

"Sure," Hacker admitted. "Shiller was in on this with me. The idea was for us to split the fortune. When you fouled your line, he saw his opportunity. He pulled the bodies out of the cabin and let them float away. Then he ripped into Pietro with his ax. The yarn about the dead bodies walking we'd made up beforehand."

"And then you killed him because you didn't want to split. You figured that now you were sure of the spot and the gold, you'd come back with a couple of hired divers and you'd just pay them wages and maybe bonuses."

Hacker shifted the tommy-gun slightly. There wasn't any hurry and he enjoyed telling us how clever he was. That's what I'd been counting on.

"That's one reason I killed him," Hacker said. "Anyway, I didn't trust him. All that hysterics wasn't just acting. I was afraid he might queer the game."

I asked: "Did you know you'd find the bodies when you hired those two to come here and haunt us? Or did you sneak into the radio room and send them a message?"

Hacker laughed. "That was a bit of luck finding those bodies. Played right into our hands. The idea was for Shiller to say he'd seen the two bodies; we didn't think there would actually be any. Tom and Margie there I'd hired before we came. The coast is only twelve miles away, and they were to come out here every night until the gold was found. They were here last night, but I was waiting for them and signaled for them to leave. Then tonight I told them to do their stuff.

"We thought at first of waiting until the gold was brought up and then kill you all, but that was too dangerous. There'd be an investigation. Simply scaring you away was safer. Tom and Margie brought the launch up to the side and the ladder was waiting for them. So was I. I told them what to do. They roamed about the ship, and as all your nerves were on edge, it wasn't hard to scare hell out of you. I ripped Shiller's throat out with an iron hook and later Tom did the same to the mate. Then we had that little game called shooting at ghosts.

"I found out that there were only two pistols on board, yours and the captain's. They were both .38 caliber and I had .38 blanks, so that was easy. I hid all the cartridges for the rifles. Some way or other I must have overlooked the gun you shot Tom with."

Well, let him think so. I clamped a dazed expression on my face and slowly pulled my revolver from my pocket. Hacker's finger tightened on the tommy-gun, and for a moment I stopped breathing. But he wasn't quite ready to shoot yet. He knew my evolver wasn't any good.

"So that's it," I muttered. "Blanks! That's why this gun is useless."

Steve Hacker shifted his feet and brought up his tommy-gun. A murmur of terror swept through the men who lined the rail. Judy held frantically to me.

Desperately I said: "Their eyes, that's what scared us most."

His gaze shifted an inch toward Margie. My fingers curled about the trigger.

Hacker chuckled. "Sure got you, didn't it? Don't blame you. It gives me the willies just to look at her eyes. Those are just thin glass shields which fit over the eyeballs." He laughed again. "Trust Steve Hacker not to overlook a thing important."

Then my revolver spoke. I knocked Judy sprawling and thumbed the hammer.

This time there was lead in the gun. At ten feet I couldn't miss. Captain Brundy leaped and knocked the tommy-gun aside. It wasn't necessary. It hadn't even been necessary for me to knock Judy down. Steve Hacker had died the instant the slug entered his heart.

About me men shouted and laughed and cursed, the way men will who have just been released from certain death. Then, as I was lifting Judy to her feet, they crowded around me, slapping my back. Even Anson Goddard.

"He overlooked one thing," I said. "That I'd break my gun with one bullet still left in the chamber and see that it was a blank. And that I had some spare bullets in the pocket of an old suit."

Judy was tight in my arms. Behind her stood her father, beaming at me. I told him: "Well, I'll bring up your gold for you tomorrow, Mr. Howell."

Judy looked up at my face, and her smile did things to me. "What do you mean, 'your gold'? She said. "Our gold. Fifty percent of it ought to go to Dad's son-in-law."

A CORPSE WIELDS THE LASH

Chapter 1: The House of Doom

ADAM TRAIN HAD DIFFICULTY hiring a taxi to take him out to the Weathers' place. It was a small town and there were only three cabs at the station. Each of the three drivers said it was too far; but he knew by the way they avoided his eyes and stubbornly refused to argue the matter that there was another reason. They were afraid . . .

He was about to phone the house for a car when a fourth taxi drove up. The driver was a young fellow who looked as if he wouldn't be afraid of the devil himself, but even so he hesitated when Adam mentioned his destination. Promise of a fat tip finally caused the driver to change his mind.

As they drove, Adam leaned forward and asked: "What's the matter with the Weathers' place? Why'd I have such a job getting a cabman to take me out there?"

"Old man Weathers died last week," the driver replied. "He was murdered. It'll be dark by the time we get there. Strange things have happened there, and most of the people who knew old Tobias Weathers or knew of him think that stranger things will happen now that he's dead."

The driver paused, then said: "I mean, they think the fact that he's buried doesn't mean that he's gone. They think that something of him stayed behind, the most evil part of him. He used to say that they'd have to do more than bury him to get rid of him."

"What did you mean by strange things?" Adam asked.

"Well, sir, it's hard to say. There's the whippings, for instance."

"Whippings!"

"Yes. They say that's the way Tobias Weathers' wife died. She was much younger than him, a beautiful woman, like all the Weathers women. There was a young fellow in town named Harrison. He worked in the bank. He was seen driving in his car with her a couple of times. Then one day Harrison left town and a couple days later Mrs. Weathers died. They say Harrison ran away because he was afraid the same thing would happen to him.

"That was a year ago. They say Mrs. Weathers didn't die naturally. They say that when the undertaker got her there wasn't any skin on her. The rumor was that old Tobias had whipped her to shreds. Landman, the undertaker, was asked about it, but of course he wouldn't talk. Some say Landman was bribed to patch her up for burial. There was a lot of heat for a while and talk of lynching Weathers and the Baron. But there wasn't anything definite to go by so it died down."

"And The Baron?" Adam asked.

He sat forward in his seat, listening. The driver obviously liked to talk.

"He's some foreign nobleman who Miss Weathers picked up. That's Miss Julie Weathers, Tobias' sister, who lives with the family. She's an old maid. Goes around collecting seedy noblemen and Hindu mystics and all such crackpots, like others collect postage stamps. She brought him to the house once a couple of years ago, and he and old Tobias sort of took to each other. So he kept coming around. If you can imagine death walking, that's the Baron. I never wanted to kill a man in my life, but once I wanted to kill him—if he can be killed. Some folks claim he can't be."

The driver stopped talking. "Tell me about that," Adam urged, "why you wanted to kill him."

"Well," said the driver reluctantly, "I never talked about it but once. The Weathers had a bad enough name, without making it worse by people knowing the kind of man they had as their guest. Then one night I got drunk and shot my mouth off. I was sorry later, because the youngest Weathers girl,

Molly, is a pretty sweet kid. She's democratic and nice. I took her to a couple of dances and . . ."

"I see," Adam said.

"One day I picked up Robert Ingram and Harold Bedford and the Baron at the station. Ingram and Bedford come from Moundville, the county seat. They're law partners. Ingram's engaged to Lucy Weathers, the old man's orphan niece who lives with them, and Bedford is engaged to Rhoda, the oldest daughter. At that time they were just beginning to court the girls. They met the Baron on the train and the three rode together to the house in my cab.

"The Baron started talking about women. About how he hates women. He said that Americans don't know how to keep women in their place. He said that when their women betray them, they weep to themselves or run away to forget or to go to a judge. That wasn't his way. And he told what he'd done to his own wife years ago in his own country.

"It seems the Baron had discovered that his wife was unfaithful to him. He'd killed the man. Mercifully, he said, at once. The woman died, too, but not all at once. A little of her died at a time and it took many weeks. He did it with a whip. Every day he used it on her—not too much. Every day he used that whip, until, he said, there was no skin on her and very little flesh.

"He was sitting just about where you are, mister, and there was a light in his eyes as he told the story that made me want to pull him out of the cab and twist his scrawny neck. The two men with him didn't say a word. I was looking at them in the mirror here, and their faces were white.

"I told you I didn't want to tell anybody that story, but I got drunk one night and I did. That was a couple of weeks before Mrs. Weathers died. I guess that story was what gave folks the idea that old man Weathers had done the same thing to his wife."

There was a silence. The driver concentrated on the road. Adam Train sat back and lit a cigarette. He was a junior member of the engineering firm with which Tobias Weathers had once been associated. After his retirement Weathers had retained advisory interest in the firm, as well as a substantial block of the stocks; and now that he was dead Adams had been sent to straighten out matters.

He'd met Tobias Weathers only once or twice. A powerful man with a face like chiseled rock.

Adam leaned forward again. "What's this you mentioned earlier about people thinking part of him isn't really dead?"

"Just superstition," the young man replied. "They say he was too hard to die just like other men. He used to say that himself. And there was something else he said. He'd become very bitter toward women after—after his wife died. He treated the women in his house pretty badly. Used to whip them, too, I think."

"His own daughters and his niece?"

"I think so. There's no way of telling. A couple of weeks ago a man who has a newspaper route picked Lucy Weathers up on the road a couple of miles from the house. It was late at night. She was crying and walking in a daze. He noticed that her dress was torn and blood was on her shoulder. He took her to the hotel in town and the next morning she went away. She never came back until after the old man's death."

"You began to tell me something else he said about women."

"Oh, yes. That the women in his family were just waiting around till he died and then they'd just jump on his money. He said that if they thought he'd let them alone after his death, they were crazy, because he'd come back, he said. Molly told me that one night at a dance. She was crying, poor kid. Something must have happened that day; I don't know what. Nobody was sorry when the old man was killed last week. Sort of retribution, if you get what I mean."

"I heard that a burglar killed him," Adam said.

"That's right. He surprised a burglar and was shot dead. Robert Ingram fought with the burglar, but he couldn't hold on to him. There was quite a manhunt in these parts that night, but he wasn't found. Ingram had come out to the house to try to locate Lucy. I drove him out that night. He couldn't sit still in that seat back there; seemed nearly frantic with worry. . . Here we are, sir. Guess I talked too much."

Adam smiled to himself. If you want gossip, ask a taxi driver. "Not at all," he said as he got out of the cab. "Thanks."

He looked at the house. It was already dark. Halfway up the steep and rocky hill the lights of the house shone. It could have been an attractive place, but for a reason he could not fathom it was the opposite. It was bleak and somber; as relentless and unsmiling as the man who had built it.

The family was just about to sit down to dinner when Adam entered the house. He was greeted cordially, but without warmth, and a place was made for him at the table.

The beauty of the Weathers women had not been exaggerated. Even Julia Weathers, sister of Tobias, retained the dignified charm of handsome middle-aged women. Molly, the younger of Tobias' two daughters, was a sweet girl of scarcely seventeen, whose perennially sad eyes enhanced her pale beauty. The other daughter, Rhoda, was by far the most stunning looking of the women. Her gorgeous sophisticated beauty literally took a man's breath away.

Yet after a while Adam found his eyes straying from the splendor of Rhoda to Lucy Weathers, the cousin of the two sisters. Hers was the ethereal, flower-like beauty which grew on one and enthralled one. He could understand why Robert Ingram looked at her every now and then with adoring eyes.

Besides the four women, there were three men, excluding himself. Harold Bedford, who was engaged to Rhoda, and Robert Ingram were pleasant and friendly sort of chaps about his own age. And there was the Baron.

He was thin, that man who was known only as the Baron. Everything about him was long and thin: his tall emaciated body, his face which looked as if the sides had been squeezed together by a giant press, his sharp beak of a nose, his dead-white fingers, his thin cruel slit of a mouth. He was like a being long dead.

It was not a cheerful meal. Not because any of the diners mourned the death of the master of the house. Adam was certain that none in that room was sorry he had died. It was as if they were all waiting in mute horror for something that was too horrible to contemplate.

Chapter 2: Return of the Dead

IT LAY AT HER FEET like a long black snake; and when she picked it up it writhed in her hand, as if it had life of its own that menaced her. Its smooth damp surface was clammy to her touch. With a little cry of horror, Lucy Weathers dropped the whip.

She had seen that whip before. She had felt its deadly tip bite into her shoulder. Now it lay half hidden in the grass, dread symbol of the man Tobias Weathers, her uncle, had been.

Seven days ago he had died and his remains had been buried deep in the ground. But they were not rid of him. The driving sadism and hatred of women which had become a mad obsession since the death of his wife lingered after him, like the effluvium from a corpse.

And now this whip was a material sign that part of him was not gone. It was the same whip that used to hang conspicuously in his study. "As a warning," he used to mock at the women. But only once had he taken it down since his wife died. And that time Lucy had answered the sting of the whip by scratching at his face. And then she had seen him no more.

How did the whip come to be here? She had passed this spot several times during the day and had not noticed it. Impossible not to have seen its long blackness against the green of the grass.

With awful fascination she stared at it. The thought of touching it again filled her with revulsion. But it must be destroyed. She sensed that with its destruction would also be destroyed the last link between Tobias Weathers and the living.

She snatched up the whip and, without daring to think, ran toward the house with it.

Suddenly she stopped. The Baron stood in her path. Light from the house revealed his deep-sunken eyes regarding her with a cynical half-smile.

His eyes moved to the whip. He stared at it as a man would stare at a desirable woman. Lust glittered in those hollow eyes. Lust not for her, but for the whip.

Lucy shrank back—then ran. She entered the house through the back door, went up to her room by the back steps, hid the whip in her closet. She wished to destroy it utterly, but that was impossible at present. It was summer and there was no fire in the furnace where she might burn it. Tomorrow she would drive to the river and throw it in.

Downstairs in the drawing room they were sipping after-dinner cordials. Robert walked across to her as soon as she entered the room.

"Where were you?" he asked. "Molly said you didn't go to your room. I was getting worried."

"I just went out for a breath of air. I had a headache."

She reached for his hand, held it in hers. His touch was comforting. In a few days, after the affairs of the estate were settled, this handsome young attorney whom she loved would take her to the city where they would be married. She would never have to go near this house again.

Later that night Lucy Weathers was awakened from sleep by the sound of a door creaking. Half asleep, she listened. It was her door. It must be one of the girls, she told herself, coming into her room for some reason.

She opened her eyes. The night was sufficiently light to outline vaguely the interior of the room. Straight ahead was the door, and it was shut tight. Yet that creaking continued, and she turned her head.

There was a man in the room. With back turned to her he was slowly opening the closet door. The outline of his back was dim, uncertain; she could not distinguish who it was. A strange horror gripped her. She opened her mouth to speak, but for a reason she could not understand she closed it again without a sound.

The man entered the closet, came out again. His feet made no sound. This time there was something in his hand. The whip! The man turned and looked at her.

It was as if she suddenly became an inanimate thing without control of any of her faculties. She wanted to cry out, but her throat refused to respond. *The man was her uncle, who had died seven days ago!*

Tobias Weathers looked at her with eyes that did not see. He moved without apparent effort. He moved without seeming to walk—and he came straight for her, the whip dangling from his hand.

Sound burst from her lips, then, but it was only an insane whisper. She sat upright, raised one arm as if to fend off that abominable presence.

The hand of the dead man went up. The whip snapped, and she felt pain sear into her chest. Even then she could not cry out. She sat in bed with an imbecilic whimper drooling from her lips; waited cringing for the second blow.

It did not come. The dead man turned and glided toward the door. The door opened and closed seemingly by itself, and he passed out of the room, the whip trailing after him.

As soon as she was again alone in the room, she snapped back to normal like a person awaking from a nightmare. She leaped out of bed, threw open the door, ran on bare feet to the staircase. It was no dream, no nightmare. There, walking down the stairs on feet which made no sound, was her uncle!

Once again she lost control of her voice. She stood clinging to the rail for support, fighting to hold on to her consciousness.

Time passed. She did not know how long. Perhaps it was only a minute. Then she looked again and the steps were empty. Downstairs faint illumination showed that there was light in the drawing room. It did not occur to her to scream, to rouse the household. She knew only that she had to see this through at once or go mad.

Desperately she fought panic as she drove her reluctant feet down the stairs. She was whimpering again as she approached the doorway to the drawing room. Then she looked in. Seated in an arm chair reading by the light of a single floor lamp was Adam Train.

She gave a little cry of relief. Adam Train looked up and gaped at her.

"Miss Weathers!" He was on his feet, coming toward her. "I didn't hear you. For a moment I thought you were a ghost."

She swayed toward him. Instinctively he reached out his arms, then dropped them to his side. Abashed, he shifted his eyes from her. She wore only a diaphanous nightgown.

"You're hurt," he cried. A thin line of blood trickled from the cut above her left breast, where the tip of the whip had struck her. He reached his handkerchief to her and she took it and pressed it against the cut.

"I have one on my shoulder too," she smiled wanly. She was recovering from the shock of her experience.

Briefly she told him what had happened. He listened quietly. When she had finished, he said: "A bad dream. This house would make anybody see things."

"It wasn't a dream," she stated with quiet conviction.

"You'd better put something on," he changed the subject. "This looks—er, compromising."

She had been aware of her semi-nudity, but she did not want to let him out of her sight. Not because of any particular attachment for him. She did not know him. She would have preferred Robert who was sleeping soundly in his room. But he was a man, real, alive, friendly; and she needed somebody like that after what had just occurred.

He followed her upstairs and waited outside her room while she put on a negligee and slippers. She looked through the closet. The whip was gone.

"Perhaps you would like to sleep," he suggested when they came out. "I'll keep guard outside the door."

She shuddered. "Good God, no." She thought of waking Robert, but she was afraid that he would laugh at her. This man, Adam Train, did not believe her, but he tried to be sympathetic and understanding. She would wait the night out with him, and tomorrow she would persuade Robert to take her away from this hellish place.

The two went down to the drawing room. He lit a cigarette for her and one for himself. He stood before her and said:

"I suppose it's none of my business, but I'm trying to understand all this. You said you have a mark on your shoulder. Was that from a whip?"

"Yes. My uncle gave that one to me, too," her voice dropped—"when he was alive. I came upon him beating Molly. He'd had that whip for some time, had been threatening to use it; but not until that day had he actually whipped any of us. Maybe once before, somebody else. I don't know."

"You mean his wife?" Adam asked. "I heard a rumor. Didn't take too much stock in it."

The girl stared at the tip of her cigarette. "I don't know. Maybe she just died. One day he sent us all away. Told us to go visiting distant relatives for a week, and his word was law. That's when he found out about that man, Harrison. He thought she'd been unfaithful. She wasn't; it was just a harmless flirtation as the result of a pretty dreary life. When we came back, she was dead. How she died, we'll never know."

"Then he whipped Molly?" Adam prompted.

"Two weeks ago I heard her scream. It was awful. I rushed to his den upstairs. He was lashing her with that horrible whip. It was ripping the clothes off her and the skin and the flesh. She still has the marks on her body. What was the most horrible of all was the expression on his face. There was the most bestial enjoyment, sheer brutal lust, I'd ever seen. I screamed to him to stop. He flicked the whip toward me and the pain on my shoulder was frightful. Then I lost my head. I leaped at him, slapped him, scratched him.

"He just gaped at me; made no effort to defend himself. Then I fell back in terror at the awful thing I'd done. It will be hard for you to understand. Nobody had ever before crossed him, much less dared to strike him. I ran out of the house. After a while a truck picked me up on the road. I took the train to a distant cousin's and stayed there till I heard of his death. I knew Molly and Rhoda would need me, so I came back."

The long speech had exhausted her. She leaned back in her chair. Adam thought that he had never seen anybody so lovely.

"And you stood for it?" Adam said. "I mean the whole thing, the whole life in this place with Tobias Weathers? You were grown women. What held you here?"

"It's not easy to explain," she said. "There are the two men Rhoda and I love—Robert Ingram and Harold Bedford. They sensed what was going on, but they knew nothing definite. We kept it from them. For they're struggling young lawyers. It's only now that they're beginning to make their way. And if we had left, we would have gone to them, and become ropes around their necks.

"And there was another thing. Call it my uncle's personality, his will. It held us to him, like something hypnotic. It was so powerful that I can still feel it after he's gone. That's why it isn't as easy for him to stay dead as it is for other people."

She huddled in her chair like a broken, frightened child, and she whispered: "And tonight he came for the whip."

Again he was about to assure her that the vision of her uncle must have been a bad dream. But he didn't say the words. He was looking out of the window at a man who was outlined in the moonlight.

There was something queer about that man. He stood on one of the boulders which dotted the side of the hill on which the house was built, and it was almost as if one could see through him. It might have been the effect of the moonlight on him, but it wasn't. That unreal, insubstantial aspect was an integral part of the man.

Adam felt Lucy Weathers' hand tighten on his arm. She had arisen from the chair and come up behind him, and he knew that she was looking at the same thing as he.

He felt the motion of her body, felt her shuddering against him, and he heard her gasp hoarsely: "Uncle Tobias!"

The man on the boulder turned slowly. His face was toward them. Now Adam recognized the man who had died a week ago. And there was something else he saw—a black whip trailing from his right hand.

The man—or thing—turned suddenly and disappeared. It was as if he had floated off the boulder.

Adam was sweating, and at the same time he felt cold chills down his back. The girl at his side was moaning, "Uncle Tobias—it's Uncle Tobias!"

Adam's hand covered hers. "No," he said, and repeated: "No." He had to deny the testimony of his eyes; deny it or know that he was mad. He grasped the girl by the shoulders. "There's something—" he began.

Far off a girl screamed. Adam and Lucy stood motionless, straining to grasp the sound. At first it sounded as if somebody might be calling in the distance, but it came again and again in recurring and more intense waves, until they knew that it was a girl screaming in terror and agony.

Then Adam Train was running.

Chapter 3: Horror on the Hill

THE SCREAMS CAME from high up the side of the hill. Beyond the lawn was a steep footpath cutting through the shrubs and undergrowth which had not been cleared.

"Mr. Train!"

Adam turned. It was Lucy. "Go back," he ordered.

"It's Rhoda or Molly," she panted. "You've got to let me come."

It would take too much time to argue. He turned and continued up the footpath. The screams had died away. They had not stopped abruptly, but rather melted into nothingness.

Both were panting from the climb when they reached a clearing to the right of the footpath. And there they saw the red and white horror.

Lucy shrieked and Adam leaped forward to catch her before she fell. She did not faint, but her body in his arms was limp and trembling. He placed himself between her and the thing that lay on the ground.

One look had been enough. He could tell at once by the copper-color hair that it was Molly Weathers. There was no other way to tell; nothing left of the body that was recognizable. A whip had done it.

A whip had cut away skin and flesh from the sweet young body; had first stripped away the silk nightgown, tattered bits of which still clung to the bloody torso. No part of the girl had been spared by the merciless lash; even her face was a gruesome welter of ragged flesh. Death had come slowly and horribly.

And on the ground lay the whip. The whip which had been stolen from Lucy's closet by a dead man; which they had seen only a few minutes ago dangling from the hands of a man who should have been rotting in his grave. The whip which was red with the blood of the dead man's youngest daughter and on which bits of her flesh and skin still adhered!

Numb horror was flowing through Adam's veins like a sluggish poison. Abomination of abominations! The dead arising! A dead man torturing and slaying his daughter!

Abruptly another woman screamed. The scream came from below, from a spot near the house.

"Rhoda!" Lucy cried. "Oh, God, he's got Rhoda now! Save her! Run! You might be in time!"

She watched Adam run down the path. Rhoda's screams had ceased. Lucy's heart stopped beating. Would he be too late? And even if he were on time, what chance would he have against a creature that was dead and walked with the living? Could one fight the dead?

Below she saw something dark and ominous rise at the side of the path down which Adam Train ran. It was as if a tree were leaning over above him. She did not know what it was, but its attitude denoted danger and she called a warning. Too late! When Adam Train was under the evil shadow she saw part of it swirl downward, and the young man dropped to the ground. He lay there, motionless.

With a cry of horror and despair, she started down the path.

"Lucy! Wait!"

The voice was not loud, but it was as incisive as a sharp knife. Lucy stopped. The Baron was coming toward her. In his hand was the bloody whip. His face was the face of death.

"Don't go down there," the Baron said, and he came closer.

Of course he wouldn't want her to go. Down there was his confederate, Tobias Weathers dead seven day.

She started to run. The Baron's hand streaked out, caught her arm. "I said don't!" he barked. She lashed out, raked his face with clawed fingers, and saw blood streak his face. With a curse he fell back, then came in again, grasped her shoulder violently.

Dry twigs snapped beneath hurried steps. The Baron whirled. Lucy cried with joy as she saw Robert Ingram approach. There was murder in his face. The Baron retreated, walking backward.

"You rat!" Robert gritted. "I've been waiting for this chance ever since I laid eyes on you."

He charged, and the Baron went down under an avalanche of blows. Then Lucy was sobbing in the strong, comforting arms of the man she loved.

"I heard screams," Robert explained. "I threw my clothes on and came out to investigate. Fortunately I was just in time."

"It wasn't I who screamed. It was—" She pointed to the grisly corpse and turned her face away. Robert gasped, his eyes bulging. He took a few steps toward the dead girl, muttering to himself in horror.

The Baron had thought to take him by surprise by feigning unconsciousness, but Robert saw him rise and whirled in time to meet his rush. But this time the Baron had discovered that he possessed a weapon stronger than Robert's fists. He avoided a crushing right and brought the butt of the whip down on Robert's head. A tremor ran through Robert, he staggered forward, then his legs collapsed under him, and he lay still.

The Baron stood looking down at the unconscious young man. The blood where Lucy's nails had ripped his skin caked on his face, making it look more like a death's-head than ever.

He looked down at Robert Ingram and the whip was in his hand. It had cut skin and flesh from Molly Weathers. It would do the same to Robert, the man she loved.

She must save him. At all cost she must save him.

The Baron's right arm which held the whip moved. She screamed. Slowly the Baron turned, looked at her. She was defenseless against him, against the whip. In a few minutes his terrible work would be done.

"Baron!" she cried. "Am I not beautiful? I have seen the way you have looked at me. You desire me. Look!"

With a single movement she stepped out of her negligee. Another movement, and her nightgown lay at her feet. Nude, like a marble statue of utmost perfection, she stood before him in the moonlight.

The Baron's tongue passed over his thin, bloodless lips. He opened his mouth and closed it again without saying anything. Then he moved toward her.

She closed her eyes, waiting for his touch as one would wait for death. Tightly she clutched her hands at her side to keep from running. She heard his voice, low, husky: "You are magnificent."

Then his hand was on her breast, gliding over the smoothness of her body. His hand was cold. Her skin squirmed under his touch; every nerve in her cried out in revulsion.

Suddenly it struck her that the Baron, like her uncle, was dead! That all along he had been dead and nobody had known it until now. A dead man was making love to her!

Darkness swooped down, engulfed her. She sensed rather than felt her body strike the ground.

There was a great stillness when she recovered consciousness some time later. She opened her eyes and the first thing she saw was the moon. It was higher in the sky, directly above her. Abruptly she sat up. The Baron was gone, Robert was gone. She was alone with the gruesome corpse of Molly.

The Baron must have removed Robert. Where had he taken him? Perhaps even now Robert was a mutilated corpse like Molly!

Snatching up her negligee and throwing it about her, she started to run down the footpath. Adam Train would help her—if he were not dead. But when she reached the spot where she had seen him knocked down, he was not there. Several small stones had dabs of what looked like brown paint on them. Adam Train's blood! Softly she called his name. It would be dangerous to raise her voice. There was no answer. The silence was laden with horror.

Desperation and fear mingled to turn her heart into a leaden mass. There was one last source of help—the house. Harold Bedford was there and Aunt Julia. She continued down the path.

Suddenly she stopped. The house was dark. Not a light in any window. It lay sprawled out a hundred feet below, like an ominous monster.

It took courage to enter the house. The house, somehow, had taken on an even more terrifying aspect than outside. She wondered why she did not go mad. It was only the danger of those she loved that gave her the strength to keep her wits, to keep from running shrieking to the main road.

Frantically she ran from one room to another, switching on every light she passed. But every room was empty. They were gone, every one of them. The Baron and her uncle had them somewhere on the hill. Her uncle had returned from the grave, as he had said he would, to wreak frightful punishment on the women he hated. And above all he hated her, for she alone of all the women had dared to strike back at him. He would come for her. There was no defense from the dead.

She fell to the floor and lay there sobbing hysterically, waiting for the doom from which there was no escape. She thought of the flashing beauty of Rhoda, of charming Aunt Julia, of Robert Ingram whom she loved, of Harold Bedford, of Adam Train. All were doomed with her. Unless—unless in some way she, who was yet free, could help them.

There was no time to be lost. She found that she was running again, running out of the house, up the hill. It had not occurred to her to telephone the town for help. She thought of nothing, permitted herself to think of nothing, save that she must save her loved ones.

She became aware of a sound that was not part of the night. Somewhere there was a scream. It went on and on. She plunged off the footpath, into the shrubs and undergrowth.

Sharp stones jabbed up through the soft soles of her slippers. Thorns and branches reached out and ripped her thin negligee, tore her skin. Her breath came in great gasps, but still she ran. Her negligee was now only a few wisps of silk that streamed after her.

Suddenly she burst into a clearing, and before she could stop she was in the midst of that scene from hell.

Tobias Weathers was there, and in his hand he held the bloody whip. He stood motionless, an intruder in the world of the living, and his eyes were fixed with the stare of the dead on the two who shrank away from him.

Rhoda Weathers and Harold Bedford were like paralyzed things without wills of their own, without power of motion. Rhoda was attired only in a nightgown, Harold in pajamas.

The whip rose, and its tip buried itself in Rhoda's arm. She screamed, then, and that awoke Harold. With an insane bellow of rage he jumped forward. The dead man did not move. With incredible speed, and yet seemingly with no motion on his part, the whip snapped back and forward, and its length curled about Harold's face.

He screamed and his hands came up to the bloody steak. The whip lashed out again and again at the crawling, writhing man who sought frantically to escape its torture.

With a cry, Rhoda turned and ran. The dead man paid no attention to her. Flight was futile. Lucy knew that he would bring Rhoda back when he wanted her.

Lucy picked up a rock, hurled it with all her remaining strength at what had once been her uncle. The rock went over his head, crashed in the bushes beyond. Then stark fear goaded her to flight. She whirled. Fire burned into her naked thighs. It was the whip! She sprawled full-length on the ground.

She did not rise. She lay there waiting for the second blow of the whip which was wielded by the hand of death. She sobbed into the ground, and her body was cold with a terror which reached the breaking point of human endurance.

Her body was cold, but not so cold as the hand of the dead man which closed on her naked shoulder.

Chapter 4: Vengeance From Hell

ADAM TRAIN felt that a vise was around his head and that skeleton that somehow resembled the Baron, was tightening the vise. He tried to fight off the skeleton, but he did not have the strength to raise his arms. Then he opened his eyes and the skeleton was gone, but his head still felt as if it were being squeezed in a vise.

He tried to lift his hands to his throbbing head, but they did not move. He was standing upright against a tree and his arms were behind him about the trunk. He was tied to the tree.

How had he come here? There had been a woman screaming—Rhoda Weathers—and he had run down the footpath, and suddenly everything had gone black, and now here he was with his head bursting with pain.

Somewhere a woman was sobbing. It was sobbing such as he had never heard before—not loud, yet with the hopeless intensity of one who had been irrevocably doomed to purgatory.

He had only to turn his head a few inches to see her. She sat on the ground, her legs under her, and her face was in her hands and her shoulders heaved. Several times she looked fearfully toward a cluster of birch trees. Something among those slim white trees had terrified her, yet she made no attempt to flee. She sat as if awaiting a fate that was inevitable. The woman was Julia Weathers.

"Miss Weathers," Adam called.

He had to call her several times before the words penetrated into her consciousness. Then slowly she turned.

"I'm tied here," Adam said. "Untie me."

The woman did not rise from the ground. She looked at him with the dull expression of an animal who does not comprehend words.

"I'm tied to this tree. It will take you only a minute to loosen the rope."

Slowly she shook her head. "He's come back, as he said he would. He told me to wait here."

"Untie me and I'll take you away."

"You can't." Her voice was low, utterly without hope. "He's not a man. He is a will. He is hatred incarnate. You can't run away from that."

Sight of the apparition of her dead brother must have broken down her mind. She no longer had a will of her own.

"Look, Miss Weathers, this rope hurts me," Adam said. "It's cutting into my arm. I'll be grateful if you'll loosen it a little."

She stood up, began to walk toward him. Then suddenly she stopped and stood as one frozen. She made no sound, did not move—waited.

Out of the cluster of birch trees came Tobias Weathers. His feet made no sound, seemed not to touch the ground as he moved toward his sister. In his hand was the whip on which were dried blood and bits of skin and flesh.

The whip which had lain besides the mangled body of poor Molly Weathers! Adam had left Lucy there when he had run toward Rhoda's screams. What had become of Lucy? There seemed to be fresh blood on the whip. Lucy's blood? God!

The dead man stopped and looked at Julia Weathers. It was horrible, that expression in his eyes, because there was no expression. There was no flicker of life in those eyes, yet they looked at the woman.

And there was no sign of life in his face. There was worse than no life. There was the beginning of putrefaction. By the light of the bright moon Adam saw the splotches of corruption on the cheeks and forehead.

The nose was shapeless. He was no longer a man. He was a corpse in the first stages of decay.

Then the thing tried to talk. But it couldn't. A straitjacket of sheer horror enclosed Adam Train as he heard the sounds that issued from its mouth, as he realized that the vocal cords and tongue were too far gone in putrefaction to be able to utter articulate words.

The lips did not move, but the sounds came slowly and agonizingly from the mouth. *"Glob . . . glob . . . glob."*

The dead man paused, then tried again. *"Glob . . . glob . . . glob,"* was all it could say.

With startling speed the whip snapped. Its murderous length curled about the woman's body. She screamed and spun with the impact. The whip snapped again, twisted her the other way. Too late she awoke from the spell in which the dead man had held her. She whirled to flee. The whip snaked about her waist and she went to her knees.

Again and again the whip flicked out, wielded with incredible speed by the arm of the dead man. He stood planted on the ground, only his arm moving back and forth like the piston of a machine. The whip was like a knife hacking away at the woman's skin and flesh.

Adam Train struggled furiously at his bonds. The woman was on the ground, writhing, screaming. On hands and knees she crawled to the feet of her torturer, and her back turned into a mass of raw flesh. What clothes remained on her were soaked with blood.

"Oh, God, Tobias, I'm your sister!" she shrieked. "Your own sister! Mercy! Have mercy on your sister!"

With deadly precision the whip snapped, snapped, endlessly.

Adam found that his own cries mingled with the screams of the woman. He fought the rope until he was exhausted.

It takes a long time to whip a person to death, even with as murderous a weapon as that lash. At last the screams of the woman stopped. For a while the cracking of the whip went on—then there was silence. . .

Wearily Adam Train looked up. The dead man was gone. On the ground lay what had once been the white body of Julia Weathers. It was now red, ragged flesh hanging in strips from raw bone. Here and there a particle of skin adhered to the flesh. Adam turned his face away and retched.

The more Adam struggled with the rope that tied him to the tree, the more deeply it bit into his wrist. What fate did that spawn of hell have in store for him? What had happened to Lucy and Rhoda Weathers? Where were the men who had been in the house? The screams of Julia Weathers must have been heard in the house. Why didn't somebody come to release him?

Somebody came. The figure walked into the path of the moonlight, stared down at the remains of Julia Weathers. The man's face was turned from him, but having seen that skeleton frame once, he could have recognized the Baron anywhere.

Adam did not call out to the Baron. Somehow he feared the Baron more than the dead man who walked the earth. The Baron gazed with what seemed like avid fascination at the horror on the ground.

Then he looked up and saw Adam Train. The Baron's body tensed, and he stood as if waiting for Adam to come forward. Adam realized then that because he stood in the shadow of the tree the Baron could not see that he was tied. To the

Baron he probably appeared to be leaning against the tree. Should he admit his helplessness?

Hesitantly the Baron stepped toward him. Suddenly Adam saw a shadow detach itself from the trees beyond the Baron and slink up behind him. It was a woman, Rhoda Weathers, and in her upraised hands she held a heavy branch. She wore only the thinnest of nightgowns and her naked feet made no sound on the ground.

Breathlessly Adam watched as the girl raised the branch higher, and then brought it down with all her strength on the skull of the Baron. He crumpled to the ground.

"Bravo!" Adam said. "Now untie me. I'm here, tied to this tree."

She turned from the Baron to Adam. Even in the moonlight Adam could see her magnificent dark eyes flash. He thought he had never seen any woman quite so beautiful.

"I wasn't sure he could be hurt," she said. "What kind of man is he—if he is a man? He brought father back from the dead. I saw father with that terrible whip in his hand and he was dead and yet he was walking, and he whipped Harold, and he whipped me. Father wasn't alive, but the whip was. It was the Baron who knew how to raise father from his grave so that he could walk with a living whip in his hand."

"Yes, yes, but untie me before he comes back," Adam urged.

She took several steps toward him. A crafty expression appeared in her face. "How do I know that you are not one of them?"

"For God's sake!" Adam exploded. "Will you untie me before it's too late, before he comes back!"

"I don't know you," she said. "You came tonight, a little while before father returned from the grave. Perhaps you brought him back."

"Believe me, I only want to help you," Adam pleaded.

The girl shook her head. "You brought him back," she said.

With a sinking heart Adam saw that inhuman terror had touched her with madness. He pleaded with her, cursed her. But she stood there shaking her head—stood there magnificently beautiful and mad!

Suddenly she turned slightly, listening. Adam listened too. The sound of moaning came from the cluster of birch trees. A woman moaning as in pain or delirium.

Rhoda Weathers scampered away, disappeared in the woods opposite from the birch trees. The moaning came nearer. There was movement among the birch trees and Tobias Weathers appeared. In his right hand was the whip, but it did not drag on the ground. It was secured to something behind, which, seemingly without effort, he was pulling after him.

Adam cried out. The end of the whip was tied about the wrists of Lucy Weathers!

Chapter 5: Mask of Death

WITH LEADEN FEET Lucy Weathers shuffled behind the dead man. Her expression was one of mingled abject resignation and appalling terror. When the dead man stopped, she kept on walking until she bumped into him. She jumped back from contact with the abomination and a violent tremor seized her body.

"Lucy!" Adam cried. Again he fought the rope which tied him to the tree. Hopeless! The heart went out of him and he sagged against the rope.

The cold fingers of the thing that had been her uncle untied the whip from her wrists. Her skin crawled under the touch of the dead hands. She glanced up at the emotionless, decaying face, and the moan that had been trickling from her lips rose up, up, until it lengthened into a shrill scream. Her eyes moved to the bloody corpse of her aunt on the ground, and again she screamed.

The whip curled lightly about her shoulders and her voice cracked. She trembled, stood waiting for the second blow with agony more intolerable than the actual sting of the lash.

She was nearly nude. Bushes and thorns had ripped her negligee until it hung from her in futile wisps. Under the moonlight her skin was like marble, save where the whip had made ugly gashes.

The whip leaped like a live thing, and a cruel red line appeared under her lovely breasts. Adam went berserk. The rope against which he strained was fire burning into his raw wrists. The bark of the tree tore into his back. He felt no pain. A mist formed before his eyes, and through it he saw the whip rise and fall, saw the girl on the ground, writhing, screaming.

Yet there was something strange. The arm of Tobias Weathers did not go far back; the whip did not snap. The blows were light and became increasingly lighter. The deadly whip, which could cut through skin and flesh, now raised no bloody welts.

Then the whip dangled idly from the dead man's hand. The vacant eyes were fixed on the near-naked girl. Once the whip was feebly raised, then dropped. The dead face was without emotion, was incapable of emotion, but the heavy body convulsed as if a desperate struggle were taking place within it.

The bloodless lips moved, tried to form words; but all that the decayed tongue could utter was the hideous *"glob. . . glob . . . glob."*

Then the Baron stirred. His eyes opened. Adam watched, trying to understand. Just where did the Baron fit in this grisly picture?

The dead man's back was to the Baron. Slowly the Baron began to crawl—not toward Tobias Weathers, not into the woods, but toward the tree to which Adam Train was tied! Foot by foot the Baron made his way over the ground. Tension gripped Adam.

The dead man did not turn, did not move. He stood like a statue staring down at the moaning, twitching body of Lucy Weathers.

After what seemed hours but could not have been more than a minute or two, the Baron reached Adam. His skeleton hands fumbled at the rope.

"It is up to you," the Baron whispered. "I am too weak. Twice I was hit over the head. Beware of the whip. It is a terrible weapon."

"Thanks," Adam muttered. "I don't understand. Who is that? What is it? I don't believe that the dead walk."

Softly the Baron cursed as he worked on the rope. "They don't," he replied.

The clear, sharp report of a pistol shattered the air. The Baron cried out and jumped upright. The gun spoke again and the Baron sprawled on his face.

Ten feet away stood Rhoda Weathers with an automatic in her right hand, her magnificent breasts heaving under her thin nightgown.

"You fool!" Adam exploded. "He was trying to release me."

Then he looked at her face. It had gone hideous with hate. Behind her Tobias Weathers had turned, but he made no other motion. She strode to him, looked from the whip to the nude body of her cousin.

"Well, why don't you finish the job?" she snapped. "The Baron would have released our star witness if it hadn't been for me."

The dead man spoke—spoke without moving his lips. A great weight lifted from Adam as he realized that this was not Tobias Weathers, dead or alive. This was a living man undoubtedly wearing a mask cleverly contrived to resemble Tobias Weathers. In the uncertain moonlight and the fear which his presence had inspired, the mask had been almost impossible to distinguish. Even now at this distance Adam was not certain that it really was a mask.

The masked man said: "Now you've spoiled it. Did you have to show yourself when you shot? Now we'll have to kill Train too, and I am tired of killing."

Adam tried to place the voice. Perhaps the masked man was Harold Bedford, Rhoda's fiancée. Perhaps somebody she had hired to arrange this massacre for hellish reasons of her own.

"We started it and we have to go through with it, whether you want to or not," she said. Her face was fiendish with mad lust for blood. "We'll be the witnesses. Our word is as good as anybody's. We'll say we shot the Baron when we caught him at it."

The Baron moaned softly. The bullets did not seem to have hit a vulnerable spot, but he was too weak to move.

"I loosened the rope a little," he whispered. "My God, she's stark mad and she's made him insane, too."

Desperately Adam squirmed his wrists. Inch by inch he twisted one hand out of the rope. His raw skin burned hellishly. He prayed for time.

"Finish her," Rhoda urged.

Lucy stared up at her cousin with unbelieving eyes. "Oh, God, Rhoda, make him stop! Please, Rhoda!" She could not bring herself to believe the role that her cousin played in the horrible events of the night.

The masked man brought the whip down on the helpless girl. Then again he paused. He turned to Rhoda. "I can't," he muttered.

Another inch and Adam's second hand would be free. His body was bathed in sweat as he worked frantically.

"You milksop!" Rhoda gritted. She snatched the whip from the hand of the masked man. Furiously she began to lash the unclad body of her cousin.

"Rhoda!" Lucy screamed. "Oh, God, Rhoda, you're killing me! Please!"

Rhoda Weathers was like one possessed as she rained blow after blow down on Lucy. The masked man stepped forward as if to stop her, then turned his head away.

Adam's hands were free. With hands that were clumsy in their haste he unwound the rope that bound his feet. Out of the birch trees a figure stumbled. It was stripped to the waist and streaked with blood. Harold Bedford! He staggered to-ward Rhoda and the masked man.

With deadly calm Rhoda stopped whipping her cousin and raised the gun which she held in her left hand. She was going to murder the man to whom she was engaged to be married!

By that time Adam was already running. He shrieked a warning to Harold. Rhoda paused, glanced around—and Harold was on her. With a blow he knocked the gun from her hand and bore her to the ground.

Adam charged straight at the masked man. His rage made him reckless, and as Adam rushed in he was met by a stiff right to the jaw which sent him back on his heels. Another blow knocked him to the ground.

Adam lay on his back, gasping for breath. It was suicide, he knew, to get to his feet. Desperately he glanced around—and not ten feet from him he saw the gun which Harold had knocked from Rhoda's hand. He threw his body up, dove for the gun. The masked man dove too, but Adam had his hands on it first. Steel fingers closed on Adam's wrist which was bruised from the rope. The fingers twisted. Adam groaned aloud, clenched his teeth, and held on.

Slowly, inexorably, the muzzle was forced against his own chest. The forefinger of the masked man pressed over his, squeezed. In another moment . . .

With a supreme effort Adam freed his foot, brought his knee up. The masked man grunted and his fingers relaxed. Adam swung the gun and fired twice.

When he staggered to his feet, Adam saw Lucy bent over a huddled heap of two bodies. "You're killing her!" she was sobbing. She tore at Harold's hands which had a death grip on Rhoda's throat.

It took all of Adam's remaining strength to pry Harold's fingers from the throat of the woman whom Harold had loved. Then it was too late. She was dead.

And when Harold realized that he had killed her, he began to sob like a child. "I loved her," he wept. "I loved her and killed her because she deserved to die."

The Baron had crawled toward them. Wounded, he had come to help. Adam wondered about him, this man whom he had imagined in league with the devil.

The Baron tore the mask from the face of the man Adam had shot. The man was not yet dead. Adam wished that he could shield Lucy from this blow, which in a way would be the most terrible of all. But she had glimpsed that pain-twisted face which she had known so well.

"Robert!" she moaned, not quite believing. She took two faltering steps forward, then would have fallen if Adam had not caught her. "Robert!" she repeated incredulously.

The Baron sat up, struggled agonizingly to speak.

"Robert Ingram, your lover," he said to Lucy. "It was not until I saw Molly's dead body that I began to suspect. I tried to warn you, but you misunderstood. Then you tried to save him from me"—he laughed harshly—"*from me* with your body—and for a while I lost my head. You fainted, and when I turned to where I had knocked him unconscious he was gone. I knew I had to stop him. I ran after him. I returned to the house, searched the hillside, and then carelessly I let Rhoda knock me out."

"Rhoda and Robert," Harold sobbed. "The woman I loved and my best friend."

"No!" Lucy cried, as she began to understand. "It can't be true."

Then Robert spoke, between racking coughs.

"I don't ask your forgiveness, Lucy. God, what I've done! I don't know how it happened. She was like a drug. Her flashing beauty, her magnificent body—I was her slave, bewitched, helpless. I think I ceased to love you, Lucy. I ceased to have any feeling but an all-consuming hunger for Rhoda. And on top of that she held Tobias Weathers' murder over my head."

"Murder!" Adam exclaimed. "Then you—"

"Yes, I killed him." Robert Ingram lay fighting for breath, then spoke again. "That night I came to the house. Lucy had run away, but I didn't care much. It was Rhoda I wanted.

And when I came in I found old Tobias screaming at Rhoda like a madman and there was the whip in his hand. He had found out about Rhoda and me. 'Harlot!' he screamed. 'A true daughter of your mother!' It seems the Baron had told him—that devil who knows everything."

"Yes, I told him," the Baron admitted. "I am very observant."

"He raised the whip at Rhoda," Robert went on, "and I knocked him down. He was a powerful man in spite of his age, and he rose with that deadly whip and lashed me across the body. I saw black then. I carry a gun; I have a law case against some racketeers and I need it for protection. I shot the old man dead. Rhoda and I arranged the murder to look as if a burglar had done it."

"But why did you kill Molly and Aunt Julia and try to kill me?" Lucy asked.

Robert went into a spasm of coughing. "I can tell you that," the Baron said. "Tobias had cut Rhoda off in his will after he found out about her and Robert. He had told me he would. Robert and Rhoda must have found out all about it."

"He told us just before I shot him," Robert explained. "That was what caused Rhoda to hatch this plan. I was against it at first. But I was mad with desire for her, mad with desire for money, mad with fear of the murder being discovered."

For a while he lay still and they thought he was dead. Then he opened his eyes. "Lucy, Lucy," he called weakly. "Believe me when I say that I wouldn't have been able to go through with your murder. Tonight, just after I appeared in your room and took the whip from your closet, I weakened again. Outside the house Rhoda was waiting for me. I told her that I was through, that she could give me over to the police and be damned. Then she showed me something through the window. You were wearing only a nightgown and you were standing close to Train. Maybe I loved you after all, because I went mad with jealousy. I became blood-mad. . . Lucy. . ."

His eyes closed. Adam bent over him, then stood up. "Dead," he said quietly. Lucy shuddered and buried her face in the crook of Adam's shoulder.

"Their diabolical scheme was based on the rumors that Tobias had whipped his wife to death," the Baron was saying wearily. "They weren't true, of course, as I happen to know; any more than the story about my whipping my wife to death—I never had a wife—which I once foolishly told to amuse myself by watching the reactions of Robert and Harold. So the death of the three women had to be a horrible one by the lash. They would blame me and the resurrection of Tobias Weathers. Mr. Train would later have testified to what he had observed. Harold they might have intended to kill in order to get him out of the way; I do not know. As for myself, I am certain they planned to shoot me and later explain that they had come upon me lashing Lucy. Fortunately for those of us who are still alive, their scheme did not quite succeed."

The Baron lay back on the ground, exhausted. "Fortunately," Adam echoed.

There was much to be done. He had to get the wounded man and Lucy and Harold, both of whom were weak from the torture of the lash, down to the house. He had to telephone for a doctor and for the police.

And after that . . . Adam Train's arm about Lucy Weathers tightened. She clung to him.

WHITE FLESH MUST ROT

Sometimes a certain house inspires fear. It may be a decrepit brick building in the midst of a teeming city; a once-stately manor in the last stages of decay; or a simple ramshackle cabin on the edge of a desolate lake. A cabin like the one which I saw before me in the failing light.

That cabin should have been a welcome sight. For I had been stumbling about the shore of the lake in desperate search for a space of ground sufficiently clear and dry to make a bed for the night. But there was nothing save slimy mud in which my feet sank to the ankles, sometimes to the knees. Nothing save dense vegetation which often rose higher than my head.

And there were vile flying insects which stung my sweat-covered body mercilessly. Time and again I glimpsed rattle-snakes and copperheads slithering close by; and once I nearly stumbled into a giant anthill shaped like a coffin.

The sun was nearly gone. Panic was swooping down on me, when I burst into a clearing and saw the cabin.

Yet I felt no joy at the sight of it. It seemed to be part of the hellish country—to be one with the muck and insects and snakes and ants and the stench of stagnant water. Why the cabin should have affected me thus, I cannot say. It was an ordinary one-room board structure, a bit over-run by vines and in need of a coat of paint, but it showed signs of habitation and looked as if it would provide a haven for the night.

Perhaps some buildings exude an atmosphere of their own; adopt, in some subtle manner, the character of their occupants. And perhaps that's why my first reaction to the cabin was an awareness of something sinister.

As I walked forward, a warning hand seemed to strive to hold me back. I laughed at myself, telling myself that my imagination was conjuring up silly fears. But my laugh was not a laugh at all but a silly frightened giggle.

My knock was not answered at once. While I waited, I wondered what kind of person would live in a place like this. A hermit, an evil old man, or most likely a criminal hiding from justice. I shoved my hand in my pocket, grasped my clasp knife.

Footsteps responded to my second knock. The door was thrown open, and to my surprise I saw a personable young man of less than thirty.

"I got tangled up in this—" I began, then paused. After all, this place appeared to be his home.

He grinned boyishly. "Go ahead, finish it—'this God forsaken place.' I quite agree with you. But come in. I was just about to sit down for a bite to eat. Join me."

He helped me off with my pack, filled a basin so that I might wash.

It was as if I'd stepped into another world. The single room of the cabin was furnished with taste. If it had had electricity and running water, it might have been mistaken for a one-room studio apartment in Greenwich Village. There was even an expensive rug on the floor. A bookcase stood along one wall. Along the opposite wall were shelves filled with what appeared to be large bell-jars, but because of the single dim kerosene light in the center of the room I could not make out what they contained.

My host smiled. "A little bit of heaven in hell, eh? Satan likes his comfort. I suppose you've found out that this is hell, this section of Long Lake, and I have the honor to be called the local Satan."

I laughed with him at that. I liked his light humor—not suspecting the monstrous truth which lay behind his words.

When we sat down to eat, with the light between us on the table, I noticed for the first time that his hair was snow white. Not grey but white, like the hair of a very old person, or of one who has had a frightful shock. And I observed, too, that his eyes sunk remarkably deep in their sockets, and that when he smiled his eyes did not also smile. They appeared to be forever brooding over a dreadful secret.

The meal, which was prepared by my host over an oil stove, was a simple one: dried corned beef, potatoes, coffee. The food was wholesome and I ate ravenously. He kept up sprightly conversation, and it was not until later that I realized that the talk was wholly about myself.

I told him I was a writer in the process of writing a novel. I had a unique way of outlining my novels. I would go hiking somewhere by myself, the less inhabited the country the better for my purpose; and as I walked along and as I lay at night under the stars I would plan the book. My memory was excellent, so I didn't have to take notes. After two weeks or a month I would return home, the book complete in my mind, requiring only to be transferred to paper. To me Long Lake had been only a place on a map. I hadn't known what I was getting into until I was in it.

"You also appear to like privacy," I observed.

"I do."

"For your work?" I inquired.

"Yes," he said, and turned to clear the table. It was obvious that he didn't want to talk about his work, whatever it was.

It was then that I began to notice the smell. It must have been present all the time, but because of the odor of the muck outside and my utter exhaustion I hadn't paid much attention to it. Now, well-fed and rested, its pungency seemed to cover me like a shroud. It came from the floor, from the walls, seeped out of the structure of the cabin—a smell of decay and death!

I looked about. There could be no other room, no closet, and there was no space curtained off. My eyes fell on the bell-jars. Did the smell come from them? While my host was piling the dishes into a basin, I walked over to them.

They were filled with life—squirming, crawling, slimy life. Some jars contained snakes of harmless species; others held ants, lice, worms, mice, wasps, spiders, and numerous other disgusting creatures which I could not identify.

But the smell did not come from the jars.

"How do you like my pets?" My host was standing behind me.

"So that's why you're here," I said. "I was wondering. You collect these?"

"Among other things, yes. I don't know much about them; can't tell you the names of the various species. I don't care to know so long as they serve my purpose."

"Your purpose?" I echoed.

His face was close to mine, and I saw that at last something had taken the place of the brooding in his eyes as he stared at the things in the jar. There was something else in his eyes now, what appeared to me to be a glint of madness.

I shuddered. Good Lord, was I isolated in this little bit of hell, as he called it, with a madman?

"They seem harmless enough in those jars, don't they?" he chuckled. "The bite or sting of none of them can harm you. Some of them may raise a tiny lump on your skin which may be slightly annoying for a little while, but that's all. But they are not harmless. They are the tiny things which bring madness."

I stared at him. He was mad and he knew it, and he was blaming the harmless creatures in the bell-jars for his plight.

"You don't believe me?" There was a sneer in his voice. "I will prove it to you. But first I will tell you how these little things drove a beautiful young girl mad."

And thus, standing before those bell-jars, with the smell as of death becoming increasingly stronger, this young man with the snow white hair told me the story of Janet Holm.

"Twelve miles north of the other end of Long Lake—my host began—is the town of Timberton. It's a cozy little place of less than a thousand people, and everybody knows everybody else. The one person in town who was ever disliked by a number of people was, odd as it may seem, Janet Holm, the loveliest, friendliest girl in Timberton. It was women who hated her—women who hadn't succeeded in getting men of their own, or who weren't sure of the men they did have.

They hated her with the furious burning hatred that can be roused only by jealousy; though the Lord knows there wasn't any reason to be jealous of her. She had a smile and a friendly word for everybody, but her heart was reserved for one individual, and that was a young lawyer named Roger Godwin. They were in love, utterly and completely, and everybody knew it and approved. Except the jealous women. They had convinced each other that she was a flirt, because the eyes of the men had a way of following her when she walked down the street.

None of them hated her more than three certain women who were fast friends. Each was convinced that Janet Holm was responsible for her troubles.

Amelia Evans, for instance, was married, but wasn't sure she could hold her husband. It was obvious that he'd stopped being fond of her a couple of years after their marriage. He would go out nearly every night and wouldn't come home until after his wife was in bed. Everybody knew where he went to, and so did Mrs. Evans. He was playing poker or drinking with some of the boys. But you can't expect a proud woman to admit even to herself that her husband preferred poker and drinking to her company. She'd seen him talking a couple of times with Janet Holm, and her jealous and outraged imagination worked on that until it convinced her that he was really spending his evenings with Janet.

The second of the three, Lillian Jason, had lost her husband within a year. He'd just packed up and moved to Timberton's one hotel. What had happened, nobody knew. It was probably that he'd found out his mistake and took the simplest way out. Like Mrs. Evans, Mrs. Jason wouldn't admit her deficiency in holding a man, and began to believe that her husband was living secretly with Janet Holm. Proof? What more proof did a jealous woman need than to see her husband waving a cheery hello to the prettiest woman in the town?

The third, Martha Cordner, hadn't yet achieved a man, but she believed she had one pretty nearly bagged. Or she would have, she was certain, if it weren't for Janet Holm. Miss

Cordner's fiancé owned the larger of the two grocery stores in town, and he'd been keeping company with her for some four years. Yet he didn't pop the question. Why? Miss Cordner looked around for a reason, and decided that it was Janet Holm who kept her grocer from her. Janet shopped in his store almost daily and he would laugh and joke with her as he served her. That was all Miss Cordner's inflamed mind needed.

And so these three women would get together afternoons and brew venomous hatred of sweet, innocent Janet Holm. As they talked of her, their jealousy grew until it became what jealousy always becomes when permitted to flourish—the most poisonous emotion on earth.

On one of their afternoons together they hatched their plot. It was a horrible enough thing they meant to do, but even they might have shrunk from it had they known what their insane jealousy would lead to.

"If she were my daughter, I'd spank her within an inch of her life." Mrs. Evans asserted.

"What she needs is a good whipping!" cried Mrs. Jason vindictively.

Several days later Mrs. Evans invited Janet Holm to take a drive with her out to the Evans' summer place. Janet was surprised, and she was even more surprised when she learned that Mrs. Jason and Miss Cordner were also to go. She knew that none of them liked her, though she didn't know why. That's why she probably went along. Her kind soul wanted to be friends with everybody and she thought that here was a chance to get on friendly terms with the three.

It was early spring and the Evanses hadn't moved into their summer place yet. Mrs. Evans said she wanted to look the place over to see that everything was all right. They drove out in Mrs. Evans' car.

When they got out of the car at the summer place, Janet noticed that Miss Cordner carried a package under her arm. They didn't go into the house but stopped in front of one of the two clothes poles outside the house. Then, without a word, the three women fell on Janet and began to rip her clothes off her. Literally, they ripped her clothes off with their nails, and ripped her flesh, too, in their fury. For a while Janet didn't make any resistance, so dazed was she. Then she put up a fight, but she didn't have a chance against those three.

When she was stark naked and bleeding, they tied her to the clothes pole. The rope was in the package Miss Cordner had brought. There was another object in the package too—a long black whip.

The sight of her lovely, nude young body, so infinitely more beautiful than theirs, infuriated them. Miss Cordner grabbed the whip first and wildly lashed the white skin. All three danced about her, gibbering their hatred, their jealousy. Now at last Janet learned the reason for her torture, and between the screams of agony which rasped from her throat she pleaded with them, tried to explain their mistake.

It wasn't any use. Her words, as well as the sight of her blood gushing in to fill the ugly welts raised on her skin, drove them to further fury. That beauty attracted their men. It must be destroyed!

When Miss Cordner's arm was weary, Mrs. Evans took her place, and then Mrs. Jason. Soon Janet's fair young body was a horror of bloody streaks. They might have been satisfied then if it hadn't been for the words Janet uttered.

As she hung against the ropes only half conscious in her unendurable pain, she wanted to do something to hurt her tormentors as they hurt her. And, being a woman, she knew what to say. Raising her head wearily from her torn breasts, she looked squarely at Mrs. Jason who was lashing her.

"You jealous old hens!"

They went crazy then, those three women whom Janet had characterized so correctly. "Hens, are we?" shouted Mrs. Jason, laying on with the whip. "You—you chicken!"

(My host paused. There was an intense, feverish expression on his face. The smell in the cabin was getting stronger, stifling.)

Maybe you can't understand the full implication of that ex-change between Janet and the three women—he continued—At first it may sound silly. But Janet, by calling them what they knew they were, jealous old hens, had cut deeper into their female vanity than ever they had cut into her with their whip. And when Mrs. Jason called Janet a chicken—a term, you remember, which used to be used quite a lot, meaning flirt—it gave her a hideous idea.

"You chicken!" Mrs. Jason gritted savagely. "All right, we'll treat you like a chicken! We'll feed you worms!"

(My host waved his hand along the bell-jars. I stared at them, wondering just what they could have done with the tiny creatures that was so horrible. He laughed—a dry, rasp-ing, low laugh, and went on.)

Perhaps what followed won't be easily understood by a man, but most women can understand. There was an old dis-carded chicken crate near the house—a remnant of several years ago when there were chickens on the place. They thrust the poor girl into it. It was so low that she could not sit up in it, could scarcely do more than wiggle from side to side. Then the three women went in search of worms. They found them in the soft rich ground under the rocks, and they dropped them into the coop.

Janet in particular felt revulsion for the slimy crawling things, and their touch was horrible to her. Her tormentors were too much consumed by furious hate to react to the worms as they ordinarily would have.

Frantically Janet brushed the worms off her. The three women picked them up and dropped them on her again. They hung over the crate, cackling now like real hens, and repeat-ing, "Give the chicken worms! Fat juicy worms!" Miss Cordner won the approbation of her two fellow fiends by stuffing some of the worms into Janet's mouth.

This was just the beginning. I said it was an early spring day, but it was an unusually hot day. As the sun rose higher and higher—they had left Timberton very early in the morn-ing—it beat down on Janet's defenseless naked body. Her perspiring body and the smell of blood which covered her attracted insects, which settled in her wounds and stung her hellishly.

That gave her tormentors another idea. Mrs. Evans found a jar of honey in the house. This they poured over her, and now myriad insects, lured by blood and sweat and honey, swarmed to the crate, and literally covered the girl. She brushed them off, beat them off; she crushed hundreds of them beneath the palms of her hands; she squirmed and twisted in the narrow confines of the crate. But none of her actions helped.

Even yet the women weren't satisfied. They moved whole anthills with a spade and dumped them on the girl. Mrs. Jason came across a garter snake which she dropped into the crate. Janet abhorred snakes, even snakes as harmless as garter snakes, and when it slithered over her naked body it was worse than all the blows of the whip. And finally Mrs. Evans located in the cellar a trap filled with mice. These too were let loose in the crate, and you know how most women react to mice.

All that afternoon those three women cackled fiendishly about the crate. They were having dreadful revenge on the lovely white body of the girl who was so much more beautiful than they. And Janet never ceased fighting against the things that covered her—frantically, hopelessly.

One thing she asked for they gave her. Her throat was parched from the sun, raw from screaming, and at length she begged for water. They gave it to her; but when she drank she felt the same slimy things which were on her gritting against her teeth, and too late she discovered that she had swallowed some. She felt them slide down her throat. She vomited—then fainted.

When she recovered, she was still in the chicken crate, still covered with the numberless disgusting creatures. And not until the sun sank did the three female fiends release her.

With darkness, reason returned to the three women. They hadn't given any thought to the consequences of their act. Now they began to realize the gravity of the situation they were in. When they returned to Timberton, Janet would tell what they had done to her, and then there would be hell to pay. Doubtless they would be arrested. Thoroughly frightened now, they brushed the creatures off her and washed her pain-wracked body. They were wondering how to clothe her—they had torn her clothes to shreds, you remember—when they noticed her strange behavior.

There were now no insects on her, but she continued to twist about and squirm. She continued to brush her hands desperately over her body and to plead piteously that the things be removed.

The women shook her, told her in frightened voices that there was nothing on her. Janet looked at them stupidly—and did not cease trying to free herself from imaginary insects.

Janet Holm was mad! Stark raving mad!. . .

Nearly a minute passed before I realized that my host's voice had ceased. I stood staring in horror at the things in the bell-jars, visualizing the hideous suffering that a sensitive girl, normally terrified by any crawling thing, must have undergone in that chicken crate—mental and physical suffering so great that it had shattered her mind.

I turned. My host was seated at the table, his head buried in his hands. I walked over to him.

"And then what?" I asked. "What happened to the girl?"

Wearily he lifted his head. There was intense suffering in his deep-sunk eyes—suffering and hate and something else which I could not understand but which chilled my blood.

"She was found next morning," he said. "Roger Godwin, the young man she loved and who loved her, found her. When she didn't return home by midnight, her parents became frantic and phoned Godwin. He organized a party of young men to search for her. Dawn was breaking when Godwin found her roaming naked along a little used road near Moundville. She was almost dead with pain and exhaustion, but she was twisting and wiping her hands over herself and mumbling wildly of horrible things on her body."

He paused, then said: "She's still that way. It happened six months ago, and she's still brushing imaginary things off her body, still begging that they be removed from her. Nobody knew what had happened to her. She was too far gone to tell. They saw the welts on her body, of course, and the stings of insects; but there was no way of knowing what was responsible. They never found out."

The smell of decay and death was becoming increasingly strong, or perhaps now I was more acutely conscious of it. It seemed to flow up from the floor and into me, gagging me.

I sank down into a chair opposite him, stared at him. I felt somehow that however dreadful the story he had just told me, there was something even more dreadful he had left untold.

"If nobody ever found out, how do you know what occurred?" I exclaimed.

"Did I say nobody? One person found out. At the sight of Roger Godwin she recovered sufficiently to mumble the names of the three women. Then she lapsed again into insanity."

"Then you—you're Roger Godwin?"

He nodded slowly, a weird light blazing in those eyes of his. So that was the reason for his snow white hair!

"And you told nobody?" I asked incredulously. "You let them get away with it?"

"I told nobody," he said.

I waited tensely for his next words. But again he lapsed into silence. The single kerosene lamp cast eerie shadows on the walls. Fear seeped into me—vague fear for which I could find no definite cause.

Suddenly a chuckle rasped against my ears. It wasn't the laugh of a human being. I looked up. Godwin's face was contorted into a hideous grin and the laughter of a wild mad thing poured from his lips.

I shrank back against my chair, fisting my hands in preparation for anything.

"Never fear, there is retribution," Godwin exulted. "Such a sin cannot go unpunished. There is retribution—if not from God, then from the devil! I will show you."

He crouched down on the floor, rolled up the expensive rug. A trapdoor was disclosed. He raised the door by an iron ring, and feeble light shone up from the depth below. I saw a pair of wooden steps leading down.

"Come," he ordered; and grabbing up the lamp from the table, he began to descend.

I hesitated, suddenly very much afraid. Where was he trying to lead me? What hell lay down there? The smell of death was overwhelming. I knew now that it came from below.

The light descended, leaving me in darkness. I would be utterly helpless in the dark. Instinctively I moved to follow the light, and I found myself walking down the wooden steps.

It was the cellar of the cabin. I stood on a hard dirt floor. I was covered by the smell now; it clogged my nostrils, stuffed my mouth, penetrated through my very soul.

Godwin's chuckles were now hysterical gasps. He stood next to me holding the lamp high, his face sickly green in its light. Another lamp hung from the ceiling near one of the walls. Under the lamp were three glass cases, each the size and shape of a coffin.

The walls of the first and second glass cases were literally covered with insects and larger creeping and crawling things. In the floor of the cases was a mass of corrupt matter over which myriads of things crawled and buzzed.

The smell, I knew then, came from the cases.

Then my eyes traveled to the third case—and a strident cry rasped from my throat. In the third case, amid the creeping, crawling, buzzing, devouring creatures was a woman—and she was alive!

Godwin's laugh sounded at my side. "That's the redoubtable Mrs. Evans, or what's left of her."

"Then those other two cases—" I gasped, as the full meaning of their contents struck me. "Good God!"

Godwin nodded. "Precisely. The two other cases are—or rather *were*—the domiciles of Martha Cordner and Lillian Jason. The mess in the case on the extreme left was once Miss Cordner. She came first. She was followed a week later by Mrs. Jason, who occupied the center case. Mrs. Evans honored us with her company last; thus she lingers longest."

Recollection flashed. I recalled a feature article in a New York newspaper about the mysterious disappearances of three women, each at intervals of one week, from the little town of—Timberton, of course! They had simply vanished, no one knew where or why, and were never heard of again.

I must have read that two months ago. And all this time . . .

"They weren't quite as sensitive to the little creatures as poor Janet Holm," Roger Godwin's dry voice went on. "But they had a longer period of it. Oh, a much longer period. And eventually madness claimed them, as it had claimed Janet. Observe what was Mrs. Evans."

Eyes stared at me from the third case. Eyes set in a blackened mass of bits of decaying flesh and exposed bones. Over one eyeball a black ant crawled, but the eye did not blink. No hand came up to flick it off. The eyes seemed divorced from anybody, were entities in themselves—entities of living pain and stark madness.

"After I put the women in the case and enclosed the little creatures with them," Roger Godwin gloated, "and they saw that their plight was hopeless, they tried to kill themselves. I would not permit them that luxury. Miss Cordner, for example, tried to break the glass of her case, with the aim, I presume, of cutting her throat on the jagged edges. But, as you notice, the glass is enormously thick and cannot be broken by naked hands."

He paused and laughed evilly as I shuddered.

"Each of the three thought at one time or another of starving themselves to death. They refused to eat the food or drink the water I shoved through a little door at the back of each case. I showed them their mistake."

He pointed to a vicious looking cat-o'-nine-tails hanging from a nail.

"Lashes on their naked bodies persuaded them to eat and drink. And they discovered that some of the little creatures enjoyed the blood which broke through the gashes made by the whip. I stood over them while they ate. If they left a crumb, it was the whip for them. So they ate, and ate too the little creatures which had a way of getting into the food."

His words before in the room upstairs: "This is a little bit of hell and I have the honor to be the local Satan!" Hell could have no more fearful tortures than those three wretched women had endured!

The weird chuckling laughter of Godwin increased in volume. This was a house of madness, and I knew that I too would go mad if I stayed here longer. Godwin's face was contorted in a hideous grimace of insane glee.

Sheer madness glinted in the far depths of his eyes.

"It took them a long time to die," that voice of madness continued. "I didn't want them to die. Janet hadn't the comfort of dying. But at last they began to disappear. Their physical bodies began to disintegrate—and all the time they continued to live!

"Other tiny creatures which I had not put into the cases began to appear in the glass cases. Corruption breeds corruption. Rotten flesh and waste matter breeds creatures of their own which devour healthy flesh. And so the mind and the body were eaten away at the same time."

Waves of nausea flowed through me. I steadied myself against the steps. I wanted to flee, knowing I had to flee; but I did not have the strength to move.

A cry such as no human throat could have uttered vibrated in the cellar. It was low, hardly more than a whisper—yet it knifed into the very core of my being.

I looked at Godwin. His body was convulsed with unholy laughter, hut he had not given voice to that cry. It came from one of the cases!

Those eyes of living pain and madness were again staring at me—the eyes of what remained of Amelia Evans. And from somewhere beyond the eyes the cry came—a cry of death, of final liberation in death!

Then the eyes closed abruptly and sank to the bottom of the case.

I found the strength to stumble frantically up the wooden steps. I groped in the darkness for my pack, couldn't find it, and fled that charnel house. Fled into the muck of the lake shore.

What followed that night is a blank spot in my mind. At noon the next day I staggered into Timberton, where incoherently I mumbled my experience. For a while the town constable and the other men who gathered about me could not understand me; and when at last they did, they did not believe me. But they went to investigate.

In the evening they returned, bringing Roger Godwin with them. He was still laughing in that weird, only half-human manner.

His mind, unhinged the day he found his sweetheart wandering naked and insane on the road, was now completely shattered.

The men who brought him back reported succinctly that he had murdered the three women in vengeance. They didn't say much more; not a word about why they hadn't brought the bodies back. They didn't say a word about the glass cases and what was in them.

The newspapers, you will remember, reported that Godwin had burned the bodies after killing the women. All things considered, that was the wisest thing to say, I think.

MY TOUCH BRINGS DEATH

Chapter 1: Death Party

AT THAT MOMENT I would have killed Stanley Wright if I had had a weapon. Black rage swirled in me as I sat on the floor feeling my jaw where Wright's fist had smashed against it. My friends and the woman I loved were looking down at me. And Wright stood above me, his hand still fisted, a contemptuous smirk twisting his lips.

Outside the rain beat down in furious solid sheets. For three days it had rained like that without let-up, and the Regans' summer home was the worst place to be in weather like that. The bungalow stood near the top of a hill, open on three sides to the roaring wind and the cold, driving rain. There was no heating system in the flimsy bungalow, and for three solid days we had huddled about the fireplace until our nerves were ragged. It was the kind of weather which could drive one to murder.

The only one who seemed to enjoy it was Stanley Wright. He could enjoy himself wherever there were pretty women. There were five couples, including Paul and Evelyn Regan, who were spending the week at the summer bungalow, which meant five women for Wright to try to play around with. He had been paired up with Jenny Lund, a cute little brunette, but like most libertines he seemed to prefer the women who were less accessible.

The third day of the rain he had been hanging around Fran Drake. He would sit next to her on the couch, too close, or lean over her chair whispering into her shell-pink ear. Fran and I were in love with each other, and whenever I wanted to get near her he was there first. That would have been bad enough if it had been anybody but Wright, but I knew his reputation with women, and anyway my temper had been set on edge by the weather.

It was evening when it happened. Leslie Hughes, concert pianist with an international reputation, was playing a Bach fugue for us. His charming wife, Thelma, was leaning against the piano. Lily Van Deusen, a luscious blond show-girl, was standing with her back to the fire, her hand tucked through Sam Bennet's arm. Evelyn and Paul Regan sat on the couch with Fran and Stanley Wright.

I stood against the wall, glowering at Wright and Fran, wishing that I were big enough to give him the beating he deserved. I am of average size and can generally take care of myself in a scrap, but Wright was three or four inches taller and at least fifty pounds heavier.

Fran smiled across the room at me to assure me that there was no need to be jealous. Then she rose from the couch to come to me. When she was on her feet, Wright's hand moved with lazy intimacy along her thigh.

That was when I flew at him. With a contemptuous laugh he stood up and knocked me down.

The piano was abruptly silent. For several seconds there was no sound but the rain and the wind. I sat on the floor rubbing my chin and trying to collect my dazed senses. Fran stepped in front of me and faced Wright. Her short brown bob reached hardly to his shoulders as she looked up at him.

She said: "You coward!"

Laughter rattled in Wright's throat. "What do you see in that weakling, Fran?" he said. "Why don't you admit to yourself that what you want is a real man like me?"

As I started to get up to my feet, I realized that I was sobbing aloud with rage and humiliation. I knew that I made anything but a gallant picture there on the floor and I hated myself for it.

The slap sounded like a pistol shot. Fran had brought her open palm sharply across Wright's face. He didn't stop laughing, but now there was something ugly in that laugh. He shoved out a hand against Fran's breast and brutally pushed her away.

By that time I was on my feet. As I swayed groggily, I made a prayer. I didn't know what I was saying and not until later did I find out that I had said it aloud.

"Dear God, give me the strength to kill him," I sobbed, *"Give me the power to kill him with my bare hands!"*

Then I hurled myself at him. Still laughing, he snapped out his right fist. Somehow I managed to come in under his blow. In the frenzy of my rage and the sense of impotence against his strength, I fought like a woman. My fingers clawed; my nails dug into his cheek, ripping through his skin.

Before he could bring up his arms for a second blow, the three other men in the room had come between us. Sam Bennet and Leslie Hughes were holding Wright back, while Paul Regan was pulling me away. I raged, struggling with Regan, begging for another chance at Wright.

Then Stanley Wright screamed. It was the most dreadful sound I had ever heard—the scream of a stricken animal coming from the throat of a husky man. He broke away from the two who held him and for a moment I tensed, thinking he was coming at me. But instead he dropped to the floor, writhing, thrashing his big body, his fingers tearing at his cheek where I had clawed him.

The nine of us gaped at him, not understanding. What kind of a man was he to carry on so because of a few scratches?

His thrashing ceased save for spasmodic twitchings of his limbs. The screams died down to moans. We were held spell-bound, looking down at him. Then the moans and the twitching stopped and his big body lay motionless in a strangely contorted position.

Sam Bennet kneeled down to Wright's side, turned him over on his back. He felt for the pulse, then dropped the arm which hit the floor with a dull plop.

"Dead," Bennet said hoarsely. "Look at his cheek."

I had been staring at the marks I had made with my nails. Impossible for me to have made that ugly red hole in his cheek, yet there it was.

A woman's voice shrilled above the roar of the storm. Jenny Lund pointed an accusing finger at me.

"You killed him!" she cried. "You prayed that God should give you power to kill him with your bare hands, and you got that power. Otherwise why should he have died from a scratch? He was strong and healthy."

I looked at my hands. "No," I whispered. "It was heart-failure. Something like that. He worked himself into a rage."

My eyes moved from face to face. I saw bewilderment—and fear. Fear of me. It was even in the face of Fran Drake.

Quietly Leslie Hughes said: "A man doesn't die that way from heart-failure. He was the healthiest specimen I ever saw. And he was clutching his cheek, not his heart."

His gaze was fixed on my fingers. So was every eye in the room. The tips of two of my fingers were slightly stained with red. Wright's blood. Paul Regan came over to me and lifted my arm by the sleeve. Closely he inspected my fingers. Then he wiped them with his handkerchief and carefully placed it in his pocket.

"Poison?" Leslie Hughes asked. "You think he might have put some poison on his fingers?"

Regan shrugged. "I doubt it. Any poison strong enough to kill so quickly would also have eaten through the skin of the fingertips. Or so I think. None of us is a doctor or a chemist. While there is a chance that this might be a police matter, the telephone wires have been down for the last twenty-four hours and I doubt if any of us relishes driving nineteen miles through the storm to the nearest town. I am sure none of us will run away and nothing will be lost if we wait until morning. Here, Sam, give me a hand with this body. We'll take it to his room."

I dropped down on the couch and sat with my hands between my knees. Regan and Bennet lifted the body and carried it out of the room. Jenny Lund was sobbing softly. As through a kind of fog I saw Fran come over and sit down beside me.

"John, dear," Fran whispered. "Don't let yourself go to pieces. You couldn't have killed him."

She swayed toward me.

Jenny Lund cried: "Don't touch him, Fran!"

Fran jerked away from me. It was a purely involuntary motion, but it was as if she had turned a knife in my heart. Fran afraid of me!

"I know he killed Stanley," Jenny went on wildly. "Somehow. Nobody else was near Stanley. He touched Stanley and he died."

"For God's sake, stop it!" Regan snapped from the doorway. Sam Bennet stood at his side. "We're grown people, not superstitious yokels."

Fran's small hand gripped my arm. "I'm sorry, John," she said. "You know I love you. I pulled away because Jenny screaming out like that startled me. I—"

I shrugged her hand off from me and stood up. I didn't want her to come near me or touch me. I didn't quite know why, but the fear must have been gnawing at the back of my mind that perhaps there was something to what Jenny had said. I loved Fran too much to take a chance. Perhaps unknown to me somebody had placed some sort of deadly poison on my fingers and I had not succeeded in quite wiping it off. It had entered Wright's bloodstream through the scratches.

I started to move across the room and suddenly there was Lily Van Deusen blocking my path.

"I'm not afraid of you, John," she said.

There was a faint smile on her lips and she held her voluptuous body thrust toward me, invitingly. Her dress was cut low and I found my eyes drawn to the revealed rounded tops of her white breasts. About a year ago I had fancied myself in love with this gorgeous showgirl. Then I had met Fran, and all other women had ceased to exist for me.

She cast a scornful glance at Fran. Then she leaned forward and pressed ,her lips hotly against mine. I stood rigid, bewildered, not knowing what to do. For all the response I made, she might have been kissing a wooden dummy. But to

Lily the kiss itself wasn't important. She wanted to show that her love for me was stronger than Fran's.

I stepped back and waited. For what? I don't know. But we all waited, staring at Lily.

The smile on Lily's lips broadened. She flashed a triumphant look at Fran, then stretched her arms above her head, the movement tightening her dress against her breasts. "And now I'm going to bed. Coming, Jenny?"

Jenny nodded and followed, her eyes not leaving Lily's back. We kept looking at the doorway through which the two girls had gone.

Leslie Hughes said: "What the hell's come over all of you? Did you really expect Lily to drop dead because John's lips touched hers?"

Did we? Maybe. The way Wright had died had had a queer effect on us.

I felt Fran's hand again on my arm. "John, darling, let's leave this place now. There is suddenly something horrible about it. I'd rather drive in the storm than stay here."

"No," I said. "I can't run away. The police will want to see me when they come tomorrow."

For a long time we stood there, her hand through my arm, her head resting against my shoulder. It occurred to neither of us to sit down. Presently I realized that we two were alone in the room. The others had all gone off to bed. I kept my hands behind my back. Fran's body was warm against my side. I ached to enclose her in my arms, to fondle her. But I didn't dare. My nerves were shot by the death of Wright and so they were susceptible to any sort of suggestion. I couldn't rid my mind of the notion that my prayer had been answered, that I had killed Stanley Wright with my bare hands.

"John, why don't you kiss me?" Fran whispered.

I turned. "Of course," I said. There was nothing to be afraid of; I was just a superstitious sap and Fran's lips were infinitely desirable. I moved my mouth down to hers.

The woman's scream shrilled above the fury of the storm. I had heard a man scream like that a short while before—like a soul in the throes of inhuman agony.

"My God!" I cried, breaking away from Fran and making for the door. As I reached the hall which led to the bedrooms, the screams faded away.

A door flew open and Paul Regan came out dressed in pajamas. He shot a startled look at me, then pounded after me as I went by. The screams had stopped, but I knew where to go. The bedroom which Lily and Jenny shared!

I pulled open the door and then stopped dead in my tracks. Jenny Lund stood in the middle of the room, her hands clutching her breasts, a crazy moan trickling from her lips. Her eyes bulged at the nude form at her feet. A single glance showed that Lily Van Deusen was dead.

Chapter 2: Death Is Where I Touch

AS I STEPPED INTO THE ROOM, Jenny Lund shrank away from me. I heard exclamations of horror behind me, but nobody came very far into the room. In various states of undress they stood huddled about the doorway, careful not to come too close to me.

For the second time my touch had killed. The interval between my touch and the coming of death had been longer with Lily Van Deusen, but that was all.

"Her mouth!" Evelyn Regan gasped from the doorway. "Look at it! That's where he kissed her."

Lily Van Deusen's provocative red lips were gone. Where her mouth had been was ugly raw flesh which looked as if it had been burned. The rest of her body was untouched as it lay nude in a crumpled position of agony. Her sightless staring eyes still mirrored the frightful pain in which she had died.

Jenny Lund had moved across the room, giving me a wide berth, to join the others at the doorway. "We were asleep," she was saying in a high-pitched, hysterical voice. "Suddenly

Lily began to scream, thrashing her body madly. I leaped out of bed and switched on the light. She was off the bed, in her agony ripping her nightgown from her. Then the screams stopped and she sank to the floor. It was all over in less than a minute."

She turned to me, yelling, "He touched her the way he touched Stanley. He prayed for the power to kill with his hands. He wanted to kill only Stanley, but that terrible power stayed with him. If he touches any of us, we'll die like that."

"Nonsense!" It was Fran's voice ringing out clearly. She pushed through the others, came into the room. "A few minutes ago John touched me. Nothing happened to me."

"How do you know?" Sam Bennet said. "Lily didn't die right away."

There was an abrupt silence. Fear shot into Fran's eyes.

"Damn you, Sam!" I blurted out. "Even if my touch does mean death, she's safe. She's wrong, I didn't touch her. I was careful not to. She touched me."

The fear in Fran's eyes receded to give way to the love which shone there.

"I don't believe that a touch can bring death," Fran said. "John, she kissed you. She wasn't afraid. I love you and I'm not afraid either."

As she stepped toward me, I moved backward. "Fran, no! For heaven's sake! Maybe my touch doesn't kill. Maybe it does. I can't take a chance. Keep her away, somebody! Don't let her near me!"

Leslie Hughes grabbed her shoulders. "He's right, Fran. None of us can take a chance until we're sure."

She twisted in his grip, crying, "I don't care. If he's like that, I want to die too. Let me go."

I saw there was only one thing to do. I crawled through the open window out into the storm. In a moment I was soaked to the skin.

In the house Fran's voice rose to a shriek. "He's going to kill himself! Stop him! John, John, they're holding me and I can't go to you! Don't do anything rash! John, darling!"

Then Jenny Lund's voice, husky with bitterness: "Let him kill himself. I hope he has the nerve. It's the only decent thing to do."

I moved away, stumbling in the utter darkness. Fran had been right: I was going to kill myself. What else was there left for me to do? I had brought the curse on myself. I was like King Midas who had prayed for the gold touch, only I had prayed for a death touch. I could never again go among men. I could never again hold Fran in my arms.

And if I did not kill myself, I would go mad. I would run amuck, spreading horrible death. There was only one way out.

Lightning flashed and I saw three forms in raincoats bowing against the storm as they came from the house. A voice shouted: "There he is." Then it was dark again and another voice shouted: "Come back, John. Wait until morning. The police will investigate—" The wind carried the rest of the words away.

I stood rooted to the spot, waiting. The beam of a flashlight came to life and neared me. The rain was clearing my head. There was something in what they said. I wasn't absolutely sure that my touch brought death. There might be some human agency involved which the police, would discover. I could lock myself into a room and wait until the police came.

Lightning showed me the white faces of Paul Regan and Leslie Hughes and Sam Bennet only a few feet from me. Darkness enveloped us again.

"Don't come too close to me," I warned. "I'll skirt around you and go to the house."

I started to move around the flash. Then I felt myself falling. My foot had hit a rock or a root or something. Instinctively my hands shot up, pawing air. My hand grabbed something solid, closed over an arm, and I held on, righting myself. The flashlight swept around to me and I saw Sam Bennet staring in horror at where my hand clutched his arm.

"God!" Sam gasped. "Oh, my God! I'm going to die!"

I dropped my hand and stepped back. I was all ice inside. The flash swerved, shone full on my face. Then the flash moved over to Sam an instant before he started to scream.

For the third time that night I heard those terrible animal howls of unbearable agony. The flash revealed the pain-contorted face and writhing body of Sam Bennet. Insanely his fingers clutched at his coat-sleeve where I had touched it. Then he was running down the hillside, his shrieks mingling with the wind and the rain.

I ran too. There was no reason in my running, no direction. I simply pumped my legs as if in a desperately impossible effort to flee from myself, to flee from the dreadful curse which had become a part of me. Above me and to my right the screams went on, endlessly, and in intervals between the screams I heard the voices of Regan and Hughes shouting.

Evidently they were pursuing him. What good could it do? He was doomed. I had touched him and he was dying.

I cannot say how long I stumbled about in the darkness and rain. My latest victim was indisputable proof that my prayer had been answered in terrible form. I knew that I had to kill myself, but I didn't know how to.

Presently I dropped with exhaustion. I was at the foot of the hill and from where I lay I could no longer see the lights of the house. From my hips down I was in a cold, muddy puddle of rainwater. I made no effort to move out of the puddle. Nothing mattered but that I wanted to die.

"God, you answered my prayer once," I muttered. "Answer it again. Let me die."

More time passed, and then out of the blackness a tiny light appeared coming toward me. The light stopped moving and sank to ground level where it remained. Through a brief lull in the storm I heard a startled exclamation.

Groggily I rose to me feet and shambled toward the light. It had a kind of hypnotic effect on me; seemed to be drawing me to it as if by invisible strings. And when I neared the light I saw that it was a storm lantern, and by its dull radiance I saw an old man staring down at a dark form on the ground.

The storm covered the sounds of my approach until I was almost on him. He straightened up with a jerk, his fingers curling around the trigger of the squirrel rifle under his arm. He wore a rubber raincoat and a crushed felt hat from which water cascaded. His face was weather-beaten. For a moment he gaped at me, then his eyes shifted to the form on the ground.

I nodded wearily. It was Sam Bennet, of course. By the light of the storm lantern I could see the ragged hole in the fabric of his sleeve where I had touched him. Right through the gabardine of his raincoat the curse of my touch had gone. I looked at my hands, flexing the fingers as if I wanted to make sure that they really belonged to me. I wanted to die!

"I live in a shack down at the foot of the hill," the old man was saying. "I thought I heard screams a couple of hours ago, but I figured it was only the wind. Then I heard screams again, this time nearer, so I went out to see." Again he looked at the corpse and repeated incredulously:

"Dead."

He swung around at me, rifle lifting.

"I'm cursed," I said wildly. "I touched him and he died. My touch is death. Give me your rifle and I'll shoot myself."

He drew his breath in scornfully. "Think I was born yesterday? So you killed 'im, eh? Guess I'll take you up to the house till we get the police."

"I'll make you kill me," I said. "If I touch you you'll die like that and I'm going to touch you, so you'll have to shoot me. Please shoot me."

The old man went back a step and ran his tongue over his lips. "You're crazy. Keep away from me."

"Please!" I said. "Just point the gun at my heart and press the trigger. I'm a murderer. I deserve to die. I—"

I froze. From up the hill the long drawn cry of a woman keened through the storm. Fran? There were only three women up there. The one who screamed might be Fran. I strained to distinguish the voice, but couldn't.

"It's Fran!" I yelled at the old man. "She touched me. I thought that because it was she who touched me the curse wouldn't work. But how do I know how it works? Oh, God, Fran, I did this to you! Fran!"

I whirled and started up the hill. The old man shouted: "Hey, wait! You can't run away."

Chapter 3: Menace in the Dark

IN A MOMENT I was swallowed up by the darkness. I no longer wanted to die. Not, at any rate, right away. First I had to see if Fran was in danger. I didn't stop to think that if Fran were a victim of my death touch there was nothing I could do for her. And all my mind could encompass was that it was probably she who had screamed and that I had to go to her.

A jagged streak of lightning momentarily revealed the bungalow flat and brooding and totally dark against the side of the hill. I had thought that the terrain of the land had shut off my view of the bungalow lights, but now I realized that the lights had been out for some time. Why?

Had the storm put the electricity out of commission? Or was something sinister happening up there? A woman wouldn't have screamed like that simply because the lights had gone out.

When I was a hundred feet from the bungalow, lightning once again illuminated the hillside. A voice shouted: "John!"

Blackness swooped down as I whirled. "Fran?" I yelled, and waited breathlessly for an answer. It came—Fran calling my name again. I could have wept with joy. Thank heaven she was safe! Calling to each other, we moved toward each other in the blackness.

The next flash revealed Fran only a few feet from me. The fleeting moments before the darkness returned seemed to hang in suspense while I drank in her beauty. I had been sure that I would never again see her, that when she next looked at me I would be dead, a suicide. At that moment, standing there with the rain pouring over her face, with her drenched dress plastered against her tall, lithe form, she was breathtakingly lovely. Then the light was gone, but the image of her beauty remained seared on my brain. She was everything worth living for—and I could not dare to take her in my arms.

"John," Fran's voice came out of the darkness, and then I felt her body against me.

I placed my hands behind my back. "You mustn't come near me," I gasped. "Sam Bennet is dead too. I stumbled against him in the darkness, touched him, and now he's dead."

"I don't care," Fran said. "I'll die in your arms then."

"Fran, keep away! Please! There might be a cure. Maybe if I pray that the curse be lifted. We'll get a doctor here somehow."

Her voice was very close to me, quivering as we stood there with the rain beating down on us. "John, darling, I'm afraid. Something terrible is happening here. There's nobody there in the house. Where could they have gone? I persuaded the three men to bring you back, to stop you from trying to kill yourself. We four women stayed in the house, Evelyn and Jenny and Thelma and I, waiting. Then we heard Sam scream. He screamed for a long time and we nearly went crazy. We didn't dare go out into the darkness without a light. And Paul and Leslie didn't come back. They haven't come back yet. Then the lights went out. The switch didn't work. The darkness was terrible. We huddled together, going mad with fear. Suddenly Thelma screamed. We heard nobody else in the room. She screamed and then she seemed to be gone. Jenny wailed that you must have touched Thelma before you left and that she'd died."

"I don't know," I said. "I don't remember, but I might have." My voice rose hysterically. "Don't you see I have no right to live?"

"No," Fran insisted. "Don't talk like that. There's something else abroad. I felt it in that dark house. We couldn't stand it in there any longer. Even the storm seemed safer. Jenny ran out first and then Evelyn and then I followed, groping my way through the door and out into the rain. All the others seemed to have vanished. Then I saw you. Oh, John, darling!"

I knew that she was throwing herself at me. I stepped away. "Fran! We can't take a chance on my touching you—yet. Perhaps there is something in the house which can explain the hellish things which are going on. We'll go there. But don't come too close to me."

It took a long time to go those hundred feet to the house. We had to wait for the occasional lightning flashes to make sure of our direction, and we had to keep close to each other without touching. I felt my way up the stairs, along the porch and finally into the bungalow. Fran and I kept up a steady whisper in order to keep together.

I groped about the living room. I remembered having seen books of matches on the table. The matches in my own pocket were of course useless. If I could find the matches, we could light our way into the kitchen. There was a kerosene lantern there for just such emergencies.

My hand touched the table top, moved over it, grasped a matchbook. I tore off a match and—

Fran's voice keened out in pure terror. I swung toward her voice, screaming, "Fran! What happened, Fran?"

Silence. No sound but the driving rain outside.

"Fran!" With trembling fingers I began the motion of striking a match. I never finished it. Something hurled itself against me, knocking me against the edge of the table.

Then I was fighting. I felt a raincoat under my hands. I lashed out wildly into the darkness with both fists. And I thought: Why doesn't he die? I've touched him and he ought to die. Does the curse work only when I don't want it to?

Abruptly my mind went blank . . .

Awareness returned gradually. I could not tell when my eyes were open because the darkness was always there. My head throbbed hellishly. Gingerly I touched my temple, felt the stickiness of blood. My assailant must have knocked me out with some sort of heavy object.

Dizzily I rose to my feet. "Fran," I called weakly. No answer. I felt what seemed to be the table against my thigh. There had been other bookmatches on the table. I found one, struck a light. The room was empty.

Lighting matches, I made my way out to the porch. As soon as I got outside, the wind whipped out the tiny flame—but not before I had seen the figure lying almost at my feet. With a choked cry I fell to my knees. My hands touched the smooth surface of a raincoat. Relief gushed through me. Not a woman's body. Not Fran's.

Hunching my body, I struck a match, nursing the flame between my cupped hands. I glimpsed the dead, upturned, horror-glazed face of the old man I had met at the bottom of the hill. Then the match went out.

I stood up. How had he died? Was he the one I had fought in the house? Had my touch killed him?

Then he must have abducted Fran? But how? If he had gotten this far before my touch killed him, how could he have taken Fran away? Perhaps she was still in the house ... dead ...

As in a trance I went to the kitchen, lit the kerosene lamp, and went through every inch of the bungalow. No sign of Fran—or of any other human being. I went out into the storm. In a second the lantern was out. I stood in the rain, not thinking, not feeling—simply stood there in an aching stupor.

A tiny cry brought me back to awareness. I tensed, listened. Then I laughed bitterly, crazily. It had only been the wind in the trees.

But, no, there it came again—a human voice riding up with the storm from somewhere at the foot of the hill. I concentrated in an effort to catch that cry once more, but I heard only the storm.

Mechanically I started to move down the hill. I could see nothing, but the slope of the ground gave me the direction. Suddenly it struck me that they all might simply have fled from me. Even Fran. There was no automobile road going up to the bungalow—the rise was too sheer—so Paul Regan had built a three-car garage at the bottom of the hill. If the cars were gone, I would know that they had merely run away.

As I neared the foot of the hill, I saw a tiny dot of light. That would be coming from the back window of the garage. Somebody was there, probably preparing to leave.

Don't go down there, an inner voice whispered to me. *Let them get away from you.*

But I kept going. I had to make sure that they were really leaving. What was it Fran had said? "Something terrible is happening around here." Aside from my death-touch? She had implied that. I would look through the back window of the garage, and if everything were all right I would go back up on the hill . . . and up there in the bungalow I would do away with myself as a creature damned, unfit to live.

The light from the window showed me the vague outline of the corner of the garage. I felt along the wall, moving toward the window.

"That'll be far enough," a voice said in my ears. "Don't turn because this is a gun in my hands."

I stood rigid. Round steel bored into the small of my back.

"Go ahead, shoot," I said. "I've been trying to kill myself."

Laughter grated harshly behind me. I was sure I knew that voice, but the wind and the rain prevented me from placing it.

"That's too easy," the voice said. "I have a more amusing scheme."

Then for a second time within thirty minutes my brain exploded into blankness.

Chapter 4: Madman's Sport

PAIN BROUGHT ME back to consciousness. For a while, I was aware only of an unendurable throbbing in my head and a violent roaring in my ears. And then through a thick haze I saw a naked woman doing a fantastic dance.

"John!"

My name was spoken softly, yet it sliced through the roaring in my skull. Was it the dancing woman who had spoken? Her mouth was open, but she wasn't looking at me. Her eyes were riveted on something above her.

"John!"

As if a sheet had been suddenly jerked away from in front of me, full awareness returned. The pain was still rioting in my head, but I knew who had called my name and where I was.

I turned my head. Agony burned through my skull with the motion, but it didn't matter. "Fran!" I cried. "Are you all right?"

She was standing against the wall only a few feet away from me with her hands raised above her head. Blood oozed slowly from her right temple and brightened the blood which plastered her cheek.

"He's mad," Fran wailed. "One by one he'll kill us like that!"

I realized that I too was standing with upraised hands against a wall. I looked up, ignoring the agony which every motion of my head brought, and saw that my wrists were tied and the rope was looped about an iron hook fastened in the wall about a foot above my head. Fran was secured in the same way, and beyond her I saw two other figures.

We were in Paul Regan's garage at the bottom of the hill, and the hooks which held our wrists were ordinarily used for hanging up work clothes and accessories. They couldn't be very firmly imbedded in the wall or very strong—or so I thought. I tested my weight against the hook and succeeded only in cutting my wrists on the rope.

"It's no use," Fran was sobbing hysterically. "Even if we did get down from the hooks, he'd get us. We're doomed."

Her dress was in rags. One of her perfect upthrust breasts was bared, but it wasn't white. It was plastered with mud. Mud covered what there was left of her dress, plastered her from head to foot. Next to her stood Evelyn Regan and next to Evelyn, Jenny Lund, their wrists fastened to hooks. Like

Fran their dresses were torn and mud-covered and like Fran blood from their heads mingled with the mud.

I realized what had happened. One by one we had been knocked out in the total darkness. That was why there had been so little sound—a quick blow from behind and then we had been dragged down the hill, through the mud and over the rough ground, and tied to these hooks.

But one of us would never recover consciousness. The blow must have been too hard. I looked at where Jenny Lund hung limply from the hook, her head hanging at a queer angle, her chin almost touching her breast.

"Dead!" Fran whispered, following the direction of my gaze. "He killed her. She was saved that—that hellish torture."

Her horror-filled eyes were drawn again to the girl who was dancing so weirdly in the center of the garage. The roaring was still pounding in my brain, but now I knew that it was the storm driving against the garage and the screaming of the woman who danced.

Why did she scream and go through those gyrations? I stared at her. It was Thelma Hughes. One end of a ten-foot chain was clamped about a slim ankle; the other end was fastened to an iron ring in the floor. She leaped out as far as the chain would let her, fell flat on her face, was up again in an instant, and, breasts joggling, ran in the opposite direction until the chain again brought her to an abrupt stop. Her nude body was bathed in sweat, her eyes fixed on something near the ceiling, and all the time she kept shrieking as if she had completely lost her mind.

"Your own wife!" Evelyn Regan cried. "You can't. She's your wife, you fool!"

A fiendish chuckle came from the ceiling. Slowly, while my head felt like a balloon that was about to burst, I moved my head back until I saw him. He was sitting astride a rafter directly above Thelma, and his face was contorted into the chortling mask of a bestial madman.

I closed my eyes, easing the pain in my head, telling myself that what I had seen couldn't be true. Wearily I tore my eyelids open. I had· seen correctly the first time. That face, almost unrecognizable in its hideous transformation, belonged to Leslie Hughes!

Holding onto the rafter with one hand, he leaned down. In his other hand he held a long metal tube which he pointed at Thelma. As she leaped about, her frantic eyes were fixed on that metal tube. Now I understood the reason for her weird dance: She was trying to keep out of the line of that tube.

I saw Hughes' thumb come down on the head of the tube, evidently pushing in a plunger. Thelma shrieked and jumped—but nothing seemed to have happened.

"He's playing with her," Fran mumbled at my side more to herself than to me. "He can hit her any time he wants to. He's making her suffer, drawing out the suspense. When he's finished with her, he'll do the same with the rest of us. Oh, God, who'll be next?"

"Hit her?" I said. "With what?"

A voice on my left said: "Acid. That's the way he killed the others."

I turned. Paul Regan, his eyes bulging, his face haggard hung from a hook on my left. Like myself and the women, he was covered with mud.

Again Hughes pushed the plunger in and this time, because I looked for it, I saw a tiny stream of liquid squirt from the tube. It hit the ground inches from Thelma. She leaped, screaming; then, grabbing the chain with both hands, she frantically tried to pull the chain from the iron ring. It was futile, of course.

"Leslie!" she shrilled. "In the name of heaven, why me? I never harmed you. I'm your wife, Thelma. You love me, Leslie, please!"

Leisurely Hughes· pulled out the plunger. "So you love me?" he laughed harshly. "Do you think you can fool me anymore? Don't you imagine I knew about you and Stanley Wright? You thought you were pulling the wool over my eyes during these days of rain, didn't you? You thought I didn't know that you and Wright would steal away whenever you got a chance to another end of the bungalow to make love? No, my beloved, I am no longer a fool."

"It's a lie!" Thelma wailed. "I had nothing to do with Stanley. I swear it. You must believe me. *Don't!*"

He aimed the tube at her.

Paul Regan shouted: "Leslie, you're being the fool. Don't you know you can't get away with this?"

Hughes shrugged. "Who will know? I'll shoot you when I'm finished with the others and blame it on you."

Desperately Regan said: "You're not as clever as you think. You didn't fool me. When John stumbled and touched Sam Bennet, I knew he couldn't have tripped over a rock. That would have been too much coincidence. You tripped John."

"But I got you anyway," Hughes gloated. "Oh, I was smarter than you. I knew that you suspected me and that you were waiting until I returned to the bungalow where you no doubt had a gun and intended to hold me until the police came. But I knocked you out before we reached the bungalow. Then I cut the electric wires and one by one I knocked the others out and brought them here. John fought me in the bungalow, but it didn't do any good. I knocked out that old man who came snooping around and while he was senseless I doused him with this nitrobenzene. He's dead now, like you'll all be dead soon, only he died easily. You'll suffer." His voice rose. "God, how you'll all suffer!"

"But why us?" Evelyn Regan implored. "We never harmed you."

Hughes swayed precariously on the rafter as he turned to her. If only he would lose his hold and fall and break his neck. It was our only hope—and a very slim hope indeed. He seemed agile as a monkey up there.

"You pretended to be my friends, but you let Wright and my wife betray me. You knew what was going on, but you said nothing to me. Now you'll all pay—and what sport I'll have!"

"You're mad!" Paul Regan yelled. "Jealousy drove you mad. You were always insanely jealous of Thelma. I put it down as the temperament of a great musician. Wright went after your wife the way he went after all women. He didn't have an affair with Thelma. But your inflamed imagination ran away with you and you determined to get revenge on both of them. You prepared that tube of nitrobenzene. It's deadly stuff. Even a few ounces on one's clothes will kill in dreadful agony. You were going to use some on Wright during his sleep and then probably frame Thelma as his murderer. You intended to plant the tube on her with her fingertips on it and it would have seemed as if she had become jealous of Wright, her lover, paying attention to other women and so had killed him."

Regan paused for breath. Hughes sat perfectly still on the rafter, listening. I knew that Regan was talking in order to mark time. Perhaps with time Hughes' homicidal madness would pass. Or perhaps help would come. But from where? Our only neighbor within miles had been the old man who lay dead on the porch of the bungalow.

Regan went on: "Then when John scratched Wright's cheek and muttered that prayer, you changed your plans. The tube of nitrobenzene was in your pocket. You palmed it and while you and Sam Bennet were holding Wright back, you managed in the excitement to squirt some of the deadly stuff on the wound in his cheek. In the hysteria resulting from the horrible way Wright had died we almost convinced ourselves that John truly possessed a death touch. Jealousy had already twisted your mind somewhat, and under the impact of murdering it cracked completely. In your madness your grievance against Wright and your wife broadened to a hatred against all of us. Everybody, it seemed to you, was against you. And you thought it a clever idea to play God and kill whomever John touched. When Lily Van Deusen kissed John you had no opportunity to use nitrobenzene on her until she was in bed. Then you sneaked into her bedroom and squirted some on her mouth and were out of the room a few seconds before Lily started screaming. After you tripped

Sam Bennet in the darkness, it was easy for you to squirt some on him. He took longer to die because the stuff had to eat through his coat. Then you—Oh, my God!"

Lesley Hughes had ceased to listen to Regan. His eyes had shifted to where his wife stood naked below him, her sweat-bathed body trembling violently with terror and exertion and the certainty of frightful death. Now Hughes' long sensitive fingers, which had enthralled multitudes throughout the world as they had glided over the keys of a piano, tightened their grip on the tube—and his thumb came down on the plunger.

His maniacal laughter mingled with Thelma's inhuman shrieks as the deadly stuff hit her bare abdomen. And all of us in that garage screamed too; and as Thelma writhed on the floor, tearing at her naked flesh with her fingers, we writhed against the wall, pulling at our bonds. I saw blood trickle down Fran's forearms where the rope had cut her wrists, and the fire in my own wrists told me that I also was bleeding.

It might have been only a few minutes or a long time before Thelma died. Presently she lay in a twisted, motionless heap—liberated at last. For her the torment was over. For us it was just beginning.

Hughes thrust the tube in his pocket and pushed himself along the rafter until he reached the high ladder which stood against the wall. Slowly, inexorably, he came to us, his insane eyes sweeping over the four of us who still lived—selecting his next victim.

Desperation seized me. If he selected me, there might be a chance. He would have to remove me from the hook in order to drag me over to the chain, and perhaps even with my hands tied I could do enough damage to him to put him out of commission. A well-directed kick . . .

I forced my lips into a contemptuous sneer. "You are a fool, after all, Leslie." I said. "You thought it was Wright who made love to your wife. It was I. Wright and I fought over your wife. We fought because I had beaten him out. And you did not know."

There was a sudden silence. The others gaped at me as if I, too, had lost my senses. Hughes' face went livid.

"So!" he grated. "I knew you were all against me, betraying me. Very well, you'll suffer twice. The first time when you watch the woman you love dying in agony."

He gripped Fran under the armpits and lifted her from the hook. She kicked at him, flailed out against him with her tied hands. But her struggles were futile. He threw her brutally to the ground, dug his fingers into her hair, and, while she squirmed and screamed, dragged her to the center of the garage.

I shouted in a tear-choked voice: "I told you I don't love Fran. She means nothing to me. It's your wife I loved. You're afraid of me. You sniveling coward!"

My taunts had no effect on him. "You love Fran, too," he said stolidly as he unfastened the chain from about Thelma's ankle while he held Fran with one hand.

I cursed myself then. If I had kept my mouth shut, he might have taken Regan or myself first. Now, even if by some miracle help would come, it would be too late.

When he had the chain about Fran's ankle, he dragged Thelma's corpse out of the way. Then he stripped every bit of clothing from Fran. She made no more resistance. She cowered under the lustful burning gaze of the madman, her palms pressed against her breasts. And even when he ran probing hands over her adorable nudity, she did no more than tremble and moan.

He did not spend much time in fondling her. His lust was of a different sort. His madness had turned all his emotions to pure sadism.

He mounted the ladder, made his way out on the rafter until he was directly above her, and pulled the deadly metal tube from his pocket.

Slowly Fran's head fell back until her eyes were on Leslie Hughes. There was no plea for mercy in her gaze, no defiance—nothing save the blankness of utter hopelessness. Then her head fell forward and still trembling but without a sound now issuing from her lips, she stood naked and in-credibly lovely waiting for agonizing death.

It was at that moment that my eyes fell on the squirrel rifle. Hughes had leaned it against the wall near the door after hav-ing taken it away from the old man, and after having held me up with it outside of the garage. But the gun might as well have been in China for all the good it did me.

Disappointment mingled with the insanity in Hughes' face as he stared down at Fran. Her lack of resistance obviously chagrined him. Thelma had been more sport. He spurted a stream of the nitrobenzene within a foot of her. She did not move, did not cry out. Knowing that death was inevitable, she seemed determined to deprive him of his sadistic sport.

I, meanwhile, was screaming and cursing and tearing at the ropes about my wrist, ignoring the fiery pain of torn skin and flesh and muscle.

Then the hook came out.

My weight snapped it. In my struggles, I had grabbed it with my hands and lifted myself a few inches from the floor. The hook, loosened by my previous efforts and never too firmly imbedded into the wall, pulled out of the wood, and I fell forward on my face. I was up in an instant, hurling my-self toward the squirrel rifle.

Hughes, intent on pulling the plunger out of the tube, did not know I was free until I had the rifle under my right arm and, in spite of my bound wrists, one finger on the trigger. Then he just stared at me, his thumb still firmly planted on the plunger.

It was a stalemate. It required no words on his part to tell me that the instant I pressed the trigger the deadly stuff, would spurt down on the girl I loved. And so we stood there, I watching Hughes, he watching both Fran and me, careful to see that the tube was pointed directly at her. He was mad, yes, but he possessed the caginess of the mad.

"Shoot!" Fran said in a strange, flat voice. "Shoot him and save yourself and Paul and Evelyn."

I remained silent, every nerve tense. He was through and he knew it. He could kill Fran before he himself died, but there was no way he could have saved himself. And then he laughed in a way that turned my blood to ice and he leaned over so that his downstretched hand was less than a foot above Fran and he could not possibly miss her.

Three things happened in the same instant. Fran threw herself forward to the end of the chain. Hughes' thumb came down on the plunger. I pressed the trigger.

The roar of the rifle vibrated in the garage, shutting out the noise of the storm. Hughes toppled on the rafter, swayed, and crashed down to the floor. His body missed Fran by inches.

I stood motionless, my heart not beating, as I stared at Fran. No cry of agony came from her lips. She rose to her knees, looked with dazed eyes at the dead body of Leslie Hughes, then at me.

"Fran!" I sobbed. "Thank heaven the stuff didn't touch you."

She went hysterical then and so did Evelyn Regan. Paul Regan and I began to laugh too, and for a moment it was as if we had all gone mad. Who can blame us?

Fran removed the cord from about my wrist and then I released her from the chain. Before we freed Paul and Evelyn Regan we threw our arms about each other, clinging. No longer was I afraid to touch her, and as we stood there we knew that out of the horror of the night had come a yearning for closeness to each other which the years would not lessen.

I SAID YES TO SATAN

Chapter 1: Marriage to the Devil

WHEN PEGGY BARNETT entered her father's sumptuous private office, Frank Hutton rose to leave. He walked past her and the door opened behind her, but it did not close at once. Peggy knew that Hutton had paused to look at her with that brazenly impudent stare of his.

Swiftly she glanced over her shoulder, and there were Hutton's black eyes on her. As always, she glimpsed something in their somber depths that made her flesh crawl.

His thin lips went crooked. Then the office doer closed behind him.

John Barnett was ruffling papers. "Sit down, Peggy," he mumbled. "I'll be with you in a minute."

She crossed her slim legs and lit a cigarette to calm her jumpy nerves. She was angry with herself for being afraid of Frank Hutton; but there it was, and no amount of reasoning could make her feel at ease in his presence or at the thought of him.

She leaned forward. "Father."

John Barrett pushed aside papers and looked up. He was a broad-shouldered man with a square face which radiated force. He beamed at his daughter, drinking in her blonde loveliness.

"You are like a breath of clean air," he said and sighed with weariness. "Dirty business, stocks and bonds—sometimes."

With nervous fingers she mutilated her cigarette in an ashtray. "Father, why do you keep that Frank Hutton?"

A cloud passed over Barnett's face and one big hand fisted. "Has he been getting fresh to you?"

"No," she said quickly. "I don't think he's ever even spoken to me. But there's something nasty about him, especially the way he looks at me."

John Barnett threw back his head and laughed. "I thought every woman likes men to look at her with admiration. Of course, you're so used to that you can afford to resent it. Hutton happens to be the most efficient secretary I've ever had. Always found him to attend strictly to business."

"You don't understand, Father," she tightly. "Whenever I come here, his eyes follow me around. They undress me, if you know what I mean, and do worse than that. I suppose I'm being foolish, but I'm actually afraid to come here because of him."

"I'm sure you're being foolish." Barnett leaned across the desk and patted her hand. "However, if he makes you at all uncomfortable, I'll fire him."

When she left her father's office ten minutes later, an oppressive sensation weighed on her heart. She told herself that it was because she regretted having caused a man to lose his livelihood, and she hesitated in the reception room, debating with herself whether to return to her father and ask him not to discharge Frank Hutton after all.

"If you have a few minutes to spare for me, Miss Barnett . . ."

Frank Hutton stood at her side. His black eyes in which strange fires flickered were unwaveringly on her. He was a thin man with a slight stoop and gaunt, ugly features.

"I can think of nothing I would care to discuss with you," she responded.

"Oh, but there is. A matter of vital importance concerning you and your father." His bloodless lips smiled. "I might say it is practically a matter of life and death. You will please step into my office."

"We can talk right here."

He kept looking at her in that way which sent little darts of ice over her. "I am afraid not." Again that pause and that crooked smile. "Certainly you do not fear to be with me in my office? You need only raise your voice to be heard by thirty people. Believe me, this concerns the future of your entire family."

The intensity of the man's voice persuaded her. After all, she had nothing to lose. She followed him into the small office which was his.

Peggy refused his offer of a chair and a cigarette. Holding her handbag with both hands, she remained standing. Hutton leaned against his desk and lit a cigarette. His smile had turned into an unpleasant smirk. She was anxious to get out of his sight.

"Now what is it you want?" she demanded.

He said: "I overheard you persuade your father to fire me."

So that was it! "I said I had nothing to discuss with you," she said, and wheeled toward the door.

"Wait!" He touched her arm. It was a light touch, yet the feel of his fingers sent a shudder through her. "I want to tell you that you wasted your breath. Several days ago I made up my mind to quit on my own account. I'm getting married."

"What's that to me?"

"Because," he said softly, "you are going to be my bride."

That should have been funny, but it wasn't, because she was convinced now that he was mad. She turned to face him and backed toward the door, ready to cry out if he made the slightest motion toward her.

"You had better remain a few more minutes," he said.

He went around to his desk and pulled open a drawer. Because he had gone away from her instead of toward her, she stopped when her hand touched the doorknob. He pulled out a sheaf of papers bound in a folder and tossed them on the desk.

"This contains evidence to send your father to jail," he declared.

She felt her knees go weak. "That's a lie!" she muttered.

He shrugged. "You will stay to listen now. I prefer that you come away from that door."

With heart throbbing, she moved halfway across the room and stopped.

"Why should I lie to you?" Frank Hutton said. "I know that you are no fool. These documents contain proof that your father used other people's money without their knowledge, juggled stocks in order to save his brokerage concern. You may excuse him by saying that he was thinking of his family, but that's no defense before a court of law. If I turned these documents over to the Securities and Exchange Commission, there would be a scandal which would shake Wall Street. Your father may be lucky to get off with a five-year jail sentence, but that will be the least of what will happen to you and your family. There would be the social disgrace. It will break your mother's heart, who prides herself on her social position. The wedding of your sister to the son of Howard Warren will certainly be called off. Your father, who is a proud, head-strong man, may even commit suicide."

She stared at the folder as if it were a repulsive, crawling thing.

"There's no reason why I should withhold these documents from the S.E.C.," Hutton went on. "I hate John Barnett. Years ago he ruined and indirectly killed my father through stock manipulations. My name isn't Frank Hutton; never mind what it was. And I hate you also—a spoiled daughter of the rich, a pampered snob living on other people's money. I could vent my hatred by making these documents public; but I have a better way, a more selfish way, if you please. You are very beautiful and very proud. I shall have my revenge by marrying you."

Peggy reached out a hand for the back of a chair. She steadied herself, then faced him with a defiant tilt to her chin.

"You lie about those documents," she asserted.

Hutton blew smoke into the air. "Take this folder with you. Needless to say, these are copies. One set is in a safe-deposit box and will be turned over to a newspaper reporter in case of my death. If you hint anything about this to your father, he might kill me. It will make him a murderer and won't conceal the facts in these papers. I give you one week to make up your mind. At the end of that period, you will either marry me or the papers will be made public."

He picked the folder up from the desk and handed it to her. Mechanically Peggy took it and stuffed it into her handbag. Then she turned and on stiff legs walked out of his office. As she closed the door behind her, she could hear him laughing softly to himself . . .

John Barnett was astounded by the interest his daughter Peggy suddenly took in his business. He joked about it to his friends during luncheon.

"You should see her button-holing everybody in the office and asking a million questions. Pretty sensible questions too. And she insists on poking through all our records. Says she's tired of being a glamour girl and wants to know what makes a brokerage office tick. Clever as she is beautiful, that daughter of mine."

On the morning of the fourth day Frank Hutton telephoned Peggy at her home.

"I suggest that you meet me at the Municipal Building at noon," he said. "You know that we must obtain our marriage license seventy-two hours in advance."

"Are you really fool enough to think that I would ever marry you?"

"That's entirely up to you. If we do not get our license to-day, we will not be able to marry when the week is up, and you know what will happen in that event."

Peggy's hand tightened on the phone. "I have a hundred thousand dollars in my own name. I will give you every cent of it if you leave my father and myself alone."

His hollow, mirthless laugh came over the wire. "My dear bride-to-be, I shall share your fortune at any rate."

She hung up the receiver and slumped back in her chair. Then she wept.

After an hour she washed her face and dressed and took a taxi to the Municipal Building. She didn't look at him, didn't speak to him. With unsteady hand she filled out the form and had it notarized with Hutton at her side, then departed. She could feel Hutton's eyes moving after her.

On the morning of the seventh day Peggy Barnett burned the papers in the folder. There was no longer any doubt in her mind that her father was guilty. Every fact in the documents checked. Her father had covered the irregularities so cleverly that they would probably never be brought to light—save through the documents. Frank Hutton had understated, if anything, the consequences to her family if the fraud became public. There was only one way to save her father and mother and sister.

She slipped out of the house with a single suitcase. She had not the courage to tell her family that she was to be married. Later she would send them a telegram.

A bevy of reporters and photographers were waiting for her at the Municipal Building. Hutton had no doubt tipped them off. The first knowledge her family and friends would receive of her marriage would be from newspaper headlines reading: "HEIRESS ELOPES WITH FATHER'S SECRETARY." And this too was part of Frank Hutton's vengeful hatred: that her family would have to endure the social disgrace of having her marriage to him smeared across every newspaper in the country.

Calling up her courage, she bravely faced the cameras. She had determined not to give Hutton the satisfaction of showing her horror of him. She forced a smile to her lips when Hutton, placing an arm intimately about her waist, gloated to the reporters over their romance. She saw society reporters who knew her look at her with puzzled frowns. They could understand her marrying a man without social position if he were especially charming and handsome, but this man's ugliness was almost repulsive.

The smile remained fastened on her face as she went through the brief civil ceremony. Then it was over and they had to kiss. His mouth pressed long and wetly against hers, and she felt something unclean slither over her heart.

Then she was sitting next to Hutton in his car. She sat as far away from him as she could without appearing to shrink from him. Never, she resolved, would she give him a chance to gloat over the maggots of horror his presence sent crawling through her.

Proud and erect she sat as they drove uptown. He made no gesture toward her; simply contented himself with twisting his thin lips into that smile of his which was no smile. He did not tell her where he was taking her and she did not ask. It didn't matter. Wherever she was with him would be a section of hell.

Chapter 2: Honeymoon In Hell

THEY LEFT THE CITY and continued upstate. It was dark when Hutton at last pulled the car up before a large cabin in the heart of the mountains. During the last half-hour she had seen no sign of any other habitation.

Two men were waiting for them on the porch, and each in his own fashion was even uglier than Frank Hutton. One was a gross, fat creature, utterly bald. The other had unhealthy, mottled skin; scarcely more than two holes for a nose and where the left part of his jaw should have been there was a gaping nothingness.

"My servants," Frank Hutton introduced her. "Carmelo Grib—he waved a hand toward the fat man—"and Al Fogel. And this, boys, is Mrs. Hutton."

They made no acknowledgment of the introduction. In the light which streamed from the open door, they stood looking at her; two pairs of evil eyes hotly penetrating through the covering of her garments. Al Fogel's tongue flicked out over his lips. Carmelo Grib's fat chest heaved.

And Peggy felt even more afraid of the two hideous servants than she did of Frank Hutton. It was somehow fitting and proper that the servants of the vile creature she had married should be so utterly repulsive. Since that afternoon a week ago when she had entered Frank Hutton's office, she had been living in a nightmare, and these two were beings out of a nightmare.

Hutton took her arm and led her into the cabin. Fogel fetched her suitcase from the car trunk while Grib set about placing the evening meal on the table. The servants sat down to eat with them.

Peggy had to force herself to bring the food to her mouth. Indomitably she was sticking to her resolution not to show any outward signs of fear. The food gagged her, but she managed to get it down. Then for a time they sat in front of the blazing fireplace.

The most dreadful moment of all was rapidly approaching. She sat absolutely motionless, hardly able to breathe.

Presently Hutton rose, stretched, and said: "Time to go to bed."

Her heart turned to a lump of ice. She found the strength to get to her feet and follow him into her bedroom. Her suitcase was on the floor. She stooped to open it and took out a pair of pajamas.

He came up behind her and snatched them out of her hand and tossed them on the floor.

"That won't be necessary, my dear," he said. "Undress."

On legs which moved mechanically, she went to a corner of the room and turned her back to him and pulled off her dress. She felt his eyes on her and it required an effort of will to keep herself from cowering. As she reached for the shoulder-straps of her slip, she heard his quick step behind her, felt his hand on her bare shoulder.

"My dear, you are being unnaturally modest before your husband. Turn around."

But he did not give her a chance to turn by her own effort. His fingers dug into her flesh and wheeled her about. He tore one shoulder-strap, then the other. The slip slid down to her hips.

"That's not necessary," she bit out defiantly. "I'm able to undress myself." She stepped out of the slip.

But he refused to let her deny him the triumph of stripping her himself, of making her cringe. He threw himself at her and ripped off her brassiere. Meekly she submitted, shoulders proudly back, head high; and her submission enraged him so that his hands were brutal on her flesh, hurting her. She did not cry out. With that forced smile, she lifted her feet for him as he pulled down the last of her undergarments.

And she still smiled, still fought down the urge to shrink from him, as his dry hands rasped over her flesh. His face was a mask of sodden lust and hate. She lay there, still smiling. With a choked cry he picked her up, staggering a little with her weight, and tossed her roughly on the bed . . .

The two hideous servants sat staring into the fire. On the floor between them stood a bottle of cheap whiskey. Every now and then one of them would lift it and tilt it down his mouth.

A big clock on the wall clicked off minutes and hours. Neither of them said a word. They appeared to be listening with strained concentration, and whenever a sound came from their master's bedroom, they would look at each other with hungry, excited expressions. Grib held a handkerchief balled in a hand with which he kept wiping sweat from his fat face.

The clock started to boom midnight. They panted as they listened. They were on their feet before the twelfth stroke died away. Side by side, wordlessly, they moved out of the room, Grib waddling grotesquely, Fogel walking with short, eager steps. They stopped before their master's bedroom and Fogel knocked on the door.

"Come in."

Grib, whimpering a little, reached past Fogel and threw open the door. They stepped into the room.

Frank Hutton, clad in a black dressing gown, was standing with his back against the dresser applying a match to a cigarette. Peggy was sitting up in bed with the covers drawn tightly up to her throat. Something had gone out of her eyes—an essential flame that had been part of her beauty.

They were dead orbs now without anything behind them. But the set of her head was still proud, undefeated. Whatever Hutton had done to her, he had not been able to break her spirit.

The two servants stared at her and their breathing became harder. She glanced at them without interest.

"It's midnight," Carmela Grib said. "You said we should come then."

Hutton puffed deeply on his cigarette and nodded casually. He turned toward Peggy.

"Go with them," he ordered.

She frowned with bewilderment. "What do you mean?"

"I said go with them."

"But I'm not dressed," she protested.

"Of course not. I'm sure they'll prefer you just as you are."

For the first time she could not keep herself from showing fear. She shrank lower in the bed, trembling a little. She still did not quite understand what the man who was her husband meant.

"By God, you'll learn to obey promptly when I give orders!" Hutton rapped.

He strode over to her and gripped an end of the blanket and jerked. It pulled down to her waist before she could catch it. She clung to it and strove to draw it up again. He jerked again and the blanket whipped off the bed.

Hungry sighs gushed from the throats of the two servants and filled the room, filled her being. They stepped closer, avidly drinking in the beauty of her naked body.

And then her pride broke. She cowered on the bed, covering the rounded fullness of her breasts with her arms, and turned imploring eyes to her husband.

"Not that!" she wailed. "Please! I'll be a dutiful wife. I'll do anything you ask. But please, you're my husband; you can't let them."

He laughed harshly and put his hands on her and pulled her off the bed. She recognized the uselessness of struggling. He twisted her around, holding her, so that she faced the two servants.

"Look at her!" he gloated. "The wealthiest men, the cream of society, would have given their souls to possess this magnificent body of hers. She would not have deigned to look at men like us. And now she's mine to lend to you if I please. And I do please!"

She twisted her head and for a long moment her eyes and Hutton's met. And there was such utter hatred in her eyes that Hutton felt little chills run along his spine. And then he laughing again as he shoved a palm between her shoulders and sent her sprawling toward his two servants.

Peggy felt eager hands on her flesh; felt herself lifted off her feet and pressed against a gross, fatty chest and borne out of the room. Hutton's laughter followed her.

And so that night Frank Hutton, with the aid of his loathsome servants, succeeded in breaking Peggy's spirit, in stripping her of the last remnants of pride and defiance as he had stripped the clothing from her glorious body. During the early hours of the night her soul died within her, and in the morning she was only an empty husk of the woman she had been. The smile which used to light up her beauty had vanished that afternoon a week ago when she had followed Hutton into his office, and now even her forced smile of contempt for him was forever gone. There was nothing left in her but hatred so deep and bitter that there was no room for anything else.

She became the servant of the servants, as well as of her husband; and she was the "wife" of all three. It pleased Hutton to degrade her as slattern and a domestic slave during the day and to share her with his repulsive servants at night.

He would stand over her as she was down on her hands and knees scrubbing the floor.

"Your father ought to see you now, and your swanky friends," he taunted.

His foot lashed out and sent her sprawling into the pail of suds. For moments she lay there, then lifted herself on all fours again, wiping the suds from her face with a dirty arm.

Hutton laughed uproariously and his servants, watching, joined in.

She turned her head to look up at him through strands of unruly blonde hair which dangled over her face, and suddenly Hutton's laughter stopped. He was frightened, although there was nothing in her face to frighten him. It was a frozen mask, but he sensed the cold, deadly hatred that lay inside of her.

He dismissed his fears, telling himself that, of course, she could do nothing to him, for his death would make public the documents. Nor could she escape by killing herself; he had made it clear to her that he would expose her father if she attempted to take that way out.

Days slid into weeks and then months. But time had stopped for her. One day was no different from another, and each by itself was an eternity in hell.

One day Frank Hutton brought a whip back with him from the city. The hideous features of Fogel and Grib lit up with sadistic anticipation when he tossed it on the table. Peggy looked at its black length dully. There would be physical pain now greater than the pain caused by the blows of their hands and feet, but even that no longer mattered.

The whip was hung on a hook next to the fireplace, and often it was taken down. The lashings were not really necessary, for she never disobeyed their slightest wish. They used the whip on her simply for their amusement.

Hatred was a living presence in that cabin. Peggy's for Hutton was locked up within her heart. Hutton's hatred for her expressed itself by degrading her to the level of an animal.

Always he would bring back from his occasional trips to the city a more fiendish way of tormenting her. The most diabolical, perhaps, was when he dumped before her a pile of newspapers. When she was alone she went through them. They were dated from the day of her marriage to several days ago—a spread of three months.

The earlier issues contained much about her, because her elopement with Frank Hutton had been something of a sensation. Members of her family had been asked for comments and all had refused to utter a word. Gossip columnists hinted at the bitterness her friends and relatives felt. Those who had known Frank Hutton suggested in almost so many words that Peggy must have lost her mind.

And there were pictures of her in all the papers. Long she stared at the photographs, then rose to her feet and studied herself in a mirror. What she saw in the glass no longer resembled the gorgeous girl of the pictures over the captions of Mrs. Frank Hutton, the former Peggy Barnett.

Indeed, the girl she saw in the mirror was no longer particularly attractive. It was a face without soul, without character, and it was sunken and lined. Her hair was stringy. She stepped back so that she could see all of her figure. She had nothing on but a thin smock, dirty and torn. Her feet and legs were bare.

She opened the smock and looked at her body. Slowly healing whip-welts marred her skin. She had become so thin that the graceful contours of her figure were gone.

She did not weep because she had long since lost the power to shed tears.

A chuckle sounded behind her. Through the mirror she saw her husband.

"Admiring yourself? I'm afraid there's not much to admire any more."

She said nothing.

"I have some papers for you to sign," he told her.

She followed him to a table and sat down and took the pen he handed her. She had signed a number of papers since she had come to this cabin, little by little turning over her money to him. This would be the last of it.

There was another paper, and she saw that it was an insurance policy for a hundred thousand dollars in her name, with Hutton her beneficiary.

"It has a double indemnity clause," he said with that queer twist of his lips.

Then she knew. He was tired of her body now, and her death would mean an additional two hundred thousand dollars for him. He would kill her and make it look like an accident. She felt a loosening of the pressure about her heart. Death would be a welcome release. How often before had she prayed for it!

She signed the policy.

A week later Hutton arrived from the city with bundles of clothing for her. He said: "I am inviting guests tomorrow. You will make yourself as attractive as possible. And you will go out of your way to be charming or I shall whip the skin off you."

"I'll do my best," she told him docilely. "I know that you want to protect yourself by having people see me living with you, so that when I die there will be no trouble about the insurance."

"Smart girl," he commented.

The gown had a high neck and long sleeves so that it covered the marks of the whip. A liberal appliance of makeup restored some of the beauty to her face, although it made her look hard, almost dissolute.

"You'll do," Hutton said after a long appraisal. "Now smile occasionally and act as if you care for me."

"I'll try," she said meekly.

That day, for the first and last time, she played the role of Frank Hutton's cherished wife. Grib and Fogel again became servants. The guests were all from the city and some of them she had known fairly well. They were a little startled by the coarseness of her appearance, and some of them whispered to each other that it was the result of loving a man like Frank Hutton. For the Huttons were an adoring couple that day. He was kind to her and attentive and apparently very much in love with her. And she, with the aid of an excuse that she was not feeling well, carried her part off rather well.

Two of the male guests stayed overnight. A hunting party had been arranged for the following morning.

As Hutton arose at dawn, he said to Peggy, who was still in bed: "Say you have a headache and prefer not to come with us. If, while we are away, the cabin should burn down by accident with you in it, you would no longer be troubled by me or Fogel or Grib."

She nodded. Then she looked squarely at him. "The only thing I have to thank you for is death. Don't think, however, that you can blackmail my father with those documents after I am gone. He will know then why I married you and he will kill you. And if you let them become public because you want to hurt my father more than you already have, there is something you must know. Once I slipped down to the village and mailed a letter to my personal lawyer. It tells everything that you have done to me."

He glowered down at her. "You little fool! Do you think anything will save your father now?"

"That letter is to be opened only if my father faces any personal danger through his business," she told him. "My lawyer is the soul of honesty. He will not even mention that he has such a letter until something happens to my father."

Hutton grinned crookedly. "So you were still able to think of that?"

"I am here because of my family, and I have thought of nothing else."

"All right, that trick's yours, baby," he said. "Not that I would have started anything because I'm pretty well satisfied with three hundred thousand dollars and"—diabolical triumph glinted in his black eyes—"what I did to the high-toned Peggy Barnett. Good-bye, now. It was a pleasure being married to you."

"Wait!"

At the door he turned. She was sitting up now. Rays of the rising sun streamed in through a window and caressed her nude torso. And at that moment she was once again beautiful, and Hutton found himself wondering if he should not delay her death. But no, he was bored with her, and with all his money he could purchase other attractive women.

Her deathless hatred broke through to the surface of her eyes. Quietly she said: "Frank Hutton, do not think that you have seen the last of me. Somehow I'll manage to come back."

He shuddered, feeling suddenly cold all over. Then he forced himself to laugh, but it was a hollow, frightened laugh.

"Don't get dramatic, my dear," he said. "Good-bye."

She heard him tell the guests that his wife had a headache. Grib and Fogel accompanied them. She lay back in bed, feeling suddenly light-headed with the coming of liberation.

The hunting party returned late in the afternoon. When they were half a mile from the cabin, one of the guests suddenly exclaimed: "Look, there's a big fire nearby!"

All stopped to stare at flames shooting up above the trees.

"My God, it's the cabin!" Grib shouted, and all of them started running.

The cabin was a huge bonfire when they reached it. "Peggy!" Hutton cried, plunging forward. The flames drove him back. He hesitated, then was about to dash directly into the fire when Al Fogel caught him. With the aid of the two guests and Grib they held him back. He struggled piteously calling Peggy's name. He was a good actor.

Suddenly the door of the cabin flew open and there stood Peggy.

Fire licked at her, made a torch of her hair. Her clothing had been burned from her body. Yet she made no outcry of pain. Hutton sensed that she was looking straight at him with hate filled eyes. A spasm of horror shook him.

She seemed to stumble backward. The door swung shut, apparently by a gust of wind. But Hutton knew that she had deliberately stepped back into that inferno and closed the door after her.

From the heart of the cabin wild laughter shrilled out above the roar of the fire. At last Peggy was able to laugh.

Chapter 3: The Return OF Peggy

CARMELO GRIB waddled down the hotel hall to Frank Hutton's swanky hotel suite. He knocked. Through the door there was the sound of whispering, of running feet, then brief silence. The door swung inward and Hutton stood there in a natty dressing gown.

Hutton scowled at the fat man. "Didn't I tell you not to bother me again? I gave you all the money I intend to." He lowered his voice. "You can't hold me up. You were as much in it as I was."

"I don't want dough." Grib ran an enormous handkerchief over his padded face. "Something's happened. We better not talk out here."

Hutton moved backward and Grib followed him into the living room. There were two glasses on an end table, and in ashtrays were half-smoked cigarettes tipped with scarlet lipstick. On a couch lay a woman's rumpled dress.

Hutton closed the bedroom door and came close to Grib. "Keep your voice low. Now what's bothering you?"

Grib was breathing heavily. He used the handkerchief again. "I seen her last night," he whispered.

"Who?"

"Peggy. Your wife."

Hutton's eyes narrowed. "What's your game? We saw her in that blazing cabin. We found her body after the flames died. She's as dead as anybody ever was."

"Yeah, I know." Grib's breath was gushing past his puffy lips now as if he had run a great distance. "But I swear I seen her. Last night when I was in bed. Something woke me up, and she was standing in my room, all naked like I often seen her, and there were marks on her like the whip used to make."

Hutton felt a cold wave sweep over him. Her last words came back to him: *"Do not think you've seen the last of me. Somehow I'll manage to come back."*

"You're crazy!" Hutton burst out. "You had a bad dream."

Grib shook his massive head. "That's what I thought. I sat up and looked at her. I pinched myself, and she was still there." His voice rose. "I tell you, I know when I'm awake and when I'm asleep. I touched her, and there was her body like I used to feel it—soft and warm and like satin. She slid away and I went after her. Then suddenly she laughed. I heard her laugh only once, that time when she was in the fire, and her laugh was just like that. I backed away from her. I admit I was scared nearly crazy. Wouldn't you be? The back of my legs hit the bed and I fell on it. Then when I looked up again, she was gone."

"And you expect me to believe that that wasn't a dream?"

"It wasn't, I tell you. I told Al Fogel and he just said I was going bugs. Maybe I am, because I seen her. Maybe that's what she's trying to do to all of us—drive us crazy. You heard the way she laughed in that fire. She was dead already when she laughed. God, nobody could have stood there in the flames and been alive and then have any voice left to laugh with! She was dead, and she laughed because she knew that she was going to get even on us."

If fear hadn't been twisted around Hutton's own heart, he wouldn't have lost his temper. "Get out of here!" he raged. "I'm not interested in your crackpot dreams. Beat it before I throw you out!"

Grib said: "All right. But she'll be after you too. She hates you the most." He left with bowed shoulders.

With unsteady hands Hutton poured himself a drink. He was lifting it to his lips when the bedroom door creaked open and a tough-looking blonde, with plenty of curves revealed by the brief undergarments she wore, came out. She threw her arms about his neck. Roughly he shoved her away.

Before he had married Peggy, he would have been satisfied with this woman, but now no woman could excite him. None of them could hold a candle to Peggy before he had debased her and stripped her of her beauty. And now, after Carmelo Grib's story, what desire he had been able to rouse for this blonde woman froze away under the mantle of ice which covered him.

Grib's story was absurd, of course. A dream. Imagination. But the ice remained. He poured himself another drink without glancing at the blonde . . .

Carmelo Grib waddled about his apartment on bare feet. Flesh joggled under the folds of his pajamas which were plastered to his gross perspiring body. His face was green; his puffy lips were working soundlessly.

Presently he picked up the phone and called Al Fogel.

"Al? Listen. She was here again."

Fogel's voice came back sleepy and annoyed. "So you managed to get yourself a woman? What do you want me to do about it?"

"You don't understand. It was Peggy—Frank's wife. I told you how she was here last night, but you just laughed at me, like Frank did."

"All right, I'm still laughing."

"For God's sake, listen to me," Grib said tightly. "She came tonight like last night and stood there by my bed. I was crazy with fear, but at the same time I couldn't keep from trying to touch her. She slid away and laughed that hellish laugh of hers and said she'd come back later. Then she just disappeared. One second she was there; next second she wasn't. Al, she's coming back and I can't stand it!"

"Well, then beat it," Fogel yawned.

"That's the hell of it," Grib whined. "I'm scared of seeing her again, and yet I want to. I keep remembering how she was in the cabin before she got skinny and worn out, and I can't run away."

"So what do you want me to do?"

"Come over here. Maybe I'm dreaming or going nuts. If she comes back and I see her and you don't, I'll know you and Frank are right. But if we both see her . . ."

Fogel said wearily "Okay, Carmelo. Anything to make you stop pestering me. I'll be over in fifteen minutes. Have some liquor ready. And frankly, I wouldn't mind if it's really a naked woman coming to visit you."

She was standing in the room when Grib hung up the receiver and turned. Fear mingled with lust to form a choking
ball in his throat. But he could not keep himself from step-
ping toward her.

Naked, she moved backward into the bedroom and he followed. She lifted a hand in invitation, and it was as if it held
a cord which drew him to her. He saw the welts of a whip on
the smooth whiteness of her skin; and he recalled how he and
the others had beaten her for their pleasure and other things
he had done to her, and terror checked him. She was an oth-
erworld creature and she hated him, but she was incredibly
beautiful and she smiled to him as she had never smiled in
the cabin. Her hips swayed provocatively.

He stumbled toward her, groping. She fell backward onto
the bed. He dropped and she rolled away and was lying beside him, with one bare arm across his heaving chest and her
red lips hovering above him. He lay on his back as one trans-
fixed, waiting for her mouth to come down to his.

"Stay here," she cooed down at him. "No matter what happens, stay here on the bed."

"Yes," he muttered. He was ready to agree to anything.

Al Fogel was outside the door to Grib's apartment when he
heard the laugh. He turned rigid. Once before he had heard a
woman laugh like that—in the heart of the blazing cabin.

Cursing himself for being as big a fool as Grib for even letting the thought cross his mind that a woman might possibly
return from the dead, he kicked in the door. At once he
smelled smoke, and a moment later he saw it billowing out
from the open bedroom door.

"Carmelo!" he yelled, plunging forward.

In the doorway he stopped dead.

The bed was a pyre, and in the midst of it lay Grib. He was
still alive and evidently not secured to the bed in any way,
yet he made no attempt to roll himself off. From his widely
distended mouth no sound issued, although agony contorted
his face.

Fogel leaped to the bed, and again he stopped, staring. Through the flames he saw Peggy standing naked on the other side of the bed. She was looking down at Grib with red lips drawn back from her teeth, and then her mouth opened wide and again he heard that horrible laugh of hers.

She glanced up and saw Fogel and she started to move toward him around the foot of the bed. Grib had been right: there wasn't any doubt that the girl was Peggy. She was as beautiful as during those first days in the cabin and the marks of the whip were on her naked body.

But she was dead—dead! Only the dead could have the ghastly power to make Grib lay on that bed while he burned to death without any effort to save himself.

"No!" Fogel shrieked. "Stay away from me!"

But she only laughed and came on. He covered his eyes with his hands; and when he removed them she was closer to him and Grib was still on the flaming bed, his blackened body still stirring slowly with agony.

She reached out a hand to Fogel. He shrank back, certain that the touch of the dead would mean horrible death. As her fingers brushed his chest, something cracked within him. He shrieked wildly and swung around and plunged wildly out of the apartment. In the dark, silent street he kept running until his breath gave out.

Chapter 4: Passion Of The Dead

FRANK HUTTON SAID: "Nuts! Carmelo Grib's ravings worked on your mind, and when you saw him burning there on the bed you got the idea that you saw her. You're not the first person who imagined he saw ghosts in flames."

Al Fogel rubbed the scar tissue on the jawless side of his face. "We saw her once in a blaze."

"Sure. And a few minutes after that she was dead. You can't make me believe that a dead girl's walking around."

"I didn't believe Carmelo either," Fogel said tautly. "He's dead now—burned up like Peggy burned." He shuddered. "You or me, Frank, will be next."

Hutton's lips found their old twist, but his eyes no longer retained their smoldering depth. There was a film over them now, a covering of fear.

He fought down the fear with assumed bravado. "You bore me, Al. Good-bye."

Al Fogel left. It was three days since Carmelo Grib had been burned alive in bed and Fogel hadn't had any real sleep in that time. He would wake suddenly at night, expecting to see her standing at his bedside. Then for the rest of the night he would sit up in bed with a gun at his side. He wasn't sure what good the gun would do. Could the dead be killed? But at least he'd try.

As he walked back to his home, he found himself praying that she would come. Not because he had overcome any of the gnawing dread of her, but because he wanted an end to the terrible suspense. Better to have it over with than to go slowly mad.

As he entered the living room of his apartment, a cold tension came over him. He sensed an unseen presence. He strode across to his bedroom. Nobody in there, and yet the feeling that he was not alone grew stronger. He turned back into the living room—and there she was.

She couldn't have come in through the door or through the window and she hadn't been in the room thirty seconds ago. She might have been hiding behind furniture, but why was it necessary for the dead to hide? They could simply materialize out of nothing.

She was naked, of course, as when he had seen her next to Grib's blazing bed, and as he had seen her so often in the cabin.

For long moments Fogel was held in a vise of terror. Then he remembered the gun in his pocket and yanked it out.

She laughed. "Do you think you can kill me?"

"I can try," he said between his teeth.

She shook her head. "Look at me," she said. She stretched out her arms to him, and the gesture lifted her splendid breasts as if in offering to him.

Once before, months ago, somebody had told him to look at her nudity—when Hutton had offered her to Grib and himself. She had been cringing then, her face and every line and curve of her body eloquent of loathing. But now there was an eagerness in her which leaped like an electric spark from her body to his.

He feared her and desired her. Desired her as if she had sprung from hell itself.

He started to go to her, then stopped, remembering Grib's fate. Hoarsely he said: "You plan to kill me?"

Delicately she shrugged bare shoulders. "In the mountains you planned to kill me and yet desired me."

She flowed toward him. He lifted the gun again, but when he saw that she ignored it, satisfied in the knowledge that bullets could not harm her, his finger went numb about the trigger. Her fingers touched his chest. He trembled with dark desire at her touch. He dropped the gun, reached out his own hand and felt the marvelous yielding softness of her flesh.

He knew that he was doomed then, and he did not much care. Living or dead, this woman, an hour of her love, was worth an eternity of damnation. Many times in the past she had been his to do with as he pleased, but then she had been a lifeless submissive thing with hatred and loathing always in her eyes. She was different now, perhaps with a passion born in hell, with an ardor to match his own.

Al Fogel crushed her to him.And as he felt the vibrancy of her against him, he heard her wild laughter in his ears which he had heard twice before—each time when a human body was consumed by flames. And terror poured back into him, but it couldn't overcome his maddening lust for her. He swept her up in his arms and carried her into the bedroom. Her laughter continued . . .

The following day Frank Hutton read in the newspaper how a man named Al Fogel had been burned in his bed dur-

ing the night. It was thought that he had fallen asleep while
smoking a cigarette which had ignited the bed sheets and
then the mattress, but it seemed odd that he had made no attempt to at least roll off the bed. He had been found a burnt
corpse lying on his back on the bedsprings amid the ashes of
the mattress.

With a savage curse Hutton threw the paper aside and
poured himself another drink. He had been keeping himself
in a constant state of drunkenness since Carmelo Grib had
told him that he had seen Peggy. And no women were able to
satisfy him any longer. The vision of Peggy before she had
lost her beauty kept flashing before his mind.

With a sense of horror, he found himself almost eager to
have her come to him.

Late that afternoon he saw her in the subway. It was
crowded and there were many people standing, and he
glimpsed her only briefly when several people left at a station. Then bodies closed in between them again.

He sat stiffly upright, covered with a cold sweat. The first
startled shock passed almost immediately and he told himself
that it had been only somebody who resembled Peggy. First
of all, Grib had always seen her naked, and this woman had
been fully clothed. And ghosts don't ride on subways. And
finally, Peggy was dead, and whatever had been Grib's and
Fogel's testimony, the dead don't return.

Several stations farther the crowd thinned out and he saw her
again. He gaped at her as if she were indeed a ghost. Good
God, it *was* Peggy! He knew every line of her face and body
and there wasn't any doubt left. Not the Peggy he had known
since that day when he had told her that she must marry him,
the Peggy who had shrank away from him and despised him.
This was the Peggy he used to watch going in and out of her
father's office—in the full bloom of womanhood—
vivacious, perfectly formed, a superb carriage, her beauty
illuminated by the joy of living.

She was looking directly at him. Her expression didn't change, but there was something subtle in it which told him that she had expected him to be there.

A part of his brain that was sane kept repeating over and over again that it couldn't be Peggy. He remembered having stared down at her body after it had been dragged out of the cold ashes—blackened and twisted, but still recognizable. Yet there she sat.

The train stopped. Suddenly she was on her feet and moving toward the door. He remained rooted to the seat, staring after her until the moving train took him away.

He got off at the next station and went to the nearest bar. He was staggering when he left, and ashamed of himself for having believed in the reality of Peggy. She'd been a drunken hallucination, of course. What a fool he had been!

The tough-looking blonde was in his hotel suite. He had arranged with her to be there and had forgotten all about it.

She threw her arms about his neck when he entered and pressed over painted lips against his mouth. He felt the avid warmth of her flesh, the mashing of her breasts against his chest, and a sense of revulsion came over him. Why should he, who had once enslaved the magnificent Peggy Barnett, bother with this lump of ordinary flesh?

He thrust her away from him, brutally told her to get out. In tears she departed. He sat down to wait.

Peggy did not come as she had come to Grib and Fogel. Her coming would mean death, perhaps, but he didn't think of that. He couldn't think of anything but her beauty.

He went through a sleepless night and a day of agonized expectancy. He didn't believe in her existence, but he couldn't believe in anything else.

Late the following afternoon he saw her the second time. She was walking on the other side of the street.

He stopped dead, staring at the perfect mold of her features, at the flowing grace of her movement. Part of him urged him to turn and plunge away in mad panic from this living-dead thing, while another part of him wanted to rush to her. The lust which had started raging within him at the sight of her won out. He hurried across the street with queer stiff steps which were eager, yet reluctant.

She was almost at the corner. Before he could reach her, she had turned it. When he himself rounded the corner, she was nowhere to be seen. He ran all the way up the block and then back; he looked in doorways; he asked people if they had seen a girl who looked like her. She had vanished suddenly and completely.

He knew then that she was taunting him, whipping up his fear and desire. And when he had returned home, he told himself that he was glad he had not caught up with her. She hated him; he recalled the hatred that had always been in her eyes.

But at night he was sleepless again for desire of her. He walked, he rode, looking for her. Two days passed. He was haggard, jumpy, half mad.

Then one evening he let himself into his hotel suite and found her there.

Chapter 5: Flames of Vengeance

HER EYES WERE ON HIM, cool, steady, and there was no hatred in them. For the first time since their marriage she looked at him without loathing. And she smiled, warmly, intimately, as she had never before smiled at the sight of him. She appeared to be wearing nothing at all save a diaphanous dress. A floor lamp behind her shone through it, bringing into relief every delectable curve and shadow of her body.

"We meet again, Frank," she said throatily.

Now that he was at last so close to her, he was more afraid than he had ever been. And yet his mind was on something beside fear.

He whispered: "You came naked to Grib and I suppose to Fogel too. Why do you cover yourself from me?"

She shifted a little so that her face was in shadows. "They saw me naked when they had no right to. They died seeing me like that."

"You killed them?" he said hoarsely, and trembled.

"They had to die. Neither was my husband and they took me against my will. You are my husband, and even death has not parted us."

She swayed toward him, moist lips parted, so infinitely beautiful and desirable that he could not keep himself from going to her. "It is a dead woman you are about to embrace," a voice gibbered within him; but he could no longer keep from going to her than he could stop breathing.

And when he felt her loveliness in his arms, horror fled completely. She lifted her mouth to his, and her mouth, her entire body, was demanding. She had never been like this in life. Alive she had been submissive, an inanimate thing for his pleasure.

Her voice was low in his ear. "You were wrong, darling. Oh, so frightfully wrong. When I knew that I had to marry you, I had made up my mind to love you, to be everything to you a wife should be. And then you threw me to your loathsome servants. That was your mistake. That ruined both our chances for happiness. And now I've come back to try once again to attain that happiness you tossed away."

"Yes," he muttered, crushing her against him. "I was a fool. I could have had you all this time—the way you are now."

"It is not yet too late—if you want me enough."

"God, yes!"

He wanted her more than he had ever wanted the living Peggy. That woman had been a shell. This woman, although dead, was a thing of passionate flame. Frantically he fumbled at the buttons of her dress.

"Wait, darling," Gently she slid from his embrace. "Not here. We'll start over again on our honeymoon. There is a cabin in the mountains, much like the one to which you took me. We will meet tomorrow and go there, with no servants, just you and me."

"Yes. Anything. But stay here with me tonight."

She shook her head. "It has to be the way I say. Listen to me. I can stay here with you on earth only if we do it right—if we start from the beginning as loving husband and wife. Tomorrow afternoon at two o'clock I shall meet you at the Municipal Building from where we started our first honeymoon."

He grasped her arm, drew her to him with the brutality she had known before. She went rigid in his arms.

"Do you want me as I was then," she said, "or as I am now?"

He released her. "I'm sorry. But suppose you don't meet me tomorrow?"

"I will. Good-bye now—husband."

She seemed to flow to the door and through it.

She was there in front of the Municipal Building at two o'clock promptly. Hutton had arrived half an hour before. There were dark bags under his eyes; his ugly face was like a skull. He had gone through another sleepless night of conflicting desire and terror.

"God, but you're lovely!" he said, devouring her with those black eyes of his. "The last time I could think only of how I hated you and your father, how I could best humiliate you and break your spirit. Now I see the mistake in not destroying the documents which would ruin your father."

"If we are to really love each other, you must have no hold over me. Before we leave, destroy those documents."

He looked at her, feeling a cold chill sweep over him. He knew, as she had known months ago when he had given her the insurance policy to sign, that it meant his death.

He said hollowly: "Damn you! You intend to kill me as you killed Grib and Fogel. You know that at my death those documents will be made public.

She leaned against him so that he felt the pressure of her breast along his arm. "You must have no hold on me. It is essential to our happiness."

"Will you promise that you will in no way try to harm me?" he demanded.

Her voice was soft. "Listen, my husband. Do you remember how, when we went to bed that first night, you tore the clothes off me? You were unnecessarily brutal then. Tonight I will have you undress me again, but this time you will be gentle, and there will be love in my eyes, and I will be more ardent than any woman has ever been with a man.

Blood drained from his fingertips at the picture she conjured. He clutched her arm in a kind of frenzy.

"But I cannot go with you as you hold the threat of those documents over me," she said.

He forgot that she had not promised not to harm him. They went to his bank. He handed her the folder containing the papers. She rifled through them, then tore them into myriad pieces and scattered them back, and that was as unreal and as unnatural as the girl sitting at his side. She was either a corpse or something worse than a corpse, or else a figment of feverish conscience-stricken imagination, yet his yearning for her was a cancer devouring his being.

Dusk was falling when, following her directions, they reached the cabin in the mountains. It was scarcely more than a shack—a single room containing only a table and chairs and a bed, but Hutton hardly noticed its bareness. They were here at last. He ran after her into the cabin and gathered her savagely in his arms.

She lay supine against him, a curious smile on her lips which was not submission or passion or anything which he could fathom. That smile gave him a queer turn, but her closeness banished every other thought. He tore at her clothes.

As he ripped the straps of her slip and as she lifted her feet to step out of it, the impression of time having reversed itself was like a physical impact. Except that when months before on their marriage night he had done the same thing, she had been proud in her hatred and contempt . . .

Then the last of her garments were off her and nothing mattered but the glory of her nudity. He put his hands on her, drew her to him. She swayed toward him—and suddenly she shuddered. His eyes were inches above hers and in them he saw revulsion crawl.

"Peggy!" he muttered and stepped back from her, as if recalling suddenly that she was a dead thing. "You still hate me. You shuddered at my touch. You brought me here to— to kill me!" He leaped to her, dug his fingers into her bare arm.

"You're not dead!" he cried. "How can the dead be cold or passionate with drink or love or breathe or walk?

She twisted toward him with that unfathomable smile and pressed her nude body against him.

"Does it matter if I am living or dead. Am I desirable?"

"You're a witch," he muttered. "A bad dream. I don't care."

Fiercely he clutched her to him. He freed one arm, picked up a glass.

"A drink first," she said. "To love." And she handed the glass to him.

He took it impatiently, anxious to get the drink over with. She picked up a second glass.

"To our love," he echoed, and they downed their drinks.

The glass fell from his hand and smashed on the floor. Slowly his head pivoted on his neck and stopped when his eyes were fixed on her.

"Poison!" he whispered "You lured me up here to poison me."

She laughed in his face—laughed like she had months ago while the flames had been licking at her. He screamed shrilly and flailed clawed hands at her. She did not move. One finger reached her breast and a speck of blood appeared on the rounded surface. Then his legs folded up under him and he dropped face first to the floor.

He felt her bending over him, felt her hands on his shoulders. He tried to rise, but every muscle was rigid. His brain

formed words to curse her, they could not go past his paralyzed throat.

"Not poison," she said. "A drug which paralyzes you. You
cannot move or speak, but you can hear me. Now you know
why Carmelo Grib and Al Fogel made no effort to leave their
beds while they burned alive. They couldn't. Poison was too
good for any of you. You will be conscious while flames
rage around you—the way Peggy was."

She bit her lip as a shadow of understanding flitted across
his frozen eyes.

"I hadn't meant you to know," she said. "Grib and Fogel
died thinking that I was Peggy returned from the dead to
avenge the things they had done to her. I'm her sister Sue.
Fortunately I was away at school and you never saw me. We
looked very much alike, Peggy and I, and the last weeks she
was with you she had changed greatly so that your memory
of her wasn't exact. With the aid of a little makeup and the
fever in your minds when you imagined you saw her, I
fooled all of you."

Sue Barnett breathed deeply and went on: "Peggy wrote everything to her lawyer. She had instructed him not to open the
letter unless something happened which threatened to disgrace Father; but the request was so unusual and suspicious,
especially in view of the fact that she was burned in an accident a week after the receipt of the letter, that he cast aside
scruples and opened it. He came to our house, intending to
show it to my father. Luckily my father was away and he
showed it to me instead. I realized at once that my father
must never know the contents. He would kill you three with
his own hands; he would hound you all over the earth if necessary. Not only would the documents which would disgrace
us all be made public, but he would be accused of murder. I
made the lawyer promise to let me handle it my own way.

"You know the rest. The documents have been destroyed.
Grib and Fogel have paid in a small measure for what they
did to Peggy. When I step out of here, the last of the debt
will be cancelled. Nobody will ever think me a murderer."

She drew her breath in harshly. "Murderer? It wasn't murder. One can murder only fellow human beings, and none of you three was that."

She turned away from him. His brain shrieked madly as helplessly he watched her pick up a five gallon can of kerosene which stood along the wall and spill its contents all over the room. She put down the can, picked a matchbook from the table, and dropped a lighted match in each corner. Flames leaped up.

Wearily she gathered her garments from the floor and went to the door. Fire closed in on Hutton.

"Look at me," she said in a voice which was suddenly very tired. "I let the three of you see me naked before you died because you had bared Peggy's body, destroying her soul before you destroyed her body." The flames were whipping dangerously close to her. "Look at me, Frank Hutton. Think of Peggy, remember her, and know that there is an infinitely hotter inferno where you are going."

A tongue of fire licked at his thigh, searing his flesh. And his mind went to pieces then and time was again reversed and he had no knowledge of a girl named Sue Barnett. That woman barely out of the reach of the flames was Peggy. Peggy as he had seen her that last time with hungry fire reaching out for her naked body.

And as at that other time, she stepped over a fiery threshold and closed a door behind her. Except that now it was Frank Hutton who was inside the cabin.

THE SINGING CORPSES

IT WAS SINGING such as no human ear had ever before heard. Hell alone could give birth to such music, and it must be sung by a soul damned to eternal torment.

Sung! Only for lack of a more accurate, more unearthly term did they call it sing . . . the tortured voice of a young girl, hoarsely emitting not a tune, but a ghastly travesty of a tune—shrieking it as if in terrible agony—each note a separate of pain.

Listening to it, Neal Dexter's blood turned into icy rivulets. Yet, unlike his two companions, he did not understand the full horror of what he heard.

Twenty minutes ago Sam Owens had picked up Neal at the Daleside station in his roadster. Lois Hilary, Neal's fiancée, was expecting him for the weekend at Hilary Manor; and Sam, a young lawyer who lived in Daleside, and who was in love with Lois' cousin, Susan Hilary, had offered to bring Neal over from the station.

With them came Hugo Gideon. He owned a tiny real estate office in Daleside. His mother was housekeeper of Hilary Manor and he was taking this opportunity to visit her.

So there they were, three self-reliant young men in the front seat of Sam Owens' roadster, suddenly frightened almost out of their wits by the sound of a young girl singing.

They heard the voice as they turned into the dirt road leading to the manor. Sam Owens brought the car to an abrupt stop. It was already dusk, yet even in the fading light Neal could see the faces of his two companions turn ashen.

"God!" Sam Owens gasped. "It's May Johnston!"

Hugo Gideon nodded solemnly, and Neal saw that Hugo's right hand, which rested on the handle of the door, was trembling.

"Something terrible is being done to her!" Neal cried. "We must help her."

His two companions did not move.

Neal looked from one to the other in unbelieving disgust. "Come on. You aren't afraid?"

Sam said huskily, "May Johnston died three days ago . . ."

Neal felt the hair on the back of his neck stiffen.

"Then why do you say it's her voice?"

"It is," Hugo assured him. "I've known May since she was a child." Then he added, as if it were conclusive proof that it was the voice of May Johnston: "And it's coming from Hermit Cave."

Sam Owens saw the bewilderment in Neal's face.

"Hermit Cave is a tradition around here," he explained. "It goes back to the beginning of the last century when Daleside was founded. A man was insulted by the townsfolk of Daleside—it has been forgotten just how—and he swore vengeance. He became a hermit, made his home in the cave, literally burying himself alive there. The cave's about a hundred yards over yonder, in the side of that hillock. It's part of the Hilary estate.

"The Hermit's vengeance was not on the living of Daleside. It was on the dead. Tradition has it that when any young girl in Daleside died, he would lure her soul to his cave and compel her to sing for his entertainment. He'd sold himself to the Devil for the privilege. And while she sang, it was said; he'd torture her terribly, and he'd accompany her singing on a mandolin or some other stringed instrument . . . Listen!"

Neal heard it. The faint twang of strings accompanying the hideous, raucous mockery of song that agonized from a dead throat . . . His own throat was dry with fear.

"They say that even after the Hermit died," Sam Owens continued, "the singing went on. When the first Hilary hewed his home out of the forest here, about a hundred years ago, the singing would be heard now and then. But long ago it stopped altogether. And now we hear . . . it again . . ."

There was a silence. The three young men sat motionless, tense, listening to the hellish sound, each trying to fight down the terror which strove to take possession of him.

Then Hugo Gideo took up the explanation where his friend had left off: "Three days ago May's body was found floating in the little lake that's part of the Hilary estate. How she got there nobody knows. There wasn't a mark on her, except for one very odd thing. All her ten fingers were swollen to twice their normal size. The police couldn't explain the swelling, though it was plainly not the cause of death. So they ignored it, merely saying that she probably committed suicide. This morning she was buried. I saw her buried! And now. . ."

Abruptly the singing ceased. In a daze Sam Owens started the car and it crawled along the dirt road until it reached the manor.

The house was a sprawling white building obviously erected many decades ago. Wings had been added from time to time to the original structure. On the large open veranda several people sat in the twilight awaiting their arrival.

Lois Hilary flew into Neal's arms. He had thought that her greeting of him before her family would be more restrained, as this was his first visit to her home and he had yet to meet Joseph Hilary, her father. But as soon as he felt her lovely body against him he realized that there was more to her impulsive action than joy at seeing him. She was quivering with fright.

"Did you hear it?" she said. "It was horrible."

Neal nodded. Together they walked up to the porch, where everybody was discussing the weird singing. Through the gloom every face was strained, fearful.

"Stuff and nonsense!" a tall, large boned woman grunted. "Grown people believing in ghosts!"

That was Mrs. Gideon. Hugo's mother, who for twenty years had been housekeeper for the Hilarys.

"But we distinctly heard the singing and it came from Hermit Cave," argued an attractive young girl. Neal guessed that she must be Lois' cousin, Susan Hilary. She was clinging to Sam Owens' arm.

"A practical joke," a deep male voice boomed. The speaker was a tall, dignified man with piercing eyes and thick white hair—Joseph Hilary, Neal was certain. "If any of you young squirts think that a joke like this—"

"We could hardly imitate May Johnston's voice," Sam protested. "That singing didn't come from a human throat. You know that as well as I do."

Joseph Hilary grunted, but said no more. Everybody on the porch knew that Sam was right; no living voice could have made those sounds.

After Neal was introduced all around, dinner was served. Mrs. Gideon and Hugo, who were like members of the family, ate with the Hilarys, in a large, gloomy room; and although everyone tried to be gay, to be cordial to Lois' intended husband, there was a pall over the group that made the meal as gloomy as the old room.

Neal had met Lois two months ago while she was visiting an aunt in Detroit, where he lived and worked; and they had discovered very quickly that they loved each other. Her conversation had been filled with affectionate references to her home in Kentucky, which she had assured him he would love as much as she did when he saw it.

But, now that he was here he disliked the place intensely. It made him feel uneasy, giving him a sense of impending danger. It was as if evil had swooped down on the house and taken possession of it.

The others at the table seemed to feel the same way. Conversation lagged. Neal felt relieved when the meal was at last over and he could be alone with Lois.

She suggested a walk in the moonlight. Ordinarily it would have been lovely, strolling around the well-kept estate on a summer evening with the girl he loved. But this night Lois was not her usual sprightly self; it was as if the spirit of evil had left the house with them and hovered over them as they walked.

They came to the lake. This was the lake Lois had told him about in Detroit—made him eager to see its romantic beauty, eager to swim there with her in the moonlight.

But tonight there was nothing romantic or tempting about it. Rather, there was something repellant . . . Low mist hung over its surface and the water had a stagnant, sinister sheen.

"It's as though something precious had gone out of my life," Lois was saying. "I was born on this estate and the lake was always the loveliest thing here. Now, since May Johnston's body was found floating in it, it seems evil."

She pressed closer to him and he slid a protecting arm about her waist.

High-pitched voices reached their ears. By the light of the pale half-moon they saw Sam Owens and Susan Hilary about a hundred yards away, moving slowly along the shore. They walked slightly apart from each other; spoke loud and heatedly, and there was a sob in Susan's voice. Obviously a lovers' quarrel.

Neal and Lois left the lake. That quarrel was none of their business. Lois led Neal to an arbor not far from the house, where they seated themselves on a bench. Presently he took her in his arms.

For the first time since his arrival at Hilary Manor Neal felt momentarily free from the brooding sense of evil. Perhaps this was the one spot where it could not follow them. Perhaps their love banished it from this place . . . They melted into each other's arms and between kisses, made glamorous plans for their future, and enjoyed, too, the long intense silences of lovers.

Thus, as they sat in the arbor, at least three hours had passed almost without their knowledge—when out of the silence of the night came sounds which sent them coldly rigid, clutching each other in terror.

It was the hellish, blood-chilling combination of sounds which resembled singing. The rasping, inhuman, agonized voice of a damned soul attempting to sing.

But it was not the same voice they had heard earlier in the evening.

"Susan!" Lois moaned.

It couldn't be. They had seen her only a few hours ago, very much alive. And those sounds came from a throat which was no longer part of a human living body.

Yet unmistakably it was the voice of Susan Hilary. Neal, after a minute of frozen silence, jumped to his feet.

"Where are you going?" Lois demanded.

"To that cave, wherever it is. That's where the singing comes from, isn't it?"

"Yes. But Neal, there might be danger. Hadn't we better get the others in the house?"

"No time," Neal yelled over his shoulder. "You go for them." He was already on his way.

"Neal—wait! I'm going with you."

He heard her feet pattering behind him and stopped to wait for her. He reached out a hand for her—it would take too much valuable time to persuade her to stay behind—and hand in hand they ran across the lawn of the house, through an apple orchard, through a field, and finally through a copse.

And as they ran they heard the twang of the strings accompanying the singing. The Hermit's mandolin accompanying the singing of the souls of dead girls whom he had tortured!

The mouth of the cave was plainly visible as they burst out of the copse. Lois hung back, her hand trembling in his.

"We've never before gone here at night," she murmured.

"Wait here for me," he ordered.

But she did not release his hand. Courageously she entered the cave with him. The weird singing was now very loud. It rasped its way to the very cores of their beings.

A dank musty odor struck them. They shivered, but it was not only the sudden cold of the cave which made them shiver. The singing seemed to come from the cave's depths. Neal strained his eyes, but saw only blackness fading into deeper blackness.

Cautiously they groped their way toward the back of the cave. Neal pulled a book of matches from his pocket, but he did not light one. It might be wisest not to make a target of themselves—if whatever was in the cave was human . . .

Lois held the back of her hand over her mouth to restrain the piteous, frightened whimpers which were coming from her lips. Neal felt a cold sweat covering him as they came nearer and nearer to the singing.

Then his outstretched hand touched a slimy stone surface. They had reached the farther wall—and had encountered nothing. There was nothing in the cave.

Yet the eerie singing continued all about them . . .

With trembling hands Neal struck a match, saw by its flickering flame that they stood in a small area surrounded by dark stone walls and a stone ceiling hardly higher than their heads, Neal lit another match and inspected the rear of the cave. There was no break in the wall, no tunnel or sign of a door.

Nothing . . . Yet that horrible singing and the twanging of a stringed instrument went on—seemingly coming out of the very ground, enveloping them!

Neal felt himself at the breaking point. Terror was entering into him, threatening to send him out of the cave a mad raving thing. And he realized Lois could stand it no longer. Then, with a wild cry Lois broke from him and ran. Neal was at her heels. Not until they were in the meadow did he catch up to her. Then she buried her face in his chest and sobbed hysterically. "What was it? Oh, God, what was it?" she kept repeating.

He could give her no answer. Could say nothing to reassure her.

The singing, he noticed, had stopped. There was no sound, not even the noises of insects. Slowly they walked to the house, gripped by a fear that stifled them.

Before they reached the house they met Lois' father, Mrs. Gideon, Hugo Gideon, and a rangy man who Neal learned later was the gardener.

"We're going to the cave to investigate this damnable nonsense," Joseph Hilary said.

Neal told them of their recent experience in the cave. "Where is Susan?" he asked. "Have you found—" he was about to say, "her body," but checked himself—"found any trace of her?"

Mrs. Gideon shook her large head. "She's gone. She's not in her room or anywhere about the house."

"Maybe she ran off with Sam Owens," Hugo muttered.

"Nonsense," Joseph Hilary protested. "Susan is too sane a girl for anything like that."

Neal said to Hugo: "I thought Sam Owens was taking you back to Daleside."

"So did I. He brought me here and the understanding was that he'd take me back. I saw his car leaving without his having said a word to me. That was rather thoughtless. I didn't want to trouble Mr. Hilary to get out his car, so I took advantage of his invitation to stay overnight. I was sitting in the library with my mother and Mr. Hilary when we heard Susan singing."

The gardener had been shaking his head from side to side. Now he said; "There's no use looking for Miss Susan."

Mr. Hilary whirled. "Why? What do you know about her disappearance?"

"All I know is that I heard her voice singing. Only the dead sing like that."

God! Could he be right? Stark terror hung like a black mantle about that little group standing in the dead of night on the lawn of that cursed estate.

The purr of a motor was heard nearby and headlights moved toward them. They waited tensely.

It was Sam Owens. He stopped the car when he saw them. His face was a question mark as he stepped out of the car.

"What's up?" he asked.

Mrs. Gideon strode up to him. "Where's Susan?" she demanded. "What have you done with her?"

"Susan?" his face blanched. "What happened to her? Where is she?"

"That's what we're asking you," Neal put in. "We heard that horrible singing again a few minutes ago—and this time the voice was Susan's."

Sam stared incredulously at him. There was sick fear in his eyes. "You're wrong," he insisted wildly. "Not *Susan's* voice. Oh, my God!"

He looked from one face to another, seeking assurance that Neal was mistaken. Suddenly he whirled. "The lake!" he cried, and started to run.

Neal followed. Was he trying to run away? He was heading for the lake—the lake where May Johnston's body had been found!

Sam Owens flew over the ground. He forged far ahead of Neal. When Neal reached the shore, he saw Sam's head bobbing in the water, swimming out. Swimming out toward a white blotch floating in the middle of the lake!

Neal waited on the shore. Sam seemed to be a strong swimmer and able to bring in—bring in what? With bated breath Neal strained his eyes toward the object floating in the uncertain moonlight.

The others arrived at the lake. Nobody spoke. Lois was whimpering. Then Sam reached the body—and the heartrending cry he uttered told them . . .

Lois gasped out a sob and collapsed in a faint. Neal jumped to her, but Mrs. Gideon reached her first.

"I'll take care of her," she said. "You might be needed here. It may be for the best that she has fainted." In powerful arms Mrs. Gideon picked Susan up, carried her to the house.

Neal waded up to his waist in the water to help Sam with his ghastly burden. But Sam would accept no help. As soon as he could stand, he gently lifted the stark white form of his dead sweetheart and waded to the shore.

"Dead!" he was mumbling to himself. "Dead!" Madness glinted in his eyes.

They persuaded him to place the body on the ground. There might still be a spark of life in her. Mr. Hilary, who had a smattering of medical knowledge, bent over the body of his niece. She was stark naked.

Mr. Hilary lifted a face from which all blood was drained. "She's been in the water for at least two hours," he said.

The gardener nodded. "She had to be dead. Only the dead sing like that. Only the dead, I say . . ."

There was no indication of whether or not she had been killed before she was thrust into the lake. An autopsy would show. Her body was unmarked save for her fingers. Each of her fingers was swollen to twice its normal size—like May Johnston's!

It was a strange procession back to the house. Sam Owens refused to let anybody else touch the body. He led with the lifeless form of the girl he had loved in his arms, and behind him came the four other men.

Sam placed Susan's body on the bed in her room. He would have stayed there all night with her, but the others forced him to accompany them downstairs to the library. They were afraid he would go mad with grief.

Mr. Hilary phoned the Daleside police. Then they waited in the library, the five men and Mrs. Gideon. Lois, Mrs. Gideon told Neal, was asleep in her room.

For a while nobody in the library said anything. Fear mingled with grief to form a giant weight which pressed down on them.

Suddenly Joseph Hilary stood up. "This place is accursed!" he burst out.

He had aged years within a half-hour. The luster was gone from his once flashing eyes. "I shall dispose of Hilary Manor. The Hermit has done enough harm. We cannot fight the dead. Our only hope lies in flight."

Neal's scalp grew taut. He knew Joseph Hilary was thinking of Lois!

Two girls had been found dead in the lake within three days, and their dead voices had been heard singing the song of the tormented damned in Hermit Cave. Lois might be the third . . .

Neal slipped out of the library, stole up the stairs. Gently he opened the door to Lois' room. Moonlight streaming through a window revealed her sleeping form.

He stood over her bed, looking down at the loveliness of her face, of the graceful lines of her bare shoulders and the firm, rounded contours of her partially uncovered breasts. He felt a catch in his throat at her beauty, and at the same time hot blood pounded in his temples with fury at any person or thing, living or dead, who would want to harm her.

"You cannot fight the dead," Joseph Hilary had said.

Neal realized that it would create an uncomfortable situation if he were found in Lois' bedroom. Against his will and better judgment—for her safety—he departed. On the stairs he heard the high voice of Mrs. Gideon and the weary, frightened voice of Mr. Hilary in argument. Mr. Hilary wanted to sell Hilary Manor and flee. Mrs. Gideon was trying to inject courage into him.

"I have no courage where my daughter's life is at stake," Mr. Hilary was protesting as Neal entered the library.

"Stuff and nonsense," Mrs. Gideon said. "I've never heard of a Hilary who was afraid of ghosts. You used to be a man, Joseph Hilary."

Mr. Hilary sank into a chair and buried his face in his hands. The death of Susan and fear of Lois' welfare had broken him utterly.

It took an hour for the police to arrive from Daleside. As soon as they entered, Neal knew that they would not accomplish anything. Daleside was a small town and hadn't much of a police force. Two men came; a constable and a deputy, and they were scared. They were local men and they knew about the Hermit.

It was plain that the constable wanted to get out of the place as soon as possible. He glanced at the body and said he was inclined to think it was suicide. Later, when he went through a desultory cross-examination of everybody in the library and learned from Neal of Susan's quarrel with Sam, he expressed himself a certain that it was suicide. She must have thrown herself in the lake as a result of the quarrel . . .

Sam, who had been staring out of a window with unseeing eyes, turned and protested vigorously. It had been a minor quarrel, he said; the kind all lovers have. He had wanted Susan to marry him within a month; Susan had wanted to wait longer. In a rage he had driven off. Several hours later he had returned, sorry for having lost his head, ready to apologize if she were not yet in bed—and had found the others outside the house looking for her. That was all he knew.

"You're on the wrong track," Hugo Gideon said to the constable. "What about the singing we heard after she was dead? You've got to explain that—if it can be explained in human terms, which I doubt."

The scared expression again came into the constable's face. He mumbled that he would put the whole matter into the hands of the sheriff in the morning; that some time tomorrow the coroner would come and after that there would be an autopsy. Then, fright glittering in his eyes, he and the deputy left.

Neal went up to his room, but he did not go to bed. He pulled a chair near the door, and, fully dressed and wide awake, he prepared to sit the night out. He left his door open several inches. Lois' room was farther down the hall, and next to it was the room where Susan's dead body now lay.

Once the sound of footsteps brought him to his feet. He peered into the dimly lit hall. A man was turning the doorknob of Susan's room. Neal recognized the stocky figure of Sam Owens. Sam let himself quietly into the room; and then there was no sound in all that house save the ticking of the grandfather clock on the landing downstairs.

Neal went back to his chair. It was understandable why Sam should want to be alone with his dead sweetheart. Neal knew that if Lois were dead he too . . .

God, don't let him get such thoughts! Nothing must be permitted to harm Lois. "We cannot fight the dead!" Cold fingers of terror played over his spine. Tomorrow he must persuade Lois to leave this accursed place with him.

The subdued creak of a door-hinge was like a pistol shot to Neal's straining ears. That must be Sam leaving Susan's room. Again he looked out into the hall. This time he saw nothing. That was odd. If that sound had been made by Sam closing the door to Susan's room. Sam would be out in the hall now.

Neal stepped into the hall. The hinge creaked again. He saw a door move an inch or two and close noiselessly. But it was not the door to Susan's room. It was the door to Lois' room!

With pounding heart and tense muscles Neal ran to the door he had seen move and pressed his ear against it. No sound inside. Had his eyes deceived him? Or was something in there that had no corporeal form?

Slowly he turned the knob—then pushed against the door and it flew open. Lois lay asleep in her bed. Nobody else was in the room. He exhaled deeply with relief and stepped into the room.

Too late he heard a sound behind him. Too late he realized that somebody could hide behind the open door ... he whirled. A blunt instrument struck him on the base of his skull, and without a sound Neal sank into oblivion.

As from a far distance Neal Dexter heard wailing. It was as if a voice from another world were calling to him. He tried to respond, to move toward the voice; but his limbs seemed bound by unseen cords and he could drive no words through his throat.

Suddenly he was sitting up, wholly conscious, and his heart was pounding madly within him. That voice calling to him—it belonged to Lois! And it wasn't calling. She was screaming the weird lament of the dead girls tortured by the Hermit!

Neal leaped to his feet. Lois' bedroom was empty. She was gone!

His head pained terrifically from the blow he had received, but he was hardly aware of the ache. *Only the dead sing like that!* Lord in heaven, was he too late? Was Lois' body floating in the lake even now while her voice sang in the cave?

Outside the house he hesitated. Should he go to the lake or to the cave? He decided to make for the cave first. If the breath of life was still in her, she would be in the cave.

There hadn't been any sign of a door in the cave leading to another chamber when he and Lois were there several hours ago. Yet that did not mean that there could not be one with a separate entrance.

Unless—unless that was truly a dead voice he heard!

When he broke out of the copse, he did not turn toward the mouth of the cave. He scrambled up the side of the hillock. It was covered with thick, almost impenetrable brush. The eerie singing was very loud now, louder than Susan's had been in the cave. Like a mad beast he crashed through the undergrowth, tearing his hands, ripping his clothes.

Presently, with a choked gasp of triumph, he found what he was looking for. Surrounded by briars was a trapdoor. Lifting the door by its iron ring, he found himself looking down into a section of a lighted chamber. A wooden ladder descended to it. In his frenzy to get to Lois he threw caution to the winds and scrambled down the ladder.

"Welcome!"

Neal turned, one hand gripping the side of the ladder, one foot on the last rung, the other on the ground. He looked into the unwavering bore of an automatic. The gun was held by a figure clad in the grey garb of a monk. The cowl completely hid his face.

"Neal! Oh, God, Neal!"

Beyond the Hermit was the living, breathing, tortured body of Lois. She was suspended from the ceiling by her ten fingers. Each finger was bound with many coils of steel wire; the wires were fastened in the ceiling separately. Her sheer nightgown hung from her in tattered strips, revealing every soft curve of her lovely body. Red welts streaked her breasts and thighs.

A great cry emitted from Neal's throat and he tensed his muscles to spring at the Hermit.

"I wouldn't if I were you," the Hermit said. "I can't miss at this distance, and I am sure the lady wouldn't like to see you with a bullet through your heart."

Neal remained motionless. The Hermit was right: resistance at this point was futile.

Meekly he obeyed the Hermit's command to turn around and hold his hands behind his back. Neal felt cold steel on his wrists, heard a click, and knew that he was handcuffed.

The Hermit passed a rope through the handcuffs; then passed the other end of the rope through a ring high on the wall and pulled down on the rope.

He was utterly helpless now. The slightest motion sent unendurable needles of agony through him. The Hermit tied the rope securely around Neal's feet; thrust a dirty gag into his mouth.

"You were a fool," the Hermit chuckled. "You should have jumped me when you were free. That was your last chance. Now your body, as well as that of the young woman's, will be found floating in the lake."

Neal cursed himself as he recognized the truth of the Hermit's words. He should have taken that desperate chance when he was still free. Now there was no hope; no release for himself and Lois—save in death.

The Hermit turned to Lois swinging from the ceiling by her fingers.

"Please!" Lois sobbed. "Not again! Oh, God, I can' stand it!"

The Hermit picked up a whip. Twice Lois screamed—the first time before the whip struck, and again when it left a narrow streak of blood under her breasts. Again and again the Hermit's arm came back, and again and again the cruel lash tore Lois' white skin.

"Stop!" Lois screamed. *"I'll sing!"*

The Hermit dropped the whip. He went to a table on which stood a small machine like a phonograph and flicked a switch. A round black disc whirled.

Now Neal understood the mystery of the singing dead. This was a recording machine. Elsewhere in the room the Hermit no doubt had a phonograph, with perhaps an amplifier attached. It was a phonograph they had heard when they had thought they were listening to the voices of girls already dead.

The Hermit climbed a ladder to a crude wooden platform as high as Lois' shoulders and which was immediately adjacent to the wires by which she was suspended—the wires which had caused the fingers of the two dead girls to swell, just as Lois' fingers were now swelling . . .

The Hermit plucked on the strings, and Neal saw that they were of varying thicknesses, so that Lois' weight pulling down on them made a crude sort of stringed instrument.

Then the Hermit played. As one would strum on a harp, the Hermit strummed on that hellish instrument. And each time a string vibrated with sound, a tremor of agony shot through Lois. It was not only an instrument of unearthly music; it was also an instrument of torture.

And Lois sang.

Fear of the whip compelled her to sing. She shrieked the melody of an eerie, nameless lament the Hermit had taught her. Her fair young body swinging from the strings writhed and gyrated in mid-air in a horrible dance of anguish as the Hermit's fingers twanged out the melody. And each note the madman struck, drew from her contorted lips an awful shriek of pain—a shriek which had in it the essence of hideous song.

And through it all Neal was powerless to move without excruciating agony, and the gag prevented him from uttering a sound. He shut his eyes to blot out the torture of the girl he loved, and he offered a silent prayer that vengeance be permitted him, or that death come quickly.

As if in answer to his prayer, an avenging agent dropped through the trapdoor.

The Hermit's covered face moved from the automatic which he had left on the table on which the recording machine stood to the disheveled, wild-eyed individual who stood below the platform glaring up at him. It was Sam Owens, and in his hand he grasped a heavy wrench.

A moment the Hermit hesitated—then leaped off the platform, landed directly on Sam. The weight of the Hermit's body threw Sam to the ground, but it gave the Hermit only a momentary advantage. Sam squirmed, disentangled the arm which held the wrench. While the Hermit pounded his face, Sam's arm drove up and forward and the wrench cracked against the Hermit's forehead.

The Hermit slumped. Sam slipped from under him; and with a fury born of grieving for his dead sweetheart, he battered the Hermit's skull.

Sam Owens released Neal, and then the two men carefully unwound the wire from Lois' fingers and lowered her to the ground. Neal stripped off his shirt and wrapped it about Lois.

"Better not," Sam said as Neal made a motion toward the body on the floor. "That face must be a bloody pulp and Lois has endured enough for one night. I can tell you who it is."

"Hugo Gideon?" Neal asked.

Sam nodded.

Neal said: "I thought so. He tried to disguise his voice; but once he slipped into his natural tone. But what I couldn't understand—and still can't—was the reason for his horrible madness."

"Madness?" Sam shrugged. "Maybe. It was cold, calculating madness born of greed. His real estate business wasn't a success. He'd started at the tail-end of a boom and nobody was buying. Then one day the agent for a wealthy syndicate of sportsmen approached him. They wanted to buy a site for a swanky golf club and they wanted Hilary Manor.

"It was a big thing for Hugo. The commission on the deal would have amounted to a fortune for him. He obtained a promise from the agent to keep the matter quiet; said Mr. Hilary would never consent to sell the old family place to be turned into a golf links. Of course his game was to buy it for as little as possible and pocket the difference, plus commission. I was the only one who knew about it. I happened to walk in on him one day while the agent was there, and overheard enough to get the idea."

"My father told me Hugo wanted to buy Hilary Manor," Lois broke in. "He scoffed at the notion."

"So Susan told me," Sam said. "I didn't butt in because I knew your father wouldn't sell. In desperation Hugo evolved his devilish scheme, with the aid of the old ghost story about the Hermit. The use of the phonograph was clever. He arranged a timing device on the phonograph to make it start automatically at a certain time, so that he was with Neal and me in my car when we hear May Johnston sing. And he was in the library with his mother and your father when Susan's voice was heard. He'd made the recording earlier in the evening."

Lois shuddered. Neal slipped his arm about her waist, held her to him.

"He had another motive besides that of money," Sam went on. "May Johnston had been his girl. He had tired of her and wanted to get rid of her. So she was the first to go. As for Susan—" Sam's voice broke—"well, he was in love with her. But she preferred me. So it was his jealous rage as well as the other thing that made Susan his second victim.

"Susan's death nearly accomplished his purpose. You heard Mr. Hilary in the library; he was ready to sell. Hugo could have bought the place for a song. And he would have—if his mother hadn't succeeded in persuading Mr. Hilary not to sell. Ironical that it should be his mother. She knew nothing of her son's scheme, of course. But nothing on earth would have prevented Mr. Hilary from selling if Lois had died like the others."

"Thanks to you, Neal and I are now alive," Lois breathed.

"It was the least I could do for Susan," Sam said. "When Mr. Hilary and Mrs. Gideon were arguing about selling the place, I got an inkling of the truth. And later, while I was in Susan's room and heard Lois singing, it suddenly struck me how Hugo arranged it. I heard the singing because I was awake. I doubt if the others in the house yet know that anything has happened. Hugo neglected to close the trapdoor which Neal left open, so it wasn't hard for me to find it . . ."

Wearily the three climbed up the ladder. The first flush of dawn tinted the sky. Neal pressed Lois' lovely throbbing body to him, and arms about each other they walked back to the house.

THE HOUSE THAT HORROR BUILT

Chapter 1: God of Vengeance and Terror

The taxi driver said: "Are you sure this is where you want to go, Miss Beaumont?"

The girl did not seem to hear. She fumbled at her expensive leather handbag, and the taxi driver saw that her hands trembled. "This is 237 Aspen Street, isn't it?" she asked, with grim determination.

The driver leaned across the seat to get a better look at the house. Barely distinguishable through the darkness—and through the muck which covered the door—was the number.

"Do you want me to go up with you?" the driver offered. "I'll be very glad to."

He knew who she was, of course. She had ridden in his cab several times, sometimes with her uncle, Calvin Beaumont, commissioner of police, sometimes with men who took her out. Her photograph and that of her sister Lorna often appeared in the society pages of the local newspapers. She lived with her uncle.

Which made it all the more strange that she should be here, after dark, in this most miserable of all slum sections, this center of depravity, disease, and filth. And the house into which she was about to go! Like most of the houses hereabouts, it had been built some sixty or seventy years ago. Its five stories were covered, inside and out, with the dirt and decay of decades. All the windows in the front were dark. In some the glass was shattered; others were boarded up. And it was in there that she was going—alone!

She handed him his fare and turned from the cab. The previous occasions on which he had seen her he had been struck by her beauty. She wasn't beautiful now. Her face was almost ugly with stark fear. She was terribly afraid of something in that house, yet she was moving toward it, driving her feet toward it through sheer force of will.

At the door of the house Emily Beaumont uttered a shrill cry and jumped back. A man lay stretched across the entrance.

She hesitated. Then, gritting her teeth, she turned the knob of the door and stepped over the prostrate body into the vestibule. She was bringing her second foot over the body—when a clammy hand grasped her silk-clad ankle.

She screamed, shamelessly, and whirled. The drunkard released her ankle. He hadn't moved any part of his body save his hand. He lay looking up at her with glazed eyes.

"You ain't goin' up there, lady?" his thick, hoarse voice asked.

She turned her eyes away from him. His face looked moldy, eaten away, and the whites of his eyes were streaked with numberless lines of blood.

The taxi driver was at her side, swearing at the drunkard, pleading: "Let me take you back, Miss Beaumont! You can't stay here!"

The man on the ground rolled his head from side to side as if in agony. "Oh, Lord!" he moaned. "A pretty young lady like you! The god lives on the blood of pretty young ladies! Thoran needs their blood and the whiteness of their bodies! Oh, Lord!"

The girl fought against the panic mounting in her. "He's in a drunken stupor," she said in a shrill voice. She whirled, pushed in, slammed the door in the taxi-man's face.

The stairs were before her, wooden, narrow, rickety. A single feeble bulb glinted at the head of the first flight. Ancient wallpaper hung in strips from the walls, and where there was no paper the plaster was sweating. The odor of dry mold clogged her nostrils. The stairs creaked beneath her feet.

Five flights. And on the fifth floor would be Lorna and whatever evil power was responsible for the change that had come over her. . .

On the second flight she heard steps high above her, steps descending. They were heavy steps—heavier, it seemed, than any man's could be; each step like a sledge hammer pounding in slow rhythm. There was no sound in all that house but the sound of those approaching steps.

Emily's heart thumped wildly. She forced herself to continue upward. It was like an ascent to meet doom.

In the middle of the third flight she saw the thing coming down. In the uncertain light it looked at first like a moving mass of flesh without definite shape and with a single large eye in the right side of what appeared to be its face, a dark shadow where the other eye should be.

Then she saw that it was a woman, a mountain of a woman with a black patch over one eye. Rolls of fat around her bare arms joggled as she lowered herself ponderously down the stairs.

Emily stood frozen. The woman would have to press against her when they passed. Emily's flesh crawled at the thought. She shrank against the banister, holding her breath to make herself as flat as possible. Then the massive female was squeezing past her. Emily felt globs of fat pushing against her slim body, shoving her against the rail.

The woman paused and turned the black patch toward her, seemed to be looking at Emily with the black patch. Fetid breath panted from her bloodless, fleshy mouth. Emily felt nausea choke her.

The rest of the way Emily ran. It was like flight—except that she ran toward the horror, not away from it!

When she reached the fifth and last floor, she was panting. She dipped trembling fingers into her handbag, looked again at a slip of paper. There was the address and then the cryptic words: "5 rear right."

That was the piece of paper Lorna had left behind her when she had departed from the house an hour ago. Lorna, Emily's younger sister, delicate, lovely, over whom a startling change had come in the last two weeks. She had suddenly lost interest in her surroundings, in parties and dances and even in James Madden, handsome young district attorney to whom she was engaged to be married. She moved about the house as in a dream and her eyes burned as with fever.

Earlier this evening Emily's uncle, James Beaumont, with whom the two sisters lived since the deaths of their parents, had drawn Emily aside after dinner. There had been a worried expression on his rugged face.

"One of my patrolmen reports that he has seen Lorna in the worst slum section of the city," he had said. "Twice within the last week, and each time it was late at night and she was alone. What in the world can she be doing there? She's sensitive and high-tempered, Emily, and frankly I don't know how to handle her. If I ask her point-blank for an explanation, she'll only get her back up and refuse to say a word. Shall I have her followed?"

"Not yet," said Emily. "Leave it to me." She had gone up to Lorna's room.

Lorna had had her hat and gloves on.

"Where are you going?" Emily had asked.

"Out."

"May I go with you? I'm bored."

Lorna had looked at her sister, and her eyes had been dots of fire in her chalk-white face. "Not yet," she had mumbled. "Later . . . perhaps . . . when he is ready for others."

"Ready for others? Who?"

"Thoran . . . God," Lorna had whispered, and her voice was tense with a feverish reverence.

Emily had felt fear tighten about her heart. She had grasped her younger sister by both shoulders. "Lorna, are you ill? What are you talking about?"

Lorna had lifted her eyes to the ceiling and whispered: "Thoran, God of vengeance and terror, who shall destroy all other gods. He is calling me."

"Lorna!"

Lorna had dashed out of the room. Emily ran after her, frantically calling her name. By the time she reached the street door, she saw Lorna pull away in a taxi. On the floor of the hall lay a piece of white paper, a sheet torn from a memorandum book. Emily stooped to pick it up. On it was scrawled an address: "237 Aspen Street, 5 rear right."

Should she give this address to her uncle and tell him what Lorna had said? Her uncle would send police to the place. There would be a raid and perhaps publicity and scandal.

Ice trickled through Emily's veins at the memory of Lorna's fanatic expression as she had whispered: "Thoran, god of vengeance and terror . . ." What had she meant? To what creature of hell had she referred?

The police could cope with mere criminal force, could arrest somebody. But this was some trickery, something elusive, sinister and subtle that held her sister in thrall. There was only one way to help Lorna, to save her, and that was to go to that address alone and investigate.

Now, in front of the right rear door on the top floor of that ancient slum dwelling, Emily hesitated. Her heart throbbed wildly with a sense of foreboding horror.

Through the door came a low humming sound. It was like the steady drone of a dynamo, its volume never increasing, never lessening. Emily tried the knob. The door opened a fraction of an inch. Her breath clogged in her throat. An inner voice warned her not to open that door! Warned her that once she was on the other side there could be no retreat.

But Lorna was in there. If evil was there, Lorna must be saved from it.

Emily pushed the door open and stepped inside.

She found herself in a long narrow room. Once it had been a slum flat, but the walls had been taken out. There was no light, save for two candles at the other end of the room. On the floor were huddled shapes, shapes of people kneeling, she made out when her eyes became accustomed to the darkness. They knelt on the bare floor, and it was from their lips that the droning sound came. They were muttering something which, at first, she could not understand.

The candles rested on what looked like an altar. Behind the altar were heavy black drapes. Otherwise the room was without any furnishings.

Behind Emily the door opened and closed again, and the enormous one-eyed woman waddled past her. She stepped behind the altar, raised one hand, and the droning stopped.

"Thoran!" she shouted. The people rose to their feet and repeated: "Thoran!"

Then suddenly there was a blinding flash of light behind the altar; and when the light was gone a man stood there.

The worshippers fell prostrate to the floor. Emily remained standing, pressing against the wall to make herself as inconspicuous as possible.

Candle light flickered on the face of the man who stood behind the altar. Man? Emily felt tremors of a strange dread pass through her as she looked at that face. It was thin, seemingly without flesh, and the skin was like parchment stretched taut as a drum over his face bones.

But it was his eyes that held her gaze, that seemed to be peering through the darkness straight into the core of her being. Deep in their sockets they were, and in their sockets they blazed with terrible intensity. They were looking at her, she felt, probing her soul, and probing, likewise, the souls of everybody in that room. . .

She swayed on her feet, felt a powerful compulsion to drop to the floor and make obeisance to him. "Thoran! Thoran!" the voices chanted—and she found to her horror that her tongue had unconsciously begun to form the syllables of that name.

Then Thoran spoke, and a silence fell over the worshippers. It was a silence so profound, so intense, that it seemed to clash against her eardrums.

"I am Thoran, god of vengeance and terror. I have made all other gods of evil my slaves, and the gods of good tremble at my name."

His voice was low, a monotone, yet there was that about it which possessed one completely, which drove all thought from one's mind save the might and awful power of Thoran.

The voice went on. "I have come from the core of the earth which is my home to wreak vengeance on those who deny me, to strike terror into the hearts of mankind so they shall know me. I am not alive as you are alive, nor am I dead as your dead. I am Thoran!"

"Thoran!" the worshippers cried. They rose to their feet. "Thoran! Thoran!" Their voices were frenzied, and Emily saw the dark shapes of the worshippers leap and gyrate in a mad dance of homage.

An overwhelming desire to join them, to be one of them in their wild, hellish rite, gripped Emily. She had to struggle with herself to keep her limbs from moving, from prostrating herself in awe before the being behind the altar.

Thoran spoke again, and at once that profound silence fell in the room.

"Thoran is not of this life. Thoran must have blood to remain with you on the surface of the earth—blood of the man-things whose form he has assumed."

The huge woman, who was evidently Thoran's high priestess, placed a copper bowl and a knife on the altar.

"Thoran needs blood," came that low, intense voice, and a man stepped forward between the candles on the altar. He pulled up the sleeve of his coat, made an incision in his wrist, and let drops of his blood trickle into the bowl.

"Enough," Thoran said. "The blood must be blood of multitudes. *And when your blood becomes part of me, I shall become part of you, and forever after you shall be the people of Thoran, and shall do homage unto Thoran, and your souls shall be the slaves of Thoran.*"

A woman stepped up to the altar, and she too made an incision in her wrist and drops of her blood fell into the bowl. And for a long time the procession continued—men and women, some well dressed, some in the filthy rags of the most disreputable inhabitants of the slums. One by one they donated their blood to Thoran.

When the bowl was full, Thoran lifted it to his lips and drank. A shout rose from the worshippers. "Thoran! Thoran!"

Fascinated, Emily watched. She felt no disgust, no horror, at the sight of a man drinking human blood. And with the force of a staggering impact, knowledge came to her that she too would go to the altar when her turn came and contribute her blood. She would go without resistance, and then she too would become a creature of Thoran.

She huddled against the wall, fighting against the irresistible power that was robbing her of will, that was making her one with those who worshipped that spawn of hell who called himself Thoran. And she knew that it was a losing fight. She was being pulled to that altar as surely as if strings were attached to her. Nearer and nearer to the altar she moved, yet she was not conscious that she walked.

A well-dressed woman turned from the bowl and one of the candles revealed her face. It was Virginia Bryan, who had been Emily's classmate in college and was one of her best friends. Somehow Emily was not surprised. Her numbed brain considered it natural that Virginia should be here, that all the world should be there to worship Thoran.

Then she cried out. It was a shriek that clashed against the walls of the room, and it ended in the name of her sister. Only the sight of Lorna, slitting her wrist at the altar, could have pierced the dominating spell of Thoran. . .

"Lorna!" Emily shrieked. "Oh, God, Lorna, don't!"

A hush fell over the room. Thoran turned his blazing eyes in the direction of Emily's voice. That gaze entered into her, shattered her resistance. She cringed before it, held her hands over her face—but she could not shut out the awful scrutiny of those eyes.

"There is a blasphemer among you," Thoran said.

Emily tore her hands from her face. Lorna stood motionless as a statue before the altar, the knife still raised in her right hand. Emily felt the last remnants of her will leaving her. She could only remember that she must do something, at once, to save herself and to save Lorna. She opened her mouth—and laughed. It was the only action of which at that moment she was capable. She laughed at Thoran.

For seconds there was no sound, no movement, in all that room. Then Thoran lifted one hand. His finger pointed directly at Emily.

Suddenly there was a burst of sound, and a bolt of fire leaped at her from the finger of Thoran. Her legs gave way under her, and with a moan she sank to the floor.

Chapter 2: Call of the Blood

DAN GIFFORD, police reporter for the *Daily Times-Record*, was with the police who conducted the raid. It was he who lifted the unconscious body of Emily Beaumont from the floor and carried her down to the street.

By the time he reached the sidewalk her eyes were open and she was urging him to set her on her feet. He did, and she swayed unsteadily. He held her in his arms and was glad of the chance.

"What happened?" she asked, her mind still dazed.

"That's what we want to know," Dan said. "The cab driver who brought you here hung around for a while. Then he became worried and told a cop that he'd seen you go up there. The cop phoned your uncle and he told them to raid the place. And here we are. What did they do to you?"

She passed a hand over her forehead. "I'm all right. I just fainted." Then she cried out: "My wrist!"

His eyes dropped to her wrist. "Just a cut. How did that happen?" The blood had already clotted.

She stared at the incision with eyes bulging with horror. After she had fainted her wrist must have been cut and held over that bowl; and her blood had been among the blood which Thoran had drunk. She felt contaminated; she felt that something darkly evil had entered into her.

A police siren screamed and an automobile containing Calvin Beaumont and James Madden, the district attorney and Lorna's fiancé, pulled up.

"Emily!" her uncle cried. "Thank heaven you're safe."

"Where's Lorna?" Madden demanded. "Wasn't she with you? Where is she?"

Lorna! Emily remembered suddenly that she had come here to save her. And now she herself would need saving!

The police were bringing down worshippers, herding them into patrol wagons. Madden leaped forward. A patrolman came out of the door, holding Lorna by one arm and Virginia Bryan by the other.

"Lorna!" Madden said. "Are you all right?"

She looked up at the man to whom she was engaged to be married and no change came over her expression. Listlessly she said: "How are you, James?"

"Aren't you glad I am here?"

"Did you send these policemen after us?" she said in a flat voice. "It was a foolish thing. Thoran will never forgive you."

"Thoran?" Madden repeated. Then he saw her expression change at last; and in her face was awed reverence and something else which he could not fathom but which filled him with vague dread. Over the street a hush had suddenly fallen.

Madden swung around. At the side of a patrolman walked a man on whom all eyes were centered. There was nothing about him that was extraordinary; at first glance he was merely another inhabitant of the slums with disheveled and ragged clothes. But then Madden looked at him again, and he saw those eyes which blazed with an inner fire and the over-powering intensity of that cadaverous face. He walked as if nobody existed in all the world but himself.

The patrolman led him to Calvin Beaumont. "This is the head guy, Chief. Calls himself God or something. A crackpot. Shall I take him in?"

"Certainly," the police commissioner said.

Dan Gifford was still supporting Emily Beaumont with one arm about her waist. Now he felt her tremble violently as she stared at the man who called himself a god. Her lips quivered and she seemed on the verge of a hysterical attack.

Thoran spoke. His voice was emotionless, impersonal, low; yet it set the heartstrings of everybody who heard it vibrating with nameless dread. There was no anger in his voice; only scorn.

"You poor, feeble, impotent mortals," he said.

Then he stepped into the patrol wagon.

The following afternoon Dan Gifford visited Emily Beaumont. She was sitting in the library with a book on her lap, but she had not been reading. She was staring out of the window when Dan entered.

She extended a hand to him. "Thank you for what you did for me last night. Are you here as a friend or as a reporter?"

"Forget I'm a reporter for a while, Miss Beaumont. I want to help you. I promise I won't write anything you don't want me to. I've just come from the district attorney's office. Madden had to release everybody who was taken at the raid last night—including Thoran. He held everybody but you and your sister and a girl named Virginia Bryan overnight. There's no law against holding religious services of any kind, no matter how weird, and there is no law against anybody calling himself God. But there are laws against certain rites. How did you get that cut on your wrist?"

She raised her wrist, dropped it. "I cut myself," she said in a lifeless voice.

"That's what every one of them said. All of them, you see, cutting themselves in the same place at the same time. . . Are you afraid of Thoran?"

She looked at him, and he saw agony in her eyes and an inward struggle.

"Won't you tell me?" he urged. "I want to help."

"Please go," she said.

Dan Gifford stood up. This was a hellish business. Every one of those people had acted the same way when questioned. What unearthly power could the man named Thoran hold over them?

Just then Calvin Beaumont and James Madden entered the library.

"We want no newspaper reporters in this house," Madden snapped.

"I'm here as a friend," Gifford explained. "I promise not to write a word."

"Let him stay," Beaumont said. He turned to his niece. "Emily, you've got to talk. Lorna refuses. She's upstairs in bed on the verge of a nervous breakdown and she became hysterical when we questioned her. You've nothing to fear. I'm the police commissioner of this city; James here is the district attorney. You'll be protected."

"There is nothing to tell," Emily said.

Beaumont shrugged hopelessly. "That's what they all say."

"Look here, Emily, there is something to tell," Madden burst out. "Last night you were screaming about blood in your sleep. The housekeeper heard you. And here's what you said, your exact words: 'My blood has become part of him and he has become part of me.' "

Emily started out of her chair, then weakly sank back.

"You see," Madden said triumphantly. "For God's sake, Emily, if you don't care about yourself, think of your sister whom you love, whom I love. That monster Thoran has done something to her. She's far worse off than you. We're the law here, your uncle and I, but we can do nothing without evidence. Please, Emily, if you love your sister."

She looked up at him with a far-away expression in her eyes. Her face was chalk-white. Without a word she rose, and as in a dream she walked out of the room.

The three men looked after her. "God in heaven!" her uncle muttered huskily.

Emily went up to her room and threw herself on her bed, sobbing as if her heart would break. She had wanted to tell them of the frightful rites, about the bolt of fire which had sprung from Thoran's finger, about the horrible drinking of the blood. Apparently the bowl and knife had been hidden as the police stormed up the stairs. But she had found that she could not tell. The words would not come.

She thought of the words of Thoran: *"And when your blood becomes part of me, I shall become part of you, and forever after you shall be the people of Thoran, and shall do homage unto Thoran, and your souls shall be the slaves of Thoran."*

She was the slave of Thoran, a creature of Thoran! He had drunk her blood. She had set out to save her sister, and now she herself was beyond saving!

Soon the worshippers of Thoran would gather and again offer up their blood to him. "Thoran must have blood to remain with you on the surface of the earth!" Her blood! The blood of multitudes!

Already she felt the call of Thoran gnawing inside of her like a horde of maggots. He wanted her, required her blood, and she was powerless to resist. And most terrible of all, she had no desire to resist. Eagerness and a desperate yearning surged in her to make obeisance to Thoran and offer up her life blood so that the god of terror and vengeance might retain human form.

She rose, dressed mechanically. In the hall stood Lorna, also fully dressed. Lorna had been waiting for her, although no word had passed between them. Together they went down the stairs and out the front door.

At the gate a patrolman stopped them. "Sorry, but the Chief gave orders that you two can't leave the house," he informed them.

The two young women ignored him, walked on. He grabbed each by an arm. "I have orders. You've got to go back to the house." He was pleading with them. After all, they were the Chief's nieces and he had to be careful how he handled them.

Suddenly the two young women turned on him. The veneer of civilization, of refinement and dignity, dropped from them, and they became primitive females fighting with teeth and nails. Lorna sank her teeth into the palm of his hand and Emily gouged flesh from his face.

The patrolman howled and released Lorna. But he managed to hold on to Emily. She fought like a wildcat. Finally, with great gasping sobs of frustration, she permitted the patrolman to lead her back into the house. His cheeks were bloody ribbons.

Emily was confined to her room. For the rest of the day and most of the night she banged on the door, begging to be let out. When the housekeeper brought her food, Emily flew at her, and in her mad frenzy might have killed the woman whom she had known since childhood had not her uncle rushed in.

Calvin Beaumont had aged perceptibly within the last twenty hours. "God, what can it be?" he muttered. "For modern healthy girls like Emily and Lorna to change so! What in the name of heaven can this Thoran be?"

In the morning they found that Emily had disappeared. She had torn up bed sheets to form a rope and had let herself down from her window, which faced the back of the house. Patrolmen had been stationed only at the front.

Twenty-four hours later Emily and Lorna Beaumont returned to their house. They were haggard, pale as death, and they refused to answer any questions. On the wrist of each was a fresh incision . . .

Chapter 3: Thoran Is Thirsty

DAN GIFFORD walked into the office of the district attorney. "How are the Beaumont girls?" was the first thing he said.

James Madden leaned back in his swivel-chair. He was in the midst of a campaign for re-election, but that was not what caused the heavy rings under his eyes or the worried lines on his face. Seven days had passed since the raid on the slum dwelling.

"I wish to God I knew," Madden said. "The way they behave is blood-chilling. Their uncle doesn't allow them out of the house. He swears that he will keep them there until they act normal again. They just sit in one spot all day, not saying much, not doing anything, just sitting there. It's maddening."

"Maybe they're ill."

Madden shook his head. "We had doctors in. They couldn't understand it. It's that damned creature that calls himself Thoran. I wish I could put him behind bars. But he's committed no crime—that is, none that we can pin on him."

Dan Gifford lit a cigarette and said: "I hear that Thoran's cult is growing by leaps and bounds. That's why I'm here. My city editor wants me to get your impression of the phenomenal growth of the number of Thoran's followers. Do you see any danger in it?"

The district attorney spread his fingers on his desk. "The phenomenal rise of cults is nothing new in the world. Let any madman preach that he is a god or a divine representative of God and there are sure to be some people who believe him. Virtually millions of people now living worship some charlatan or other who has persuaded them that he is a god. But I'll say this much as far as Thoran is concerned. He has me scared. He seems to have power over people that is really frightening. And it's a power for terrible evil. Sometimes I am almost ready to admit that—that he isn't human after all; that he is what he says he is, a god of evil in human form."

"Does your office intend to do anything about him?"

"As soon as he breaks a law, certainly. He hasn't yet, as far as we know. Persons who could testify against him refuse to. They seem to have lost control of their own wills, like Lorna and Emily Beaumont. We have had undercover men and women attend the services he has held during the last few days. He has preached his gospel of vengeance and terror and that is all."

"There are rumors that he also holds services elsewhere," Dan said. "Rumors of blood sacrifices and other hideous practices."

"As far as this office knows they are just rumors," the district attorney said, and picked up a sheaf of papers to indicate that the interview was at an end.

Dan Gifford rose to leave. As he neared the door a young man burst into the room. His hair was disheveled and his eyes were wild.

"My name's Martin Rolfe," he stammered to Madden. "I'm the fiancé of Virginia Bryan."

Dan Gifford remained in the office, standing near the door.

"Oh, yes," Madden nodded and stuck out his hand. "She's a friend of Lorna. She's one of the girls who—" He hesitated.

"Who was picked up at the raid on Thoran's temple or whatever it was," Martin Rolfe finished. "You can say it. She's in the same boat as your fiancée—or was. Now she's disappeared. Been gone three days. Her family is almost crazy. So am I. She's with Thoran, I know. There's nowhere else she would have gone."

The last sentences had been uttered in a shaking, hoarse voice. Now he was gasping:

"God, why did this have to happen to her? She was so sweet, so lovely, before . . . before . . . What hellish thing has that monster done to her? What good are the police if they couldn't save her?"

With a sob the young man sank into a chair and covered his face with his hands. Madden walked around the desk and placed a hand on his shoulder. "I know how you feel," he murmured. "Lorna . . ."

Dan Gifford's hands were clenched into tight balls at his side. He thought of Emily Beaumont. She too was one of Thoran's creatures. He choked with emotion at the thought of her. She was the loveliest girl he had ever seen. If not for Thoran, perhaps he and she . . .

If only he could get his fingers around the scrawny neck of that monster! Law or no law, he'd choke the life out of him and forever rid the world of him.

A telephone jangled. Madden picked up the receiver.

He listened for several seconds, then barked: "I'll be right over."

He was in motion before the receiver was on the cradle. "You'd better come, Rolfe," he said, troubled. "A girl's been found—dead. It may be Miss Bryan . . . You come too, Gifford."

Madden's car took them to the slum section of the city. A patrolman led them through a dark, narrow alley.

"Some boys who were playing found her about twenty minutes ago," the patrolman explained as they picked their way over accumulated filth.

At the end of the alley there was a group of detectives and patrolmen. At their feet was the nude body of a woman.

"Virginia!" Martin Rolfe gasped and leaped forward.

A detective grasped his arm. "Easy, sonny," he said, then turned to Madden. "Been dead maybe twenty-four hours. There's no blood in her."

The body of the once attractive young woman was propped in a sitting position against the wall, the head hanging grotesquely limp. Her legs were doubled up under her. The color of her skin was nauseating. The color! It had no color. It was as if all the color pigments in her skin had been removed, leaving it shrunken, grey . . .

She had no hands. They had been severed at the wrists.

"That's the way she died," a detective said. "She bled to death. And she wasn't killed here where she was found. There's no blood on any part of her body, and there's none anywhere around here."

"Thoran!" Dan Gifford burst out. "Now he's gone in for murder."

Madden turned to him. "You think it's Thoran?"

"His cult has something to do with blood. You remember what Emily Beaumont shouted in her sleep. There's a rumor that he drinks it. And this girl was a follower of his. The whole thing ties up."

Madden nodded. "We'll pick him up for questioning."

For questioning! And Thoran of course would establish an alibi, Dan Gifford thought bitterly. He would be questioned as before and then released to continue his hellish religious rites.

The police did not find Thoran. He was not at the place where his religious rites were held. And nobody would talk. Even the underworld characters who made a living out of passing information to the police vigorously denied that they

had ever heard the name. The police broadcast an alarm for
Thoran.

That night Dan Gifford roamed through the slum sections of
the city. He had filed his story of the murder of Virginia
Bryan and was out looking for material for a follow-up story.
If by any chance Thoran was picked up, he wanted to be near
the spot.

At about midnight he dropped into a greasy little saloon for
a beer. The place was empty except for the bartender.

"I hear this Thoran is the real thing," Dan said conversa-
tionally as he gnawed on a pretzel.

"Yeah?" the bartender replied. "Who's this what's-his-
name?"

He lied, of course. Dan could tell by the way he shifted his
eyes, by the way the color of his pasty face went one shade
whiter.

Dan tried a different angle. "The police will pick him up
any minute now, and they'll clip his wings all right. Or his
horns, rather, if what I hear about him is true."

"The police!" The bartender spat the word out. "Did you
ever see a man look down at an anthill? Well, all of us, the
police and you and me and everybody, we're the ants, and
the one who can crush us out with his foot is—" his voice
dropped to a whisper—"Thoran."

"Maybe. But the police have guns if necessary. Ants haven't."

"Guns!" The bartender was contemptuous. "Guns will stop
you and me all right. They won't stop one who takes human
form only for . . . for convenience."

Dan looked at him with steady eyes. "And he needs fresh
warm blood to retain human form."

The bartender was suddenly busy wiping the bar. "Fill 'er
up again?" he growled.

Neatly he had fallen into Dan's verbal trap. He had said
enough to show the hold Thoran had over certain people, the
awe they felt for him. That was understandable. Dan felt it
too. He had seen what Thoran was able to do to sensible

women like Emily and Lorna Beaumont. What in the name of heaven was this creature who called himself a god and appeared to have the awful power of a god?

He slapped a nickel on the bar and sauntered out. Conspicuously he did not hurry. Through the window he had glimpsed an enormously fat woman with a black patch over one eye waddle down the street. He had seen her before; she was one of those caught in the police raid last week. Perhaps she could lead him to Thoran.

Four or five blocks he trailed her. Then she turned into an alley, at the end of which was a high board fence. She went through the door sideways, squeezing through, and shut it behind her.

Cautiously Dan went to the door. He was about to push it in when a voice checked him. A voice he had heard once before and would remember to the last day of his life. Thoran was on the other side of the fence!

Now to call the police. He turned to leave, then stopped. That voice was saying: "I am growing thirsty again. I must drink. Thoran must have the blood of the man-things."

The fat woman mumbled something; then there was a silence. Dan stood frozen. More blood! The blood of another like Virginia Bryan—beautiful and young and who believed him a god. Like Emily Beaumont! Good Lord, perhaps she would be Thoran's next victim!

His blood ran cold at the thought. The police couldn't save Emily or any other intended victim of Thoran, because they couldn't legally hold him for more than questioning. There was only one thing to do, and that was to wipe this abomination off the face of the earth.

Slowly Dan pushed the door open. There, standing in a filthy little tenement house back yard, was Thoran. The misted moon provided only enough light to outline his form dimly. His back was to Dan. The fat woman was gone.

Dan sprang, and together the two went down to the ground. Dan landed on top and his fingers were gripped around the scrawny neck of Thoran. There was no sound. The thin fingers of the man who called himself God tore at his hands. Relentlessly Dan held on.

Little by little Thoran's struggles grew feebler. Then he lay without sound, without motion; only his fiery eyes burned with the intensity of hell. Dan turned his face away from that intolerable gaze—and held on.

At last the man was dead. His tongue protruded horribly between his teeth and his eyes were wide open, staring, still seeming to blaze. But he was dead, all right. Dan made sure of that. He felt the pulse, the heart. No slightest flutter.

Dan Gifford stole away. The body would be found, and nobody would know who was responsible for the murder . . .

Chapter 4: The Return of Thoran

Emily awoke as if from a sleep which had lasted a week. That sleep had transported her to a nightmare world in which an evil god had enslaved her soul and her mind by drinking her blood. And now Thoran was dead and she was free.

Dan Gifford told her of the death of Thoran. He was vague about how he had died, but he swore that he had seen the dead body.

"That means that you have nothing to fear," Dan kept repeating over and over as if the words were a kind of ritual. And they were. He had to break down the terror for Thoran which had been rooted in her subconscious.

They were sitting in the library of the Beaumont home. His eyes were fixed on her face, searching for the effect of what he had just told her. His heart leaped with joy as he observed her return to normal.

"But what had he done to me?" she quavered. "What spell did he cast over me?"

Impulsively Dan placed his arm protectingly about her. His lips dropped to hers, and her lips were sweetly responsive. Lord, she was adorable! When he lifted his head, she stroked his face tenderly and then stood up.

"Come upstairs," she said. "We must tell Lorna about Thoran."

Lorna sat knitting at the window in her bedroom. She did not look up when they entered.

"Lorna, Thoran is dead," Emily burst out. "Dan—Mr. Gifford—says he saw his dead body. He's dead and there is no more reason to fear him."

Lorna looked up with vacant eyes. "Thoran cannot die. Thoran is greater than death, the master of death."

"Lorna get a grip on yourself. Thoran was mortal. He was some hideous trick. Now he is dead."

"Thoran . . . dead? No Thoran cannot die."

There was nothing they could do with Lorna no way they could break the spell.

When they left Lorna's bedroom, Emily was sobbing. In the hall she clung to Dan. "I'm afraid, Dan. Terribly afraid. Thoran may be dead, but his evil influence is not. It still possesses Lorna, and I feel that I, too, am not completely free."

"It's your frayed nerves, that's all," Dan assured her. "Same thing wrong with Lorna, only her nerves must be completely shattered."

A maid came up the stairs. "Telephone call for Mr. Gifford."

It was Burke, city editor of the *Times-Record*. Dan had left the telephone number at the office.

"Another girl has been found," Burke told him. "Exactly the same as that Virginia Bryan. Stark naked and not a drop of blood in her. Her hands chopped off at the wrists. Must be another of Thoran's victims. Body's in an empty lot at Pine and Wilmot."

"Okay, Chief," Dan mumbled and slowly hung up the receiver.

Emily was standing at his side. He looked as if he had seen a ghost. "What's the matter? Has anything happened?"

"Happened?" he echoed, trying to collect his thoughts. "No. Just a—just a hold-up. The Chief wants me to cover it . . ."

He flagged a taxicab. He leaned back in the seat and lit a cigarette. The hand which held the match trembled. Frantically he groped for a rational explanation.

He had to find an explanation, he told himself, or go mad.

He had told nobody that Thoran was dead. In the eyes of the law he was a murderer. All day he had expected to hear word that the police had found the body. When evening came and the body had not yet been discovered, he had assumed that Thoran's followers had come upon it first and had hidden it. Thoran was dead, all right. Last night he, Dan Gilford, had choked the life out of him. And now . . .

Last night, just before his death, Thoran had said: "I am growing thirsty again. Thoran must have the blood of the man-things." And now another nude woman was found with the blood drained from her body. Was Lorna Beaumont right? Was Thoran beyond death, greater than death?

Perhaps the woman had been killed before Thoran's death. Dan clung to that thought until he reached the vacant lot where the nude, bloodless body of a pretty young girl lay among a pile of debris.

"How long has she been dead?" Dan asked the police medical examiner.

"About ten hours, I should say. Maybe twelve, but not more."

Dan had killed Thoran twenty hours ago! Perhaps it had not been Thoran but one of his followers who had slain this girl. But that thought was small comfort. He knew that it had not been so. He knew that it had been Thoran and nobody else who had drunk the blood of the girl. Drunk her blood after she had died!

That meant that Emily was again in danger. While Thoran walked the earth, his baleful influence was all-powerful.

He rushed back to the Beaumont residence in a taxi. Outside the house were two police prowl cars. Well, that was all right. It was the house of the police commissioner, and since the night the spell of Thoran had possessed his nieces, Calvin Beaumont had maintained a police guard outside his house.

But all the same, something was decidedly wrong. The spot of fear around his heart grew.

The police commissioner was in the house with six or seven policemen. The housekeeper was in a corner of the room sobbing. A patrolman sat in a chair. He was hatless and there was an ugly patch of caked blood on the side of his head.

"Where's Emily?" Dan demanded. "For God's sake, what happened?"

"Emily . . . Lorna . . . they're gone," Beaumont muttered. Suddenly he turned savagely on the wounded patrolman. "Now tell me exactly what happened. My God, my own police can't protect my nieces!"

"You came out and told me that it was all right to let Miss Emily have perfect freedom to come and go," the wounded patrolman said. "You said she was cured and that—"

"So she was," Beaumont interrupted. "But I didn't say you should let Lorna out of the house."

"I didn't, sir. That is, I didn't know it was her. At about ten o'clock a young lady come out wearin' the blue coat I'd seen Miss Emily wear lots of times. It was pretty dark, sir, and bein' sisters they look pretty much alike. I didn't think Miss Lorna would try to go out. It wasn't more than a minute or two later that Miss Emily come flyin' out of the house without a coat or hat and she was yellin', 'Did Lorna go this way?' Then I seen my mistake, sir. 'Quick,' she says, 'before we're too late,' and starts runnin' down the street with me at her heels.

"When we turned the corner we seen Miss Lorna just about to get into a black sedan. There was two men there. They wasn't forcin' her in. She looked like she wanted to go. They heard us comin' when we were twenty feet away. I had my gun out, but I couldn't use it because they held Miss Lorna in front of them. So I closed in on them. One of the men had a gun and he pumped a slug past my ear. I took a chance with my gun then and I think I got him in the arm. Then the other guy swung and I swung back and dropped him with one on the jaw. There must have been a third one in the shadows. I felt something like a mountain fall on my head and that's the last thing I knew for a while."

"You incompetent fool!" Beaumont yelled. "Do you think they took both girls in the car?"

"Yes, sir, I do. It seemed to me while I was fallin' that I saw Miss Emily strugglin' with one of the men."

"And you haven't any idea who they were?"

"Well, sir, Miss Emily yelled something that sounded like 'She's goin' to Thoran,' while we were runnin'."

"You've got to do something," Dan broke in. "He's killed two girls already that we know of. If we don't hurry—"

"You're damned right we'll do something." Beaumont snapped orders. "Get every available man. Comb the town. I mean comb it! Pick up everybody you think knows this Thoran or might have heard of him and sweat the truth out of them."

Dan did not wait for more. He slammed out of the house.

Later that night a madman wandered through dark and dirty streets mumbling to himself, "Thoran . . . I must find Thoran." He stopped staggering drunkards, approached tenement dwellers who sat on their front steps to escape the stuffy heat of their flats, awoke human derelicts who slept in doorways; and always his words were the same. "I must find Thoran or I am lost."

Some growled at him, some laughed at him, but there were many who trembled and averted their eyes from his own gaze.

For an hour Dan Gifford played the role of a mad follower of Thoran. As time went on his madness became less and less a role. Thoran had Emily . . . and Thoran drank the blood of beautiful women. Thoran was a creature of hell whom he had killed and yet seemed to be alive . . .

Every man on the police force was out. Prowl cars sped through the streets. Detectives and patrolmen stopped every-body who passed, invaded homes, questioned, threatened, conducted a score of raids. Time after time Dan was stopped, released when he flashed his press card.

Damn the police! They were driving Thoran and his wor-shippers deeper and deeper into their hiding place, and there were places in the city where one could hide forever.

Dan pulled a knife from his pocket, gashed his left wrist, and held his handkerchief over the cut until the blood had clotted. He held a wad of bills of sizeable denominations in his hand. But men who would murder for five dollars turned away from him. They saw the cut on his wrist and were even afraid to try to rob him.

He stood on a street which was utterly deserted. The police had combed it and found nothing.

A voice whispered in his ear: "Go home. Thoran orders that you go home."

There were two men in the shadow of a building. They were shabbily dressed.

"Thoran, god of terror and vengeance," Dan mumbled. "I must find Thoran or I am lost." He held out the money. "I am rich. I have much more. Thoran is calling me, but I don't know where he is. I was not met."

The eyes of the men licked greedily at the money. One of them said: "Where did you get that cut wrist?"

He remembered the words which the Beaumont house-keeper had reported Emily had screamed in her sleep, and in a dull tone he repeated them: "My blood has become part of him and he has become part of me."

There was a silence. Then one of the men said: "All right, come."

"You better not, George," the other warned. "There's no telling . . ."

"He's all right. I can tell." He took the money from Dan and said again: "Come."

They stepped into a doorway and then went through a long hall which was pitch dark. The second man remained out-side. Dan groped after his guide. They descended into a cel-lar, came up into another hall which was in another house; then went through a yard and into a third house. There was still another hall, another descent into a cellar. They stopped before a heavy wooden door. On the other side of the door there was a sound like the droning of many bees.

The man knocked twice, then three times, then twice. The door opened and Dan stepped inside.

Chapter 5: Temple of Evil

The room was dark save for two lighted candles which rested on an altar. Dim shapes on hands and knees mumbled to themselves. Dan dropped to the stone floor on his knees. His hands patted the side of his coat. The feel of the snub-nosed automatic was reassuring. He had wasted valuable time by going home for it after he had heard of Emily's disappearance.

Suddenly the drone of voices stopped. The enormously fat woman who had unwittingly led him to Thoran last night mounted the platform behind the altar and raised two pudgy arms. There was a roar and a brilliant burst of light, and Thoran stood at the altar.

Dan almost cried out. He gaped. No question that it was the man he had choked to death last night! What was the awful explanation? Was he a being that could not be killed because he was not alive? Absurd. But there was Thoran, resurrected from the dead.

The voice of Thoran, unforgettable in its dread intensity, spoke. "I am Thoran, god of vengeance and terror. Through the blood of the man-things which I drink I appear to you in human form that you may know my might. I am Thoran!"

"Thoran! Thoran!" the cry arose from every side of the room.

Another form stepped behind the altar. It was a man dressed in flowing black robes and over his face was a black cowl.

"Thoran is mighty," he intoned. "Thoran is all-powerful. Before the greatness of Thoran we insignificant man-things grovel. We are the slaves of Thoran. We have nothing that is not Thoran's—our souls, our bodies, our wealth. As a sign of our deathless devotion to Thoran we give of our blood. As another sign we give of our earthly possession."

He held money and jewels in his outstretched hand. "This then, I offer to Thoran, as a token of my undying devotion." He dropped the money and jewels into a huge copper bowl which the fat woman had placed on the altar.

The worshippers went mad. They leaped to their feet, dancing and shouting, and rushed to the altar. Women stripped jewels from their fingers and ears and throats and dropped them into the bowl. Men poured money into it. They fought with each other like wild beasts to reach the bowl.

Their fervor was contagious. Dan felt it. A hellish power sought to gain possession of him, to make him one with these howling, crazed fanatics. He fought it down without difficulty because he understood now the reason for Thoran's extraordinary power.

Thoran was a man who possessed remarkable hypnotic power. Seeing him standing at the altar, motionless except for his blazing eyes which swept over the milling mob, it was easy to understand how he was able to convince rational people that he was a god. Mass hypnotism had been used since man first roamed the earth by the priest-craft of a thousand cults and religions.

Mass hypnotism and one other thing. Self-hypnosis. Once people believed that Thoran was truly a god because of the hypnotism of those eyes of his and the awful ceremony of the drinking of the blood, they had reached a stage where they hypnotized themselves.

Dan had suspected as much when he had told Emily that Thoran was dead and had observed her reaction. Once sure that Thoran was no god, Thoran's spell over her and the spell of her own convictions were broken.

Dan moved forward to the altar with the rest. He dropped some money in the copper bowl. His eyes roamed the room for a sight of Emily. He saw Lorna, saw her pull a ring from her finger and toss it in with the others. Her dress was ripped at the shoulder, exposing half of her breast, but she seemed unconscious of it.

Where was Emily? The only masked person in the room was the man with the cowl. The others appeared heedless of who knew them or recognized them. Dan observed that most of the men and women were well-dressed. This must be Thoran's inner temple, where only the wealthiest were permitted to attend.

The copper bowl was rapidly filling. There must be a fortune in there. The whole thing, then, was nothing but a racket to make money. Money for Thoran? Dan again looked at Thoran and doubted it. The man was no doubt a fanatic, mad probably, and convinced that he really was a god.

Somebody else must be behind this, profiting enormously from Thoran's fanaticism. The man in the cowl, perhaps . . .

When no more money and jewels fell into the copper bowl, the fat woman raised her hands. The worshippers fell back from the altar, subsided on the floor.

Again there was that roar and flash of fire, and a woman stood next to Thoran. She was naked, and she struggled furiously in the grip of two men who held each of her arms. Emily Beaumont!

Without thought Dan leaped forward, shouting her name. The next instant he was sprawling on the ground. A strange numbness possessed his body. He tried to lift his hand, but it was as if he had no hand. It seemed as if he was without existence save for a brain which could think and eyes which could see.

He saw the man who had led him here stand over him with a club in his hand. The man must have been suspicious of him all along, had been ready with that club. Dan shut his eyes. Perhaps the paralysis would pass in a short while. If it did not . . .

He opened his eyes. The feet of the man who had struck him were moving away. He probably thought he had knocked Dan out for good. Perhaps he had.

Emily was screaming as they lashed her to the altar. She lay stomach down, her head dangling over the front of the altar. Futilely she tore at the ropes.

The fat woman placed the huge copper bowl under Emily's head. It was empty now. Soon again it would be full—this time with the red blood of Emily!

The fat woman now picked up a machete from behind the altar and, kissing it, handed the murderous weapon to Thoran. Thoran lifted it high and intoned: "Fresh young blood for Thoran."

The candles glowed yellow on the lovely nude body of Emily. Insanely she shrieked: "Stop him! He's not a god. He's mortal like all of us. Oh, God, stop him, please! Please, God, stop him! Oh! . . ."

A solemn hush had settled over the room. Heads leaned forward to see better. Desperately Dan strove to move. He had felt life return to the muscles of his hands, his feet. He could move his fingers, but that was all. That was all—and in another minute it would be too late!

There was an interruption. The man in the cowl stepped forward.

"Thoran needs the blood of multitudes," he said. "Has not Thoran himself said that time and again? Rather than the blood of one puny woman, let us all contribute our blood to the might and glory of Thoran."

"Fresh young blood for Thoran," Thoran repeated, and he stepped to the front of the altar. Two men grasped each of Emily's arms and held her wrists above the bowl. Thoran raised the machete.

Two shrieks rose simultaneously. One was Emily's. The other who shrieked was now fighting her way to the altar.

"Emily! Not Emily! That's my sister Emily!"

The sight of her sister about to be killed had snapped the spell. Thoran turned slowly, majestically, and faced Lorna Beaumont.

"Please!" Lorna sobbed. "She is my sister."

Thoran said not a word. Again he raised the machete.

"You fiend!" Lorna screamed.

Thoran fixed his burning eyes on her. She trembled violently, but she did not cringe.

"Blasphemer!" Thoran pointed a finger at her and a bolt of fire leaped from his finger to Lorna. "Untie this first woman. Thoran will drink the blood of the blasphemer first."

Dan felt strength returning. That bolt of fire was simply a cheap magician's trick to inspire awe. Probably a battery and a concealed wire up his sleeve. Dan flexed his fingers. But still he could not move his arm. Sweat covered his body as he struggled to drop his hand to his pocket. He could not. He stifled a sob of frustration.

"No, Thoran!"

It was the man's voice this time—the man in the cowl. He repeated in a voice that quavered: "I ask this one favor, Thoran. Spare this girl."

There was no sound in the room save the heavy breathing of the worshippers. Thoran said slowly: "You defy Thoran?"

The man in the cowl fell back. "No, Thoran. I ask but this favor. Spare that woman."

Thoran turned to his worshippers and looked at them a long time before speaking. Dan could feel them cringe under his gaze.

"Are there any more blasphemers here?"

Silence.

Again fire leaped from his finger, this time at the man in the cowl. "Then tear this blasphemer limb from limb!"

The man in the cowl screamed. Then they were on him. They were a milling, snarling horde, a pack of wild dogs tearing a man to pieces. Men and women gorged at flesh, ripped his eyeballs from their sockets.

They could have left nothing but a pile of blood and bones if Thoran had not raised a hand. They fell back.

"Such shall be the fate of all blasphemers," Thoran said. "Now shall the woman blasphemer be punished."

The two men untied Emily from the altar, began to tear the clothes from Lorna.

"I defy you, Thoran! You are a fraud, a mortal like any of us. I defy you and I shall kill you!"

It was Dan Gifford who spoke. The paralysis caused by the blow had departed to an extent sufficient to enable Dan to rise feebly to his feet and grope his way along the wall until now he stood only a few feet from Thoran. His snub-nosed automatic was in his hand as he shouted his defiance.

"Another!" Thoran screamed in rage. "Serve him as you did the other."

The report of the gun filled the room, vibrated from the walls. Then there were two more reports. At that distance Dan knew that he could not miss, but he pumped two more bullets into Thoran to make sure.

The worshippers surged toward Dan. "Look!" Dan cried. "Look at the man who called himself God!"

They stopped, bewildered. Thoran lay at the foot of the altar. A lead slug had driven a hole through his nose and there was another between his eyes.

Women screamed. Men knocked aside women in a stampede for the door. The spell of Thoran was broken.

When the police, brought by the hysterical jabberings of the former worshippers, poured into the place, they found it empty save for Dan Gifford, Emily and Lorna Beaumont, and two dead bodies. Dan had torn down the black drapes which hung behind the altar and had wrapped them about the two women. Emily was in his arms.

Calvin Beaumont arrived several minutes later. "Thank God!" he exclaimed when he saw his nieces alive and unharmed. Then, as he looked down at the dead body of the man who had worn the cowl, he cried: "Madden!"

Dan nodded. "The power behind Thoran.

The police commissioner stared incredulously at the corpse of the district attorney.

"He wasn't quite dead and managed to say a few words to me before the police arrived," Dan said. "Not much, and what he said was disconnected and jumbled, but enough to straighten out the whole thing. He wasn't in with Thoran at first. The first time he met him was last week when Thoran was picked up in the raid. While questioning him, Madden realized the possibility for making large sums of money through a fanatical cult like Thoran's.

"Election Day is not far off, and Madden was convinced that he would not be re-elected. He had been swept in on a reform wave, but the old political machine is again as strong as ever. The district attorney's job doesn't pay much, and even if Madden had wanted to go in for graft the reform party kept too close a watch. Here was a chance to gain a fortune quickly, and Madden grabbed it. He pretended to become one of Thoran's converts.

"I think that Thoran was an honest fanatic—honest in a horribly perverted and evil way. He probably believed that he really was a god. He wasn't interested in wealth or money; only in power and blood for his perverted thirst. So Madden had an easy time of it. He had nothing to do with the kidnapping of Emily and he thought the police would prevent Lorna from coming here. He tried to save Emily without endangering his standing with Thoran. But when Lorna was to be killed too, it was too much for Madden. Chances are he really did love her. So in the end he gave his life for her."

Lorna was sobbing convulsively. Beaumont placed a comforting arm about her.

There was one thing Dan did not tell the police commissioner: that he had had to kill twice. Madden had gasped out the explanation for Thoran's apparent resurrection. Just three words: "Doctor . . . adrenalin . . . revived." Which doubtless meant that Thoran had been found immediately after Dan had choked him; that a doctor had been nearby; that a feeble spark of vitality had still been in Thoran and that injections of adrenalin had restored him to life.

In the eyes of the police, Dan had taken the law into his own hands when he had choked Thoran. This second time he had killed to save innocent lives.

Dan had to rush away to phone the story to his newspaper. Before he left he kissed Emily, shamelessly, with the police looking on. He did not care who saw. And neither, for that matter, did Emily.

DARLINGS OF THE BLACK MASTER

Chapter 1: The Thing on the Table

ELAINE SCREAMED. It was the full-throated scream of a woman in the grip of unspeakable terror.

I rushed into the bedroom. Elaine, clad only in a brief chemise, stood near her dresser, and the expression on her face drained the blood from me. Only the small lamp over the dressing table was on, but its light was sufficient to show my quick glance that there was nothing in the room which could have frightened her.

In an instant my arms were about her.

"In the drawer," she gasped against my chest.

The second drawer of her dresser was partly open. I pulled it all the way out. The silken undergarments which lay in it were in disorder, which was odd, for Elaine was fanatically neat.

She clutched my arm. "Under the clothes," she said. "I felt it."

I thrust my hand into the silk. There was something cold and clammy—smooth as marble but a great deal softer.

Years ago a friend of mine had drowned while swimming. We had worked over him long after he was dead in the desperate hope that a feeble spark of life might yet be in him. His skin had felt like this.

It was not easy to thrust my hand in that drawer again. I forced myself to push the garments aside. The dim light from the dressing table revealed a human forearm and hand.

Elaine shrieked again. Gently I led her into the living room. "It's a practical joke," I tried to comfort her. "The thing's a fake."

She shook her head. "That was Fanny Woodworth's. One glance was enough. The emerald-cut diamond ring on her finger—I could recognize it anywhere."

The door bell rang furiously. Elaine put on a negligee and accompanied me to the door. She said that she could not bear to be left alone for a moment.

It was Victor Joseffy, out next-door neighbor and one of my best friends. He wore a dressing gown over his pajamas.

"I heard Elaine scream," he said. "Is there anything wrong?"

In as few words as possible I told him.

"I went to the drawer for a fresh nightgown," Elaine supplemented. "There wasn't much light—I had not troubled to put on the ceiling light—so I groped in the drawer for a moment. Then I felt it." She shuddered.

Victor scoffed. "Of course it's somebody's grisly idea of a joke. Have you taken a good look at it?"

I admitted that I had not, and he was for going into the bedroom at once. But I suggested that we take Elaine over to his house first. She could stay there with Victor's wife Mady while we investigated. I had become convinced that the thing in the drawer was a hoax; but if it was not I wanted Elaine out of the way.

Well, that thing in the drawer of my wife's dresser was a human arm and hand—and it was not. That is, the skin was human. The inside was packed with cold, wet sawdust.

"That's Fanny Woodworth's ring all right," Victor said.

We had removed the gruesome object from the drawer and had placed it over a layer of newspapers on a table in the living room.

"But that does not necessarily mean that the rest is Fanny's," I pointed out. "Somebody with a perverted idea of a joke might have stripped the skin from a fresh corpse and stolen Fanny's ring."

Victor nodded. "Probably. I saw Fanny yesterday afternoon. I don't doubt that if you call up the Woodworth home you'll find her there all in one piece."

I dialed the Woodworth telephone number. Reynold Woodworth answered.

"Fanny? No, Fanny's not home. She's on a visit to her mother's at Pinemount. Left late yesterday. I expect her home tomorrow. Anything I can do?"

"Yes," I said. "Come over here at once."

"I was just about to go to bed," he protested.

"Dress and come over," I insisted in a strained voice. "There is something here that's—that might be tremendously important."

I had been about to say, "That might be a matter of life or death." But I did not even want to allow myself to think that thought, much less frighten Reynold, probably unduly.

Reynold Woodworth lived only a few blocks from my house. He arrived in less than ten minutes. I let him into the house.

"Was Fanny's engagement ring stolen or mislaid?" I asked as he removed his coat.

"Her diamond ring? Of course not. She wore it when she left yesterday. It never leaves her finger. As a matter of fact, it's grown tight on her. It would be hard to remove it from her without"—he laughed lightly—"without removing her hand. No, the ring's safe enough as long as she is. Why?"

As long as she is! echoed in my brain. Lord, what horror were we confronted with?

"A queer thing happened," I said. "A dastardly hoax. Somebody had an imitation of her ring made, placed it on something like a hand, and left it here."

A lame way of preparing him. But I had not the heart to break it to him any other way.

"What?" he cried. His face blanched. "In God's name, where is—is it?"

I led him into the living room. Victor was staring down at the thing on the table with morbid fascination. Reynold took one look at it, and then stood stock still. He did not say a word. He did not go closer. His ruddy face went deathly white.

Suddenly he whirled and went to the phone in the foyer. Victor and I followed him. His trembling fingers dialed the wrong number twice before he could get the proper connection.

"Hello, put Fanny on the wire," he barked into the mouthpiece when at last there was an answer.

A dreadful silence save for the muffled sound of the voice on the other end of the wire.

"What? Absurd! She arrived yesterday. I saw her off myself on the 6:27 train . . . She has to be there . . . My God! . . . Are you sure? . . . God in heaven!"

Slowly he placed the receiver on the cradle. When he turned to us, his face was terrible. He was a hearty man of thirty-two or so, but at that moment he looked twenty years older.

"She never got to her mother's," he muttered.

Wordlessly we returned to the living room. With horror-filled eyes Reynold Woodworth stared down at the table.

"That's Fanny's hand—skin," he said. "The ring is not an imitation. And that polish on the nails is the tint of ruby red she always uses. That cut on the middle finger—she cut herself two days ago with a can opener."

"That means," Victor whispered, "that she is dead."

Reynold sat down heavily on the couch. He spoke as if to himself. "It might mean that she is—worse than dead."

"Worse than dead!" Victor echoed. He looked at Reynold as if he thought the man had lost his senses because of grief.

Reynold said: "You remember Luke Strawn. 'A limb for a limb,' he swore. It was I who killed his daughter, and Fanny was my wife. Fanny was the only one of us to take his curse seriously. It worried her. At times she actually believed that he would carry out his threat—and he has!"

"But Strawn is dead!" I protested.

Vividly etched in our minds was the accident who had taken the life of Luke Strawn's young daughter two months ago. We were driving home from a jolly day of picnicking, we four married couples who were firm friends. We were all young; all lived near each other in the neat little frame houses in Hope Valley's residential section.

There was Victor Joseffy, tall and lean, whose fame as an architect was spreading beyond the state, and his wife, Mady, lovely and fragile as a porcelain doll. Reynolds Woodworth, successful insurance broker and sportsman, and vivacious blonde Fanny Woodworth. Douglas Kemble, owner of the Hope Valley garage, good-natured, pudgy, inches shorter than his attractive statuesque wife, Marie. And myself, Andrew Bradner, up and coming lawyer, I hope, and Elaine whom I considered the most beautiful woman any man ever had the good fortune to call his wife.

We had had a jolly time all day, and when night began to fall we started back in high spirits. We drove in two cars— Elaine and I with the Joseffy's, and the Kembles in the Woodworths' car.

It happened a few miles from Hope Valley. Victor was keeping about thirty feet behind the rear bumper of Reynold's car. Suddenly there was a shriek of agony, a grinding of brakes. Victor had to swerve into the dirt on the side of the road to avoid hitting Reynold's car.

Then Victor and I were slamming out of the car, yelling to our wives to remain behind. Auto accidents produce some pretty bad sights.

"I didn't see her," Reynold was saying when we reached the front of his car. "She ran right in front. I tried to avoid her."

He held the girl in his arms. The headlights of the car shone on her. Her white dress was drenched in blood and blood poured on Reynold's suit. The blood gushed from her arm—or rather from where her arm had been. The front mudguard had amputated the arm just below the elbow. It hung from her by the merest thread of skin.

As we watched with sick horror, the weight of the arm broke the skin and the arm fell to the ground. In the car Fanny Woodworth shrieked.

Another voice shrieked. A man's.

"You killed her! Curse you, you murdered my daughter!"

It was old Luke Strawn, a queer character who lived in a tiny tumble-down shack on the outskirts of Hope Valley. How he supported himself and his wild sixteen-year-old daughter nobody knew. There were rumors that he had traffic with the devil, that the soul of his daughter had been sold to Satan, that it was certain death in the most agonizing manner for anybody who crossed him. The usual tales started by superstitious folk.

At that moment, however, I could believe anything about him. He looked like the devil himself as he cursed us.

"She's not dead," I cried. "Rush her to the hospital."

Reynold snapped out of the daze which had gripped him. Hurriedly we transferred the women to Victor's car and Reynold got into the back of his own car with the moaning girl. Luke Strawn got in too. In his hands he held that severed, bloody arm; held it tenderly as if it had a life of its own.

I took the wheel. Never in my life shall I forget that ride to the hospital. With my hand never leaving the horn for an instant, I drove like mad. And as I weaved in and out of traffic, Luke Strawn's bitter curses poured into my ear.

Soon after we reached the hospital the girl died. She had lost too much blood.

As we were leaving the hospital, Luke Strawn confronted us in the lobby. His ragged clothes were blood-streaked from the stump of his daughter's arm. An attendant had told me that they had had to struggle with him before he would give up the bloody limb.

"Give back my daughter's arm!" he stormed. "Give back her arm!"

It was an odd thing that he refused to accept the fact that his daughter was dead. He did not ask that her life be returned to her, but asked for her arm.

Reynold told him that he was well covered by insurance and that the settlement would be generous. This only enraged the old man.

"I want her arm! She was all I had, and you took her arm!"

He swung at the four of us standing in the lobby, Reynold, Victor, Douglas and myself, and his black eyes pierced into us. "You have wives. Pretty creatures. I've seen them. They have arms—smooth, soft, white arms like my daughter. Give me their arms to take the place of her arm!"

We gaped at him. The man was mad.

The following day Luke Strawn was killed by a truck. Ironic coincidence that he should be killed the day after his daughter, and like her, by a motor vehicle. He lived for a few minutes after the accident. The interne, who heard his last words in the ambulance on the way to the hospital, was an acquaintance of mine.

"He died raving about arms," the interne told me. "Kept screaming with his last breath, 'They think they've saved themselves by killing me. They think they've saved their wives' arms. But I'll come back. I'll came back for the white arms of their wives to replace the one they took from my daughter.' Poor chap was off his nut."

Two months ago that had occurred, and now here we were in the living room of my house, and on the table was the skin of the arm of Fanny Woodworth whose husband had killed Luke Strawn's daughter.

"But Luke Strawn is dead," I repeated.

Reynold Woodworth lifted his face from his hands. "You remember his dying words. He said he would come back."

"Nonsense!" Victor said. "The dead remain dead. This is a case for the police."

I nodded, went to the phone and called the police. As I waited for the answer, terror slithered through my veins like a slimy snake. I had a feeling that this was only the beginning of something more horrible than I could guess.

Chapter 2: Hell Demands Tribute

FROM THE MOMENT that Fanny Woodworth had stepped off the train at Pinehurst, all trace of her was gone. One of the conductors identified her from a photograph as the woman he had assisted off the train. After that nobody had seen her. She had vanished as completely as if the earth had opened there at the depot and swallowed her. A nation-wide search for her and front-page newspaper publicity revealed nothing further.

A change had come over Elaine. Naturally she was deeply shocked at the probability that a hideous fate had overcome her friend. But I knew that that was not the whole explanation. It was not so much grief as—fear. Fear for herself.

I could see it in her eyes as she sat in silent abstraction in one place for hours at a time. I could tell by her moody smilelessness, by the way she would start violently at the slightest unusual sound.

I could have put it down to concern over her friend, if I did not recall that she had acted like that for several days before the disappearance of Fanny Woodworth. I had thought at the time that she had not been feeling well; but now I sensed that it was something else, something that she was keeping from me.

I tried to comfort her. It was three days since she had found that ghastly limb in the drawer of her dresser. "What's wrong, sweetheart," I asked as I placed an arm about her. "Aren't you feeling well?"

She did not look at me when she replied after a short silence. "It's—it's nothing . . . Yes, it is, Andy. I need money."

"Money? Is that all? I've always been liberal with you."

"But I need a great deal of money." She hesitated. "A thousand dollars."

"A thousand dollars!" I sputtered.

She had about twenty-five hundred dollars in the bank in her own name—a legacy from an uncle. Hadn't she touched that? I put the question to her. And why did she want the money?

"Please, Andy! You know I'm not unreasonable. I need the money, and you mustn't ask me why." Her voice rose hysterically. "You mustn't ask me why!"

Just then the telephone rang.

"Come right over," Douglas Kemble said tersely. "Something terrible has happened."

Elaine stood white-faced behind me. "What is it?"

"I don't know," I yelled over my shoulder. I was already running out of the house. Behind me I heard Elaine wail: "Oh, God, again!"

I picked up Victor Joseffy next door and together we ran the two blocks to Kemble's house. A police prowl car was standing outside. Reynold Woodworth was slumped in a chair, staring fixedly before him. Marie Kemble nodded toward the bedrooms upstairs. Her eyes were wide with terror; and I knew somehow that it was not terror alone at what was in the bedroom. It was something even more frightful. She was afraid of the some thing as Elaine.

There were two patrolmen in the bedroom, and Douglas Kemble. And on the floor—

Douglas explained. Several minutes ago Marie had stepped into the bedroom closet to hang up her dress. With a little cry she had jumped back. It appeared as if a woman stood among the dresses. There was a woman's foot and calf clad in shoe and stocking.

Douglas dashed in. When Marie pointed out the foot to him, he went to a drawer for his gun.

"Come out of there," he demanded.

No answer.

He went into the closet, gun ready, and swept his hand through the row of dresses. The limb moved, fell to the floor with a sickening thud. There was a leg up to the hip—and nothing else.

As it lay on the bedroom floor, we did not have to examine it to know that it was only human skin filled with wet sawdust. And because it was not flesh and bone inside, it was worse. A human bloody limb would have been bad enough. But this—it was skin rolled down from the hip without a break, without a scar. Rolled down from the limb of a woman who had just died or—and this thought was even more horrible—from a woman who lived!

And what was most nerve-shattering of all was the fact that the limb was fully clothed; saucy shoe on the foot, sheer stocking covering the graceful leg, a lacy black garter just above the knee cap.

"Fanny Woodworth's leg," Douglas said soberly. "Reynold identified the shoe and a birthmark. And there is the—" He pointed down at the thigh.

There were markings on the tapering thigh which appeared to be handwriting. "Done with a tattoo needle," one of the patrolmen observed.

I dropped to my knees. The writing was scrawled, wavy, there was no punctuation, but the hellish words could be made out.

he is making me write this on my own thigh there is no skin on my left arm I am very weak pray God that I die before he uses the skin for his daughters arm Strawn gloats as I write this and says I will not die he has turned away if I can keep writing until I am de—

The writing stopped abruptly with the last letter as if her hand had been suddenly snatched away.

I stood up, looked from one to another of the strained faces of the men. "Strawn!" I gasped. "His daughter! Both dead!"

"They're in hell where they've taken Fanny to avenge themselves on me through her!" Reynold Woodworth stood in the doorway of the bedroom. "The damned are having their vengeance!"

For some time Victor and I said nothing as we walked back to our homes. It was Victor who broke the silence.

"I'm not a coward. I think I'm as brave as the next man. But the fear that's been in me these last few days is turning my blood to water. And it's worse because I'm not afraid for myself but for Mady."

I nodded understandingly. I felt that way too.

"It's not only that I am afraid that the same thing will happen to her as has happened to Fanny," he went on. "In some way which I cannot understand it's even more terrible than that, if you can imagine anything more terrible. It's something that goes beyond what happened to Fanny, that started some time before she disappeared. For instance, there's the money."

"Has she been asking you for money too?" I stopped walking, faced him.

"So Elaine has been doing the same? All of Mady's jewels are gone—even her marriage ring. When I questioned her, she said they had not been stolen, but refused to tell me what had become of them. And the money in the bank, several thousand dollars. We held it in a joint account; either of us could draw it. I discovered today that she had drawn all of it."

By that time we had reached his house. Just before he went in, Victor turned to me.

"Can the devil demand tribute in cash? Have the damned use for money?"

"What do you mean?"

"I wish to God I knew. You read what Fanny wrote on her skin. The vengeance of Strawn."

"You're mad!" I exclaimed. The next moment I was sorry I had really said it. Sorry because maybe Victor really was mad.

He laughed harshly. "Maybe I am. A few days ago I'd have called anybody who spoke like that mad. Now . . ." He went into his house.

I found Mady Joseffy keeping my wife company. I had let myself into the house quietly, thinking that Elaine might be asleep; and when I walked into the living room, they jumped as if I were a ghost. Their eyes were red from weeping, and stark terror had changed the loveliness of their faces into something which made my flesh crawl.

A minute later Victor charged into the house, shouting, "Where's Mady? My God, she's not in the house!"

Mady stood up. "Here I am, dear."

Victor sank into a chair with a sigh of relief. "It's awful," he said, "thinking every minute that your wife—"

He left the thought unfinished. Our nerves were at the breaking point.

Later, as I lay side by side with my wife in bed, she said suddenly: "Andy, you will give me that money? That thousand dollars I spoke to you about."

"You still refuse to tell me what you want it for?"

"Please, darling, trust me. I need it desperately."

My hand gripped hers under the cover. "Don't be afraid of blackmail, Elaine. You have nothing to fear from me."

"If it were only that!"

"It's worse?"

"Yes, Andy."

"Afraid of the same thing happening to you as happened to Fanny? I'll get the police."

I felt her body tremble against mine. "The police won't help. Nobody can. The police are good only against human beings."

"Elaine! What are you saying?"

She stopped my mouth with her soft lips, pressed her warm body against mine. "Darling, if you love me, you'll do what I ask. It's our only hope."

I held her tightly to me. "All right," I said.

The following morning I telephoned from my office the bank where Elaine kept her money. I was informed that my wife had withdrawn her money a week ago.

One is more rational in the morning, and I resolved not to let Elaine have the thousand dollars after all. I was about to call the police and inform them that my wife was apparently the victim of a blackmail plot when the telephone rang.

"She's gone," Douglas Kemble's agitated voice came over the wire. "Marie is gone. She disappeared during the night. She wasn't kidnapped. She was there in bed with me, and when I awoke she wasn't there. Nobody could have come into the house because the police had placed a guard outside.

I'd asked them to after what we found last night. She must have slipped out past the police. She must have left because I would not give her the money."

"She asked for money?" The receiver shook in my hand.

"Several times during the past week. Kept nagging me constantly. Naturally I refused unless she would tell me what she wanted it for, and that she would not do. Last night before we went to bed she went into hysterics when I would not give her the money. Said I would regret it for the rest of my life. And now she is gone."

Fortunately for him he thought that she had simply deserted him. Tragic enough, but how much more so was what I suspected had happened!

There was some hellish power at work, some frightful compulsion, which had forced both Fanny Woodworth and Marie Kemble to seek out their doom. Fanny could not have been abducted against her will at the crowded railroad depot or on the busy street between the station and her mother's house. And Marie had left her home of her own will.

Her own will? Had she control of her will?

Of the four friends, two were gone. The four women, I thought with mounting terror, who had been in the party which Luke Strawn had held responsible for the death of his daughter. Those dying words of Strawn: *"I'll come back for the white arms of their wives to replace the one they took from my daughter."* Strawn, who they said had sold himself to the devil!

Fanny and Marie gone. Mady and Elaine left . . .

Chapter 3: "Strawn Wants Them"

A MILKMAN NODDED sleepily behind his trudging horse. The street was bathed in the mellow half light of breaking dawn. Suddenly the milkman's eyes opened wide and he pulled up his horse. He gaped. A stark naked woman stood in front of one of the one-family houses which lined the street.

Just inside the iron fence which surrounded the house she stood, one hand resting lightly on the gate, one foot advanced a little before the other as if she were about to walk into the street. Every line of her statuesque body, the upthrust of her splendid breasts, the manner in which she held her hips, was eloquent of invitation.

A milkman becomes accustomed to strange sights and experiences, but this was the first time he had ever seen anything so blatantly brazen. He continued to gape. He began to feel uneasy. Why didn't she move?

Jumping down from the wagon, he cautiously approached her. He had decided that it was a statute, a statute made by a master who had paid marvelous attention to detail. A hell of a place for a statue like that. The closer he came to the gate, the more uneasy he grew.

A breathless morning hush was in the air. Timidly he reached out a hand. Then he was running like mad.

It was the day after the disappearance of Marie Kemble.

The patrolman whom the milkman called telephoned the homicide squad. "The damnedest thing," he said over the phone. "She seems to be dead all right, but she's standing without any support, like she's alive. There's nothing holding her up. I'll be damned."

Then the patrolman roused the occupant of the house. Douglas Kemble came down in a bathrobe which was hastily thrown over his pajamas. He took one look at the thing at the gate, and the patrolman grabbed his arm. He thought Kemble was about to faint.

"Marie!" Kemble wailed.

The skin was Marie. Nothing else was. Her skin had been tightly stretched over a plaster cast of her body. The few slits in the skin had been skillfully sewed together. It was a masterpiece of flaying.

I saw the thing later in the morning at the station house where the police had taken it. Its beauty was startling, but when I looked at it I became sick to my stomach.

Fanny and Marie . . .

I went home from the police station. No use trying to keep it from Elaine. The papers were already full of it. I found her huddled in a chair, staring with incredulous eyes at the glaring headlines of a newspaper.

"If you'll only tell me what it is, we can do something," I stormed at her. "God, don't you even want to save yourself from—that?"

"There's nothing to tell," she muttered. "There's nothing you can do."

I glanced down at her left hand. Her rings were gone!

I flung out of the house in a rage, went next door to Victor Joseffy's house. Didn't Elaine trust me? Didn't she realize that I would willingly have laid down my life to save her from harm? Perhaps Victor and I together could figure out a way to compel our wives to talk for their own good.

On the porch I could hear the bell ring hollowly in the interior of Victor's house. No answer. That was odd. Yesterday Victor had told me that he would spend the day at home to work on some drawings. He could do more work in the quiet of his home than in his office.

Why didn't Victor or Mady answer? Probably they'd gone out for a while. A little spot of fear in me grew bigger and bigger. I tried the front door. Locked. Then I went around to the back. The door was open. That was wrong. I knew how Mady felt about doors; always kept them securely locked, even when Victor was at home.

I walked in, went through the kitchen, the dining room. On the foot of the staircase I found him.

Victor Joseffy looked as if he had been torn apart by a giant. Blood spattered the carpet, the first few steps leading upstairs. Where his face had been, there was now a pulpy mass of gore.

Like an automaton I went through the motions of phoning the police, of waiting there until they arrived, of answering the questions they shot at me.

The lieutenant of the homicide squad asked me if I lived next door. Then why hadn't I heard the sound of the struggle?

And Mrs. Joseffy would certainly have cried out. I should have heard it, shouldn't I?

Yes, I replied. I was a light sleeper. But there hadn't been any sounds of a struggle. Mady hadn't cried out. I was sure of it.

The lieutenant looked at me suspiciously. "Then how do you explain this?" he demanded. "The medical examiner says he was killed about two o'clock this morning. You say you were in bed then and that your bedroom window faces this hall window. Your window was open and this window was open. Your house is not twenty feet away. Your wife didn't hear anything either?"

Elaine was in the house. I would have given anything to have spared her that sight, but the sirens of the police cars had brought her. She was in a chair with her face buried in her arms. Now she looked up.

"We heard nothing because there was nothing to hear," she said.

"Impossible!" the lieutenant exploded. "You can't tell me that a man is murdered like this and his wife kidnapped without a sound being made. At least one of them was sure to have cried out."

"No," Elaine said obstinately. "Mady couldn't have cried out because she was out of the house when—when Victor was killed. And a little while after she'd left, Victor must have awakened and came down after her. Somebody must have been waiting at the bottom of the stairs for him. He hit Victor on the head, then tore him apart.

"Just a minute, madam. You mean to say Mrs. Joseffy left the house at night just before her husband was murdered?"

"Yes."

"Just like this Mrs. Kemble last night?"

"Yes."

"And you think the two disappearances tie up?"

"Yes. And Fanny Woodworth's."

The lieutenant stared down at her with a puzzled frown. "Why?" he asked.

I leaned forward. Perhaps Elaine would tell the police officer what she would not tell me. Elaine hesitated. Suddenly she jumped up from the chair.

"Because Luke Strawn wanted them!" she shrieked.

I took her in my arms. She sobbed hysterically against my chest.

"Strawn?" the lieutenant repeated. "Wasn't that the old beggar who lived in that shack beyond the tracks? I thought he was killed in an accident a couple of months ago."

"He was," Elaine sobbed. "Oh, God!"

The lieutenant shook his head. He was quite certain that she was stark mad. He agreed readily enough to my request for a police guard. Two men would be detailed to watch her day and night.

In the afternoon I went to my bank and drew out one thousand dollars in bills. Without a word I gave the money to Elaine. I did not even return to my office.

Of the four women, only Elaine was left . . .

Chapter 4: The Demon

THAT NIGHT I went to bed much later than Elaine. I told her that I had work to do. When I was certain that she was asleep, I methodically went through all the drawers in the house in which she kept her personal possessions. Perhaps I would find something which would give me a clue to the thing she feared.

Hidden away amid her very old letters in a drawer which was seldom opened, I found it. I had to check myself from crying out aloud, and even when I examined it under the light in another room, it took some time before I would believe my eyes.

The thing I held in my hand was a photograph of Elaine in—Even now I shudder as I think of the picture of my wife, sweet adorable Elaine, the central figure in that obscene orgy—the most indecent of those unspeakable degenerates!

No! It could not be true. But neither could I deny the testimony of my eyes. I knew every line of her body—every line of that wanton in the photograph.

I returned the photograph where I had found it. Heartbroken, I lay down in bed beside Elaine. Needless to say, sleep would not come. Tomorrow I would have it out with her. No wonder the women had refused to tell us why they wanted the money. For their lewd rites, of course. They must belong to some obscene cult. Perhaps Fanny Woodworth and Marie Kemble had tried to break away and as a result had suffered a dreadful penalty.

Incredible thought! Elaine, my wife! Yet there was that photograph.

Hours must have passed. My tumultuous mind could not keep track of time. Suddenly I was very wide awake. Elaine was stirring beside me. Instinctively I pretended to be asleep. I felt Elaine leaning over me, listening to my regular breathing. Then she slipped out of the bed and I heard her bare feet glide over the floor. She went downstairs.

The two policemen downstairs would stop her. When I had gone to bed, one of them had been on the front porch, the other in the living room. I heard her whispering voice, heard a policeman answer. The voices stopped. Half a minute later the back door opened softly.

It was then that I got out of bed. Two of the bedroom windows faced the side of the house, one the back. Through the window which faced the flower garden in back of the house I saw Elaine pick her way through rows of tulips. She wore a negligee over her nightgown, and in the moonlight she was breathtakingly beautiful.

The garden was enclosed by a low picket fence which separated our property from a strip of woods. Without hesitation she climbed the fence. Her negligee lifted above her thighs, revealing lovely white flesh on which moonbeams danced.

I was under a kind of spell which held me motionless as I watched her, and which was broken only when she disappeared into the woods. I rushed downstairs. The policeman heard me and came out to the living room. He was seated comfortably in an easy chair and smoking a fat cigar, evidently quite at home.

"Your wife's in the kitchen," he said. "She told me that she got hungry and was going for a bite to eat."

I nodded, went into the kitchen, and out the back door. Naturally I did not want the policeman to accompany me. Perhaps a lover awaited her there in the woods, or perhaps she was on the way to one of the orgies so vividly and obscenely depicted in the photograph. Whatever it was, it was necessary that I confront it alone. There must be no scandal.

I heard the voices when I entered the woods. One was Elaine's. The other—well, it was like nothing I had ever heard from a human throat. It was a voice pitched lower than the deepest bass and seemed to come from the bowels of the earth.

Cautiously I kept behind trees and shrubs as I edged forward. Then I saw!

It was not human, that thing that was talking to my wife. It reached hardly to her waist. Like a spider it crawled on all its limbs, using hands and feet to scamper over the ground, and its body was round and bloated. Its eyes were protruding black pinpoints and its mouth a crooked slit without lips. Red material which was tight as a sheath over its body looked like a second skin.

If ever a demon of hell appeared on earth, that was it!

And the way that monstrosity gaped at Elaine! Its tiny eyes were glued at the point where her negligee fell open at the throat, half exposing her perfect breasts. Its lipless mouth drooled with a lust which could have been learned only in Hell.

My wife did not cringe before that gaze of unholy lust; she made no effort to draw the negligee over her breasts. Indeed, she moved her hand up coyly to arrange her hair, and the gesture caused the negligee to fall open still further. Brazenly she stood motionless in the moonlight while the creature reveled in the display of her semi-nudity.

Was I dreaming? Was this the woman I had loved beyond anything on earth?

Elaine stretched out a hand to the demon. In the hand was the money I had given her that day.

Greedily the demon snatched at the bills. "Good. My master is jealous of the welfare of his people. My master demands retribution."

It was then that I charged out of my hiding place. The demon uttered a sound that was like the rumble of the earth and squarely met my assault. My fist flew downward and sent him tumbling. In a split second he was up and at me. In my fury I was determined to tear him to pieces, but as soon as his hands were on me I realized that it would be the other way around.

Those arms were incredibly strong. Arms like that must have killed Victor Joseffy. I was fighting now not to destroy this creature but to save myself. Elaine was screaming. Another voice was calling; a heavy body crashed through shrubs.

Suddenly those deadly arms fell away from me. Stiffly I rose to my feet. The two policemen who had been in the house stood with drawn guns. The demon was gone. Elaine was gone.

The policemen and I went over every inch of the woods. No sign of either the demon or Elaine. When we returned to the house at last, the police sent out a general alarm for Elaine.

I dressed, spent precious minutes looking for my gun. It was not in the drawer of my desk where I always kept it. No matter. I set out.

I had no idea where I was going. I roamed up and down dark streets, for periods at a time lost all track of where I was. If by some miracle I found Elaine, what would I do? I did not know.

Several times I told myself that I would kill her. There might have been a good explanation for that photograph, for the money she gave to that demon, for her refusal to confide in me. But there could be no explanation of the fact that of her own free will she had gone off with the demon. For he had not forced her to go with him. Even had he wanted to, he could not have managed to do so in the short space of time before the arrival of the policemen. And I had seen how he had disappeared into the woods and how she had followed him.

Followed him to what abominable lair, to what hellish rites?

What had the creature meant by his words, "My master demands retribution?" Who was his master? Who would be the master of a demon but the devil himself? "My master is jealous of the welfare of his people." And one of the people of the devil had been—or still was—Luke Strawn who had vowed vengeance on four women, all of whom had disappeared!

Presently I found myself on the outskirts of the city, and I stood before the ramshackle hut which had been the abode of Luke Strawn and his daughter. I do not remember having thought of going there. It was as if my feet had taken me there of their own volition.

I went around to the side, tried to look through a filth-covered window. Utter darkness inside. As I was about to turn the corner of the house, I saw something scamper toward me.

For a moment I thought it was a dog: then I whirled around to the side of the house. It was the demon, the creature I had fought in the woods an hour ago. He scampered on all fours, like something that was more beast than man.

The rusty hinges of the door creaked open, then shut. Something else creaked inside, and then there was a silence.

It was not easy for me to enter that house. I had felt the terrible power of those arms before, and—I admit it—I was afraid. And there was something else I feared: that my eyes would reveal Elaine in a scene similar to the one depicted in the photograph. My love for her clung to the hope that the picture might be a hoax in spite of the fact that she had willingly gone off with the demon. If I should find out beyond doubt that it was true, I do not think that I should have wanted to live.

I opened that door finally, slowly so that as little sound as possible be made. A smell of decay and mold struck me. No sound inside; no light filtered through the grimy windows.

A match revealed a filthy bed, a crude table and two chairs, a coal stove. Nothing else. There was but the single room and no second floor. Where was the demon?

Again the hinges of the door creaked. I flicked out the match, squeezed myself into the darkest corner. The door opened, and for an instant moonlight revealed Elaine. Then she closed the door behind her, and again the darkness.

We were there, shut in by the darkness, my wife and I. My first impulse had been to call out to her. I fought it down, crouched in the corner, waited. And as I stood in the darkness, my heart broke. Alone she had come here. Nobody had forced her to. She could have gone to the police where she would be safe.

Sound of the table moving, of other hinges creaking. Then again silence, terrible in its intensity.

This time I knew what to do. A match revealed a trapdoor. When I raised the trapdoor, I saw only darkness below. I lit another match. Wooden steps led downward.

Cautiously I descended the steps. Halfway down the steps I distinguished the hard dirt floor below. Light trickled from somewhere close by. Turning at the last step, I found myself in a small room which was completely empty. Beyond was a second room, the door of which stood open a few inches.

Elaine's voice rang out sharply, "Now release her!"

She was in the other room. Carefully, so that my feet made no sound on the dirt floor, I moved toward the door, until I was able to look into the room.

Elaine's back with to me, but I could see the line of her right arm and the automatic which was clutched in her fist. My gun which I had not been able to find!

In the middle of the room stood the demon; and behind him hanging from the ceiling by her wrists, was Mady Joseffy, stark naked.

"Release her!" Elaine repeated.

The demon's black eyes blazed hatred at her, and I could sense the tension of his muscles as he prepared to leap. Stupidly I acted out of impulse. Yanking the door open, I cried, "Elaine, it's me, Andy!"

Elaine turned her head an inch or two; her vigilance relaxed momentarily. I should have guessed that that was what would happen. The demon sprang, and the gun in Elaine's hand fell to the ground.

Then I was fighting. Out of the corner of my eye I saw Elaine lying motionless on the ground, the result of a single blow of that powerful arm. I fought with the desperate fury of one who battles for all he holds dear in the world.

Perhaps eventually I might have overpowered him. I do not know. A shadow loomed up behind me. There was no other person in the room besides we two and two helpless women, I could have sworn that, and I sensed that the thing behind me was without material reality, without physical substance.

But the object I glimpsed descending toward my skull was real enough. I tried to pull away, but the arms of the demon beneath me held me. I did not even feel the blow. Darkness came in a split second.

Chapter 5: Woman Without Skin

I OPENED MY EYES. Mady Joseffy danced grotesquely above me. With the stiff, convulsive movements of a marionette she jerked and twisted from the ropes which tied her wrists to an iron ring in the ceiling.

As she writhed in the air, her eyes never left the spider-like demon who gloated up at the delicate contours of her nude body. Lust contorted his lipless mouth and his pinpoint eyes bulged even further than usual from their sockets. In one hand he held a thin razor-edged knife.

"I'll give you money, everything I possess!" Mady shrieked frantically.

I was lying on the floor, my arms beneath my body, my hands and feet tied with heavy rope. Others cries joined those of Mady Joseffy. I turned my head. Elaine lay a foot or two from me, tied in the same manner as I.

I tugged at the rope which bound me. It felt as if it would forever hold me helpless. On a bench against the opposite wall lay my automatic which had been knocked out of Elaine's hand by the demon.

The demon lifted himself on his feet and ran a hand over Mady's white body. Talon-like fingers probed the smooth flesh, rested finally on her right thigh. Then his knife moved.

The two women screamed at the same time, and I think that I cried out too. Mady's body swung forward, and her knees struck the demon, knocking him off his feet. In a flash he was up. He scampered to a corner of the room and obtained more rope. Around each of her ankles he tied one end, then secured the middle of the rope to a second iron ring which came up from the ground. She was now held rigid between the ring above and the ring below.

Again his hand holding the knife moved up. There were words in her screams which were hardly distinguishable.

"You can't! Oh God, please! I'll give you anything! I'll—"

When the tip of the murderous knife bit into her skin, the shriek she emitted froze the blood in my veins. It could not have hurt a great deal, even when he drew the knife around the plump thigh.

It was not the pain that caused her to shriek, but the knowledge of what was to come. And as soon as the circle was completed the agony began, which must have been as unendurable as any torture ever inflicted upon a human being. The sensitive blade of the knife slid under the break in the skin, loosening the top of the skin from the flesh. Then the demon worked with both fingers and knife.

He was a master at his hellish task. I closed my eyes to shut out the hideous sight. Beside me Elaine rolled on the ground and moaned. Mady's screams went on and on end-lessly.

When at last I opened my eyes again, he was finished with that limb. He rolled the skin off the leg like a silk stocking. Then he went to work on the other thigh.

It seemed an eternity that the frightful agony of Mady went on. I tried to keep my eyes closed, but could not. The second time I opened them, there was no skin on her other leg.

My stomach turned when I saw those raw red limbs. A pool of blood had formed under them. The bloody skins lay on the ground. The demon was now working higher up, holding her shoulder with one hand, the knife with the other. Her screams had turned into low groans which were even more terrible to hear.

The third time I opened my eyes was when I heard the thud. The demon had cut the body loose from the ring in the ceiling. The thing which lay on the ground, which had a short time before been the charming, delicately proportioned body of Mady Joseffy, was a nightmare of raw flesh.

And she was not yet dead. That was the ultimate horror, the sight of that skinless body still twitching in the final spasms of agony!

The demon scampered over the ground on his feet and one hand. His second hand held the blood-stained knife.

Wildly I yelled at him; "Keep away from her! I'll kill you! I'll tear you apart bit by bit if you touch her!"

He ignored me. Elaine's eyes were wide with fear, and fear paralyzed her throat so that she could utter no sound. Grasp-ing an ankle, he dragged her, feet first, over the ground. He climbed a short ladder which was in the room, placed two ropes through the iron ring in the ceiling. Slashing the rope which bound her, he tied an end of each of the dangling ropes to her wrists.

His hand reached up to the neck of her negligee and fabric ripped. Then he cut the sleeves, and Elaine hung there with her gorgeous nude body exposed to the obscene gaze of that creature of the devil.

In a short while Elaine would be like her three friends—raw ugly flesh without skin!

As I desperately fought the rope, I suddenly remembered having heard that it was impossible to tie a man's hands and feet securely with one length of rope. Especially not with rope as thick as this. In my frantic effort to free myself, I had been merely consuming energy. Forcing myself to be calm through sheer effort of will, I twisted my wrists, worked the rope away with the tips of my fingers.

For the first time since I entered the hellish underground room, the demon spoke. "This will be my masterpiece," he chuckled in his inhuman voice. "The loveliest of them all. First those magnificent breasts; with what care I shall remove the skin and stuff it. And finally your face. Only the face itself, like a death-mask."

Elaine's mouth was open, but still she made no sound. She did not struggle.

One of my hands was almost free. A few more inches. Dear God, don't let me be too late!

One of the talons of the creature slid over her breasts. The bloody knife rose. Elaine found her voice when the tip of the knife drew blood over her right breast, leaving a thin line of blood in its trail. Elaine's voice rose, rose—a scream of mad terror and pain.

My hand was free! Through the loosened rope I pulled out my other hand. The demon's back was toward me and so fortunately he could not see me throw the rope off from about my legs.

My charge bore him to the ground. I went for the knife first, grasping the wrist that held it with both hands. He had no chance to turn; my weight was on his back, pressing his chest down against the ground. With all the strength at my command I twisted his wrist. He cried out with pain, thrashed his body under me, dug teeth into the back of my hand.

God knows how I held on, but I did. Bone snapped and the knife fell from his hand. Then we both struggled to reach the knife.

Elaine shrilled a warning. I felt that shape behind me which had knocked me unconscious before, sensed it waiting for an opening again to bring a club down on my head. When that club descended, Elaine and I were through.

I flung my body away from the demon, springing to my feet with the same motion. I had gained a few seconds, but the demon now had the knife and behind him stood a man with a blackjack in his hand.

"Reynold!" I exclaimed, gaping at him in bewilderment.

For a moment I thought that somehow Reynold Woodworth had found this place and had come to help; but then I saw that the demon carelessly turned his back to him and faced me, knife in hand.

"Andy, the gun!" Elaine cried.

I moved the instant she spoke. The three of us had forgotten about my gun. Whirling, I snatched up the gun and turned. The knife flashed in the demon's hand. I twisted aside, at the same time crashing the barrel of the gun down into the demon's face. The bridge of his nose cracked just as his knife grated against my hipbone.

With a cry of pain the demon staggered back. Reynold's blackjack was in the air, descending. I had no opportunity to use my gun, so I lashed out with my left fist, rocking Reynold on his heels.

Then I backed away rapidly, bringing up my gun. The demon was coming for me again, and so was Reynold. A single shot stopped the demon, and then Reynold lost his nerve and fell back.

"Andy, for God's sake, don't!" he wailed.

I had no more compassion for him than for a venomous snake. Deliberately I poured lead slugs into him.

After I cut down Elaine, she and I bound up the incision around her breast and the wound in my hip with strips torn from my shirt.

"Reynold Woodworth!" I mumbled incredulously, staring down at the corpse of the man I had considered my friend. "He must have been hiding there"—I pointed to a space curtained off near the door—"from where he sadistically watched the flayings without being seen. But why . . ."

"I think I can explain that," Elaine said as I tied the improvised bandage about her chest. "He had two motives—revenge on Fanny, and greed. Several weeks ago he came home unexpectedly and found Fanny in the arms of another man. Fanny didn't tell me who the man was, but she told me everything else. Reynold had been mean to her, especially after he lost a great deal playing the stock market, and Fanny sought comfort and affection with another man. She told me several days before she disappeared.

"The loss of the money and of his wife's love at the same time must have embittered him terribly. He conceived the diabolical idea of punishing his wife and starting an extortion scheme at the same time. He used the dying curse of Luke Strawn and hired a hideous freak in order to heighten the sense of horror. I don't think he meant to stop with his wife and we other three women. After all, none of us had great sums of money. I think he wanted to prepare the ground with us; set the scene with horror, so that wealthier women would be terrorized into giving freely.

"He did one other thing. He obtained photographs of us—Fanny had an album full—and superimposed our faces on bodies resembling ours and then photographed the whole thing. They were pictures of . . . of . . ."

"I saw them," I put in. "For a while they fooled me. If I hadn't been half mad with worry . . ."

"I don't blame you. They were very cleverly done. It would have been difficult to explain them. He sent them to us, warned us that he would distribute them far and wide. When Marie and Mady had given him every cent and piece of jewelry they possessed, they became desperate and went to him to beg for mercy. Mercy! He did not know the meaning of the word.

"Not that any of us knew that the monster was Reynold Woodworth. His intermediary was the freak. I was the only one who suspected—because of what Fanny had told me.

"But I had no facts. The police would have laughed at me. I knew that only I would be able to find this place. So I took your gun and—and you know the rest."

I held her in my arms. She shuddered against my chest. "You brave, adorable girl," I muttered.

So we left that charnel room, climbed up through the trapdoor, and, arms about each other, stood again in the clean air.

THE DEVIL IS OUR LANDLORD

Chapter 1: The Coming of Madness

THE SPECIAL POLICEMAN at the entrance to the Rose Hill Apartments kept glancing behind him with fear in his eyes. Martin Wright couldn't help but notice it as he came down the wide stairs into the courtyard. He hesitated, put down his valise.

He had a distinct impression that people were scurrying frantically across the court, although of course they weren't, really. But there was something different this evening about the way they came through the two main entrances and rushed across the flagstone walks to the five units which housed two thousand tenants. There was an urgency in their movements, a suppressed desire to break into a run, as if they were anxious to get to the safety of their apartments before a terrible fate caught up with them.

Two uniformed policemen stood before the guardhouse in the center of the court, not talking to each other, their eyes continually sweeping the unit entrances. Martin Wright bent to pick up his valise—then straightened up with a jerk and gaped.

People stopped in their tracks, too bewildered even to cry out. A hush was abruptly in the court, as if all sound, all movement, had been snapped off by a switch.

There was no sound but the patter of bare feet on the flagstones and a long-drawn scream on a single key incredibly high-pitched. The girl who ran across the court was stark naked.

Oddly, the first thought which entered Martin Wright's mind was that the girl must be very cold, for the collar of his topcoat was raised over his neck against the autumn chill. She was coming right toward him, blindly, running without direction. Her scream stopped. She glanced once behind her, without slowing down, then screamed again. This time there were words in her scream.

The policemen were the first to move. One raced in the direction from which she had come, revolver in his hand. The second chased the girl.

The words that shrieked from the girl's lips began to take on meaning.

"The hands! Oh, God, stop the hands! No! Stop them, please stop them! God, you can't let the hands . . ."

She was only a few feet from Martin Wright when he flung his arms out. He caught her about the waist. She didn't struggle, didn't resist; simply collapsed limply in his arms, still shrieking.

The policeman pounded up. "Here," he ordered. "Let's carry her into the guardhouse."

Martin shrugged the policeman away, lifted her in his arms. The policeman walked at his side. The people who had been in the courtyard edged closer, staring wide-eyed; a hundred windows were open out of which people looked. And they were all strangely quiet.

The girl was lovely, in the full bloom of maturity. But it wasn't at her nudity, Martin felt, that any of the people were looking. In the eyes of the people nearest him he saw stark horror . . . and fear.

She lay supinely in his arms, but her voice didn't stop. "Stop the hands! Oh God, no!" The lines of her face were twisted into a mask of hideous terror.

Martin carried her into the guardhouse, placed her on the cot which was there for emergencies. He stripped off his topcoat, draped it over her. As soon as the material of the coat touched her body, she leaped off the cot.

"Not again! God in heaven, no!"

She fought the policeman and Martin, clawing, scratching. They overpowered her, held her down on the cot until she subsided. She lay there, breathing in great gasps, still screaming. It didn't seem as if a human throat could scream so long or so loud.

John Mackey, superintendent of the building, came rushing in. "Another one!" he grated. "The third in a week! Who is it this time?"

"Ruth Chambers," Martin Wright told him. "Bertram Chambers' wife! You say the third in a week?"

"There've been two others since Monday," Mackey said. "Stark raving mad, all of them. They appeared in the building like Mrs. Chambers, suddenly, naked, and their minds were completely shattered. It's inhuman . . ."

The second policeman entered the guardhouse.

"Couldn't find a thing," he reported. "Nobody seen where she came from. People say she was suddenly there in the court, running, like the earth had opened and thrown her up."

Another scream ripped out in the guardhouse. Bertram Chambers was in the doorway. He leaped across to the cot, gathered his wife in his arms.

"Ruth, what did they do to you? I'll kill them! I'll tear down every stone in the building until I find them! Ruth, look at me! My God, don't you know me? It's Bert, darling, your husband."

There wasn't any change in the expression of her eyes. Terror was stamped there . . . forever. She turned away, her voice now a hoarse wail.

"The hands!"

Through the window Martin saw Victor Lowry making his way through the crowd which was gathered outside. He was resident manager of the Rose Hill Apartments. His lean handsome face was deadly white.

Bertram Chambers spun around when he saw Victor Lowry. "You let this happen. Two days ago my wife disappeared. She wasn't even out of the house; wasn't dressed for the street. She couldn't have been taken out because there was a guard at every exit. I said she was in the building. What did you do to find her?"

"We went through every square inch of the house and the basement," Victor Lowry replied wearily. "We had the police in. We did all we could."

"It wasn't enough," Chambers sobbed. "You should have done more."

"But what?" Victor asked as if to himself. "We seem to be helpless; women are suddenly vanishing and then reappearing out of the thin air, stark mad." He slumped down into a chair.

Martin placed a hand on Victor's shoulder. "Buck up, old boy. You're in charge here. If you go to pieces, panic will grip this place."

Victor looked up. "Hello, Martin. Just get back from your vacation? You were lucky to be away. It's pretty awful."

"Let's get out of here," Martin suggested. "You can't do any more. The cop phoned for an ambulance and it should be here any minute."

The two young men brushed through the crowd outside. People fell away before them. Martin heard voices mumble: "I'm moving out of here." . . . "If it were something human, it could be fought, but I tell you this is devil's work." . . . "My God, to go insane like that! It's more horrible than being murdered."

"I was having dinner at Susan's," Victor said as they walked into one of the units. "When I heard the screaming, I rushed down. Why don't you come up with me? You probably haven't eaten yet and there is plenty."

That was like Victor Lowry, asking him to come up to the apartment of the girl they both loved. The fact that they were rivals for the love of Susan Hall did not come between their rather cordial friendship. That was the intelligent, civilized way.

"I don't understand," Martin said. "What's happened to the three women? What's behind all this?"

Victor Lowry pressed the elevator button and replied: "You understand as much as any of us. Monday afternoon Mary Norton, the daughter of Spencer Norton, appeared in the foyer of C unit. The elevator operator, one of the porters, and several tenants were in the lobby at the time. Suddenly she appeared, bursting into their midst from nowhere. She was stark naked, clawing her body, shrieking something about hands, just like Mrs. Chambers.

"We discovered from her parents that she had been gone for several days. She's a spoiled, willful girl and her parents thought that she had left without telling them, to spend a few days with her friends. She'd done that before. When she was examined in the hospital, it was found that her mind was completely shattered.

"That same evening Emmery Liddle, our renting agent, told the police that his wife had disappeared. He'd come home from work and she was gone. The police sent out an alarm. Two days later Kate Liddle returned. She was found walking along the seventh floor hall in A unit, yelling like Mary Norton that somebody was coming for her. She too was raving mad.

"We had police stationed everywhere, at every exit and entrance in the building. The following day Ruth Chambers vanished. Her husband insisted that she was still somewhere in the house and we made as thorough a search as is humanly possible. We found no trace of her. Then a few minutes ago she . . . came back."

The elevator door opened and the two men stepped in. The hands of the Negro elevator operator were trembling as he worked the controls.

"Scared, Charlie?" Victor said.

The Negro attempted a smile, but it was rather sickish. "No sir, Mr. Lowry. They don't go after no men. Only girls; young and pretty ones."

"Whom do you mean by 'they,' Charlie?" Victor asked. "Who do you think is behind this?"

"The devil," Charlie asserted soberly. "The devil and his friends. They take away the soul of the girls and push their bodies right up through the earth again."

When they got out at the floor on which Susan Hall lived, Victor said to Martin: "There are others in this building who believe Charlie's right. I'm almost beginning to think so myself."

Susan Hall opened the door for them. Her presence always took Martin's breath away. He had thought that some of the constant ache for her would disappear if he didn't see her for a couple of weeks, but his two weeks' vacation hadn't made any difference.

She held out a hand to him. "So you're back, Martin. I'm glad you came up. We were just about to eat. You must join us."

She turned to Victor. "That screaming. Was it . . ."

"Yes," Victor said quietly. "Another one."

She shuddered. "That screaming coming all the way here from the court. It wasn't a scream of pain or of fear, but something far worse."

Victor's arm went protectingly about Susan's shoulder. Martin saw her lean against Victor and a stab of jealousy shot through him.

There were two other people in the apartment—Ellen Clay and Walter Miller. Ellen, a school teacher, shared the apartment with Susan. She was pretty in a plump fashion, jovial, friendly. Walter Miller, a very lean and very quiet account-ant, was her most persistent suitor.

Susan sat between Martin and Victor at the table. Judi-ciously she divided her attention equally between the two men. That made Martin feel better. He still stood as good a chance with her as did Victor.

Or did he? Victor Lowry was resident manager of the larg-est apartment house in the city, with a good income, living in the swankiest penthouse in the building with his aunt and uncle. It was his uncle, Wilbur Lowry, president of the syn-dicate which owned the Rose Hill Apartments, who had got Victor the position.

Some people had all the luck. He, Martin Wright, had had to struggle all his life, was now only one of a myriad of un-derpaid lawyers who worked for the law firm of Hewitt, Kling and Schwab. That's where he had met Susan Hall. She was a law stenographer in his office. And he had moved from his single room in a boarding house to furnish his own apartment in this building in order to be near Susan. He couldn't afford it, but just to be able to ride home with Susan every day was worth it.

"What I don't understand is what's been done to the women?" Walter Miller questioned.

Victor shook his head. "Nobody knows. That's the most hideous part of it. We've had the foremost brain specialists in the country examine the girls. All they say is that their minds are completely shattered, and that it is unlikely that they will ever recover. They gave a number of tests to find out what caused the insanity. All they could get was one thought repeated endlessly and hysterically by the girls— something about hands."

"Hands?" Martin said. "I was wondering what Ruth Chambers meant. What hands? And why are they afraid of them?"

Victor toyed with the food on his plate.

"We have no idea," he replied.

"Possibly they were tortured into madness by somebody's hands," Martin suggested.

"There is no mark or bruise on them. They are as healthy and normal physically as they were before they disappeared."

"Maybe a drug or an injection," Ellen Clay put in.

"They've had every conceivable blood test," Victor said. "There is no foreign matter in their systems."

"Then what in the name of heaven is it?" Susan cried.

Victor sighed. "The elevator operator's guess is as good as any. He says it's the devil who's robbed them of their souls and thrust them back to earth again."

"But that's ridiculous," Walter Miller scoffed.

"Of course," Victor agreed. "We mustn't take him seriously. But I've seen what happened to each of those three normal healthy girls and I have a feeling that the true explanation isn't much different."

Chapter 2: Satan's Apartment House

THE FOLLOWING MORNING Emmery Liddle, the renting agent, phoned up from the renting office downstairs while Victor Lowry was still at breakfast. When Victor returned to the table, his uncle, Wilbur Lowry, looked up at him inquiringly.

"Liddle says that they started coming in as soon as they opened the office," Victor explained. "The tenants. They want to break their leases, move out. Poor Liddle! His wife turned stark mad, and now it's his job to tell tenants there is nothing to be afraid of."

Wilbur Lowry stabbed into his grapefruit.

Wilbur was a short-set, pouchy man with iron-grey hair. His life had been a sort of see-saw between wealth and poverty. Well, that was the real estate business, Victor reflected—sudden rises to riches and then just as sudden plunges to poverty.

Wilbur Lowry said: "Is that what you're going to tell them?"

Victor shrugged. "I suppose it's my duty to."

"But you don't believe that there is nothing to be afraid of?"

"Something utterly hellish and unexplainable has happened to three women within a week and there is no reason to think that the same won't happen to other women," Victor retorted.

"I thought so," his uncle sneered. "You're like the others, scared yellow because a few women go crazy. A lot of people live here; it's almost a city. People are born here, die here, commit suicide, marry, get murdered, go mad just like anywhere else."

"But not like that," Victor argued.

"The members of the Board of Directors blame me for these insane women too," his uncle raged. "They don't dare say it, but I can see it in their faces. They've blamed me for everything. All right, the Rose Hill Apartments was my idea, and a damned good idea too. An apartment house capable of housing eight hundred families built in the suburbs where rent can be cheaper—why, it seemed a natural money-maker. Is it my fault that the place was never more than half filled? Is it my fault that prospective tenants object to the journey to the business section—just because a bus line failed? Damn that Board of Directors, I'll buy them out, that's what I'll do."

"You haven't the money," Victor reminded him.

Wilbur Lowry subsided in his chair. "No, I haven't," he admitted.

Cora Lowry came in without a glance at her husband. She muttered a good-morning to Victor, ignored her husband entirely. Victor had lived with them since he was a boy and he never remembered his aunt and uncle on affectionate terms. When they weren't actually quarrelling, there was a cold formality between them. Last night they had had another quarrel—a violent exchange of words which had reached Victor in his room.

Victor put down his coffee cup and left. He found himself glancing continually around him as he waited for an elevator, half expecting to see a mad, shrieking woman yelling to stop the hands. But there couldn't be. The women returned only after they had been gone for two days, and as far as he knew no woman had mysteriously disappeared within the last two days.

But there might be another one—more than one, an endless number. There was no reason to think that whatever evil power was responsible for the madness would stop at three. The next one might be . . . Susan!

Cold sweat was on his brow as he dropped down to the renting office on the ground floor.

He entered his office through a back door. He could hear tenants clamoring for the privilege to break their leases, and Liddle trying to put them off in a dead, toneless voice. Victor admitted to himself that he hadn't the courage to face the tenants. He couldn't tell them there was nothing to be afraid of.

The door opened and Police Sergeant O'Neal entered. "Well, there's going to be no more women kidnapped from this house," he announced. "Got this place airtight. Our men are watching everybody and everything that leaves and enters. Every package big enough to hold a human body is inspected."

"So you think, Sergeant, that the women were removed from this building, in some way made mad, and then returned here?"

"Sure. We went through every inch of the building while two of the women were missing. Combed the basement with a fine-tooth comb."

"I can't agree with you," Victor said. "Those women were never removed from the building. Whatever caused their madness is right here."

"And where were they kept?"

"Perhaps in one of the apartments. There are eight hundred in the building."

The sergeant smiled patronizingly. "Then how'd they go mad? It wasn't a drug or anything like that. There's only one answer, and the brain specialists agree with me: shock. And it takes plenty of room and sound and stage props to make them as completely off their nuts as that. These apartments aren't sound proof. You can hear your neighbor argue in the next apartment. One squeak or groan or anything like that and it would have been heard."

Victor bounced the rubber of his pencil on his desk. "Then why, Sergeant, weren't these women kidnapped when they were out of the building? Certainly it would be easier to have kidnapped them while they were shopping or out walking alone than to carry them out of a place like this."

"Maybe," the sergeant said. "But I promise you no more women will be taken out of this building in a hurry."

The telephone jangled. Victor picked up the phone on his desk. It was his Aunt Cora.

"Victor, I'm afraid!"

"Afraid? Of what?"

Her voice was agitated, quavering. "I don't know. I feel something closing in on me. I felt like that ever since Wilbur left about ten minutes ago. We had another quarrel. He said he wished he could get rid of me. I was brooding about that and suddenly I had the strangest feeling, as if . . . as if I were going to go mad like the others."

"Nonsense, Aunt Cora."

"Victor, I'm afraid of being alone. It's Margie's day off. I feel . . ."

"Have you locked the door?"

"Yes. But that's no good. Whatever it is isn't stopped by locked doors."

"Aunt Cora, I'm surprised at you," Victor scolded her as if she were a child. "There are police all over the building. Nobody can get near you. You're just frightening yourself because of the argument you had with Uncle Wilbur. Now just relax, try to calm your nerves."

"I suppose you're right," she faltered. "I'll take a hot bath. That usually calms me."

"That's a good girl," Victor said and hung up. He turned to Sergeant O'Neal. "My aunt's jittery. I guess every woman in the building is." Victor stood up. "Think I'll go up for a minute and see how she is."

The policeman grinned. "Seems it's not only the women who are scared stiff. You haven't much confidence in us, yourself, have you?"

"I have when it's a case of protection from ordinary human beings," Victor declared. "But this isn't."

He let himself into the penthouse apartment and called his aunt's name. She didn't answer and he told himself that she was probably in the bathroom taking the hot bath. He went through the foyer, into the living room, then stopped abruptly, looking down at a crumpled silk material which lay on the floor. There was something odd about that. Aunt Cora was the most fastidious person in the world; she would never tolerate anything like that lying on the floor.

He picked up the silk. It was a negligee, slightly damp to the touch. Under the negligee were a pair of house slippers. The insteps were moist.

"Aunt Cora!"

There were two bathrooms in the apartment, one leading into Aunt Cora's bedroom. He raced into the bedroom. The bathroom door was open. He went across the room, calling his aunt's name. The bathroom was empty. The tub was filled with water. Dipping a hand into the water, he found that it was still hot.

Victor ran to the phone, called the office downstairs. Five minutes later Sergeant O'Neal panted into the apartment, followed by two detectives.

"I had double guards placed at every exit as soon as they told me you thought your aunt was abducted," he said. "What makes you think she has been?"

"She's not here," Victor replied. "You remember she told me over the phone that she was about to take a bath. I came up seven minutes later—I looked at my watch—and she was gone. The tub was full and the water hot."

"Maybe she changed her mind. She might have walked out, visited a neighbor."

Victor showed him the negligee and bath slippers. "Not without clothes on. Conceivably she might not yet have undressed for her bath, but then she certainly wouldn't have dropped her negligee here. And they're damp; feel them. The negligee is damp on the inside only and the same with the slippers. That means that she put the negligee on over her wet body, stepped into the slippers with her wet feet."

O'Neal nodded. "I get it. She was already in the tub when something happened to make her get out again. Maybe the doorbell rang. She got into the negligee and slippers and came into the living room."

"Maybe she opened the front door to let whoever rang in and then came in here with him," Victor put in.

"That's right," the sergeant agreed, "Then whoever it was knocked her out, and for some reason removed her negligee and carried her out."

"Carried her out to where?" Victor demanded. "It's not yet eleven o'clock in the morning. Tenants are constantly walking through the halls. There are police all over the place. He couldn't be in these halls a minute carrying a woman, even if she weren't nude, without being noticed."

"Sure," the sergeant asserted. "That's why we'll nab him any minute. My men might have caught him already. Your aunt will be back here safe and unharmed in less than no time."

But the heaviness which clamped Victor's heart didn't leave. His aunt had been like a mother to him since his childhood, and now she was in the grip of whatever terrible beings delighted in turning women into raving maniacs!

Late that afternoon Sergeant O'Neal came into Victor's office and dropped wearily into a chair. He wiped perspiration from his brow with a great square of linen.

"It beats me," he declared. "There's no way your aunt could have been taken all the way from the penthouse without having been seen. She couldn't have been taken down the elevator because of course the operator would have known about it. The only other way down is the single flight of stairs and they lead out into other floors or the lobby where a cop was stationed. There is only one place where we haven't looked—the apartments . . ."

It required the rest of the afternoon and until midnight to go through every occupied and vacant apartment. And when the police completed their search it was clear that Cora Lowry could not possibly be in the building and at the same time could not possibly have been carried out of the building.

Chapter 3: Horror at the Door

Martin Wright said: "Why don't you leave, too, Susan? I'm half crazy worrying over you."

He had pulled his second-hand car up to the curb in front of the Rose Hill Apartments. It had been hard to find space to park, for the street was crowded with moving vans. The

moving men were carrying furniture in only one direction—
out of the building.

Susan Hall huddled in the front seat of the car. She had
driven home with Martin from the law office where they
both worked.

"I can't run out on Victor like the others," she said.

"You've got to think of yourself," Martin argued. "It's you
who are in real danger, not Victor. My God, if you should
become like those other girls!"

"Don't!" She turned a fear-lined face to him. "Don't talk
like that. Don't you think that's all I've been thinking of—
what every woman in this building is thinking of? I lay
awake all last night, choking with ghastly terror. One can be
afraid of being murdered in bed, and that must be pretty awful, but at least you know that there are those about who can
protect you.

"But there is a fear that's worse than that, the fear that's
always with me. And that is that no police or guns or locked
doors can save you from whatever horrible power is responsible for what is happening here—once your doom has been
decreed. You simply vanish and then you come back stark
mad without a mark on you, without a sign of how you became mad. Do you think it is easy to restrain myself from
running away in panic like the others?"

"Then why don't you?" Martin urged.

"Because Victor is our friend and we must stay with him
when he needs us most."

Martin nodded slowly. "I guess you're right." He covered
her hand with his. "But if anything happens to you, hell itself
won't hide the fiend from me."

She smiled wanly. "Let's stop off at Victor's office. It's
been even harder on him since his aunt vanished yesterday
morning."

Wilbur Lowry and Sergeant O'Neal were in the manager's
office with Victor. Victor rose when he saw Susan enter,
took several steps toward her. His face was ghastly, his eyes
dark-rimmed from lack of sleep.

Impulsively Susan flew to him. "Oh, Victor, it's so awful! Have they found any trace of your aunt?"

He shook his head, held her to him as if he never wanted to let her go.

Wilbur Lowry was striding back and forth, muttering: "I'm ruined. We can't keep them from moving out. A house like this, it was a perfect idea. We would yet have made money." He swung around to Sergeant O'Neal. "Damn you, why don't you do something? Sitting around here, your police standing about in the halls of the building, while I am being ruined!"

Victor released Susan, grabbed his uncle's arm. His fist went up as if to strike him. He was trembling with rage.

"How can you! Your wife in the hands of those fiends and you worrying only about losing money!"

Martin Wright stepped between them. "Come, come, get a grip on yourself, Victor. This is no time for quarreling."

"Sorry," Victor mumbled and dropped down in the chair behind his desk. "But this waiting," his voice went on. "Waiting for Aunt Cora to come back. If only we could do something, had something to fight against. I'll go mad myself knowing that I have to fight and that there's nothing tangible to fight against."

The back door flew open. Every head in the room went up, every pair of eyes turned to the door. Sergeant O'Neal moved forward to shut it. Then he fell back, gasping, "Mother of God!"

Cora Lowry stood in the doorway.

Without a stitch of clothing on her, she stood motionless, her heavy breasts heaving, her eyes bottomless pools in which bewilderment mingled with stark terror.

"Cora!" Wilbur Lowry groaned and took a step toward her. That was when the scream started. It trickled up in a thin wail from the depth of her throat and it rose until it clashed against the walls, knifed insanely into the brains of all who heard it. She shrank back, one hand clawing her breasts, the other tearing wildly at her hair.

"The hands are moving! You've got to stop them! Oh, God, stop the hands! Please!"

Sergeant O'Neal swept past the woman, tugging at his gun. Victor and Martin sprang to her side, tried to hold her arms, to lead her to a chair. She fought like a tigress, clawing, biting, and kept on yelling, "Don't let them come! You can't let them come again!"

Patrolmen pounded in from the outer office, helped the two young men subdue the mad woman. Her screams didn't stop nor her struggles, even after it seemed that there could not possibly be any more strength left in her. The patrolmen threw a coat over her, held her in a chair until an ambulance should come.

O'Neal came back, revolver in his hand, his forehead creased in a frown.

"I'll be damned," he said. "She had to come from somewhere, but it seems as if she just shot out of the ground. The door to this office is at the end of the hall. It's only about thirty feet between the door and the lobby of D unit, and there's no door between. There was a cop and a porter and a couple of tenants in the lobby and they say they didn't see a thing. The cop's been there steadily for three hours. Where in the world did she come from?"

Susan huddled in Victor's arms, sobbing. Wilbur Lowry gaped at his wife, mumbling, "Cora, it can't be! What did they do to you?"

For the second time within ten minutes Victor swung out of Susan's arms and confronted his uncle.

"You know damn well where she was!" Victor rasped. "For years you've wanted her out of the way and she knew it. Dead or insane, the result would be the same as far as you were concerned; you'd be rid of her. Last night you had a violent quarrel which made you come to a final decision."

"Victor!" Wilbur Lowry cried. "You don't know what you're saying!"

"She tried to warn me yesterday morning just before she disappeared," Victor went on. "What a fool I was to have forgotten. She was afraid of you. That's why she phoned me."

His uncle's eyes were bewildered, hurt. "How can you say such a thing about your own uncle? Cora and I might not have been on the best of terms, but, good Lord, I'd have to be a monster to do anything like that. And what about the other women—am I responsible for their madness, too? These horrors are ruining this house, are ruining me. Do you think I am mad too?"

Victor was relentless. "You can buy out the other members of the syndicate for a song now and become sole owner. You always chafed under the control of the Board; said that they were a bunch of nitwits; that if you had complete control you could make the house pay."

Wilbur Lowry wiped his florid face with a handkerchief. "So that's it?" he sneered. "How do we know you aren't in back of all this yourself? You'd like to get control yourself. You always insisted that you had your own ideas about running the building."

Susan gripped Victor's arm. "Victor, I'm surprised at you. At such a time as this, with your poor aunt still in the room, losing your head like a hysterical child."

"I'm sorry," Victor muttered. "Guess my nerves are all shot."

Without another word he went out the back door. Sergeant O'Neal looked after him, his eyes narrowed. Wilbur Lowry sank into a chair, running the handkerchief endlessly over his face. Cora Lowry's voice started again. "Oh, God, please stop the hands!"

"Let's get out of here," Martin whispered in Susan's ear. "This is no place for you."

She allowed him to lead her out of the office. Then she said: "I am going up to see Victor. Poor boy, the strain has been terrible and I was much too harsh with him."

"I'll go with you," Martin offered.

"Thanks, but I'd rather go alone."

The maid answered the door of the Lowry penthouse. No, young Mr. Lowry wasn't in; he hadn't been in since noon. Susan went to her own apartment, wondering where Victor could have gone. She hoped he wouldn't do anything foolish because of the way she had spoken to him.

In her own apartment Susan found a note from Ellen Clay that she wouldn't be home until late that night. She and Walter Miller were going to a dance. Susan stood a long time with the note in her hand, feeling her limbs grow weak with terror. The thought of being alone in the apartment sent slivers of ice through her veins.

With an effort she fought down an impulse to rush out of the apartment. She had scolded Victor for acting like a hysterical child. She mustn't act like one herself.

Why was everything so strangely quiet in spite of the hundreds of people who lived in the building, there was now no whisper of sound. It was as if she were shut off by herself, isolated from the rest of the world.

Abruptly she was aware of the darkening room. Gloom was seeping out of the walls, drifting down like a grey-black sheet from the ceiling. She leaped to the switch in a frenzy to snap on the light. Fool, to be afraid of the twilight!

But why was darkness coming so suddenly? Why was the darkness so eerie, so laden with premonition of evil? And why wasn't there any sound in the house? What had happened to the ordinary street noises below?

She moved to the window, stopped abruptly. What was that sound like distant thunder which was growing louder, coming closer and closer? It didn't come from the street. It was right here in the house, right in the walls of her apartment, seemed to be coming through the walls. She stood stock still, fighting down a scream. Every nerve in her body was strained toward that sound, trembling before it, trying to understand it.

Suddenly she burst into wild, uncontrolled laughter. Idiot! She had heard that sound numberless times before. In order to reassure herself, she threw open the front door. There, sure enough, was Elmer Heft, one of the porters, pushing the hand-truck in which he kept his mops and brooms and into which he piled the refuse from the incinerators.

Susan shut the door, still laughing. It was laughter which bordered on hysteria.

Ten minutes later, as she was preparing supper for herself in the kitchen, her doorbell rang. Instantly beads of perspiration formed on her body and her hand which gripped the frying pan trembled. What in the world was the matter with her, frightened half to death by the bell? Again she was working herself into a frenzy for no reason at all.

The bell rang persistently, urgently. Slowly she walked toward the door, having to force her limbs forward. The bell was a magnet, drawing her to the door against her will. And while her heart was clamped tighter and tighter in a vise of fear, she kept scolding herself. Certainly whoever was responsible for the disappearance of the four other women would not announce himself by ringing the bell. Once she opened the door a single cry by her would be heard by every tenant on the floor.

It required an exertion of will to turn the doorknob. The bell rang in her ears, penetrated into the core of her being, and a tiny voice within her warned her not to open that door. But once that door was open her voice could be heard by her neighbors. Indeed, even if she cried out right here, she would be heard by the tenants in the apartments on either side of her and above and below her. There was really nothing to fear.

She opened the door. A sigh of relief gushed from her lips and she forced a weak smile.

"Yes?" she said.

Chapter 4: Master of Madness

ELMER HEFT, THE PORTER, stood in the hall, and behind him was his hand-truck. He was squat, his features as well as his body looking as if they had been squeezed in a press. Tiny watery eyes swam in deep-set sockets.

Susan had seen him a hundred times before without having given him a second glance. But as he stood in the doorway looking up at her, fear crawled up her spine.

"Yes?" she demanded. "What is it?"

He stepped over the threshold, not taking his pale eyes from her. A warning voice within her urged her to shout for help before it was too late. She started to scream, but the screams died in her throat. A knife had appeared in his hand, a long slender blade, the deadly point of which was pressed against her abdomen.

"One peep out of you and this knife goes through you like it would through butter," he said in a flat, emotionless voice. "You won't die right away. You'll suffer a long time."

Her eyes bulged. "What do you want?" she managed to whisper.

"Do what I say."

She hadn't any choice. A single cry would bring police, but that cry would also mean horrible death. While she lived, there was the probability that the police would save her. He couldn't take her from the apartment without being seen by the police.

"All right," she said.

Without moving the knife, the porter glanced behind him. There was nobody in the hall.

"Get into my hand-truck," he ordered.

She hesitated. The tip of the blade dug into her. She moved toward the truck. Even if somebody were to step into the hall, it wouldn't help. It would look as if she were talking to the porter; the knife wouldn't be seen.

"Climb in backward," Elmer Heft said.

She lifted herself over the side boards of the hand-truck, the knife point sticking to her abdomen as if it were fastened there. There was a heavy tarpaulin on the bottom of the hand-truck. It was used to cover the garbage. Heft pulled it aside with his free hand. The truck was empty, but a thin layer of scum covered the bottom and bits of garbage adhered to the sides. The smell was nauseating. But the knife was there against her and she lay down.

Suddenly she knew what was going to happen to her and she moved to sit up again. Better a clean death by the knife than the madness which had come to the other women. Her shoulders jerked upward, her arms clawed up toward him, but it was too late. A wet cloth covered her face, a rough hand pushed it back. She held her breath . . . tried to scream . . . gagged. The cloth was saturated with chloroform.

And as she felt consciousness slipping from her, she saw in a flash how it would be. When she was unconscious, he would throw the tarpaulin over her. Nobody would suspect, as he wheeled the hand-truck into an elevator and down to the basement, that it was not garbage at the bottom. And the tarpaulin and the odor of garbage would keep the smell of chloroform confined. It would appear as if she had simply vanished. And then would come the madness.

She sank back and lay in the filth and the slime, motionless . . .

Susan fought her way up from the thick fog which enveloped her. Consciousness returned slowly, as when a person is awakening from a deep sleep. Then she became aware of the pain in her arms; they felt as if they were being pulled from their sockets. She attempted to rub the stiff joints with her hands and to her surprise found that she could not. There was nothing wrong with her hands; she could flex her fingers. But her hands simply could not move to be directed toward her body.

Her eyes opened and she was looking directly into the face of a clock. The hands, which were less than two feet from her eyes, said 8:19. It must have been about 7:15 when she had stepped into that hand-truck.

Her arms were stretched above her. Looking up, she saw a sort of stocks above her, with two round openings in which her wrists were enclosed. She could bend her knees two or three inches, no more. When she stood upright, the pull on her arms was lessened, but her muscles kept on hurting.

The room was small, low-ceilinged, dim. It was utterly bare save for that clock on a pedestal in front of her eyes. At her feet there was a swirl of clothes—her clothes. There were her shoes and stockings and dress and the lacy pink of her chemise.

But she wasn't nude. She was wearing a single garment, a robe of very heavy material which dropped from her shoulders to her ankles.

The clock ticked, ticked, ticked. That was the only sound in the room. It was now 8:22.

She was in the building, she knew. It would have been impossible for even Elmer Heft to have taken her out of the apartment house. The police would not suspect a hand-truck rumbling through the halls on its accustomed rounds, but they were letting nothing which could contain a human body out of the building without inspection.

She started to scream for help, but her mouth would not open. Her lips seemed stuck together. She tried to force her lips apart, could not, and she knew that her mouth was taped.

There was a low chuckle. Elmer Heft said: "So you are conscious. Good. There is no reason to lose any more time."

He stepped in front of her. In his hand was a black object. It was about two feet long, six inches wide, and more than an inch thick. One end tapered down into a short handle. It seemed to be made of rubber.

Elmer Heft slapped it lightly against his thigh, then walked around her. "Oh, God, he is going to beat me!" Susan thought and tensed her body for the blow. When he struck her, her body jerked forward from her fettered wrists and a scream gushed to her taped mouth, remained stuck in her throat soundlessly.

A second blow came and a third. The heavy robe protected her somewhat, and she began to wonder why the porter had stripped her naked and then dressed her in the robe. Without the robe the pain would have been even greater and it would seem that the object of those blows was to inflict pain on her.

Then she realized that something else had been done in order to lessen her torment. The stocks which enclosed her wrists were lined with heavy material, probably velvet, in order to protect her skin from being chafed.

Why? What manner of madman was this to fasten her to these stocks and yet be careful not to bruise her skin, to beat her with a rubber flail, yet clothe her in a heavy garment to mitigate the pain?

Elmer Heft was standing in front of her again. His watery eyes ran over the slim length of her body as if regretting that he had clothed her in the robe.

He said: "It is now 8:30. In fifteen minutes I shall beat you again. Three blows. And at nine o'clock three more blows. Every fifteen minutes you will receive three blows and that will go on forever."

He lifted the clock from the pedestal; wound it, and chuckling under his breath returned it. It was now 8:33. In twelve minutes he would beat her again. At the thought of the blows that were to come, her flesh flinched.

The porter pulled a stool from a corner of the room, sat down on it, and began to read a magazine. The minute hand of the clock moved slowly, inexorably, toward the nine. She could actually see the hand move, rush as if time had suddenly been stepped up by some hellish force, and then it was 8:45.

At precisely 8:45 Elmer Heft rose, picked up the flail. Susan screamed silently, inwardly, before the first blow struck. The pain seemed greater now. Her body quivered, trembled in anticipation of the second blow. It seemed an eternity before the flat rubber flail slapped her back with a force which seemed to cave in her backbone. And then the third blow smashed against her quivering back.

And fifteen minutes later three more. And after that . . .

Elmer Heft was again reading the magazine. Her arms began to feel like leaden weights. Her legs ached, could hardly hold up her body. But when she sagged down the full weight of her body was on her wrists, and that was even more painful than standing erect with her arms above her.

8:51. Nine more minutes before she would be beaten again. Eight minutes more . . . seven . . . six . . . The hands of the clock were racing as they could race only in a nightmare.

Four minutes . . . three . . . two. Oh, God, only two minutes! It couldn't have been thirteen minutes ago that . . .

Nine o'clock! Elmer Heft rose from his stool, picked up the rubber flail. If only she could scream! Her body thrashed wildly from her fettered wrists, her voiceless tongue shrieked silent agony, even before the first of the blows struck.

On, on the hands of that clock moved—moved as relentlessly as death. 9:15. 9:30 . . . 9:45 . . . 10:00 . . . And each time those three blows.

Everything in the world disappeared but the hands of the clock. There was no room in her mind for anything but those hands. Nothing existed but those hands which every fifteen minutes announced further torture.

A man was in the room. He must have been there a long time before she became aware of him. A black mask covered all of his face. Came down to below his chin. He stood looking at her for a long time, watching the fear-contracted pupils of her eyes, watching how the muscles of her mouth worked against the tape every time the clock neared the quarter hour and Elmer Heft stood ready.

Only once he spoke. It was a voice which she had heard before, but which she could not place. He said: "She'll go quicker than the others, Elmer. She's more sensitive, has more imagination. I'll relieve you at midnight."

He went out through a door which she could not see because it was behind her.

She knew now, of course, what it was that had made the other women stark, raving mad. Sooner or later she would be like that, her mind cracked by a horrible variation of the Chinese torture of allowing drops of cold water to fall on the forehead in regular intervals, or of lightly and rhythmically tapping the soles of the victim's bare feet.

And then she would appear somewhere in the apartment house, naked, thrust out of Elmer Heft's hand-truck, and in her madness she would be shrieking about hands, and nobody would guess that it was the hands of a clock that she meant. And they would wonder how her madness had come and why there were no marks on her body, not knowing the diabolical cleverness of the fiends who had taken pains that no slightest bruise appear on her.

She sagged at last from the stocks, her legs having given way under her. Her throat was burning. If only she had a drink, if only the weight on her arms were released. But no, that was part of the torment—that and the blows and the clock endlessly moving in front of her eyes. The inexorable hands which would drive her, like the others, to madness.

Elmer Heft sat suddenly upright and fear leaped into his watery eyes. He half rose from his stool, and a voice barked: "Sit down!" Then the same voice gasped: "God, Susan! . . . I'm going to kill you for this, Heft. I'm going to shoot you down like a dog."

Victor Lowry stepped into her line of vision, a gun in his hand. Dear, sweet Victor! She was saved!

Heft crouched back on the stool. "Mr. Lowry, don't! It wasn't me. Don't shoot, and I'll talk."

Victor moved forward until he stood above Heft. "All right, talk. Who's your boss? You haven't the brains to do this alone."

Martin Wright was in the room too. She wanted to shout her gratitude to the two men who loved her and who had managed to find her, but her mouth was taped. Martin also had a gun in his hand. He walked on feet that made no sound.

What was the matter with Martin? What did the strange expression in his eyes as they were fixed on Victor's back mean—an expression like a jungle beast stalking prey? Why was he raising the butt of the gun over Victor's head?

No! If only she could call out to Victor, warn him to turn! Victor did turn, after what seemed an eternity, and then it was too late. The butt of Martin's gun descended on Victor's skull and he crumpled.

Mutely she had to watch while Martin and Heft tied Victor with heavy rope. The blow had only stunned Victor, for within a few minutes he opened his eyes.

"So it's you?" Victor gasped.

Martin nodded. "When I saw you in the basement headed this way and followed you, I hadn't time to put on my mask. I always wear a mask in front of my victims; they might mention my name in their ravings after they are mad. So I think I shall kill you instead of treating you like the others. But first I'm curious to know how you found this place."

"It wasn't hard after I established one fact," Victor said. "I went over the reports and found that every time one of the mad women appeared there was a porter nearby, and then I established that the porter was always Elmer Heft. It became plain then—his hand-truck explained how the women had been abducted. So I came to this store-room in the basement where hand-trucks and mops and pails are kept. I looked behind the tarpaulin which hangs down one wall, as the police no doubt did, and when I saw nothing 1 searched elsewhere. But I continued to wonder about that store-room—I returned. I felt about until I hit on the button which opens the sliding door, and here I am."

"Bright boy," Martin said, "but not bright enough. In your hurry to get down here you fortunately didn't think of telling the police."

Victor tore futilely at his bonds. "You can't get away with this. The police will find you the way I did."

Martin shook his head, grinning. "They'll come too late to find anything. I've accomplished my purpose. And I'll be able to buy Rose Hill Apartments for a song."

"So that's it," Victor said. "I suspected that somebody wanted to ruin the place, then buy it up cheap. The fact that every one of the women who went mad was the wife or daughter of a member of the Board of Directors showed that. But I thought it was my uncle. Why you? You haven't any money."

"But I've something worth more than money," Martin gloated. "You know I work in the offices of Hewitt, Kling and Schwab. Mr. Kling is attorney for the city traction commission. One day about a month ago I came across a confidential report on Mr. Kling's desk and surreptitiously I glanced through it. From the report I learned that within a year the city plans to build a subway from the business section of the city which will run right past this house. The Rose Hill Apartments will be worth a fortune, and anybody who could purchase it at its present low price would become wealthy.

"I approached a former college chum who has some money, took him into my confidence. He couldn't raise more than twenty per cent of the cash that was needed and neither of us knew anybody else whom we could trust with our information. After all, I had no money to invest; I could easily be left out in the cold.

"I was desperate. A fortune was in my grasp. And there was Susan. I was certain then that the only thing which kept her from marrying me was my poverty. I knew of this chamber. Elmer Heft had told me about it. It had been built according to the original plan and during construction, when it was found that there would be no use for it, it had been walled up. I promised Elmer Heft a share of the money, and during the night we quietly cut through the door. During the last week of my vacation I was really in this room, eating and sleeping here and driving women to madness."

He lit a cigarette. "But enough of talking," he said. "Elmer, you are neglecting your duty."

The porter stood up, the rubber flail in his hand.

"But why Susan?" Victor pleaded. "I don't care what you do to me, but you can't make the woman you love mad!"

"Love?" Martin sneered. His eyes were livid balls of fever—the eyes of a man who was himself mad. "I loved her more than any man ever loved a woman until she turned me down for you. Oh, yes, she did. She mightn't have said it in so many words, but I could see it in her eyes, I could tell by her actions. She was only concerned over you. It was clear then that she didn't give a damn about me. So my love turned to hate. And now—"

"And now you'll reach for the ceiling!"

Martin Wright wheeled. The sliding door was open and Sergeant O'Neal stood there with leveled gun. Behind him were the blue uniforms of patrolmen.

Martin's automatic, which was still in his hand, jerked up. Two shots, one after the other, roared in the small room— both from the sergeant's service revolver. Without a sound Martin sank to the floor.

"I was hoping he'd do that," O'Neal said. He turned to Elmer Heft who cowered against the wall. "Take him away, men."

Several minutes later, when Susan had been released from the stocks and Victor's bonds had been cut, Sergeant O'Neal explained: "One of my men who was stationed in the basement saw you go into the store-room, and a minute later saw Wright go in, too. When neither of you came out after some time, he began to suspect something and went in himself. When he saw the room was empty he called me down. After a while we found the sliding door."

"Thank heaven!" Victor muttered fervently. He was holding Susan in his arms. "God, to think that the fiend might have driven you insane!"

"I am insane," she said, smiling up at him. "At least crazy—crazy about you!"

VALLEY OF THE RED DEATH

Chapter 1: Scalped!

OAK VALLEY'S ONLY business block consisted of seven stores. From one of these—the combination restaurant and curio shop—stepped Paul Shepard. He stood for a moment, blinking in the dazzling sun.

It was a hot, lazy summer day. On the opposite sidewalk six or seven men and boys lounged on the porch of the post office. Their eyes were focused on a girl who had come out of the butcher shop and was walking up the street.

Paul Shepard lit a cigarette. He, too, followed the graceful undulation of the girl's tall slim body. She was very pretty. Still watching her, he moved toward his car, which was parked in front of the restaurant. Then he stopped.

The stillness which hung stiflingly over the sun-baked thoroughfare deepened suddenly into a hush so intense that it could be felt. The girl was standing with one foot on the running board of a sedan, motionless. One of the men on the post office porch had started to raise a pipe to his mouth; the pipe remained suspended in mid-air.

Nobody thought of moving, not even when that other girl—who seemed suddenly to have appeared in the middle of the street—started to scream.

She must have come from around one of the store buildings. Now she was there before their eyes, staggering, stumbling, flopping about as if there were no bones in her limbs. There were clothes on her, but she would have been less shamefully exposed if she hadn't had a stitch on. There were strips and rags of a dress and wisps of undergarments which only accentuated the lovely curves of her flesh.

But her face wasn't lovely, although it, like her body, was unmarked. It was contorted into an agonized grimace of horror and suffering. She hadn't any hair. There didn't seem to be any top to her head. It was a nauseating red, and the red flowed down over her face and body.

Then she screamed. It must have been only a few seconds after her appearance, but it seemed an eternity, as if time had held its breath in horrified suspense. She stopped trying to move; stood there with her mouth wide open, emitting a shrill soul-chilling scream.

Abruptly the scream broke into a gurgle like water seeping down a drain. She swayed, thrust out her arms before her as if to ward off something which stood there, and collapsed, limp as a rag doll.

Everybody moved at once, then. Paul Shepard was the first at her side. During his days as a newspaperman, he had seen bodies hideously mangled, but he had never before seen anything which struck him with so great an impact of horror.

Above him voices mumbled, shouted. "Mother in Heaven! . . . It's Irene Blakely! . . . Lordy, look at her head!"

A face was close to Paul Shepard's, kneeling on the other side of the body. A lean, rugged face with tiny eyes. Across the body those eyes met his.

"She's dead," Paul said.

The other nodded grimly. A woman began to whimper. Paul glanced up. It was the girl he had seen come out of the butcher shop. She was mashing the packages she was carrying against her breast, sobbing, "Irene! Oh, God, what happened to her?"

The lean man with the rugged face stood up. "She's been scalped," he announced.

A horrified mutter went through the crowd. Paul stood up too. There was nothing that could be done for the girl. The crowd had grown; remarkable how the sleepy town had awakened. Men, women and children pushed forward to see the horror which lay on the ground, and then shrank back with exclamations and screams.

"Scalped alive," the lean man added.

"But who?" voices demanded. "Why'd anybody want to do that to Judge Morrison's girl?"

"Who?" The lean man balled his fists. "Who'd scalp a person but an *Indian*? And who's the only Indian living within five miles of Oak Valley?"

"No!" The girl faced the lean man, her magnificent blue eyes flashing. Paul thought that he had never seen any woman so beautiful. "Hank Somerville, if you are accusing Eddie Badger, you know that's a lie. Eddie wouldn't hurt a soul, especially Irene, who was my very dearest friend."

Hank Somerville's tiny eyes shifted from the girl's direct gaze. "Who then?" he said. He turned to the crowd. "Who but an Indian would—There he is now, the murdering, scalping rat."

Every eye followed the direction of his pointing hand. Paul Shepard had glimpsed the man in the chauffeur's seat of the car which the girl had been about to enter. He had come out of the car, was standing some twenty feet from the crowd. He was tall and straight as a birch; the sleek flat muscles of perfect physical condition rippled under his copper skin.

He stepped forward, calm, impassive, save for an angry twitching of the skin over his high cheek-bone.

"I was in the car for the past fifteen minutes while Miss Addams was shopping," he told Somerville. "You saw me there."

"It's Indian's work," Somerville repeated stubbornly. "If not you, maybe that squaw of yours."

Paul saw the Indian rise to the balls of his feet, saw his right hand clench. Somerville saw too and struck first. The blow didn't reach the Indian. It was stopped by the shoulder of the girl who had leaped between the two. She spun, would have fallen if Paul hadn't caught her in his arms.

The following minute was chaotic. The Indian had leaped past the girl, lifted Somerville in the air, and dropped him to the ground. Somebody else struck at the Indian and a third man came to the Indian's aid. Then there was a free-for-all.

Paul held one hand about the girl's shoulders; with the other he tried to keep her clear of the mob.

Women shrieked; one voice yelled, "Shame on you, with that poor girl lying there." The men fought taking sides. It was as if a baleful influence were goading them on, had changed them suddenly into savages.

"You fools." It was a thin, cracked voice, but it spoke with authority. "Fools! Fighting amongst yourselves when we're all in danger. Don't you know who scalped the girl? Chief Flying Hawk!"

The fight stopped. Men dropped their arms to their sides, turned to look at the very old man whose frail body stooped over a cane. Shadows of fear flitted across the faces of the mob.

"Chief Flying Hawk." the old man repeated. "He said he'd come back for revenge. Every generation he'd come back, he swore, when our forefathers wiped out his village. He hasn't been among us for many years and now it's time. The girl is the first."

Voices babbled, strained, fearfully. "The Indian curse! . . . The Chief's come back. My grandpa said— . . . God, then none of us is safe!"

The girl tugged at Paul Shepard's arm. "Come, we can get away now. They might be whipped up against Eddie Badger again."

Paul Shepard went with her to the car, the Indian walking on the other side of her. Once again Eddie Badger seemed impassive, save for his coal-black eyes. In them Paul saw fear glint. He knew that the Indian wasn't afraid of Somerville or any of the other men. It wasn't physical fear that Paul saw in his eyes.

Eddie Badger opened the back door of the car and got into the front. The girl turned with one hand on the door, extended the other to Paul.

"Thank you ever so much. My name is Claire Addams. My father owns the Addams farm three miles up the road. You must come to see us."

He held her soft hand in his. She was tall and slim and her blue eyes were the deepest Paul had ever looked into. He hated to release her hand.

"My name's Paul Shepard."

It didn't mean anything to her. She said: "I've never seen you about town. Are you a stranger?"

"Yes, just drifting about."

"Looking for work?" she asked.

He smiled. "In a way."

Well, that was more or less accurate. He was traveling through New York State looking for material for a book. Obviously she had never heard of Paul Shepard, novelist and writer of travelogues. Certainly at that moment he looked like a migratory worker. He had had a flat tire just before entering Oak Valley and grease had smeared his grey slacks and white shirt.

"I heard my father talking about taking on extra help for haying," Claire Addams said. "If you want to come back with me . . ."

"Do I!" he burst out. He wanted to be wherever this adorable girl was. He felt that she needed him.

Two men were carrying the body into the general store. The rest were in two distinct groups. One was about the very old man, the other listening to Hank Somerville. "We'd better hurry," Claire Addams urged. Paul got in beside her in the back seat and Eddie Badger started the car.

When they reached an isolated section of the road about half a mile from the town, the Indian stopped the car. He turned around to the back seat. Stark terror had replaced the fear in his eyes.

"What's the matter, Eddie?" Claire asked.

"Something's beside me on the front seat," Eddie Badger said in a contrite tone. "It's been there since I got into the car. I didn't want to say anything in town because of the mob. They mightn't have understood. I don't understand myself."

"What—" Claire began and impulsively leaned forward.

"Don't, please!" Eddie Badger cried.

She sank back, puzzled. It was Paul who looked over to the front seat. He saw a mop of long black hair next to the Indian. At first glance it looked like a wig. Then he saw the blood which dyed the seat, and strands of the hair, and he saw the skin and ragged flesh at the roots of the hair.

"A scalp!" he ejaculated.

Claire Addams was looking at it too, then. She couldn't keep herself from looking. She let out a little scream and sank back in the seat.

"Irene Blakely's scalp!" she moaned.

Chapter 2: Flying Hawk's Curse

EDDIE BADGER drove a short distance further, stopping by a small lake. He got out carrying a newspaper wadded into a roll the size of a large melon. Drops of red were beginning to seep through the newspaper. The Indian stooped and picked up several rocks. Then he disappeared behind a cluster of trees which lined the shore of the pond.

Paul Shepard felt his throat burn with the urgency to say something, but he couldn't think of the appropriate words. He dipped into his pocket for a cigarette, offered one to Claire Addams. She shook her head. She had shrunk into a pathetic bundle in the corner of the seat, staring vacantly.

Eddie Badger returned. He didn't look at the two in the back seat. He slid behind the wheel, but he didn't start the car. He just sat there.

At last Claire Addams spoke. "Are you going to tell?"

Paul shrugged. He had been waiting for that. "Wouldn't it have been wiser to have turned the scalp over to the police? Eddie Badger has a good alibi."

"The police of Oak Valley is a constable named Ned Lewis," she said. "He's a doddering old fool. He'd tell everybody in the county that Eddie Badger had been found with Irene's scalp in his possession. Do you think that many people could be convinced that he hadn't done it?"

Paul regarded the tip of his cigarette before he spoke. "And Eddie's alibi wouldn't hold water, especially if anybody else noticed what I did. He says he was in the parked car for fifteen minutes while you were shopping. I saw him when I stepped out of the restaurant; but when I passed the general store a few minutes later, I noticed that it was impossible to see the front seat of this car from the porch of the post office."

Eddie Badger's back tensed. Paul went on relentlessly. "It's conceivable that he slipped out of the car, murdered the girl, then returned without having been seen."

"He didn't!" Claire exclaimed. "Why would he murder Irene?"

Eddie Badger turned. He said quietly: "I didn't kill her. I swear I was in the car all the time. And it wasn't the scalping alone that killed her. Why should a girl fall down dead all of a sudden a couple minutes after she had been scalped? She might have died finally, yes, but not like that."

"Then you think something besides the scalping killed her?" Paul asked.

"That and one other thing." The Indian's face muscles twitched. "Horror."

"Horror?"

Gravely the Indian nodded. "She saw the spirit of Chief Flying Hawk. It was he who took her scalp. Irene Blakely was a Morrison before she married."

Paul flipped the cigarette butt out of the window. "That yarn the old man was ranting about over the girl's body? What's it all about?"

Claire Addams said: "It goes back to the Revolution. Most of the Iroquois nations joined the armies of the British against the American colonists. The Americans were taking the land from the People of the Long House, and the British made them all sorts of promises. The British and their Indian allies massacred hundreds in their raids. And Congress did almost nothing until nearly the end of the war. Then it sent an army against the Iroquois.

"Not all the Iroquois nations had taken the side of the British. Some Seneca tribes remained friendly to the Americans. Flying Hawk, chief of the Seneca tribe which occupies the edge of this valley, was one of them. But when the avenging army of the Americans came, they made no distinctions.

"Especially bitter were the three first families that had settled here. There were the Addamses, my family, the Morrisons and the Prescotts. One day my ancestor, Joseph Addams, returned to his home to find his cabin burned to the ground. The scalped bodies of his wife and three children were lying nearby. The Prescotts were wiped out in the same way, leaving only one son to carry on the name. And the Morrison's oldest daughter—she was carried off by the British renegades, made their slave, then brutally killed when she was of no more use.

"And so this army of Americans, guided by what men of the Addamses and Morrisons and Prescotts remained, wiped out entire villages, burned granaries, slaughtered every man, woman and child whose skin was red. When they came to the tribe of Flying Hawk, the Indians did not flee, for they felt they had nothing to fear from the white men whom they had not harmed. But, as I said, our forefathers, in their bitterness, could see no distinction, and burned and massacred until none was alive.

"The story goes that with his dying breath Chief Flying Hawk cursed the men who could have saved his people and did not. And the curse was that he would return generation after generation to have vengeance on the three families."

Paul could not restrain a smile. "So what you want me to believe is that the Chief came back and scalped the girl?"

Eddie Badger shrugged. "I don't know what to believe. Records will show that men and women of the three families have died in queer and violent ways since the curse of Chief Flying Hawk. Joseph Addams himself was eventually shot by Indians. A generation later the head of the Prescotts was found dead in this lake; they say Chief Flying Hawk pulled him under. A Morrison was killed fighting Indians in Kentucky; they say Chief Flying Hawk had appeared just to shoot that one bullet. And so on it went in every generation one member of each family died violently or by accident. Thirty years ago Miss Addams' grandfather died when a horse threw him and two weeks later Judge Morrison's father died the same way; the spirit of the Chief, they say, had entered into the horses. And now there is a new generation."

"Coincidence," Paul scoffed.

"Perhaps," Claire said. "But how do you explain Irene Blakely's death?"

A car flew by, racing in the direction of Oak Valley. Paul glimpsed a young man at the wheel and next to him an older man who, in spite of the heat, wore a frock coat, a flowing bow tie and a severe black hat. Their faces were tense.

"Judge Morrison and Raymond Blakely!" Claire exclaimed. "Poor men, they must have heard by telephone."

"The murdered girl's family?" Paul asked.

"Yes. Judge Morrison was her father and Raymond Blakely her husband. Raymond and Irene were married only a little over a year. He was madly in love with her. He'll take this terribly hard."

"Too bad," Paul muttered. Then he saw that Eddie Badger was still turned in his front seat, looking at him with his steady black eyes. There was something which had not yet been decided.

"Hadn't we better get going?" Paul said.

The Indian didn't move. Claire was also looking at Paul. She said: "You don't know this Hank Somerville. He worked for us until a couple of weeks ago. Eddie caught him trying to make love to his wife and he thrashed him. Father fired Hank. He wouldn't stop at anything to get even with Eddie. All he'd need was to hear that Irene's scalp was found in this car."

Paul lit a fresh cigarette. It wasn't easy to make up his mind. It was his duty to go with this information to the police; he might be aiding a murderer.

"All right," he said finally. "I won't say anything until I have more definite information."

Claire's splendid blue eyes expressed silent gratitude. Eddie Badger said, "Thanks," and started the car. Paul found that he and Claire were somehow sitting closer to each other. He felt that he had been bribed and he didn't care . . .

The Addams place was a dairy farm, with only a few acres given over to truck farming. A rambling, freshly-painted house stood several hundred feet off the road. Three men and a girl sitting on the open porch rose when the car pulled up. The girl flew down the stairs into Claire's arms, weeping.

"Isn't it terrible?" the girl cried. "We heard about Irene by telephone."

"I hear Hank Somerville tried to blame Eddie Badger," a wiry man with a bristling white mustache said to Claire. "And that the skunk hit you. I'll break his neck when I see him."

Paul stood among them uncomfortably. He had never been a farm hand before and did not know how to conduct himself. Claire solved the problem for the moment by placing her hand on his arm and saying: "Paul Shepard here, helped us get away from the mob. He is looking for a job. I told him you needed an able-bodied man to help Eddie get the hay in."

The man with the white mustache stuck out his hand. "Thanks a lot, son. Glad to hire you. I'm Judson Addams, Claire's dad."

Then as if Paul weren't a hired hand at all, Judson Addams introduced him to the others. The girl who had run to Claire was Joan Prescott, pretty in a full blown, rural way, her yellow hair a mad whirl above her head. One of the two young men was Warren Addams; unlike either his father or sister, he was short and broad, with a virile, ruddy complexion. But his face, at the moment, was yellowish and his lower lip was trembling, no doubt caused by grief for Irene Blakely whom he must have known all his life. Glen Tyson, the other young man, was the only one there dressed in city clothes. From conversation Paul gathered that he was a lawyer and Joan Prescott's fiancé.

"It will be a frightful blow to Ray Blakely," Joan was saying. "I've never seen a man so terribly in love with a woman as he was with Irene."

"He's not only lost a wife but her money as well," Glen Tyson commented cynically. "He hasn't a cent of his own; been living on Judge Morrison's money since their marriage."

"Glen, how can you speak like that at such a time!" Claire reprimanded him.

They had begun to move off toward the house as they talked. Eddie Badger plucked Paul's arm and said, "Come with me," which brought home to Paul the fact that he was, after all, a hired hand.

Eddie Badger led him to a one-story frame house not far from the huge white barn and installed him in a tiny room. Eddie Badger and his wife shared two rooms in a wing of the house. In other parts of the house other hired hands slept.

Solemnly the Indian introduced Paul to his wife as, "My friend, Paul Shepard." Mary Badger was small, with delicate features and a willowy body which Paul could have lifted with one hand. He could easily see why Hank Somerville had tried to make love to her.

For the five hours until supper time he worked on a field pitching hay with Eddie Badger. Two minutes after they started Eddie must have known that Paul had never before held a pitch-fork in his hand; but he said nothing, worked practically for two. Paul began to feel pretty certain that a man like Eddie Badger could never have brutally slain Irene Blakely.

Paul ate supper in the large kitchen of the main house with the rest of the help. In the dining room the Addamses were eating. Paul had only to say a word, to tell who he really was, in order to be eating in there with them. But then, as a guest, he would have to leave after a day or two. This way he could say on indefinitely. And he wanted to, in spite of the fact that his hands were swollen and his shoulders felt as if they were coming apart. He had looked into a pair of blue eyes and was lost.

After supper he hung around the house, but he didn't get a chance to see Claire. A sticky, breathless night descended and the weary farm hands went to bed. He wandered through the meadows, entered a small birch forest and wondered if for the first time in his life he was making a fool of himself over a woman.

Suddenly he stopped in his tracks, every sense alert. A shadow had flitted past soundlessly, was lost behind some trees—a shadow of an Indian, naked save for a breech-cloth and moccasins. In his right hand he held a hunting knife.

Chapter 3: The Second Scalp

PAUL SHEPARD laughed softly to himself. The fact that the shadow had been that of an Indian proved, of course, that it had simply been his imagination. No Indians around here would dress, or undress, like that. At night they could not be distinguished from white farmers.

He had been hearing too much about Indians. No doubt, he sneered at himself, it had been the ghost of Chief Flying Hawk.

Then he saw the Indian again, this time clearly outlined under the bright half-moon as he ran along the fringe of the birch trees. Paul saw now that he was attired like an Indian on the war-path, his scalp-lock standing up from his hairless skull, his face and naked chest covered with bright paint.

Breath clogged in Paul's throat. He closed his eyes, opened them. There the Indian was, running on feet which made no sound. Then once again trees hid him from sight.

Without being aware of it, Paul lit a cigarette, trying to think. He was either having hallucinations, or—suddenly he whirled about and ran toward the main house. Ran in the same direction as the Indian.

Claire Addams' forefather had been one of those whose had been responsible for the massacre of the Senecas and the death of Chief Flying Hawk. The curse had struck Irene Blakely. Claire, or her father or brother, might be next!

There wasn't any breath left in him when he got to the house. Light shone in a single ground floor window. He looked in. Claire was reading in the living room; her father was listening to a radio lecture. Paul made a tour of the grounds, saw nothing. Then he hung around outside the lighted window, tense and alert, until he saw both Claire and her father go upstairs to bed.

Slowly Paul walked back to the house where he slept, deep frowns furrowing his forehead. The Indian had been headed for the house. Had he disappeared into thin air, as a spirit might?

Fool! Was he, a sophisticated writer, falling for the legend of Chief Flying Hawk?

Then he saw a second Indian. Like the other, this one was stripped to the waist, but there all resemblance ended. There was no war-paint on him; instead of a scalp-lock he had a shock of thick black hair, and he wore a pair of pajama trousers. It was Eddie Badger.

Furtively Eddie Badger was moving away from the house. He saw Paul, stopped, then started to run. Paul raced after him. For the moonlight had revealed the object Eddie Badger held in his hand. It was a mop of yellow hair!

The Indian was fleet as a deer and easily outdistanced Paul. Then abruptly he stopped, waiting for Paul to catch up to him. He waited half-crouching, holding the grisly object behind his back.

Paul halted a few feet from him, tensing to meet the Indian's spring. His eyes met the Indian's, and there was neither anger nor defiance in them. They were livid with fear, not, apparently, of Paul, but of the thing he held behind his back.

"Another scalp!" Paul panted at last.

Eddie Badger nodded, drew his hand from behind him. Drops of blood fell to the ground like water from a slowly dripping faucet. Paul had seen that hair in a chaotic whirl on the head of an attractive farm girl.

"Joan Prescott!" Paul whispered.

"I didn't do it!" Eddie Badger burst out. "I swear I didn't! I woke up, found it beside me on my bed."

"Like the other scalp?"

"Yes."

"And like the other scalp you were planning to get rid of it?"

"Yes."

"Quite a coincidence, isn't it?" Paul said in a voice that bit.

The Indian looked up sharply. "You don't think—"

"What do you imagine I would think?"

"I swear—" Eddie Badger stopped, his voice breaking. He ran a hand over his face, appeared dazed. "Maybe I did it," he whispered. "I don't know. Maybe Chief Flying Hawk . . ."

Paul was peering at Eddie Badger. He could have been the painted Indian he had seen running toward the house. In the fifty minutes or so which had passed between then and now, he could have washed the paint off him. He had thought at the time that the Indian was bound for the Addams house. But he might have been returning instead from the Prescott farm which, he had been told, was less than a mile away.

"It's very convenient to blame an Indian chief who's been dead since the Revolution," Paul said.

"You don't understand," Eddie Barger mumbled. "Chief Flying Hawk took the scalps through me. His spirit entered into me while I slept, used my body. It's true that this afternoon I was in the car while Irene Blakely was being murdered. You pointed out how I could have slipped in and out without being seen. That gave me the first hint of what might have happened. I fell asleep in the car while I waited for Miss Addams. I slept for about ten minutes. When I awoke I had a frightful headache and for a reason I could not understand, I felt afraid. And then tonight, shortly after I'd gone to sleep, I awoke with the same headache, the same feeling of fear. I sat up, covered with cold sweat, and put on a light. I saw the scalp."

"I see," Paul sneered. "Chief Flying Hawk came along, booted your spirit out of your body, stepped in himself and used your body for a couple of minutes each time to do his dirty work."

"Yes," Eddie Badger said.

The simplicity with which Eddie Badger uttered that one word startled Paul. There was no guile in the Indian; he seemed incapable of deceit. Did he have a dual personality, lead a sort of Jekyll and Hyde existence—one part of him a civilized, educated man, the other part a primitive savage?

Far off a bell rang. Paul saw lights go on in the second story of the main house. Eddie Badger stood like a rock. The gruesome thing in his hand still dripped blood. He said: "I don't care what you do now. Maybe I ought to be killed."

A shudder ran through his frame. "Miss Adams will be next!"

More lights went on in the house. Paul saw a man's shape run toward the garage, heard the kick of a starter and then the sputter of a motor.

Paul grabbed Eddie Badger's bare shoulder. "What do you mean, Miss Addams will be next? You think that you—"

"I'd give my life for her. But when the spirit of Chief Flying Hawk takes possession of my body, my own spirit sleeps. Chief Flying Hawk has skipped a generation. He might have a reason. There were four of the youngest generation of the Addamses, the Morrisons and the Prescotts. Two died today. Claire and Warren Addams remain."

The car pulled out of the garage. Paul saw a woman run from the house to the car. Impulsively Paul wheeled and raced for the car. At all costs he had to be near Claire Addams. Maybe Eddie Badger was the murderer; maybe the spirit of Chief Flying Hawk; maybe somebody else. He could protect her best by being at her side.

The car had started to roll when Paul jumped on the running board. Claire and her father were in the front seat.

"Can I help?" Paul said.

Claire turned a drawn face to him on which horror had stamped harsh lines. "Joan Prescott . . . her mother just phoned. They found her near the house—scalped."

Paul rode the running board all the way to the Prescott farm. There wasn't anybody outside the house, which was odd, and inside the house were only Mrs. Prescott, Glen Tyson and the dead girl.

Joan Prescott's body had been carried up to a bedroom. A sheet covered it, but Paul seemed to see through the sheet, could picture vividly the appalling thing that lay beneath— an attractive, buxom girl, almost nude, her face a death-mask of horror, the top of her head hairless and hideously raw.

Glen Tyson sat at the head of the bed, his clasped hands between his knees, staring dry-eyed at the floor. Mrs. Prescott sat in another chair, weeping. Neither looked up when the three entered.

"How did it happen?" Judson Addams asked. "My God, if I get my hands on the murderer!"

Mrs. Prescott started to speak without moving, words gasping from her lips between sobs.

"After Glen left—just as I was about to go to bed—Joan said she was going to walk over to see Warren. She said . . . it was very important. I told her to wait until . . . morning or else to phone him. She said no, she had to see him personally at once. She was a strong-willed girl and . . . since my husband died I haven't been able to do anything with her, so she started out. I was worried on account of the terrible thing that happened to Irene Blakely . . . so I couldn't sleep. After a long time . . . I thought I heard a faint moan outside. I thought I'd . . . dreamed it at first, but it went on and on . . . and at last I went downstairs and I found her."

Her voice broke. Convulsive sobs wracked her frame.

"Where's everybody?" Judson Addams demanded. "Where are the farm hands?"

"They went out with the others," Mrs. Prescott sobbed. "I called the town, the constable, the doctor, everybody, after my men carried her in here. They came. After a while they left and I grew afraid with just Glen and myself here, so I phoned you.

"Left?" Claire asked in a tight voice. "Where did they go?"

Glen Tyson looked up at last. "To get that damned Indian of yours, of course. He did it. Who else but an Indian would do it? I would have gone along to pull the rope, by God, but I can't . . . I can't leave Joan."

"Oh, God, they're going to lynch Eddie Badger!" Claire cried. "It's that Hank Somerville who has it in for him. Dad, we must stop them!"

"They must have cut across the fields while we were coming here by the road," Addams said. "Let's go!"

They made the distance back in a couple of minutes. From the car they saw the flashlights, the huge mass of the mob. They tumbled out of the car and ran.

Paul found himself lagging behind Claire Addams and her father. Doubt slowed his legs. He had promised to say nothing about the scalp which Eddie Badger had found in the car; but that promise did not commit him to silence about every bloody scalp which he found in the Indian's possession.

But if he mentioned that second scalp now, he would only be adding fuel to the lynch spirit of the mob. And he was against any man being lynched under any circumstances; against any man being condemned without a fair trial.

Flashlights flickered on Eddie Badger's impassive face as he stood under an oak tree surrounded by a mob. A rope dangled from the lowest branch of the tree, swayed against the Indian's shoulder. He made no gesture to defend himself, uttered no plea of mercy. He did not seem to care.

But his wife, Mary Badger, was a wildcat, clawing and screaming and weeping. Two men held her at the edge of the mob, and they weren't having an easy time of it.

"What's going on here?" Judson Addams demanded.

The mob grew still. Eyes shifted uneasily. Out of the mob a man stepped—Hank Somerville.

"Sending him to where he won't go around killing and scalping girls," Somerville stated. There was a roar of assent.

Judson Addams pushed men aside until he stood next to Eddie Badger. "You can't do this. If you've no conscience, no shame, at least get off my property. You, Sam Johnston, and you Joe Hammer, you work for me. I order you to release this man."

The men whom Addams had named didn't seem to know what to do. One kicked a toe against a heel, the other shifted a shotgun from one arm to another and looked timorously at Somerville.

"He's your boss while you're working," Somerville said, "but you're not working now. You're human beings with the right to protect yourselves and the women of the community."

"If he's guilty, there's the law," Judson Addams argued.

"We're the law this minute," Somerville asserted. "Are we going to let him stop us, men?"

"No!" tore from a score of throats.

A hand shoved Judson Addams aside. Paul Shepard tensed, moved toward Claire's side. Something had happened to these men. A few hours ago they had been normal, law-abiding citizens. Now cruelty contorted their faces, the lust to kill glinted in their eyes, as if suddenly they had been converted into beasts.

Chapter 4: Encounter With Horror

JUDSON ADDAMS struck out against the man who had shoved him. A gnarled, brown hand grasped Claire's arm, and the next moment the owner of the hand found himself on the ground, knocked down by Paul's right fist. Another man pivoted, raised a rifle over Paul's head.

"Stop!"

It was a deep, authoritative voice, used to giving orders and having them instantly obeyed. All eyes turned toward the two men who were striding toward the mob. Paul recognized them as the two he had glimpsed in the passing car on the road that afternoon—Judge Morrison and his son-in-law, Raymond Blakely.

"Hank Somerville, who gave you the authority to do this?" Judge Morrison boomed.

"He murdered your daughter, Judge, and the Prescott girl."

"How do you know?"

"Well, he's an Indian and—"

"Fools!" the Judge roared. "Release that man at once!"

Nobody moved. Several of the men raised their guns threateningly. The madness to kill Eddie Badger was in them.

Then Raymond Blakely spoke. His voice was soft, musical, and he did not raise it. "Listen, men. Irene was my wife and I am more anxious than any of you that her murderer be brought to justice. But because she meant so much to me, I'll do all in my power to prevent the wrong man from being harmed. That is why I demand a fair trial by the official authorities for this man. Why, you haven't a scrap of real evidence against him. I'll say this: my father-in-law, Mr. and Miss Addams here, and myself know every one of you, and we'll see that you are punished to the fullest extent of the law, if you do not release him at once. And remember, what you plan to do here is murder."

The effect of his words was immediate. The men seemed to awaken from the spell which had gripped them. They looked from one to the other uncertainly, knowing that Raymond Blakely would keep his word and that tomorrow they would be hunted down by the forces of the law. One by one they slid into the shadows.

"Thank you, Raymond," Claire said.

Eddie Badger was holding his wife's trembling body in his arms. The experience seemed to have had no effect on him. Quietly he said: "Chief Flying Hawk killed her because she is a Morrison.

"You mean—" Raymond Blakely sputtered. "Why, man, that legend! I thought you Indians were civilized."

Eddie Badger shrugged, walked toward his house with his wife. The others walked toward the main house. Paul was left standing there alone. He began to move after them, then stopped. There was something important he had to tell them, about having come across Eddie Badger with the second scalp. But somehow he couldn't bring himself to do it. Blakely might lose his head, might in blind rage and grief kill the Indian right then and there.

Several minutes later Judge Morrison and Raymond Blakely left in their car. That was when Paul went to the house to seek out Claire Addams.

She was standing on the front porch, smoking a final cigarette before going up to bed, when Paul mounted the steps.

"You must have collected a great deal of interesting material out of our tragedies," she said with a touch of bitterness in her tone. "No doubt it will all go into your next book."

"Then you know?"

"Yes. Raymond Blakely told me. He thought he recognized you, but he wasn't sure. He heard you lecture once."

"Well, so I am a writer," Paul admitted. "That's no crime."

"It's a crime prying into other people's business," she snapped.

Whirling, she went into the house before Paul could say another word.

No doubt the experiences of the night had set her nerves on edge so that she was ready to pick a quarrel with anybody. In the morning he would explain to her in detail why he had concealed his identity.

Footsteps sounded behind him. The short, broad figure of Warren Addams came up the walk. He nodded abruptly to Paul, was about to go past him when Paul reached out a hand and stopped him.

"Joan Prescott was murdered," Paul told him.

"So I've heard."

"Did you hear that she was on the way to see you when she was killed?"

"No. Why would she want to do that?"

"I don't know. I thought you'd be interested."

"I'm not," Warren Addams said. "Good-night."

Paul walked away from the house, but not far. The danger to Claire, if she really were in danger, wasn't by any means over.

Paul continued standing guard near the house until his eyes began to droop with weariness. After a while he saw Warren Addams leave the house and walk in the direction of the garage.

Then for the second time that night Paul saw the naked Indian. He was running at right angles from the house on feet which made no sound in the grass. Moonlight glistened on the bright war-paint which covered his chest and face. A hunting knife was clutched in his right hand.

Paul cut across his path, was almost on him before the Indian, hearing Paul's shoes crunch the ground, swung around, the knife upraised. For a moment Paul hesitated before the deadly menace of that knife—then he dove in a football tackle which he had not used since college days.

Paul concentrated on the knife, grabbed the wrist which held it, twisted with both hands. The Indian's free hand drove short, chopping blows into Paul's face; but Paul held on until the hand opened and the knife dropped out.

One of the Indian's hands was on his throat. The other snaked up; strong fingers tightened. Too late Paul regretted that he had not cried out for help. Now he had all he could do to move, and breathing was becoming more difficult.

With all his strength he jabbed a knee into the pit of the Indian's stomach. The Indian grunted, his fingers loosened, and this time it was Paul who had him by the throat. The slippery naked body squirmed under him, thrashed desperately. The Indian was hideous in his war-paint. Paul strove to see through the paint, to distinguish the features, but a cloud had covered the moon and there was not enough light.

And there was not enough light to see the rock which the Indian's frantically thrashing arms had struck. The rock was mere inches from his head before Paul was aware of it. He tried to duck, his chin hit the Indian's forehead, and then it was as if his skull had suddenly split in two. He clung to the Indian's throat, fighting to retain consciousness.

The rock descended a second time, and Paul sank into a bottomless pit which was utterly black . . .

He had no idea how much time had passed when he opened his eyes. He lay where he had fallen, every nerve in his head throbbing with agony. The moon rode serenely in a sky which was now without a cloud. The Indian was gone, as was the knife.

Groggily he stood up, holding his temples to ease the pain. The first time he had seen the Indian that night, Joan Prescott had been killed. This time—God, was Claire safe?

The house was dark, silent. That could mean anything or nothing. Paul found himself running. He approached from the back of the house, turned around the side—and then he stopped, frozen!

Eddie Badger stood over a figure which lay sprawled on the ground.

Paul moved forward, suspense robbing him of breath. A gasp of relief poured from his throat as he saw that the body wore men's clothing. Thank God it wasn't Claire! Then his stomach turned. Not Claire, but Claire's brother!

An expression of utmost horror twisted the features of the dead face, bulged the open eyes from their sockets. Where his hair had been was raw flesh. The grass near the head was dyed red.

Eddie Badger turned slowly, faced Paul. His tall, straight body seemed to have suddenly shrunk, as if his bones were growing soft. He looked old and afraid.

"Another one!" Eddie Badger choked. "There's no way to fight the curse of Chief Flying Hawk. I didn't care if the mob killed me. I wanted to die. I thought if I died, Miss Addams would be safe."

"The man who did this was human," Paul said.

"His flesh and blood was human, but the spirit of Chief Flying Hawk had taken possession of him. I am that man. I did not go to sleep after the mob left. I was afraid. I thought if I remained awake, Chief Flying Hawk's spirit could not enter into me. So I walked and walked. Maybe for a while I slept as I walked. I do not know. Then I found myself here."

He raised his voice. "Call the police! Tell the mob! *Let them hang me!* Twice today you found me with scalps and now you find me with this body. I swear I am not guilty, but I have no defense."

"Stop raving like a hysterical woman," Paul snapped. "You didn't do it and Chief Flying Hawk's ghost didn't either. A short while ago I fought with the person who did. He knocked me out or I would have had him and would have saved Warren Addams' life, too."

"Then Chief Flying Hawk returned himself," Eddie Badger muttered.

"I tell you he was human."

Eddie Badger shook his head. "He could take that shape for his purpose."

"And also turn his eyes blue?" Paul said.

Eddie Badger straightened up. "What?"

"The so-called Indian I fought had blue eyes. A cloud covered the moon while we were fighting, but there was enough light for me to see his eyes. Chief Flying Hawk could hardly have had blue eyes."

"No," Eddie Badger said bewildered. "Indians don't have blue eyes."

"Which means that our Indian was not an Indian," Paul said.

Eddie Badger looked down at the corpse, clenched his fists. "I'll have to tell them in the house," he muttered.

Hurrying feet sounded on the stairs in the house. Judson Addams came around the side, Eddie Badger behind him.

"My God!" Judson Addams gasped as he went down on his knees beside the body of his son. He looked up with a face as grim as death. "Who did it? Warren never harmed a soul. He had no enemies."

Paul told him about his fight with the man disguised as an Indian. "Because the three people the murderer wanted to kill belonged to families cursed by Chief Flying Hawk, he hit upon this scheme to throw the blame either on the curse, or, if people didn't fall for that, on an Indian in the neighborhood."

Eddie Badger nodded. "That's why the scalps of the two women were placed so that they would be found near me. Luckily I found them first each time; otherwise the mob couldn't have been stopped from lynching me."

"The scalps near you?" Addams said. "What are you talking about?"

Eddie Badger explained. "I was to be the scapegoat. With me lynched, the police would never look for the real murderer. They would think it was me." He paused; his eyes opened wide. "Hank Somerville! He hates me. Twice he tried to get the mob to lynch me. He has blue eyes."

Judson Addams stood up. "I'm phoning the police. Then I'm going to Oak Valley."

"I'll go with you," Eddie Badger said.

Paul watched them go into the house. There was something grim and deadly in the quiet manner in which they had spoken and in which they now moved which was as terrible and unreasoning as the fury of the lynch mob had been. They were going to Oak Valley for Hank Somerville and he could expect as much mercy and justice at their hands as Eddie Badger had from the mob.

A cry as from a hurt animal came from the house. Paul pounded through the front door, up a flight of stairs to the second floor. Judson Addams and Eddie Badger stood at the head of the stairs.

"She's gone," Addams blurted. "Claire's not in her room. My God, if a hair of her head is touched, I'll—"

Paul's heart contracted. Claire completed the pattern of vengeance against the youngest generation of the families cursed by Chief Flying Hawk. But he could swear that it wasn't an Indian with whom he had fought. Then what in the name of heaven was the answer?

Within five minutes the farm was roused. Hired hands went over the grounds with lanterns and flashlights. Judson Addams sat at the telephone making a dozen calls.

Paul joined the searchers. It wasn't easy to push aside the darkness with the beam of a flashlight, expecting any moment to come across the dead, scalpless body of Claire Addams. "I love her," Paul sobbed to himself. "I love her and I'll never see her alive again."

Chapter 5: Madman's Vengeance

PAUL SHEPARD raced back to the house. Judson Addams sat on the porch, a rifle on his knee. He had been searching with the others, but now he seemed to have lost the energy or ability to move.

"You're sure Claire went up to bed when you did?" Paul asked.

Addams nodded wearily. "I said goodnight to her at the door of her bedroom."

"She couldn't have been taken out of the house forcibly," Paul thought aloud. "You would have been sure to have heard. She must have gone out of her free will. Somebody must have called her from beneath her window, urged her to come down; somebody whose voice she could recognize at once and whom she trusted."

Addams fingered the trigger of his rifle. "Yes. Hank Somerville."

"Not Somerville," Paul said. "He'd been on the post office porch fifteen minutes before Irene Blakely appeared in the street, scalped. It was obvious that she'd been scalped only a couple of minutes before. Somerville might be the murderer's accomplice, but I don't think so. Eddie Badger was right in saying that the murderer would want him lynched so that the police would take for granted that he was the criminal—but it would spoil the whole plan if Eddie were lynched before all intended victims were slain. Indeed, the murderer would fight against Eddie being lynched until all the murders were completed. He'd—Say!"

Suddenly the whole diabolical picture became clear, save for one missing section. He opened his mouth to question Addams, closed it again and dashed down the porch steps. Addams hadn't been listening. He was gazing abstractedly into space, thinking of the horrible fate his daughter might have met or was about to meet.

Mary Badger was in her bedroom, sitting on the edge of her bed and weeping bitterly when Paul burst in.

"Look, you do the housework for the Addamses," Paul blurted. "That means you know about everything that goes on. Do you know anybody who had cause to hate Irene Blakely, Joan Prescott, and Claire and Warren Addams?"

She looked up dully. "Hate? Nobody hates them. Everybody loves Claire."

"Loves?" he said. He thought about that. "Does Claire love anybody?"

"Not yet."

"And Warren?"

"I don't know. They all used to play together when they were young, Claire and Warren and Irene and Joan. When they grew older, Warren began to go out with Joan Prescott. I used to see them walking together at night toward the fort."

"The fort?"

"That's a place they built when they were young. There's a clearing surrounded by oak trees about half a mile directly behind the Prescott farm. The ground is strewn with rocks, and Warren and the three girls built what they called the fort. It's just a rock enclosure without any ceiling. Well, Warren used to go there with Joan Prescott and later with Irene Morrison."

"I see," Paul said. "Why did he break with the girls?"

"He stopped going with Joan because of Irene. Everybody expected Warren and Irene to get married. Then a little over a year ago they had a fight about something and a few weeks later Irene married Raymond Blakely. Then Warren started going around with Joan again, but last month Joan became engaged to Glen Tyson."

"Blakely was crazy over his wife, wasn't he?"

"Everybody noticed it," Mary Badger said. "The way he looked at her when they were together! I always said it's not good for one person to love another so much. What will happen to him now?"

"Thanks, Mary."

Paul was out of the house, running. After a while breath left him and he slowed down to a walk. He had only a general idea of the direction and he had no light; but most of the way was over meadows.

When his breath returned, he again broke into a run. Please God, don't let him be too late! He should have called others, he should have fetched a weapon; but there hadn't been time. He would have had to explain to Judson Addams, and every second counted.

A gun barked. Paul halted abruptly, his heart turning over within him. Then once again he was running at top speed. He was in an oak wood now, clumsily breaking through the underbrush.

He burst into a clearing, pulled up short before a stone wall. It was the fort, crudely built by piling rocks one on top of the other to the height of three or four feet. In the exact center of the stone enclosure was a single tree—and to it Claire Addams was tied!

The moonlight clearly revealed her horror-stricken face as she stared at something at her feet. And the moonlight showed something else—the Indian with whom Paul had fought standing several feet away from him and calmly pointing an automatic at Paul's heart.

"I'm afraid you're a better writer than a woodsman," the pseudo-Indian said. "The way you went crashing through the woods was a perfect announcement of your arrival. This way, please."

Paul stepped through the entrance into the stone enclosure, the man with the gun right behind him. Claire's eyes were wide with horror as she stood with her back against the tree, her arms fastened behind her around the trunk.

Now he saw at what Claire had been staring. Eddie Badger's motionless body lay at her feet.

"I shot him down in cold blood," Paul's captor gloated. "Just as I shall shoot you down."

Paul turned slowly, leaned with his back against the wall, facing the pseudo-Indian. Death was a matter of minutes or seconds. There was one chance in a thousand that somebody else had heard the shot and was coming to investigate. If he could stave off the bullet as long as possible, there was that chance, otherwise none at all.

"It's clear, of course," Paul said. "In the morning three dead bodies will be found here. Claire Addams will be scalped like the others, after having been outraged. Eddie Badger and myself will have been shot. You will be the one to find us, and your story will be that you and I, while searching for Claire, came upon Eddie Badger and Claire's scalped corpse. In the struggle I was shot by Eddie Badger and then you shot him. Perfect."

"Right!" his captor agreed. "You're clever, but not clever enough to get out of this."

The gun raised. Paul tensed, ready to leap, although he knew there wasn't a chance.

He said. "Even cleverer than you think, Raymond Blakely."

His captor shrugged. "Penetrating my disguise isn't an ac- complishment. I knew this Indian get-up and paint wouldn't fool anybody who saw me at close hand."

"That's because you didn't intend that anybody get a good look at you," Paul told him. "You assumed that disguise only so that if anybody caught sight of you near the scene of the crimes before or after they were committed, it would heighten the impression you wanted to spread—either that Chief Flying Hawk had returned from the dead or that Eddie Badger had dressed like his ancestors when he went mad and ran amok, killing and scalping. At night you would be hard to recognize. It fooled me because of the darkness and because I'd only glimpsed you twice without the disguise."

"It doesn't matter," Raymond Blakely muttered. "Neither you nor Claire will be able to tell."

Again he raised the gun.

"It will matter to you," Paul said desperately. "I left word that you are the murderer. They are looking for you even now."

The gun wavered. "You lie!"

Of course it was a lie, a desperate lie. But it needn't have been. Fool for not having told what he knew before he had left to find Claire!

"Your crimes were too logical, formed too perfect a design," Paul said. "When I attained possession of all the facts, the design filled out. Would I have come straight to this place otherwise?"

The muscles of Raymond Blakely's face worked with indecision. Paul eyed the gun, watching it droop. If he were five feet closer . . .

"The broad outline of the design was clear from the first," Paul went on. "The murderer was out to slay a number of people and pin the crime on Eddie Badger. It was important that Eddie remain alive until the last crime. When that occurred to me while I was talking to Judson Addams a short while ago, I recalled that it was you who had gone out of your way to save Eddie from the mob. I found that odd, because if you really loved your wife as much as you were supposed to, you either wouldn't have bothered about the lynch mob, like Glen Tyson, or else you would have been with the mob.

"Then another thing. Claire was attracted down from her bedroom by a voice she knew and trusted. That didn't exclude others, but it certainly included you.

"But why, if it were you, would you murder the woman you loved so much, and the woman whose death would deprive you of rather easy living? Mary Badger gave me the answer, although she didn't know it. Warren Addams and

Irene were once in love with each other. You were probably jealous of your wife; men who love their wives as much as you did generally are. Irene married you on the rebound after a quarrel with Warren. She probably still loved him. After a year of married life with you, she again continued to see Warren. Somehow or other you found out about it. And you went blood-mad with hatred. Violent love can turn to violent hatred!"

"Stay where you are!" Raymond Blakely snapped. Paul had been moving forward almost perceptibly. Paul stopped, went on talking.

"First you murdered Irene, then you intended to murder Warren and pin both crimes on Eddie Badger. But two unforeseen complications came up. First, Joan Prescott must have suspected you and set out to warn Warren. You discovered that and killed her. Then the lynch mob was about to get rid of your scapegoat before you had a chance to kill Warren. Warren probably had gone away somewhere to nurse his grief, so you had to mark time for a few hours.

"After you killed Warren, your hatred possessed you to such an extent that you decided on your final stroke of vengeance. Your mad mind thought of Claire sleeping in her room, thought of how her brother had taken your wife from you, and that your vengeance would be complete if you were to take his sister. So you lured her down, brought her here, tied her to this tree while you went to get Eddie Badger, who was roaming the woods looking for her. You brought him here, shot him, and your plan would—"

Paul leaped while the words were still pouring from his lips. The gun spoke in instant later.

But another form had moved even before that. Eddie Badger! He seemed to skim over the ground, grasping Raymond Blakely's ankle; and the murderer stumbled. The shot went wild.

Before he could shoot again, Paul was on him, and for the second time that night the two men were locked in desperate struggle. Paul went for the gun hand, strained to keep the muzzle away from him.

Suddenly Raymond Blakely went limp. A hideous gurgling sound trembled on his lips, died in his throat, and he slumped to the ground, dead. Eddie Badger's knife protruded from his left side.

The Indian was sitting on the ground, holding his head in his hands. He looked up smiling.

"His bullet only creased my skull. It knocked me out and he thought I was dead. Luckily I recovered in time. I've got the most hellish headache."

Paul untied Claire, tore the gag from her mouth. She fell into his arms, sobbing.

"Still think it's a crime to pry into other people's business?" Paul asked.

She pulled his face down to hers. "I'm glad you pried into mine. I want you to keep on doing it."

"Forever?" he said.

She kissed him.

RAMBLE HOUSE's

HARRY STEPHEN KEELER WEBWORK MYSTERIES

(RH) indicates the title is available ONLY in the RAMBLE HOUSE edition

The Ace of Spades Murder
The Affair of the Bottled Deuce (RH)
The Amazing Web
The Barking Clock
Behind That Mask
The Book with the Orange Leaves
The Bottle with the Green Wax Seal
The Box from Japan
The Case of the Canny Killer
The Case of the Crazy Corpse (RH)
The Case of the Flying Hands (RH)
The Case of the Ivory Arrow
The Case of the Jeweled Ragpicker
The Case of the Lavender Gripsack
The Case of the Mysterious Moll
The Case of the 16 Beans
The Case of the Transparent Nude (RH)
The Case of the Transposed Legs
The Case of the Two-Headed Idiot (RH)
The Case of the Two Strange Ladies
The Circus Stealers (RH)
Cleopatra's Tears
A Copy of Beowulf (RH)
The Crimson Cube (RH)
The Face of the Man From Saturn
Find the Clock
The Five Silver Buddhas
The 4th King
The Gallows Waits, My Lord! (RH)
The Green Jade Hand
Finger! Finger!
Hangman's Nights (RH)
I, Chameleon (RH)
I Killed Lincoln at 10:13! (RH)
The Iron Ring
The Man Who Changed His Skin (RH)
The Man with the Crimson Box
The Man with the Magic Eardrums
The Man with the Wooden Spectacles
The Marceau Case
The Matilda Hunter Murder

The Monocled Monster
The Murder of London Lew
The Murdered Mathematician
The Mysterious Card (RH)
The Mysterious Ivory Ball of Wong Shing Li (RH)
The Mystery of the Fiddling Cracksman
The Peacock Fan
The Photo of Lady X (RH)
The Portrait of Jirjohn Cobb
Report on Vanessa Hewstone (RH)
Riddle of the Travelling Skull
Riddle of the Wooden Parrakeet (RH)
The Scarlet Mummy (RH)
The Search for X-Y-Z
The Sharkskin Book
Sing Sing Nights
The Six From Nowhere (RH)
The Skull of the Waltzing Clown
The Spectacles of Mr. Cagliostro
Stand By—London Calling!
The Steeltown Strangler
The Stolen Gravestone (RH)
Strange Journey (RH)
The Strange Will
The Straw Hat Murders (RH)
The Street of 1000 Eyes (RH)
Thieves' Nights
Three Novellos (RH)
The Tiger Snake
The Trap (RH)
Vagabond Nights (Defrauded Yeggman)
Vagabond Nights 2 (10 Hours)
The Vanishing Gold Truck
The Voice of the Seven Sparrows
The Washington Square Enigma
When Thief Meets Thief
The White Circle (RH)
The Wonderful Scheme of Mr. Christopher Thorne
X. Jones—of Scotland Yard
Y. Cheung, Business Detective

Keeler Related Works

A To Izzard: A Harry Stephen Keeler Companion by Fender Tucker · Articles and stories about Harry, by Harry, and in his style. Included is a compleat bibliography.

Wild About Harry: Reviews of Keeler Novels — Edited by Richard Polt & Fender Tucker — 22 reviews of works by Harry Stephen Keeler from *Keeler News*. A perfect introduction to the author.

The Keeler Keyhole Collection: Annotated newsletter rants from Harry Stephen Keeler, edited by Francis M. Nevins. Over 400 pages of incredibly personal Keeleriana.

Fakealoo — Pastiches of the style of Harry Stephen Keeler by selected demented members of the HSK Society. Updated every year with the new winner.

Strands of the Web: Short Stories of Harry Stephen Keeler — 29 stories, just about all that Keeler wrote, are edited and introduced by Fred Cleaver.

RAMBLE HOUSE's LOON SANCTUARY

A Clear Path to Cross — Sharon Knowles short mystery stories by Ed Lynskey.

A Corpse Walks in Brooklyn and Other Stories — Volume 5 in the Day Keene in the Detective Pulps series.

A Jimmy Starr Omnibus — Three 40s novels by Jimmy Starr.

A Niche in Time and Other Stories — Classic SF by William F. Temple

A Roland Daniel Double: The Signal and The Return of Wu Fang — Classic thrillers from the 30s.

A Shot Rang Out — Three decades of reviews and articles by today's Anthony Boucher, Jon Breen. An essential book for any mystery lover's library.

A Smell of Smoke — A 1951 English countryside thriller by Miles Burton.

A Snark Selection — Lewis Carroll's *The Hunting of the Snark* with two Snarkian chapters by Harry Stephen Keeler — Illustrated by Gavin L. O'Keefe.

A Young Man's Heart — A forgotten early classic by Cornell Woolrich.

Alexander Laing Novels — *The Motives of Nicholas Holtz* and *Dr. Scarlett*, stories of medical mayhem and intrigue from the 30s.

An Angel in the Street — Modern hardboiled noir by Peter Genovese.

Automaton — Brilliant treatise on robotics: 1928-style! By H. Stafford Hatfield.

Away From the Here and Now — Clare Winger Harris stories, collected by Richard A. Lupoff

Beast or Man? — A 1930 novel of racism and horror by Sean M'Guire. Introduced by John Pelan.

Black Beadle — A 1939 thriller by E.C.R. Lorac.

Black Hogan Strikes Again — Australia's Peter Renwick pens a tale of the 30s outback.

Black River Falls — Suspense from the master, Ed Gorman.

Blondy's Boy Friend — A snappy 1930 story by Philip Wylie, writing as Leatrice Homesley.

Blood in a Snap — The *Finnegan's Wake* of the 21st century, by Jim Weiler.

Blood Moon — The first of the Robert Payne series by Ed Gorman.

Bogart '48 — Hollywood action with Bogie by John Stanley and Kenn Davis

Calling Lou Largo! — Two Lou Largo novels by William Ard.

Cornucopia of Crime — Francis M. Nevins assembled this huge collection of his writings about crime literature and the people who write it. Essential for any serious mystery library.

Corpse Without Flesh — Strange novel of forensics by George Bruce

Crimson Clown Novels — By Johnston McCulley, author of the Zorro novels, *The Crimson Clown* and *The Crimson Clown Again*.

Dago Red — 22 tales of dark suspense by Bill Pronzini.

Dark Sanctuary — Weird Menace story by H. B. Gregory

David Hume Novels — *Corpses Never Argue, Cemetery First Stop, Make Way for the Mourners, Eternity Here I Come*. 1930s British hardboiled fiction with an attitude.

Dead Man Talks Too Much — Hollywood boozer by Weed Dickenson.

Death Leaves No Card — One of the most unusual murdered-in-the-tub mysteries you'll ever read. By Miles Burton.

Death March of the Dancing Dolls and Other Stories — Volume Three in the Day Keene in the Detective Pulps series. Introduced by Bill Crider.

Deep Space and other Stories — A collection of SF gems by Richard A. Lupoff.

Detective Duff Unravels It — Episodic mysteries by Harvey O'Higgins.

Diabolic Candelabra — Classic 30s mystery by E.R. Punshon

Dictator's Way — Another D.S. Bobby Owen mystery from E.R. Punshon

Dime Novels: Ramble House's 10-Cent Books — *Knife in the Dark* by Robert Leslie Bellem, *Hot Lead* and *Song of Death* by Ed Earl Repp, *A Hashish House in New York* by H.H. Kane, and five more.

Doctor Arnoldi — Tiffany Thayer's story of the death of death.

Don Diablo: Book of a Lost Film — Two-volume treatment of a western by Paul Landres, with diagrams. Intro by Francis M. Nevins.

Dope and Swastikas — Two strange novels from 1922 by Edmund Snell

Dope Tales #1 — Two dope-riddled classics; *Dope Runners* by Gerald Grantham and *Death Takes the Joystick* by Phillip Condé.

Dope Tales #2 — Two more narco-classics; *The Invisible Hand* by Rex Dark and *The Smokers of Hashish* by Norman Berrow.

Dope Tales #3 — Two enchanting novels of opium by the master, Sax Rohmer. *Dope* and *The Yellow Claw*.

Double Hot — Two 60s softcore sex novels by Morris Hershman.

Double Sex — Yet two more panting thrillers from Morris Hershman.

Dr. Odin — Douglas Newton's 1933 racial potboiler comes back to life.

Evangelical Cockroach — Jack Woodford writes about writing.

Evidence in Blue — 1938 mystery by E. Charles Vivian.

Fatal Accident — Murder by automobile, a 1936 mystery by Cecil M. Wills.

Fighting Mad — Todd Robbins' 1922 novel about boxing and life

Finger-prints Never Lie — A 1939 classic detective novel by John G. Brandon.

Freaks and Fantasies — Eerie tales by Tod Robbins, collaborator of Tod Browning on the film FREAKS.

Gadsby — A lipogram (a novel without the letter E). Ernest Vincent Wright's last work, published in 1939 right before his death.

Gelett Burgess Novels — *The Master of Mysteries, The White Cat, Two O'Clock Courage, Ladies in Boxes, Find the Woman, The Heart Line, The Picaroons* and *Lady Mechante*. Recently added is A Gelett Burgess Sampler, edited by Alfred Jan. All are introduced by Richard A. Lupoff.

Geronimo — S. M. Barrett's 1905 autobiography of a noble American.

Hake Talbot Novels — *Rim of the Pit, The Hangman's Handyman.* Classic locked room mysteries, with mapback covers by Gavin O'Keefe.

Hands Out of Hell and Other Stories — John H. Knox's eerie hallucinations

Hell is a City — William Ard's masterpiece.

Hollywood Dreams — A novel of Tinsel Town and the Depression by Richard O'Brien.

Hostesses in Hell and Other Stories — Russell Gray's most graphic stories

House of the Restless Dead — Strange and ominous tales by Hugh B. Cave

I Stole $16,000,000 — A true story by cracksman Herbert E. Wilson.

Inclination to Murder — 1966 thriller by New Zealand's Harriet Hunter.

Invaders from the Dark — Classic werewolf tale from Greye La Spina.

J. Poindexter, Colored — Classic satirical black novel by Irvin S. Cobb.

Jack Mann Novels — Strange murder in the English countryside. *Gees' First Case, Nightmare Farm, Grey Shapes, The Ninth Life, The Glass Too Many, Her Ways Are Death, The Kleinert Case* and *Maker of Shadows*.

Jake Hardy — A lusty western tale from Wesley Tallant.

Jim Harmon Double Novels — *Vixen Hollow/Celluloid Scandal, The Man Who Made Maniacs/Silent Siren, Ape Rape/Wanton Witch, Sex Burns Like Fire/Twist Session, Sudden Lust/Passion Strip, Sin Unlimited/Harlot Master, Twilight Girls/Sex Institution*. Written in the early 60s and never reprinted until now.

Joel Townsley Rogers Novels and Short Stories — By the author of *The Red Right Hand: Once In a Red Moon, Lady With the Dice, The Stopped Clock, Never Leave My Bed.* Also two short story collections: *Night of Horror* and *Killing Time*.

John Carstairs, Space Detective — Arboreal Sci-fi by Frank Belknap Long

Joseph Shallit Novels — *The Case of the Billion Dollar Body, Lady Don't Die on My Doorstep, Kiss the Killer, Yell Bloody Murder, Take Your Last Look.* One of America's best 50's authors and a favorite of author Bill Pronzini.

Keller Memento — 45 short stories of the amazing and weird by Dr. David Keller.

Killer's Caress — Cary Moran's 1936 hardboiled thriller.

Lady of the Yellow Death and Other Stories — More stories by Wyatt Blassingame.

League of the Grateful Dead and Other Stories — Volume One in the Day Keene in the Detective Pulps series.

Library of Death — Ghastly tale by Ronald S. L. Harding, introduced by John Pelan

Malcolm Jameson Novels and Short Stories — *Astonishing! Astounding!, Tarnished Bomb, The Alien Envoy and Other Stories* and *The Chariots of San Fernando and Other Stories.* All introduced and edited by John Pelan or Richard A. Lupoff.

Man Out of Hell and Other Stories — Volume II of the John H. Knox weird pulps collection.

Marblehead: A Novel of H.P. Lovecraft — A long-lost masterpiece from Richard A. Lupoff. This is the "director's cut", the long version that has never been published before.

Mark of the Laughing Death and Other Stories — Shockers from the pulps by Francis James, introduced by John Pelan.

Master of Souls — Mark Hansom's 1937 shocker is introduced by weirdologist John Pelan.

Max Afford Novels — *Owl of Darkness, Death's Mannikins, Blood on His Hands, The Dead Are Blind, The Sheep and the Wolves, Sinners in Paradise* and *Two Locked Room Mysteries and a Ripping Yarn* by one of Australia's finest mystery novelists.

Money Brawl — Two books about the writing business by Jack Woodford and H. Bedford-Jones. Introduced by Richard A. Lupoff.

More Secret Adventures of Sherlock Holmes — Gary Lovisi's second collection of tales about the unknown sides of the great detective.

Muddled Mind: Complete Works of Ed Wood, Jr. — David Hayes and Hayden Davis deconstruct the life and works of the mad, but canny, genius.

Murder among the Nudists — A mystery from 1934 by Peter Hunt, featuring a naked Detective-Inspector going undercover in a nudist colony.

Murder in Black and White — 1931 classic tennis whodunit by Evelyn Elder.

Murder in Shawnee — Two novels of the Alleghenies by John Douglas: *Shawnee Alley Fire* and *Haunts*.

Murder in Silk — A 1937 Yellow Peril novel of the silk trade by Ralph Trevor.

My Deadly Angel — 1955 Cold War drama by John Chelton.

My First Time: The One Experience You Never Forget — Michael Birchwood — 64 true first-person narratives of how they lost it.

Mysterious Martin, the Master of Murder — Two versions of a strange 1912 novel by Tod Robbins about a man who writes books that can kill.

Norman Berrow Novels — *The Bishop's Sword, Ghost House, Don't Go Out After Dark, Claws of the Cougar, The Smokers of Hashish, The Secret Dancer, Don't Jump Mr. Boland!, The Footprints of Satan, Fingers for Ransom, The Three Tiers of Fantasy, The Spaniard's Thumb, The Eleventh Plague, Words Have Wings, One Thrilling Night, The Lady's in Danger, It Howls at Night, The Terror in the Fog, Oil Under the Window, Murder in the Melody, The Singing Room.* This is the complete Norman Berrow library of locked-room mysteries, several of which are masterpieces.

Old Faithful and Other Stories — SF classic tales by Raymond Z. Gallun.

Old Times' Sake — Short stories by James Reasoner from Mike Shayne Magazine.

One Dreadful Night — A classic mystery by Ronald S. L. Harding.

Pair O' Jacks — A mystery novel and a diatribe about publishing by Jack Woodford.

Perfect .38 — Two early Timothy Dane novels by William Ard. More to come.

Prince Pax — Devilish intrigue by George Sylvester Viereck and Philip Eldridge.

Prose Bowl — Futuristic satire of a world where hack writing has replaced football as our national obsession, by Bill Pronzini and Barry N. Malzberg.

Red Light — The history of legal prostitution in Shreveport Louisiana by Eric Brock. Includes wonderful photos of the houses and the ladies.

Researching American-Made Toy Soldiers — A 276-page collection of a lifetime of articles by toy soldier expert Richard O'Brien.

Reunion in Hell — Volume One of the John H. Knox series of weird stories from the pulps. Introduced by horror expert John Pelan.

Ripped from the Headlines! — The Jack the Ripper story as told in the newspaper articles in the *New York* and *London Times*.

Rough Cut & New, Improved Murder — Ed Gorman's first two novels.

R.R. Ryan Novels — Freak Museum and The Subjugated Beast, two horror classics.

Ruby of a Thousand Dreams — The villain Wu Fang returns in this Roland Daniel novel.

Ruled By Radio — 1925 futuristic novel by Robert L. Hadfield & Frank E. Farncombe.

Rupert Penny Novels — *Policeman's Holiday, Policeman's Evidence, Lucky Policeman, Policeman in Armour, Sealed Room Murder, Sweet Poison, The Talkative Policeman, She had to Have Gas* and *Cut and Run* (by Martin Tanner.) Rupert Penny is the pseudonym of Australian Charles Thornett, a master of the locked room, impossible crime plot.

Sacred Locomotive Flies — Richard A. Lupoff's psychedelic SF story.

Sam — Early gay novel by Lonnie Coleman.

Sand's Game — Spectacular hard-boiled noir from Ennis Willie, edited by Lynn Myers and Stephen Mertz, with contributions from Max Allan Collins, Bill Crider, Wayne Dundee, Bill Pronzini, Gary Lovisi and James Reasoner.

Sand's War — More violent fiction from the typewriter of Ennis Willie

Satan's Den Exposed — True crime in Truth or Consequences New Mexico — Award-winning journalism by the *Desert Journal*.

Satans of Saturn — Novellas from the pulps by Otis Adelbert Kline and E. H. Price

Satan's Sin House and Other Stories — Horrific gore by Wayne Rogers

Secrets of a Teenage Superhero — Graphic lit by Jonathan Sweet

Sex Slave — Potboiler of lust in the days of Cleopatra by Dion Leclerq, 1966.

Sideslip — 1968 SF masterpiece by Ted White and Dave Van Arnam.

Slammer Days — Two full-length prison memoirs: *Men into Beasts* (1952) by George Sylvester Viereck and *Home Away From Home* (1962) by Jack Woodford.

Slippery Staircase — 1930s whodunit from E.C.R. Lorac

Sorcerer's Chessmen — John Pelan introduces this 1939 classic by Mark Hansom.

Star Griffin — Michael Kurland's 1987 masterpiece of SF drollery is back.

Stakeout on Millennium Drive — Award-winning Indianapolis Noir by Ian Woollen.

Strands of the Web: Short Stories of Harry Stephen Keeler — Edited and Introduced by Fred Cleaver.

Summer Camp for Corpses and Other Stories — Weird Menace tales from Arthur Leo Zagat; introduced by John Pelan.

Suzy — A collection of comic strips by Richard O'Brien and Bob Vojtko from 1970.

Tales of the Macabre and Ordinary — Modern twisted horror by Chris Mikul, author of the *Bizarrism* series.

Tales of Terror and Torment #1 — John Pelan selects and introduces this sampler of weird menace tales from the pulps.

Tenebrae — Ernest G. Henham's 1898 horror tale brought back.

The Amorous Intrigues & Adventures of Aaron Burr — by Anonymous. Hot historical action about the man who almost became Emperor of Mexico.

The Anthony Boucher Chronicles — edited by Francis M. Nevins. Book reviews by Anthony Boucher written for the *San Francisco Chronicle,* 1942 – 1947. Essential and fascinating reading by the best book reviewer there ever was.

The Barclay Catalogs — Two essential books about toy soldier collecting by Richard O'Brien

The Basil Wells Omnibus — A collection of Wells' stories by Richard A. Lupoff

The Beautiful Dead and Other Stories — Dreadful tales from Donald Dale

The Best of 10-Story Book — edited by Chris Mikul, over 35 stories from the literary magazine Harry Stephen Keeler edited.

The Black Dark Murders — Vintage 50s college murder yarn by Milt Ozaki, writing as Robert O. Saber.

The Book of Time — The classic novel by H.G. Wells is joined by sequels by Wells himself and three stories by Richard A. Lupoff. Illustrated by Gavin L. O'Keefe.

The Case in the Clinic — One of E.C.R. Lorac's finest.

The Strange Case of the Antlered Man — A mystery of superstition by Edwy Searles Brooks.

The Case of the Bearded Bride — #4 in the Day Keene in the Detective Pulps series

The Case of the Little Green Men — Mack Reynolds wrote this love song to sci-fi fans back in 1951 and it's now back in print.

The Case of the Withered Hand — 1936 potboiler by John G. Brandon.

The Charlie Chaplin Murder Mystery — A 2004 tribute by noted film scholar, Wes D. Gehring.

The Chinese Jar Mystery — Murder in the manor by John Stephen Strange, 1934.

The Cloudbuilders and Other Stories — SF tales from Colin Kapp.

The Compleat Calhoon — All of Fender Tucker's works: Includes *Totah Six-Pack, Weed, Women and Song* and *Tales from the Tower,* plus a CD of all of his songs.

The Compleat Ova Hamlet — Parodies of SF authors by Richard A. Lupoff. This is a brand new edition with more stories and more illustrations by Trina Robbins.

The Shadow on the House — Mark Hansom's 1934 masterpiece of horror is introduced by John Pelan.

The Sign of the Scorpion — A 1935 Edmund Snell tale of oriental evil.

The Singular Problem of the Stygian House-Boat — Two classic tales by John Kendrick Bangs about the denizens of Hades.

The Smiling Corpse — Philip Wylie and Bernard Bergman's odd 1935 novel.

The Spider: Satan's Murder Machines — A thesis about Iron Man

The Stench of Death: An Odoriferous Omnibus by Jack Moskovitz — Two complete novels and two novellas from 60's sleaze author, Jack Moskovitz.

The Story Writer and Other Stories — Classic SF from Richard Wilson

The Strange Case of the Antlered Man — 1935 dementia from Edwy Searles Brooks

The Strange Thirteen — Richard B. Gamon's odd stories about Raj India.

The Technique of the Mystery Story — Carolyn Wells' tips about writing.

The Threat of Nostalgia — A collection of his most obscure stories by Jon Breen

The Time Armada — Fox B. Holden's 1953 SF gem.

The Tongueless Horror and Other Stories — Volume One of the series of short stories from the weird pulps by Wyatt Blassingame.

The Town from Planet Five — From Richard Wilson, two SF classics, *And Then the Town Took Off* and *The Girls from Planet 5*

The Tracer of Lost Persons — From 1906, an episodic novel that became a hit radio series in the 30s. Introduced by Richard A. Lupoff.

The Trail of the Cloven Hoof — Diabolical horror from 1935 by Arlton Eadie. Introduced by John Pelan.

The Triune Man — Mindscrambling science fiction from Richard A. Lupoff.

The Unholy Goddess and Other Stories — Wyatt Blassingame's first DTP compilation

The Universal Holmes — Richard A. Lupoff's 2007 collection of five Holmesian pastiches and a recipe for giant rat stew.

The Werewolf vs the Vampire Woman — Hard to believe ultraviolence by either Arthur M. Scarm or Arthur M. Scram.

The Whistling Ancestors — A 1936 classic of weirdness by Richard E. Goddard and introduced by John Pelan.

The White Owl — A vintage thriller from Edmund Snell

The White Peril in the Far East — Sidney Lewis Gulick's 1905 indictment of the West and assurance that Japan would never attack the U.S.

The Wizard of Berner's Abbey — A 1935 horror gem written by Mark Hansom and introduced by John Pelan.

The Wonderful Wizard of Oz — by L. Frank Baum and illustrated by Gavin L. O'Keefe

Through the Looking Glass — Lewis Carroll wrote it; Gavin L. O'Keefe illustrated it.

Time Line — Ramble House artist Gavin O'Keefe selects his most evocative art inspired by the twisted literature he reads and designs.

Tiresias — Psychotic modern horror novel by Jonathan M. Sweet.

Tortures and Towers — Two novellas of terror by Dexter Dayle.

Totah Six-Pack — Fender Tucker's six tales about Farmington in one sleek volume.

Tree of Life, Book of Death — Grania Davis' book of her life.

Triple Quest — An arty mystery from the 30s by E.R. Punshon.

Trail of the Spirit Warrior — Roger Haley's saga of life in the Indian Territories.

Two Kinds of Bad — Two 50s novels by William Ard about Danny Fontaine

Two Suns of Morcali and Other Stories — Evelyn E. Smith's SF tour-de-force

Ultra-Boiled — 23 gut-wrenching tales by our Man in Brooklyn, Gary Lovisi.

Up Front From Behind — A 2011 satire of Wall Street by James B. Kobak.

Victims & Villains — Intriguing Sherlockiana from Derham Groves.

Wade Wright Novels — *Echo of Fear, Death At Nostalgia Street, It Leads to Murder* and *Shadows' Edge*, a double book featuring *Shadows Don't Bleed* and *The Sharp Edge*.

Walter S. Masterman Novels — *The Green Toad, The Flying Beast, The Yellow Mistletoe, The Wrong Verdict, The Perjured Alibi, The Border Line, The Bloodhounds Bay, The Curse of Cantire* and *The Baddington Horror*. Masterman wrote horror and mystery, some introduced by John Pelan.

We Are the Dead and Other Stories — Volume Two in the Day Keene in the Detective Pulps series, introduced by Ed Gorman. When done, there may be 11 in the series.

Welsh Rarebit Tales — Charming stories from 1902 by Harle Oren Cummins
West Texas War and Other Western Stories — by Gary Lovisi.
What If? Volume 1, 2 and 3 — Richard A. Lupoff introduces three decades worth of SF short stories that should have won a Hugo, but didn't.
When the Batman Thirsts and Other Stories — Weird tales from Frederick C. Davis.
Whip Dodge: Man Hunter — Wesley Tallant's saga of a bounty hunter of the old West.
Win, Place and Die! — The first new mystery by Milt Ozaki in decades. The ultimate novel of 70s Reno.
Writer 1 and 2 — A magnus opus from Richard A. Lupoff summing up his life as writer.
You'll Die Laughing — Bruce Elliott's 1945 novel of murder at a practical joker's English countryside manor.

RAMBLE HOUSE
Fender Tucker, Prop.   Gavin L. O'Keefe, Graphics
www.ramblehouse.com   fender@ramblehouse.com
228-826-1783   10329 Sheephead Drive, Vancleave MS 39565